Magical praise for Elizabeth Bass and

A Letter to Three Witches!

"Bass delivers an enchanting paranormal rom-com replete with laugh-out-loud banter . . . as the tale takes on an almost episodic form, moving between quirky blunders, it achieves sitcom-level humor that will have readers cackling. The ending feels a bit tidy, but it's a charming ride to get there. Fans of *Practical Magic* will be delighted." —*Publishers Weekly*

"What happens when a family of witches is forced to suppress their powers? . . . A lighthearted supernatural romp."
—*Kirkus Reviews*

Books by Elizabeth Bass

MISS YOU MOST OF ALL
WHEREVER GRACE IS NEEDED
THE WAY BACK TO HAPPINESS
LIFE IS SWEET
A LETTER TO THREE WITCHES
THE WITCH HITCH

And writing as Liz Ireland

Mrs. Claus Mysteries
MRS. CLAUS AND THE SANTALAND SLAYINGS
MRS. CLAUS AND THE HALLOWEEN HOMICIDE
MRS. CLAUS AND THE EVIL ELVES
MRS. CLAUS AND THE TROUBLE WITH TURKEYS

HALLOWEEN CUPCAKE MURDER
(with Carlene O'Connor and Carol Perry)

Published by Kensington Publishing Corp.

The Witch Hitch

ELIZABETH BASS

KENSINGTON
PUBLISHING CORP.

www.kensingtonbooks.com

KENSINGTON BOOKS are published by

Kensington Publishing Corp.
119 West 40th Street
New York, NY 10018

Special book excerpts or customized printings can also be created to fit specific needs. For details, write or phone the office of the Kensington Sales Manager: Kensington Publishing Corp., 119 West 40th Street, New York, NY 10018. Attn. Sales Department. Phone: 1-800-221-2647.

The K with book logo Reg US Pat. & TM Off.

ISBN: 978-1-4967-3435-8 (ebook)

ISBN: 978-1-4967-3434-1

First Kensington Trade Paperback Printing: August 2023

10 9 8 7 6 5 4 3 2 1

Printed in the United States of America

The Witch Hitch

Chapter 1

"Boutonnieres."

The word, spoken like a warning, froze me on my bridal pedestal.

Olivia, one of my bridesmaids and sister of Wes Haverman, my fiancé, sprawled in a powder-blue poof chair, eyes glued to her phone screen.

Boutonnieres? I locked gazes with Sarah, my best friend and maid of honor, to see if she had a clue what this was about. She shook her head.

"It's a text from Katrina," Olivia explained without looking up. She spent so much time staring down at her screen, it wouldn't have been surprising to see some kind of primordial eyeball evolving on her scalp. "You're supposed to pick the boutonnieres for the groomsmen, Bailey. Or okay them or something."

Katrina, the wedding planner my future in-laws had generously hired, spray hosed me daily with texts. I now twitched at my phone's every vibration or ping, knowing another request for consultation on wedding minutiae was incoming.

"Katrina's texting *you* now?" I asked Olivia.

"Yes, and it's annoying." Her voice didn't convey any more annoyance than usual, however. Exhausted irritation was her steady state. "Oh, and I'm supposed to tell you that Dads wants to walk you down the aisle."

I gaped at her. "Katrina told you *that?*"

"No, Mother did."

It sounded like something Joan Haverman, my future mother-in-law, would suggest. She'd also "suggested" the venue, including Olivia as a bridesmaid, and having Wes's adolescent nephew and niece, Parker and Aida, provide the music for the ceremony. Which is why in three weeks I would be marching toward a bower set up by the country club putting green, behind the world's least enthusiastic bridesmaid, serenaded by a middle school cello-oboe combo.

Sarah was about to bite into a complimentary macaron, but now mouthed *Dads?* at me incredulously.

I turned away quickly to keep from laughing—and immediately regretted it. Blanche Bridal Boutique was a nightmare of mirrors. Everywhere I looked, there I was, standing in the strangest dress yet while Blanche, the owner, flitted about, alternately tugging at me and topping off champagne glasses.

Less than three weeks out from the wedding, I was scrambling to locate the ultimate dress. With Katrina and Joan tackling everything else, this was my one big designated wedding task. Unfortunately, I couldn't find a dress special enough. I had holds on three gowns in boutiques all over western New York, including one strong option I considered my backup dress. But the more I tried on, the more I dithered.

Three weeks. My waffling was rapidly becoming a crisis.

The boutique was empty except for me, Olivia, Sarah, Blanche, and one woman with brassy red hair who'd wandered in after we arrived and hovered around various racks and displays, peering at us. The exclusive shop was reserved for a half-hour private fitting, but I resisted the urge to ask Blanche to expel the red-haired woman or to pull the curtain to cut off the viewing area with its comfy armchairs, table of complimentary champagne and macarons, and all the mirrors from the showroom. I was trying not to be a bridezilla, although it was difficult not to feel self-conscious while swathed head-to-toe in strange white silk material, wearing foundation garments not in vogue since 1902.

Now I had to refuse my future father-in-law—"Dads" to his two children but still Mr. Haverman to me—offering to walk me down the aisle. How did I say no without causing a family-wide kerfuffle?

Thank God Mom wasn't here yet to hear this latest proposal. This wedding was already straining our relationship. I could tell that Mom thought Joan Haverman and her wedding planning had usurped her own role as mother of the bride. The thought of Mr. Haverman standing in my late father's place might just break her.

Where was Mom? She liked to come to these dress appointments, which was quite a concession since I knew she was upset that I'd chosen not to wear her old wedding dress.

I checked my phone. Nothing from Mom. I fired off a text. **Did you forget Blanche Bridal Boutique?**

When I snapped my phone closed, Sarah was regarding me with a pensive frown. "It's weird."

"It's worse than weird," Olivia declared, her smoky eyes finally darting up from her screen. "Whatever they've done to that fabric makes you look like Bride of the Michelin Man."

I agreed. Blanche had called to tell me that she had a newly arrived dress that was *totalement unique.* It was that, but not in a good way. The designer had put strange, tufted gathers everywhere, giving the material a quilted effect. "It's like bridal bubble wrap."

"I'm not talking about the dress," Sarah said. "I'm talking

about Bailey walking down the aisle with her future father-in-law. *That's* weird." Her gaze met mine, anxious in a way I'd been seeing more and more lately. "You're going to say no, right?"

This was where things could get awkward. I mean, Olivia was sitting right there. In addition to being a bridesmaid, I suspected she was Joan Haverman's spy. My phone pinged. I grabbed it.

MOM: I forgot! So sorry!!! I'm at the hairdresser's. In the chair. If I weren't halfway done . . .

I tapped out a reply. **No biggie.**

MOM: I'll be at the next shopping expedition. I promise. WTF.

Frowning, I tapped, **What?**

MOM: Wednesday, Thursday, or Friday after noon. I'm free all those days.

LOL.

MOM: LOL to you too!

No matter how many times I told her, I couldn't convince Mom that LOL didn't stand for "lots of love."

In the time it had taken me to text with Mom, the lines on Sarah's forehead had deepened. She was my best friend since our Zenobia College days, my confidante of fifteen years, and now she saw herself as the last guardrail from my becoming a Haver-monster. A word I really needed to expunge from my vocabulary sometime before June 1.

"Mr. Haverman's not your father," Sarah said.

Olivia snorted. "Genius observation."

I tried to joke it off. "Actually, I'm thinking of having Django walk me down the aisle." Django was my parrot, a colorful, and until recently, stubbornly silent green-cheeked conure. I'd adopted him a couple of years ago, when I was grieving for my dad. It was around the same time I'd taken up guitar, so I'd named him for my favorite guitarist, Django Reinhardt. "Did I tell you that he finally started talking to me?"

Sarah brightened. Getting Django to say anything had been our discouraging, longtime project. "What did he say?"

"He said, 'Are you sure?' Freakin' amazing. He's got an English accent, too. Like a BBC announcer."

Olivia finally glanced up at me, her face wearing the same perplexed expression as Sarah's. "Why would you teach a bird to say that?"

"I didn't. He thought of it all on his own. And it's funny, because at the time I was so distracted I was about to pour orange juice instead of milk into my coffee. And then he came out with, 'Are you sure?' and I caught my mistake just in time."

Sarah shook her head. "Remember that parrot documentary we watched, Bailey? That's not how the talking thing works. They don't just 'come up' with stuff. Or speak with foreign accents."

"He probably picked it up from television." I was addicted to BritBox.

"I need to witness this for myself," Sarah's blue eyes brightened in her round face. "Maybe I can come over and help you finish packing."

"Finish?" I laughed. Right now I lived in a one-bedroom duplex, but after the honeymoon I was going to live with Wes, of course, in his townhouse, which was a little bigger and nicer. I'd been putting off packing, though. "So far all I've done is scavenge a bunch of boxes."

Sarah smiled. "I have an idea—let's have a packing-up party."

Olivia choked on her champagne. "I have a better idea—let's not." She shook her head at me. "Honestly, Bailey, just hire a mover who'll do it for you. Why waste your time working?"

Why waste your time working could have been Olivia's motto. She had a job in the PR department of the Haverman family's grocery store chain, but she never seemed to let it get in the way of her free time.

She unfolded herself from her chair. "Are we done here?"

I nodded. "Sure—I need to get back to work."

Sarah sighed. "Me too."

"Another day, another dress fail." Olivia made a ticking sound.

An odd feeling I'd experienced lately jolted me—an electric current traveling across my nerve endings. All my life I'd occasionally had tingling in my extremities, which worried my parents, since my dad had diabetes. But lately the hot-and-cold prickling in my fingertips was getting extreme. Wedding jitters, I told myself. Or full-fledged wedding panic. Three weeks . . . still no dress . . . and I obviously wasn't going to find *the one* today. What if I never did?

I took a breath. There was always the backup dress—a white silk shift that everyone agreed looked fine. Wes's family was pulling out all the stops for this wedding, though. Did I really want to get married in a backup dress?

Sarah rounded on Olivia. "There's no reason to put pressure on her, Olivia. Everything else is almost done. And we have our bridesmaid dresses—even Martine's."

"And we're just assuming it will fit her?" Olivia asked, brow arched.

I wasn't just assuming, I was certain. Martine—Sarah's and my French-Canadian roommate from our Zenobia College days—was a flight attendant and hadn't seemed to gain or lose an ounce since freshman orientation fifteen years ago. Anyway, she would be flying into town two days before the wedding—plenty of time to make a last-minute adjustment.

"You don't have to be negative all the time just because you don't like the dress," Sarah told Olivia. "You had a vote."

Olivia was less than thrilled with the bridesmaid outfits. She hadn't minded the design—a classic strapless sheath in raw silk. It was the colors she objected to.

"Oh, right—me against the pastel caucus."

Sarah planted her hands on her hips. She was a half foot shorter than Olivia. Watching them scrap was like seeing a terrier face off with a greyhound. "Bridesmaids' dresses shouldn't be black."

"You've never heard of Truman Capote's Black and White Ball?" Olivia asked. "It's classic—much more original than being part of this Necco Wafer bridal chorus line."

Sarah sputtered, "How original can it be when you're referencing a party some writer threw over fifty years ago?"

While Olivia and Sarah sniped at each other, I drained the last of my champagne—I only allowed myself a half glass per fitting, just to make the trying-on experience less cringe-inducing. Then I stepped off the pedestal and walked over to inform Blanche that this dress didn't suit me, but that if she got anything new this week with simpler lines, maybe she could call me? ASAP, s'il vous plaît?

Before I could escape to the dressing room, the woman with the frizzy red hair darted in front of me. I'd forgotten all about her. Now my fingertips sparked, causing me to jump like I'd just touched a static surface. Did I know this woman? There was something familiar about her. . . .

"Didn't like the dress?" she asked.

We were the same height, so I was looking straight into her eyes, which, strangely, were brimming with tears. As if she were emotionally invested in the outcome of my dress hunt. Was she the dress designer?

"It's just not my style," I said.

"No," she agreed, sighing, "it's not. Of course you'd be beautiful in anything, but that getup looks like what you'd wear to be crowned Miss Miniature Marshmallow."

Okay, not the dress designer. Maybe she just had seasonal allergies.

"Your silhouette cries out for something less fussy, with straight lines," she continued.

Was she some kind of bridal boutique junkie? Was that even a thing?

I imitated Olivia's deadpan verbal fry as I backed away. "Thanks, that's so nice of you to say. I'm in a hurry, so . . ."

I retreated to the dressing room and collapsed on a button-tufted chair. Then I remembered I was wrinkling the dress—and that I had squillions of little buttons to undo on my back.

My phone rang. Katrina. *Again?* The woman's birth had pre-dated the deadly hurricane of 2005 by several years, so her parents had shown an eerie foresight in naming a baby who would grow up to deluge me in messages every day.

"Boutonnieres?" her impatient voice asked as soon as I picked up. "I sent you three options. All you have to do is pick one."

"I'm so sorry. I will—I'm at a bridal boutique and I need to get back to work, so . . ."

"Please tell me you're not straying from our color palette," she said in a rush of despair.

"The dresses I'm looking at are mostly white." *As bridal gowns tend to be.*

"White?" She sputtered at my ignorance. "You mean pearl white, or cotton, or alabaster? Or maybe parchment white? Linen? Cream, or—God help us—ecru?"

"Ecru isn't white, is it?"

A sigh gusted over the line. "All I'm saying, Bailey, is that white covers a lot of territory, and we decided *months* ago on a Spring Blush color scheme. If you veer too far toward blinding white, you're going to push yourself into Summer Fancy and send your entire visual scheme completely off the rails."

"I won't veer," I promised.

"Just get back to me today about those boutonnieres. Even if you decide to walk down the aisle in a bathrobe, we need to fi-nalize the florist order."

"I understand."

A soft knock at the dressing room door gave me an excuse to hang up and stand.

Sarah poked her head into the dressing room. "Olivia took off, and now I need to run. I have a one-o'clock appointment. A pa-tient's getting four wisdom teeth extracted at once."

I winced in sympathy for her patient. "Okay, can you help me with all these buttons before you go?"

She cast a baffled gaze at my back, which I'd twisted toward her. "You're already undone."

I looked in the mirror. She was right. The back of the dress was gaping open. When had I done that, and how? It had taken Blanche five minutes to do up all the little pearl buttons when I put it on.

On top of everything else, I seemed to be losing my mind.

"The owner lady must have helped you," Sarah said.

"And I just forgot having her undo fifty buttons?"

"It's called wedding jitters. Frankly, who can blame you? Just being in the same room with Olivia gives me the jitters. One more crack about Necco Wafers and I'll be ready to shove that cell phone up her patrician nose."

"Don't take anything she says personally. She's equally awful to everyone."

Sarah smiled. "It's good that Wes isn't like her, or your maid of honor would be objecting at the wedding."

I gave her a grateful hug. "Thanks for going through all of this with me. You're all that's keeping me from being sucked into the Havermonster vortex."

She laughed, then checked herself. "We should really stop using that word."

"We really should." I lowered my voice. "Is that woman still out there?"

"The store owner?"

"No, the lady with the red hair."

Sarah blinked. "What lady with red hair?"

"You didn't see her? She's been lurking the whole time we've been here."

Sarah's expression remained a puzzled frown.

Maybe I really was losing my mind. The store wasn't that big. "I was talking to her. You heard me talking to her, right?"

"I heard you say something to Blanche."

"I didn't just dream up a strange red-headed woman." *Did I?* How could Sarah have missed her? "I think she might be some bridal boutique kook," I said, noting that Sarah was looking even more anxious now. "I've seen her around somewhere before. She was just my height, with blue-green eyes, and red hair—curly, like mine used to be."

"So she looked like . . . you?"

"Well, no." Well, yes. "She's a lot older than me."

Sarah crooked her head. "You think maybe she's a long-lost relative of yours, like an aunt or something?"

"If there's one thing I don't have to worry about, it's relations crawling out of the woodwork." Both my parents, who'd adopted me when they were in their late thirties had been only children. Not counting my aunt Janet in Florida, we were a family of three—until my dad's final heart attack two years ago had winnowed us down to two.

Sarah hitched her purse higher on her shoulder. "You really are okay, aren't you?"

"Of course."

"Good." She smiled. "I'm so excited about the wedding. Dave said he's buying an actual suit for it. It'll be the first time we're in public together with him wearing something other than jeans or a dentist smock."

Dave, an orthodontist, was her longtime—very longtime—boyfriend.

After she left, I wriggled out of the weird corset thing that Joan Haverman had convinced me was essential when trying on wedding dresses. Freed, my diaphragm sucked in a healthy lungful of air. No wonder my hands were feeling funny. My circulation was being squeezed off by my underwear. How had women survived centuries of that kind of torture? How was I going to survive one day?

I took care returning the dress to its hanger, then hurriedly got back into my work clothes. In just a few minutes, I was my usual business casual self again. I unclipped my hair. I missed the curls sometimes, but that kooky lady made me glad I'd taken Olivia's advice and gone to her stylist to straighten it. Anton had deepened the color, too. "Makes it look less clown orange," Olivia had declared in her usual flattering way.

The woman in the store had been clown orange.

Could I have really been hallucinating? Maybe some trick of my mind, oxygen-deprived from my wedding bra, had made me imagine an older version of myself looking at current me trying on wedding dresses. Was Future Me attempting to tell Current Me something?

A sound popped into my head. A literal popping sound. *Popcorn. Someone crunching popcorn.* The memory was so distinct, I could smell the butter flavoring. The last time Wes and I had gone to the movies, there had been a loud popcorn cruncher behind us. I'd reflexively twisted to glare and noticed a woman with the jumbo-sized bag cradled in her lap, scooping little handfuls methodically to her mouth. A woman with curly red hair.

She'd smiled at me, which had been annoying at the time. Now . . .

I picked up my purse and hurried out. The mysterious woman was loitering in front of the store. I might have sagged in relief— she wasn't a hallucination—except that I was more than a little wigged out that she seemed to be lying in wait for me.

A warning klaxon in my head told me to walk past the red-haired woman, but my feet stopped right in front of her. "Were you at the movies last week?" I asked.

"I was, but that's not where you know me from." She tilted her head. "You don't remember me? I'm Esme Zimmer."

The name jolted something in my memory. Esme Zimmer. Esme Zimmer . . .

Finally, it clicked. She was one of my customers—one of my best customers, if you went by how many policies she'd taken out with Genesee Insurance. We insured her business, car, house (homeowner with extra contents coverage *and* earthquake coverage), and life. If I wasn't mistaken, there was a premium traveler's insurance policy in the mix, too. I'd seen her at the office a few times.

So. Not future me. A client.

I was about to laugh, but it died in my throat as doubts bubbled back to the surface. The Esme Zimmer who was my customer had not looked like this woman. Esme Zimmer had been . . . well, unattractive. To say the least. In a Grimm's fairy tale, she'd have been the old lady in a forest handing out poisoned apples. This woman, while odd, was not hag material.

"You look different than the last time I saw you."

"New hairdo." Her smile revealed newly whitened teeth, too. "You know, if you're still in need of a wedding dress, I can make you the gown of your dreams."

"Are you a designer?"

"In a manner of speaking. You might call me a sorceress with a Singer."

"I thought you had some other business . . ."

"I'm a woman of many talents. As are you."

She leveled that strange gaze on me again. The intensity of it made me step back as I would from a snake I couldn't identify. She spoke as if *she* knew me well, which was downright creepy.

"Well, thanks. I'll give it some thought. The dress, I mean."

"Any time of the day or the night," she said. "Just look me up. I'll make whatever you want in a jiffy."

She made it sound as if she had fairy godmother–like abilities. "You're just going to snap your fingers or wave a wand or something?"

She blasted out another laugh. "Right. Bippity-boppity-flippin'-boo."

Oh, boy. I smiled and kept edging away.

The sharp tattoo of high heels on sidewalk came toward us, then stopped abruptly. "Bailey!"

At the sound of the hyperenthusiastic greeting, my guts clenched in dread. A tall, lanky brunette whipped off her sunglasses to reveal perfect, long-lashed doe eyes.

"Madeleine!" I said, with no enthusiasm. "What are you doing here?"

Madeleine was Olivia's best friend. More significantly, she was Wes's ex-girlfriend. And not just any ex-girlfriend. They dated *all through* school, to hear them tell it, practically from Montessori right up to the day after she'd confessed to a debauched spring break one-night stand with a teammate on Wes's college lacrosse team. Wes had never forgiven her—and Madeleine never forgave any woman who'd dated Wes since then. Olivia had even hinted that Madeleine had caused the breakup of Wes's first marriage . . . although the Havermans had never confirmed whose idea it had been to hire the private investigator who discovered Wes's wife, Lydia, and her personal trainer having a workout session in a motel.

"I thought you were in France," I said.

After we'd announced our engagement, Madeleine had taken off on an open-ended grief tour of Europe. I should have known our Madeleine hiatus was too good to last.

"I'm back!" Her smile broadened. "O told me to meet her here."

My lips froze in a tight smile. Why hadn't Olivia—or Wes—warned me that Madeleine was back in Rochester?

"Olivia left a little while ago," I said. "You missed her."

"Too bad. But it's *such* a kick to see you." Her insincere smile transferred from me to Esme Zimmer. "Is this a relative of yours?"

"No," I said quickly. "A client, actually. We just bumped into each other."

"How odd. You're practically Twinkies." She hiked her voluminous fringed leather shoulder bag higher on her shoulder, and put her sunglasses back on. "Well, I guess I'll catch up with O somewhere. *Great* to see you, though."

She flashed a parting smile, turned, and tottered off in the direction she'd come from.

"Friend of yours?" Esme asked.

"She's my fiancé's ex."

"Really."

As we watched Madeleine sashay toward her MINI Cooper like a model on a Milan catwalk, an amazing thing happened. The heels of her shoes disintegrated, crumbling under her weight like dried cork. First Madeleine's long colt legs wobbled, then she wheeled her arms, and finally she stumble-fell to the sidewalk.

I ran over to help her. "My God, are you okay? What happened?" I'd never seen Madeleine move awkwardly before, much less face-plant on the pavement.

She was having even more trouble processing how she'd ended up sprawled on the sidewalk than I was. "These are Christian Louboutins! From their Paris store."

I helped Madeleine hobble to her car and watched her drive away.

"*Quel dommage*," Esme Zimmer said.

I'd been so distracted and puzzled by Madeleine's weird shoe malfunction, I'd almost forgotten that the strange woman was still there. Now she was right at my elbow. It was disconcerting.

"Don't forget about my dress offer, Iz," Esme told me.

"My name's Bailey."

"Oh, right." She smiled, and there was a little sadness in it. "I keep forgetting."

What did *that* mean?

Come to think of it, I didn't want to know. I'd had my full quota of weirdness for one day. I said a quick goodbye and hurried to my car. After I got in and pulled into the street, the strange woman was still standing where I'd left her, watching me.

Chapter 2

Madeleine was back.

At my desk in my gray office at Genesee Insurance, I picked up my phone to call Sarah with this alarming news bulletin, but then I remembered she was extracting four wisdom teeth. I had work to do, too.

And yet . . .

Madeleine was back, and no one had told me. Shouldn't I have been given a heads-up? A simple *Oh, by the way, your nemesis is back*?

Not that she was *really* my nemesis. She was just Wes's ex-girlfriend. From long ago. She wasn't even his ex-wife. He had one of those, too. Most adults had a string of broken relationships behind them by the time they got married. There was no reason to freak out over an ex-girlfriend.

Of course, not every ex was entrenched in your fiancé's life as your future sister-in-law's bestie and all-round family friend. And one who hailed from his world. Wes, Olivia, Madeleine, and I had all grown up here. Rochester, New York, wasn't exactly a mega-metropolis, but I hadn't crossed paths with any of them in my youth, because they'd inhabited a parallel universe of country clubs, big vacations, and private schools. Even now, it sometimes felt as if they were communicating in a secret code I would never crack.

That was why Madeleine brought out the worst in me, like my secret glee at seeing her fall on her butt on the sidewalk today. Not something I was proud of.

The gleam in that red-headed woman's eyes came back to me. She'd been delighted by the sight of Madeleine toppling off her Louboutins, too. The more I considered it, the stranger it seemed that some client of mine would pop up twice in the past week. And looking so different than she used to.

Was I being paranoid? Did I not have enough to worry me already?

Someone knocked on my office door. It was Paige Wilkins.

Speaking of worries.

"Oh, hey, you're finally here." Paige's studied casualness couldn't disguise that *finally*. In the past weeks, she'd been not-so-subtly undermining my position in the company where I'd worked since college. The company my father had cofounded and that my mother still had a stake in.

"I've been here for the past hour," I said, fudging fifteen minutes in my favor. And yes, thirty minutes of those forty-five had been spent researching Esme Zimmer and worrying that Madeleine had jetted back from Paris to sabotage my wedding.

Paige pushed a few locks of jet-black hair behind her ear. She wore it long, with straight bangs. Wire-frame glasses perched on her nose, and she'd encased her curvaceous figure in a fitted jersey dress with a tight melon-colored cardigan. "I came by an hour ago," she said, not buying my timeline. "You must have been out dress shopping." A smile pulled at her lips. "Again."

"Did you need something?"

"Just wanted to let you know I'm forwarding some files. Frank Raditzky from Insta-Lube came by today to go over their coverage. Maybe you forgot the appointment?"

My brows knit. "I didn't forget. I didn't know."

"Really? I left a Post-it on your desk last week. Guess you didn't see it."

More like she didn't actually leave it.

"No worries," she said. "I stepped up. Frank and I actually get along super well, so it's all good." She smiled brightly. "I know you've got a hundred things on your plate—and who knows? You'll probably want to be downsizing your client list soon, right?"

I leaned back, fixing her with a hard stare. "Why would I do that?"

"Because you'll have a fabulous guy waiting at home? Anyway, I'm sure there'll soon be the patter of little Haverman feet."

"We're not in any rush about that."

Paige made a show of scanning the hallway and lowering her voice to a confidential purr. "Of course you have to *say* that, but I get it. Once you hit your midthirties, you slough off healthy eggs like Siberian huskies shedding fur in August."

With Herculean effort, I made myself smile. "Thanks for looking after Insta-Lube."

She sent me a smart salute. "Glad to be of service. Like I told Ron, we don't want to lose an account just because you're so distracted with wedding stuff." She about-faced and walked out.

Ron was our boss.

This was no joke. The last woman Paige had decided to step over to get promoted had spent months weeping in the washroom before quitting to attend a phlebotomist training program.

Two minutes later, I was standing in Ron's office. He and my late father had founded the business, and even though my mom couldn't stand him, Ron and I had a solid working relationship.

"I honestly didn't know Insta-Lube was coming in today," I told him. "Their policy wasn't due for renewal for another month and a half."

Ron, stocky but fit, dismissed my anxiety with a wave. "Don't worry about it. Everybody gets distracted before their wedding."

"It wasn't that—"

He was grinning. "Boy, wouldn't Lloyd have been proud. His little Bailey-Bee, marrying a Haverman!"

Granted, this man had known me since I was running around in homemade rompers Mom had sewn for me. He and my dad had been best friends—Ron was a little like Dad's rascally brother. But I didn't like being called Bailey-Bee in a professional setting. Also, even after two years, thoughts of my dad could bring on a spontaneous eruption of tears—that wasn't very professional, either.

I bit my lip. "I'm sure he would have been, but I'm as dedicated to the job as ever."

He stood up and put an avuncular hand on my shoulder. "Didn't I just say don't worry about it? Enjoy your wedding and all the hoopla around it. Find out where you're going on your honeymoon yet?"

I shook my head. Wes was not a traditionalist in all things, but he loved the idea of keeping the honeymoon destination a big secret until the last minute. "I suspect Jamaica."

"Fantastic. Burn some sun into that Vampira complexion of yours, drink cocktails with little umbrellas in 'em, and when you get back, we'll talk over your future. Right?"

"My future is here."

"Of course it is." For a split second, his ever-present smile broke. "How's your mother?"

"Fine." Although something about her text this morning still jangled in my brain. "She's fine."

He shook his head. "Headstrong woman."

Ron was the only person on the planet who would use the word *headstrong* to describe Deb Tomlin. That was because she inherited my father's share of the business and refused to let Ron buy her out. It was probably the one thing she'd stood firm on in her entire life, besides making me wear my retainer for six months beyond the time the orthodontist officially freed me from it. After what my parents paid for my teeth, she'd declared, they would not move back a fraction of a millimeter on her watch.

I returned to my office, far from reassured by my conversation with Ron. A two-week honeymoon would be two weeks Paige could spend knifing me in the back.

I couldn't deal with work stress *and* wedding stress. I shouldn't even have wedding stress. That's what Katrina was for. All I had to do, as everyone kept reminding me, was buy a dress. And I hadn't even been able to do that.

And now Madeleine was back. Madeleine wouldn't have trouble figuring out what to wear on her wedding day.

You had one job. . . .

Maybe taking Esme Zimmer up on her offer wasn't such a bad idea. *If* she could design. Or sew. According to her Genesee Insurance paperwork, she was a CPA. There was nothing in all the policies she'd taken out with us to indicate a dressmaking sideline. But why would a woman offer to make a wedding dress for someone unless she was certain of her skill?

At dinner at the country club that night, Wes and I sat at our usual table by a window offering a spectacular view. The clubhouse was situated on a bluff overlooking Lake Ontario, our city's sweetwater sea. Sunset was drawing near, but boats still dotted the water. Once spring arrived, it was hard to keep the locals inside.

The view made me nostalgic. Not that I'd ever stepped foot in this club while growing up—my dad loved golf, but he was frugal and played on public courses. It was the lake that reminded me of childhood. My parents lived in the Charlotte neighborhood, and some of my earliest memories were of flying kites on the beach, or the three of us strolling on the boardwalk with a frozen custard.

It would make a beautiful setting for the wedding. The thought made my hands vibrate—that weird feeling again. It was really uncomfortable.

As Wes and I perused menus we both had memorized, Madeleine was our invisible dinner companion, our unseen third wheel. I was afraid to speak of her for fear of sounding the wrong note, so I strained to think of some other subject. My brain naturally flitted to my other preoccupation: the dress. I told Wes about an insurance client offering to whip up the wedding gown of my dreams.

Wes was classically handsome, with a face that looked like it had been chiseled by a long-ago sculptor to represent an upstanding community leader of ancient times. Thanks to his strict morning workout regimen, his thirty-six years hadn't added an ounce of doughiness to him. His face rarely crumpled into a comical worried expression, but it did now at the thought of me asking some strange woman to sew a wedding dress for the society wedding his mother was planning.

"Just let Olivia and Mom take you to the city this weekend," he said. "They'll have you fixed up in no time. We'll pay."

"Your family's already paying for everything." Before he could object, I added, "I'm sure I'll find something. If not, I'll just rent a tux and we can be twinsies."

He paled, then shook his head. "You're joking." It wasn't a question, but a statement of relief.

I laughed and looked down at my menu again. Before our

engagement, he would have laughed, too. The moment he'd slipped the engagement ring on my finger, something had shifted.

The food here was on the dull side, but the club was like a home away from home to Wes. It was beginning to seem like home to me, too. We came here so often that I knew the menu as well as I'd known the dishes my mom made when I was growing up. Some of them even overlapped—like salmon croquettes. Although I doubt this place used canned salmon as my mother had. Still, it seemed almost like comfort food, and I needed that today.

After we told the waiter what we wanted, Wes topped up our glasses with the wine he'd ordered before I'd arrived. "You might want a drink when I tell you what's happened," he said. "It's Madeleine. She's back."

I sagged with relief that he'd mentioned her first. "I know. I saw her today. What does she want?"

Aside from my death.

He hesitated. "I think she wants to be part of the wedding."

"I can guess what part she wants to play," I said, reaching again for my wine.

"Not to be a bridesmaid," he assured me quickly, as if that's what I'd meant. "Mad just wants to be involved."

I always cringed when he called her Mad, as appropriate as the nickname was on so many levels. I wasn't sure if it was a Haverman tic or just a prep school thing generally, but I struggled with the chummy diminutives he, his friends, and his family tended to use.

"Involved, how?" I asked.

"O suggests that we put her on guest book."

I mulled over having the first person all our wedding guests encountered be someone who hated the bride's guts. A long tug of malbec was required to reconcile me to the idea. Madeleine was going to find a way to insert herself into the ceremony some-how. Sidelining her to a country club corridor with the guest book might not be the worst strategy.

"Okay," I said.

"Really?" He exhaled in relief. "Thanks for being such a brick about it. Mad can be such a pain in the neck. I swear, one of the first rules of life should be never to date your sibling's best friend."

"Like never getting involved in a land war in Asia," I said.

He laughed at the hat tip to *The Princess Bride*, a movie we both loved. It had always seemed especially funny that Wes's full name was Wesley—so close to the Westley that Cary Elwes played in the movie.

"Or going against a Sicilian when death is on the line," he said.

I had an idea. "Why don't we chuck everything and go to your place and watch a movie."

The suggestion caused a spark in his eyes, although he hesitated, thinking it through.

"The only correct answer is 'As you wish,'" I reminded him.

The spark in his eyes flamed out like a falling star. "It sounds great, but I've got to go back to the office after dinner."

I took a sip of wine to cover my disappointment. "Never mind—I just had a wild hair."

"I'm trying to get my desk cleared out for the wedding."

Of course he was. He was responsible—a rock. That was one of the things that had made me fall in love with him. My father died not long after we met, and Wes's love and steadiness got me through those terrible days. I couldn't begrudge him that same steadiness now.

"I've got a guitar lesson anyway." With all that had happened today, the lesson had slipped my mind. I couldn't help asking, "Why didn't Olivia tell me about Madeleine this afternoon?"

"O thought it might go over better if the request to involve

Mad in the wedding came from me. She told me you already shot down the idea of Dads walking you down the aisle."

I could tell he was disappointed about that. "It doesn't seem right. He's not my father."

"Your own father wasn't your real father, either. What's the difference?"

I thumped my glass down and drew my hands together in my lap to keep myself from shaking. The moment my fingertips touched, an electric current bolted through me. Again! Did I need to see a doctor? An internet search this afternoon had informed me that electric fingertips could be a symptom of anything from carpal tunnel syndrome to a brain tumor. The Mayo Clinic website didn't mention bridal nerves. Or adopted child rage.

I sucked in a breath. "I might have been adopted, but to me, Mom and Dad were my real parents, my entire family, my whole life. They took care of me and nurtured me, loved me and educated me. Dad would have laid down his life for me. I owe him so much, and not having him here for the wedding—"

My throat closed up, choking my words.

"Oh, God." Wes reached across the table and grabbed my elbow. "Bailey, I'm sorry."

I could still barely think about Dad without feeling as if there were a boa constrictor squeezing my chest. "No one could be his substitute."

Wes lifted his hands in surrender. "I should have realized."

Tears welled in my eyes. It was foolish to get so riled up, but I couldn't help it. Dad had been such an oversized presence in my life. I still went to work every day in the office of the business he'd started forty years ago and brought me into after college.

"I really respected your dad," Wes continued, his voice warm.

"I know." My constricted throat expelled the words in a squeak.

And my dad had liked Wes, too. In fact, one of my last conversations with Dad had been *about* Wes. "That one's a good egg," he'd told me.

If he'd lived, he would've been over-the-moon happy for me now. His own father had been an electrician, and while Dad never would have brushed the working-class chip off his shoulder, he would have gotten a kick out of hobnobbing with the Havermans. I could imagine him meeting Wes here for lunches, and the two of them playing golf. Dad would have needled Wes about his expensive tastes, and then splurged and sent the Havermans a bottle of Glenlivet for the holidays.

Thankfully, our dinners arrived. Salmon for me, steak for Wes. In a strange way, seeing Wes cut into his steak calmed me. Steak was what my dad would have ordered. "Solid food," he would have declared it.

Wes caught me staring at his plate and looked up, worried. "Something the matter?"

Probably best not to analyze why similarities between my late father and my fiancé were so comforting. *Daddy complex much?* I shook my head, took a bite of salmon, and foraged through my mind for something else to talk about. No surprise what I came up with.

"It's been a strange day. That woman at the bridal shop, the one who offered to make the dress? I'd seen her before."

"Rochester's a small world."

"No kidding. She's one of my clients. But the times I saw her before, she looked completely different. She used to be"—I hesitated—"well, almost a crone. It sounds mean, but she really was a mess. She had a dowager's hump, a face like a desiccated apple, and this crazy, frizzy gray hair."

"And now?"

"I would swear she's thirty years younger. No hump, no wrinkles. And her hair isn't gray anymore." Just orangey-red.

"It's amazing what plastic surgeons can do. One of Mother's friends came back from a trip to California totally transformed."

I was about to take another bite of salmon, but I put my fork down. "Do you remember a woman was sitting behind us at the movies eating popcorn last week?"

"No, but a lot of people eat popcorn at the movies."

"But loudly, like she wanted me to notice her. You don't remember?"

"Uh, no."

Was I the only person who could see this woman? "It was her."

"Who, the woman from the dress shop?"

I nodded. "That's twice in one week," I pointed out. "In two very different places."

He leaned forward. "Do you think one of your clients is stalking you?"

Stalking. That was the word I'd been avoiding all day. "I don't know."

"I doubt people become obsessed with their insurance agents, but if you're worried, Dads could have a word with the police. They could keep an eye on your condo."

Police? I tried to imagine myself explaining about popcorn and dream wedding dresses to a guy in uniform. "Probably not necessary. Thanks, though."

Wes launched into an anecdote from his day involving the building of Haverman's newest grocery store, which was going to cater to the high-end food shopper. Something about a wood-fired oven not fitting. I tried to listen, I really did. But as soon as he stopped to take a sip of water, I jumped in again.

"You know what's the weirdest thing? This woman—Esme—said she could make me the wedding dress of my dreams, but she's a tax accountant."

His brow furrowed. "If you're having that much trouble finding a wedding dress here, please let Olivia or Mom take you to the city. They'd love to, you know."

He'd completely missed my point. "I just meant, it's *really* weird that a CPA is offering to make me a wedding dress, don't you think?"

"I wouldn't trust it. Honestly, a trip to the city would be fun, wouldn't it? You and Mother could stay at the Plaza—have a ball."

It was on the tip of my tongue to ask him how much of a ball he'd have spending the night at the Plaza with *my* mother, but I stopped myself and chewed an asparagus spear instead.

"Sarah says my description of her makes her sound like me."

Wes looked confused. "You and Mother?"

"No, me and the kooky accountant."

He nearly dropped his fork. "Your best friend is saying you resemble some old crone?"

"She's not a crone now," I reminded him. "It's just . . . odd."

I also considered telling him about Django's remarkable powers of speech, and my electric hands. But he would be incredulous about those, too, so I let it drop. The trouble was, I had difficulty thinking about anything else. Our conversation flatlined. There were married couples at tables around us who looked *Cocoon* years old and seemed more animated than we were.

I couldn't help remembering the times—not so long ago—when Wes and I used to talk nonstop. Okay, maybe *I* was the one who'd done most of the chattering, but part of what I loved about him was what a great listener he was. We laughed so much, too, when we'd first started dating. Of course, it was hard to find anything funny after my father died. Along the way, our humor biceps had gotten a little flabby.

Maybe it was time to work them out a little.

I took a sip of wine and cleared my throat. "Did I tell you I sold my vacuum?"

He looked up at me with startled eyes. "What? Why?"

"It was just collecting dust."

It took a moment for his lips to quirk up. "For a minute I thought you were talking about downsizing all that stuff in your house. You won't need to move *everything* over to my place, you know."

I nodded. Talking about packing up my stuff wasn't side-splittingly funny, but it was better than eating salmon croquettes in silence.

Still, I wasn't sad to glance at my watch and tell him I had to go. "I need to get to my lesson."

"With what's-his-name? Phil?"

"Gil." I had guitar lessons every Tuesday night with a guy who owned a music store downtown, where I used to give piano lessons to beginner students on weekends. I'd cut that out six months ago to have more time for Wes and the wedding, but I missed both my pupils and hanging around the music store.

"Do you still have time for these lessons?" he asked as we were walking out.

"Practicing music keeps me sane. And I've already given up my piano students."

"Well, whatever makes you happy," he said, obviously not quite convinced. Music was one area where our minds didn't meet and probably never would. I loved music—especially old jazz and swing music that spoke of sweeping cobwebs off the moon and the strings of one's heart going zing—all the happy, corny, crazy sentiments that touched that tiny non-realist corner of me.

"If I didn't know you better," Wes said, "I'd probably be jealous."

"Of Gil?" The thought made me smile. Gil was a grizzled fiftysomething.

He reached out and took my hand. "Of any man you wanted to spend so much time with. The great thing is I can trust you."

Our eyes met, and once again I thought about all the tiny accidents and missteps that led to the very right step that this engagement was for us both: Madeleine and the lacrosse player; Wes's failed first marriage to Lydia, who'd cheated on him with her personal trainer; my own trail of flaky or failed relationships; and finally, a shady insurance salesman who'd embezzled money from his Haverman Foods account, opening the way for me to meet with Wes and make a bid for the biggest account of my career. "Love at First Business Liability Estimate," we sometimes joked.

He lifted my knuckles to his lips, and I felt that old desire skitter through me. That muscle was still working, at least. Who cared about how many silly jokes we told now, or whether we chattered over dinner like teenagers? This was something deeper.

"Maybe I should skip the lesson after all," I said.

He smiled in that stoic way of his. "Nah. I've got some work to finish up tonight. I'll see you tomorrow anyway."

"Tomorrow?" My smile melted. I needed to keep a calendar on my phone, or tattoo my schedule on my arm. "What's tomorrow?"

"Dinner with the folks." The prospect of dinner with the Havermans was as effective a libido killer as a cold shower. "They're going to announce what their wedding present to us will be."

Was he joking? "They're already paying for the lion's share of the wedding."

"Sure, but they'll still want to give us something."

I nodded numbly. Yes, they were my future in-laws, but somehow I felt as if I were tallying up a debt with their every extravagance. They were doing so much, while I . . .

You have one job: the dress. And so far I'd bungled it. After Wes drove off, I sat in my car, tapping my fingers on the steering wheel. *I'm a sorceress with a Singer,* Esme Zimmer had said. Maybe, just maybe, the strange woman really could whip up my dream dress. That would be one thing I could cross off my list. It was a long shot, but what did I have to lose?

I called Gil, canceled my guitar lesson, and pointed my car south toward Zenobia.

Chapter 3

When I drove by, Esme Zimmer's office in Zenobia wasn't just closed for the day; it also had butcher paper over the inside of the windows and a FOR RENT sign posted. Strange that a CPA of all people would be wasting money insuring a business that no longer existed.

She'd bought home insurance from me, as well, so I had her home address and sort of knew where it was, in a neighborhood across the Genesee River from central Zenobia, the quaint college town where I'd spent some of the happiest years of my life, along with Sarah and Martine. According to my file, Esme's farmhouse dated back to the 1880s, so I was surprised to see that her neighborhood was one of two-story homes of a more recent vintage on small lots. Her property was set apart from the others, lending its weathered stone, ivory-covered walls a "one of these things is not like the other" look from its neighbors. It gave off a dilapidated air—mossy roof, crooked gutters, shutters askew. Had Esme abandoned this place, too? I might have concluded that, if not for the vehicle standing in the drive and a dim light shining through the curtains on the front windows.

I approached the porch warily. Nothing indicated a home business being operated here—no hand-painted DESIGNS BY ESME placard, or anything like that. At least not that I could see. The sun was going down, but the porch light wasn't on. I squinted up at a tree branch scraping the roof—as if that roof didn't have enough problems. This place was an insurance claim waiting to happen.

I rang the bell and stood back, contemplating the NO SOLICITA-TIONS warning on the door, underneath which someone had scrawled the addendum *Unless you're selling Girl Scout cookies!* After a moment, the sounds of multiple bolts being unlocked and chains unfastening sounded through the door. I couldn't fault the security measures here, at least. When at last the door opened, I found myself face-to-face not with Esme, but with a woman my age or a bit younger. She was taller than me, with long hair worn in a braid, and dressed in a flannel shirt and jeans.

She looked me over, confused at first. Then, rapid-fire, she asked, "You changed *again*? Did you find him?"

"I don't think I—"

At the sound of my voice, the woman's eyes widened. "Oh! Sorry!" She reached to her right and snapped the porch light on. "Who are you?"

"My name's Bailey Tomlin. Esme Zimmer told me I should talk to her about a wedding dress."

She stepped back and crossed her arms, clearly perplexed. And mistrustful.

"Ms. Zimmer doesn't design bridal apparel?" I asked.

A laugh burbled out of her. Just as quickly, she sobered. "Uh, no."

"I'd like to speak with her. Any idea when she'll be back?"

"Could be any moment. Or days." She leaned in, squinting at me. "Has anyone ever told you that you look a lot like Esme?"

I could feel my molars grinding. "It's been noted."

The woman gazed straight into my eyes. After an awkward pause, she shook her head. "Sorry, it's just—" She laughed, and asked in louder, well-enunciated syllables, "This isn't some kind of test, is it?"

She was talking at me as if I had a transmitter in my skull that she was trying to reach. I leaned away from her. Something very weird was going on here. "If it is, I think I'm failing." I wondered if Genesee Insurance was getting scammed. This obviously wasn't a dress shop, and now I wasn't even sure Esme Zimmer lived there. "Who are you?" I asked.

"My name is Gwen Engel."

"There's no mention of tenants in Mrs. Zimmer's policy."

She blinked. "What policy?"

"I'm an insurance agent. We're providing coverage for a business she no longer runs, evidently. We also insure this house and her car." I glanced again at the driveway. The Kia Soul parked there had some kind of business logo affixed to the passenger door; it was not the ancient Gremlin Esme Zimmer had a policy for.

The woman's demeanor grew more guarded, almost hostile. "You said you were here about a wedding dress."

"I am. I'm also Ms. Zimmer's insurance agent." I dug through my purse and pulled out my business card. "Here."

She plucked it from my hand. After giving it a quick scan, she had the grace to look slightly embarrassed. "Oh. Okay, I'm Esme's niece, and I've been living here because she's been away a lot."

"Traveling?"

"Um, yeah. She's had . . . distractions."

That sounded fishy, too. And vague. Traveling where? Surely Esme Zimmer didn't need someone to housesit while she was seeing me in Rochester, a twenty-minute drive up the highway. The words Gwen had spoken when she first opened the door came back to me. *You changed* again? *Did you find him?* What had that meant?

Something furry rubbed against my legs, launching me out of my thoughts into pure terror. I jumped, only to look down at a black cat winding between my calves.

Gwen seemed as surprised as I was. "Wow, he seems to like you—he's not usually so friendly." She bent down and scooped the cat into her arms. "What do you think, Griz?" They both fixed me with penetrating stares. The cat meowed.

She smiled. "Griz mistook you, too."

"Uh-huh." Nothing weird about talking with and speaking for your cat. Did I want to have anything more to do with these people? No.

I took a step back. "I'll be going now."

"I'll give Aunt Esme your card."

Damn. My fingers itched to grab that card back. In fact, they'd been tingling like crazy the whole time I'd been standing on the porch. The card was immaterial, though. Esme clearly knew where to find me, and she apparently knew my schedule. Knew it too well. "Your aunt doesn't have a criminal record, does she?"

The woman's face went slack. "Why are you asking?"

"She's been turning up in my life a lot lately. I need to know she's not, you know, dangerous."

She laughed. "Of course she's not." The cat meowed, and Gwen tilted her head as if listening to her feline friend voicing an objection. "Right. But *she's* okay."

She, who? It was like Gwen was talking to her cat, not to me.

I stepped off the porch and began backing away. "Never mind."

"I'll tell Aunt Esme you were here," she called after me.

I hurried to my car, got in, and pulled away as fast as possible without actually peeling off down the street. Coming to Zenobia had been a huge mistake. Whatever was happening with Esme Zimmer, I was done with both her and her cat-whisperer niece.

Tomorrow I'd drive to Buffalo and buy the backup dress. *Done is as good as perfect*, my dad used to say.

As I pulled onto the road leading away from Esme Zimmer's neighborhood, a movement flashed behind me. In my rearview, two eyes were peering back at me from the back seat. I shrieked and swerved the car.

"Watch out!" a man's voice yelled.

Thank God there was no oncoming traffic in the next lane. I'd lost control for a second, but I gripped the wheel in a white-knuckle ten-to-two clench. My heart pounded against my ribs.

"Who are you?" I barked as I careened toward the shoulder of the road. "What are you doing in my car?"

The man in the back seat held up his hands as if he were under arrest. "Don't be frightened."

Too damn late.

I screeched to a stop, tossing us both forward. "Get out!"

"Please—only listen to me for a moment."

My gaze was pinned to the rearview. This creepy guy must have crawled into the back seat when I was parked on the street near Esme Zimmer's. Had I left the car unlocked? Maybe. I hadn't expected the neighborhood to be harboring carjackers. Was he armed?

"I'm not carrying much money," I said, fumbling for the wallet in my purse, "but you can take whatever's in there and go."

He drew back, offended. "Believe me, miss, stealing wasn't my objective when I climbed into this contraption."

His voice had such a strange cadence—he didn't sound like a carjacker, armed robber, or serial killer. Then again, my ideas of those things were straight out of Hollywood. And if he wasn't a criminal, what was he doing crouched in the back seat of my car? No matter how straitlaced and normal a guy looked, there was always the Ted Bundy exception.

And no, it wasn't a good idea to remind myself of Ted Bundy at this precise moment.

"What do you want?" I asked, hating the quaver in my voice. "Y-you don't talk like a murderer."

"I should say not. Please, I just need to get away."

"From the police?"

"No, from that woman back there."

"Gwen?"

"Her, too, but especially the one with red hair."

What had Gwen asked me when she opened the door? *Did you find him?*

I seemed to have solved the mystery of whom she'd meant by *him.*

"I had to escape from that house," he said.

I couldn't blame him for that. "So you decided to stow away in my car?"

"I didn't feel like spending the entire night hiding in the neighbor's holly bush. I saw a Buster Keaton picture once where a man sneaked into a car to get away."

Something in me thawed at the mentioned of Buster Keaton. I loved old movies. "Which one—"

"THAT'S HER!" he shrieked.

Headlights swept toward us and the man dove behind the seat. Instinctively, I also slammed my body flat onto the passenger seat, out of sight. I didn't want Esme Zimmer to see me either—but now there was no way of knowing if that car really was hers. The vehicle that passed us sounded more like a diesel truck. Then again, she drove an ancient Gremlin.

After a few moments, the light and noise passed, and I straightened out of my hiding position just as the guy poked his head over the back seat. His eyes were wider than ever, and when I got another look at him, I saw his sandy brown hair was parted in the center and looked to be slicked back with hair product. There was something freakish about him.

And I had just wasted my best chance to flag someone down for help. *Smart, Bailey.*

"Is she gone?" he asked, his voice reedy with fear.

I plucked up some courage. "Look, I don't know you, and I barely know the people back in that house. But I don't let strangers into my car. Get out now or I'll call the police."

"No!" He sounded like a wounded animal. "Coppers will never understand. They might even send me back to the witch house." His gaze locked on mine. "Please help me."

Beads of sweat popped out on the man's brow. The guy really was terrified. And obviously not of sound mind.

Witch house, he'd said.

Trying to sound calm, I asked, "You think Esme Zimmer and her niece are . . . witches?"

He nodded frantically. "I *know* they are. What's more, I can prove it."

Chapter 4

His name was Seton Atterbury, from New York City. That was all the information I managed to extract from him during the ensuing drive. I didn't want to be alone with this guy, or even sit with him in a semi-deserted fast food joint, which most of the places along that strip of highway were. So I sped toward Zenobia's town center, while Seton gripped the sides of his seat the whole way, his eyes pinned on the road ahead and his face white-green, like a passenger on a 747 nose-diving toward a crash landing.

As if he weren't the one who'd just scared the daylights out of me.

He retained that same look of shock as I dragged him into the Owl's Nest, a hangout from my college days. The bar-café had been a Zenobia institution for decades. The owner hadn't changed the décor, menu, or the playlist since about 1982. Boy George bleated "Karma Chameleon" from the corner speakers, and the air was heavy with the smells of fried cheese sticks and stale beer.

In the comparatively brighter light of the bar, I got my first long look at the strange guy I'd picked up. I was surprised by how tall Seton was—his height had been hard to judge when he'd been cowering in my LEAF. He reminded me a little of Gary Cooper in his younger, dapper days. His eyes had the same dazzling glint. Or maybe I just thought of classic movie actors because Seton's suit was an elaborate period costume—a subtle salt-and-pepper tweed over a herringbone vest, with a tie kept in place with a silver tie pin. If I wasn't mistaken, his shirt cuffs were fastened with actual cufflinks. He turned heads—although that might have been because he was acting like a goggle-eyed tourist. I had to jab him toward an empty booth.

That jab sent a shock through my system. He felt it, too, and turned to me. "What was that?"

"Static electricity?" I guessed.

He was still rubbing his arm as he folded himself into the booth.

I plucked a laminated menu from between the salt-and-pepper shakers and the box of Trivial Pursuit cards—probably the same cards Sarah, Martine, and I had quizzed each other on fifteen years ago.

Seton didn't reach for a menu. His neck crooked and his gaze darted overhead. "What is this noise?"

"Not a Boy George fan, I guess."

His confusion only grew. "Is there a wireless hidden?"

I pointed to the black box mounted on a wall in the opposite corner. "The music's coming from there."

"That's *music*?"

I handed him a menu. "I should have guessed you were a snob from the cufflinks. The city doesn't have dives like this?"

"No . . ." His attention had snagged on a guy sporting a goatee and a man bun at a nearby table.

I cleared my throat. The sooner I got this over with and dumped this guy, the better. "All right. Tell me what you have to say."

I'd hear him out and then leave. At least he'd be in downtown

Zenobia rather than out on the outskirts of town. He'd wanted to get away from Esme, and I'd obliged him.

What an evening. First Esme's cat-whispering niece, and then this catatonic carjacker. Served me right for skipping my guitar lesson.

Before he could answer me, our server sauntered over. She was clearly a student. A Penguin Classic poked out of her apron pocket next to a ketchup bottle. "Something to drink?"

I felt the need for something strong, but I was driving. A decade of reviewing clients' car insurance accident claims had made me prudent. "Coffee for me."

Seton didn't answer. He was too focused on the server's nose ring to notice her impatient expression. Under the table, I nudged his calf with my foot. "What do you want?" I prompted.

He pivoted toward me. "Is this a speak?"

What kind of slang was that? I spoke more slowly. "Do. You. Want. A. Drink?"

"People seem to be drinking beer. I'll have one of those." He eyed me and lowered his voice. "If you don't mind risking it."

Risking what? Come to think of it, I wasn't sure if this guy should be drinking. No telling what kind of meds he was on. But that wasn't my lookout. I was leaving him here.

At my shrug, Seton turned to the waitress and affirmed, "A beer please, miss."

The server sighed and rattled off a list of brands the Owl's Nest carried on tap.

His face went slack. "I just want a beer."

"Genesee Cream Ale," I answered for him, smiling apologetically at the server. "He's not from here."

"Who is?" she said, then sloped off to the bar.

Seton sat rigidly straight. Staring at everything with wide, astonished eyes, he resembled a lemur in a vintage suit. "This place is very modern."

"Oh yeah." Imagine calling this 1980s relic *modern*. "Look, I need to get back to Rochester soon. You were going to tell me something about Esme Zimmer, but—"

"She's a witch," he blurted out. "I think maybe that niece of hers is, too, but definitely the older one."

I tried to keep an open mind. Some people really believed in astrology, or the healing power of magnets, or, yes, witches.

"And you think this because . . . ?"

He eyed me as if the answer was self-evident. "She brought me here."

"To Zenobia?" I frowned. "Kidnapped you, you mean?"

He nodded, encouraged that I was finally catching on. "From New York City. And from 1930."

The waitress appeared with our drinks. She gave him his glass of beer and clunked a mug of coffee down on the table. A handful of tiny plastic creamers tumbled down after it. Across from me, Seton was sniffing his beer as if he didn't quite trust it.

Had he said *1930*?

Yes, he had.

"On second thought," I told the waitress, "I'll have a gin and tonic."

Her face screwed up doubtfully. "Instead of coffee?"

I guarded my cup. "No, I'll drink this, too." Caffeine, alcohol—right now I was up for any potable drug she could push in front of me.

Seton finally chanced a sip of his beer. Once he'd tested it, he took a longer swig. "I hope we don't get raided before I can finish."

Oh, Lord. Did this poor soul really think he'd been kidnapped from 1930? That explained why he was dressed like an escapee from *The Great Gatsby*. In his head, the man was living in the world of gangsters and speakeasies.

And witches. I wasn't sure how witches fit into his Roaring Twenties cosplay. I wasn't sure I wanted to know.

He read the doubt in my expression. "You don't believe me." A long sigh deflated him. "It's difficult to believe it myself."

I nodded at his outfit. "Is that the reason for the strange suit—to convince yourself?"

A laugh blurted out of him. "I strike *you* as strange? I don't understand the fashions of these times at all. People dress in rags, and men have all manner of scraggly hair, and did you get a load of that girl's poor nostril?"

"Okay, Grandpa, let's rewind a little. What makes you think you're from 1930?"

He bristled. "I don't think, *I know*. I'm jumbled up about a lot of things, but that's one thing I'm sure of. It was April thirteenth, 1930. A Saturday. I was at work."

"What do—did—you do for a living?"

"I work downtown in an investment house."

"You were at work on a Saturday?"

"Indeed I was. Mr. Waymire insists on half days on Saturdays."

My gin and tonic arrived. I downed half in one gulp. "And exactly how did you get from your investment house to here?"

"That woman! It was all her doing. She even admits it—just ask her!" He caught the edge of hysteria in his voice and frowned. "No, don't ask her. I'm sorry for being so agitated. You seem nice. You don't want to have anything to do with her if you can help it."

That was one thing we agreed on. "So you were at your office when Esme Zimmer plucked you up and somehow teleported you over ninety years into the future."

"I'm not familiar with that word—teleported—but she did *something*."

"What was Esme doing in 1930?"

"How should I know? She's a witch!"

"A time-traveling witch." I was unable to keep the disbelief out of my voice. "Okay, I'll bite. Why don't you ask her to send you back?"

"She says she can't. Her explanation is that sending me back would be unethical because I'll die."

An aching pressure started up in my temples. I couldn't decide if slugging down the rest of that gin and tonic would help or make it worse. An hour ago, I'd been worried about a wedding dress. Now I had a man gabbling at me about witch ethics and time travel.

Seton explained, "In the matter of my possibly dying, I can't fault her. When she snatched me, or whatever you would call it, I was falling from a window on the nineteenth floor." He took a long sip of his beer, steadying the glass with both hands. Whatever psychosis had caused him to cook up this preposterous story, he clearly was convinced it had actually happened.

"So you're telling me that Esme actually *saved* you from a certain death."

He shifted, then emitted a grudging "Yes."

"Why were you falling? Were you committing suicide?"

He drew back. "Certainly not! I was pushed. By my friend, Burt. Rather, I *thought* he was my friend, until the four-flusher informed me that he was having a love affair with my wife. Ruthie and I are—were—having problems. I thought we'd fallen out of love. I didn't know that she'd fallen *in* love with Burt."

So now he was ladling soap opera into his science fiction.

He registered my skepticism but soldiered on. "It probably seems strange for you to see a man still shaken by events that happened so long ago, but to me it was just last week. And since then"—he lifted his hand in a vague gesture to indicate not only the Owl's Nest, but the whole world—"well, there's been a lot to adjust to."

I wondered how much of this was true. Not the time travel nonsense, of course. But was there really an unfaithful wife or girlfriend in the picture, and a friend who wanted to shove him out a window? Maybe the trauma of learning of the infidelity had caused his brain to snap.

But how had Esme Zimmer come into the picture?

"So in the seconds after Bill pushed you—"

"Burt."

"—after Burt pushed you out the window, and in the moment before you hit the sidewalk, Esme Zimmer just happened to be wandering past and zapped you forward to present-day Zenobia."

"Precisely."

It was all preposterous. And, happily, not my problem.

"You don't believe me." His shoulders slumped. "I don't blame you. I wouldn't have believed it myself."

"I believe that you *think* the story is true."

Disappointment filled his eyes. "I see. You think I'm screwy." He took another drink, then shook his head. "Sometimes I imagine that I'm still falling, or I've hit that sidewalk and this is the afterlife—a very strange one."

"That would make me an angel. Believe me, no one has ever called me that."

His face almost twitched into a smile, but he continued, dead serious, "Some people believe in a thing called reincarnation, don't they? I've even felt it myself sometimes, haven't you?"

"That I was Cleopatra or a hummingbird in a former life?" I shook my head. "No."

"You've never felt you've landed in the wrong place? I have, even before now. Sometimes I'd be sitting at my dinner table, alone with Ruthie, both of us eating silently as the mantel clock ticked and chimed through the meal with never a word between us. We might as well have been cows out in a field chewing our cud. And I'd wonder how I'd arrived there. I'd think that if I could call up Aladdin's genie, I'd change it all in a snap. Live some other life. Maybe that's what happened." His fingers drummed on the waxy tabletop.

"You need help, Seton."

"The kind of help available at the nearest lunatic asylum, you mean." His lips flattened. "I haven't gone goofy."

"Lunatic asylums don't really exist anymore—not the way they used to."

He looked around the bar. "That would explain a lot."

I realized I'd just spoken to him as if his hallucination were real, as if he actually were a man from 1930. I'd intended to find a way to offload this character and head home and spend what was left of the evening with my bird, but abandoning him didn't seem so easy now. There was such a vulnerability about him.

"Will you help me, Bailey?" he asked. "You're the only person I know here at the moment, and you seem kind."

Where could I possibly park this oddball? I flipped through the roster of possibilities in my mental Rolodex. I wasn't going to allow a strange man to stay overnight in my one-room duplex, and I couldn't ask Wes. He would definitely not understand my having picked a strange man up off the street. Nor did I feel comfortable asking my mom or any of my female friends to put him up.

Then I remembered my guitar teacher. Gil owned a music shop and had ties to a shelter in town. Sometimes he gave free music lessons to the kids living there. He would be able to advise me.

I pulled out my phone and tapped out a text. **Are you home this evening? I met a homeless guy who needs help.**

I wasn't expecting a reply right away, but even before I could snap my phone's cover closed, the dots were blinking. A moment later a message from Gil popped up.

Sure, bring him by and I'll see what I can do.

Thank you! I was so relieved, I added three smiley faces before I hit Send.

When I looked up again, Seton was eyeing my phone with that rigid, pop-eyed look of terror he'd had in the car.

"What's the matter?"

"You're one of them," he whispered in a fearful rasp. "You have one of those thingamabobs like Esme and her niece have."

"You mean a phone?"

"That's not a phone—it's a witch communicator. Were you sending the witches a message?"

As his voice looped up in agitation, the next table turned to stare at him.

I leaned toward him. "Calm down. I don't know where you've been for the past twenty-five years—"

"I *told* you."

He was really sticking to his ridiculous story. And he seemed so convinced that my phone was some kind of supernatural device shared by only a select few that perspiration was beading along his forehead.

"Seton, this *is* a phone. Look around you. *Everyone* has them."

He scoped the surrounding tables, most of which had at least one person staring down at their screen. His eyes narrowed suspiciously on the black rectangle lying on the table. "Doesn't it need a wire to work?"

"Um, no." How could I explain wireless technology to someone who was convinced he'd skipped ninety years? Especially when I had only the faintest grasp on how it all worked myself. "It's more like a . . . telegram? I was messaging my friend Gil, who's going to find you a place to sleep."

"Gil's not a witch?" He couldn't take his eye off my phone, as if he suspected I was summoning evil forces to storm into the café and seize him.

"Gil's my guitar instructor."

"You weren't talking to him, though."

"I was typing." I held up my phone. "These do everything—I can even take your picture." I pressed the picture icon and snapped a photo. The flash made him jump. But that was nothing next to his astonishment when I showed him the picture.

"How did it develop so fast?" he asked.

"It . . . well, it just does. It's digital."

He shuddered. "It's fantastical, like something from H. G. Wells."

"We should go," I said. "We have a twenty-minute drive ahead of us in case you need to use the washroom. I'll get the check."

"I can't let you do that," he protested. "You think I'm a moocher?"

"No, but—" I was about to ask what he was going to use for money when he pulled a wad of bills from his pocket. "Lucky for me I'd just gone to the bank." He peeled off two dollar bills and laid them on the table. "That should cover two drinks and a coffee, plus tip." He stood and strode off to the men's room.

I narrowed my eyes on the money he'd put down. Something wasn't right. I picked up one of the dollars. George Washington was on the front—the same as he ever was—but on the back was simply written "One Dollar" in large letters. No pyramid. No seal. Was Seton some sort of counterfeiter?

Also . . . two dollars for two drinks and a coffee?

Quickly, I pulled out my wallet, paid the waitress, and pocketed the fake bills.

I was standing up and ready to go when Seton returned. He looked bizarrely distinguished in this college bar. Other customers tracked him with their eyes, probably assuming he was one of the more eccentric profs at the university. A few women, I noticed, had something more than curiosity in their gazes as we walked out. He was handsome—at least in those rare moments when he didn't look panicked and demented. As he held the door open for me and I looked up into his eyes, my stomach fluttered.

Then I remembered he was a stranger. Possibly a lunatic. And I was getting back in a car with him, driving down a dark highway.

"Hang on a sec."

I texted Sarah. **I'm in Zenobia. I'm giving a guy a ride home. He says his name is Seton Atterbury. ICOE, he looks like this:** I attached the picture I'd taken of him and hit Send.

As we settled into the front seat, I said, "By the way, I just sent your name and picture to my best friend. She'll be able to identify you in case you turn out to be a serial killer."

"A . . . ?" He shook his head. "You mean, like Jack the Ripper?"

"Right. So if you are, you'd better take tonight off."

"Maybe I should just go . . ."

I laughed. "I'm just joking." Sort of. "Fasten your seat belt."

"My *what?*" He reacted as if I'd said something lewd.

"Seat belt." I pulled out my shoulder belt to demonstrate. "You know—the thing the law says you have to wear in a car?"

"There's a law?" He pawed around the seat looking for it.

"Right side." He found the shoulder belt and extended it in front of him, puzzled. The struggle to figure out what to do next didn't appear feigned. I'd seen toddlers buckle themselves in faster.

When we finally got on the road, he assumed the posture of terror he'd had on the way to the bar. I glanced over at him. "You look like you think your seat might eject you."

His eyes widened even more. "Is that possible?"

"Seton, this is a LEAF, not a jet fighter."

He shifted uneasily. "I'm not sure what you mean by that remark, but we're going very fast."

"It's a forty mile an hour zone. Hardly hot-rodding." He'd really flip out on the highway.

Nothing I said seemed to make him any calmer, so I switched on my favorite streaming station. Louis Armstrong and His Hot Seven piped out of the speakers.

Seton was flabbergasted. "That's incredible! It's like he's *right here!*"

"I just bought the basic package," I said, "but the sound's pretty decent."

Stopping at a light, I looked at my phone on its charger station. Sarah had replied to my text in all caps. **HAVE YOU LOST YOUR MIND?**

I glanced over at Seton, who was still gaping at the speaker, which at least seemed to get his mind off the terror of riding in a modern car. His leg bobbed along to "Muskrat Ramble." If he was putting on an act, he was making it look pretty damned convincing.

"I saw these guys," he said.

"*You* saw Louis Armstrong?"

"They play around town a lot," he said, as if they were still around. "I went to the Roseland Ballroom a few times when they were headlining there."

He'd *seen* him. Incredible.

Incredible if true, I meant. Which it wasn't. How could it be?

Behind us, a horn honked. The light had turned green. I pressed on the accelerator. Weird money, old clothes, and a knowledge of 1920s music didn't authenticate his story. There were lots of jazz fanatics in the world. It didn't mean . . .

Did it?

That I was even entertaining the notion that his story was true disturbed me.

HAVE YOU LOST YOUR MIND?

Maybe I had.

Chapter 5

Gil lived in the apartment above his music shop. Seton and I passed in front of the store's long display window on our way to the outside door that led upstairs.

He stopped, pressing his hands against the plate glass. "That's my saxophone!"

I peered at the ancient instrument he was eyeing.

"It's a Buescher True Tone," he said, "just like I played in college."

"You're a musician?" A saxophone playing banker.

"I was in a college band—Boyd and His Hot Beavers. We played a lot of dances. Not exactly the big time, but it helped pay for my last year of school. My Atterbury grandparents were well-to-do, but when my father died suddenly while I was in college, I discovered that Father hadn't been careful with money. As a matter of fact, he'd been living like a Rockefeller and had squandered away most of what had been left to him. Luckily there was only me to be disappointed by that time. It turned me into a saver."

"You were all alone?"

A cloud passed over his expression. "My mother and little brother, Toby, died in 1918. Influenza."

"How awful. And then to lose your father, too."

"By the time Father passed away there had been five years with just the two of us. If I hadn't been such a selfish pup I might have noticed that the pater was living a sham sort of existence. But I was young and caught up in my own concerns. Flaming youth." He shook his head. "Father's heart attack made me realize what a fool I'd been. After college, I put away ridiculous things."

"Like the saxophone?"

"Eventually." Although he had a wistful gaze pinned on the one in the window.

"And so you gave up music and embraced the business life." Why did that sound familiar?

"My father's death came as such a shock, I became very serious about making money and being the grown-up he hadn't been. The market turned out to be about as stable as a house of cards, of course—although I've done quite well." At my puzzled look, he said, "Commodities."

There had to be a grain of truth in his tale somewhere. His ravings about falling from a window and being teleported in time by a witch were lunacy, but when he spoke of his family, I believed him.

I pushed Gil's doorbell. I needed to get rid of Seton before I swallowed the whole nutty story.

The door swung open. Gil was wiry and slightly leathery looking, with deep lines etched in his face. He was about fifty, but in his early thirties he'd found himself living in his car until he finally received help from an aid society. Then he'd gotten a job at the music store and started giving lessons. He'd scraped enough money together to take over the shop when the former owner retired, but Gil had never forgotten what desperation felt like.

That was why I'd suspected that he would be willing to help Seton.

I introduced the two men and we all tromped up the narrow staircase. The apartment was a two-bedroom and fairly spacious . . . or would have been had not so much of the square footage been taken up by Gil's various projects—battered instruments he'd rescued from garage sales, boxes of musty sheet music from estate sales, and a harpsichord he was building himself from a design he'd found on the internet.

"You guys take a seat," Gil said.

That necessitated picking our way through a maze of junk to reach Gil's table and chairs. The kitchen-dining area was a tidy oasis in a sea of music-related mess.

When we were finally sitting down, Gil said to Seton, "Tell me about yourself."

Oh, no, I thought as Seton launched into his story of betrayal, time travel, and sorcery. I hadn't warned Gil about Seton's delusions.

But Gil didn't interrupt Seton's rambling tale, nor did he shoot me any accusing looks for involving him with this eccentric. Instead, he listened and nodded until Seton had him all up-to-date.

"Sounds like you've had a hard time of it," he said.

Seton laughed nervously, but seemed pleased that Gil hadn't reacted skeptically, as I had. "You can say that again. I'm not certain what to do next. That is, if there's anything I *can* do. Esme Zimmer said she wasn't sure she could help me, and I'm not certain I'd want her to in any case."

"Right, the whole falling-out-of-a-building thing," Gil agreed placidly, as if this were just an ordinary convo. "You're in a tough spot. How about a sandwich?"

Ten minutes later, the two of them were eating grilled ham and cheese sandwiches. I was impressed. Instinctively, Gil had known how to get Seton to open up and how to keep his agitation down.

Seton mentioned the saxophone downstairs.

"The True Tone." Gil nodded. "I haven't received much interest in that. It's the later-vintage models that sax collectors go for these days."

I clenched back a yawn and stood up. A sax gear discussion would put me to sleep. It seemed like two decades since I'd left my duplex that morning. I was ready to have a glass of wine, read a chapter of a book, and fall asleep.

"I should go. Did you find a place for Seton?"

"I did. I just thought he might like to have some food, a shower, and a shave before I drive him over. The shelter facilities are pretty decent, but there's a little more privacy here."

"Thank you," Seton said. "I appreciate your kindness."

I echoed the thanks. What would I have done without Gil?

"I'll leave you to it, then." I looked at Seton. "It's been . . ." I couldn't think of anything positive to say. "Anyway, good luck to you." Impulsively, I stuck out my hand.

He rose and clasped my hand in his. At once, my whole arm felt as if I'd stuck my finger into a light socket. Both Seton and I jumped and snatched our hands back.

"What *is* that?" he asked.

"I don't know." My fingertip problem was getting worse. This couldn't be good. I would have to consult a doctor.

I got out of there as soon as I could.

Once at home, I opened the door and, ignoring the disorder caused by the empty packing boxes stacked around, I headed straight for the wide parrot cage that now took up half the dining room area of the living room. On the opposite wall from the cage stood my little studio piano, now gathering dust.

Django thought I'd been away too long, too. He side-stepped across the branch inside his cage and was bobbing at the wire door even before I got across the room to open it for him. He hopped on my hand and quickly climbed to my shoulder, where he perched while I poured wine.

I put two grapes on a dessert plate and placed it on the table so he could join me. As soon as I was seated, he scrambled down my arm to get his snack.

I'd found Django at the local animal shelter. I'd gone there to adopt a cat, but as I walked in, a bird with half his feathers plucked tugged at my heart—especially when I approached the cage and he climbed straight over to me, sticking his black beak out between the bars. I'd changed my mind about the cat then and there and become a bird woman instead. I loved the sound his toenails made when he walked across wood or Formica. The turn of his head when he looked at me never failed to delight me. And his every little coo or squawk seemed wonderful to me.

"Are you sure?" I prompted him, remembering his words of this morning.

He'd been bending down for a grape, but now he cocked his head and eyed me curiously.

"Not talking tonight?" I asked.

"No," he said.

My mouth dropped open at the same time my phone rang. I picked it up. Sarah.

"He did it again," I told her excitedly.

"Who did what?"

"Django. He talked to me."

"What did he say?"

"'No.'"

"Uh-huh. Are you sure it wasn't a birdie burp or something?"

"He answered a question like he really understood me. I swear, I think he's got this communication thing all figured out."

"Tomorrow he'll be delivering the Gettysburg Address."

"You of all people should understand how exciting this is." We'd been trying to get him to speak for almost two years.

"I was worried you were dead, Bailey. The last thing I heard from you was a text two hours ago telling me that you'd picked up a hitchhiker or something. Excuse me if I'm not over the moon about Django's mumbles."

"His words were very distinct."

"What possessed you to pick up a hitchhiker?" She was clearly not interested in my parrot.

"He wasn't a hitchhiker so much as—" Saying he was a hijacker wouldn't soothe her fears any. "He was some guy I met in Zenobia."

"What were you doing there?"

"Looking for that woman we saw in the bridal boutique this afternoon—she was really there. I talked to her outside the place after you left. She's an insurance client of mine—that's why she looked so familiar. And Madeleine saw her, too."

Sarah gasped. "Madeleine? I thought she was in Europe."

"She's back."

"Oh, no." She sounded more distressed about it than I was. I'd had too many distractions this evening to dwell much on the Madeleine problem.

"She offered to make me a dress."

"*Madeleine?*"

I laughed. "No, Esme Zimmer. The woman at the bridal boutique."

"Oh, God. You're not going to get some rando to sew your wedding dress, are you?"

"I considered it, but no. I even went to her house in Zenobia and met her niece, who is as odd as Esme. Then I ran into Seton and got completely sidetracked."

Mentioning Seton brought Sarah back to her reason for phoning me. "What happened?"

"Nothing, really. He's a little off his rocker, but not in a dangerous way—you know, a lot of loony supernatural crap. Remember sophomore year when Martine's boyfriend got hold of the magic mushrooms? It was a lot like that."

"What did you do?"

"We just went to the Owl's Nest and talked, and then I drove him to Gil's. Gil was great."

"I wish you'd answered my text. I was getting ready to call the police."

An idea occurred to me. Sarah was a genealogy nut—she even volunteered weekends at the local genealogy library. She knew all about researching the past. "Hey, what's the name of the website with all the old newspapers? I need to look up something from the 1930s."

She gave me a name of a website, which I scribbled down on my grocery list pad on the fridge.

I could hear her yawn over the line. "I'm sorry," she said. "I should probably go to bed now. I've got a root canal in the morning. I just wanted to make sure you weren't lying in a shallow grave along the highway. If I'd known that Madeleine was back, I would've been even more worried."

I grunted in agreement as I booted up my computer.

"Just in time for the wedding," Sarah said. "I wonder what she has up her sleeve?"

"I wondered that, too. I've agreed to put her on guest book at the wedding."

Sarah made ominous noises, but we said good night. As soon as she'd hung up, I was in the newspaper website, looking up papers that existed in New York in 1930. There were scads of them. I ponied up for a premium membership to have access to them all. I looked up one, the *New York Courier-Sun* and typed in *Seton Atterbury*, not really expecting to get any hits.

To my surprise, a couple of articles popped right up. More startling, when I clicked on the first, in the middle of a scan of a densely typeset page was a blotchy picture that looked a lot like Seton. I enlarged my screen and then leaned in to read.

DOWNTOWN BANKER DISAPPEARS
Distraught Wife Pleads for Public's Help
Seton Atterbury III went missing from his office
Saturday morning, according to colleagues. "He just

vanished," his secretary, Miss Effie Levine, told this reporter. "I wandered down the hall to deliver a phone message to someone, and when I got back, Mr. Atterbury wasn't there anymore."

A visitor to the office at the time, Burton Lane, said he was mystified as to what had transpired. "One moment Seton was there, and the next there was just an open window."

Mr. Atterbury's wife, Ruth Atterbury, pleads with the public to inform the police if her husband is sighted. Seton Atterbury is tall, with light brown hair and blue eyes. He was last seen wearing a salt-and-pepper suit with a ruby tie clip. According to Mrs. Atterbury, her husband is in perfect health and does not suffer from despondency.

I frowned and studied the picture again. It looked so much like Seton, but it had to be his grandfather—or great-grandfather. It couldn't be the man I'd spoken with tonight.

The second article was from weeks later. MYSTERY OF MISSING BANKER REMAINS UNSOLVED, the headline read.

This time the paper didn't bother with a photograph. I supposed those were expensive to include, and now that the story was off the front page, the paper clearly didn't feel the disappearance was worth wasting capital on.

The article was "no new developments" boilerplate.

After that, the only item about Seton I found was from three years later, when Ruthie married Burton Lane. The article mentioned that her first husband, Seton Atterbury III, had never been found after his mysterious disappearance, but had been declared legally dead.

And the police didn't think it was suspicious that the supposed widow was marrying the man who'd been in the room when Seton had vanished? I felt outraged on Seton's behalf.

Or on Seton's great-grandfather's behalf.

Is that how Seton had come up with this story? It must have been something he'd heard relatives talk about. For all I knew, he might have checked out this website and gotten the details there. But why pretend to be his own ancestor?

Of course, people had been known to have mental breaks and imagine they were figures from the past. Believing you were your own great-grandfather was no stranger than believing yourself to be Genghis Khan or Benjamin Franklin.

And what if it isn't a delusion? The question was ridiculous, but I couldn't dislodge it from my mind. I remembered looking into Seton's eyes, so readable. With his open face, he didn't seem to have a deceitful bone in his body.

If Seton *wasn't* pretending, though, that would mean that he really had been snatched from the air during his Burt-spurred freefall from his office window.

And that Esme Zimmer really was a witch.

I reached into my purse and pulled out the bills I'd stashed there when I was at the restaurant. I switched browser tabs and typed *1920s US dollar* into the search engine's window.

My dollar bill came on-screen, along with a description. Apparently, the seal wasn't added to the back of the one-dollar bill until the midthirties. The bill from the twenties until that change was made had featured a much plainer background, just like the bill in my hand. According to the website, modern collectors call these bills Funnyback dollars.

Maybe Seton knew about that, too, and just decided to put a telling detail into his cosplay to make his tale more believable. But that seemed like an awful lot of trouble to go through to fool . . . who? Me? What motive would he have for that? He didn't seem to be trying to scam me. He didn't even know my last name. Then again, that wouldn't be difficult information to discover. And in the meantime . . .

I worried about Gil. He was streetwise, but he was also a sweet, caring person. A perfect mark.

I picked up my phone and messaged him. **Did the shelter turn out okay?**

It was a little while before the response popped onto the screen. **Decided to let him stay overnight. Dude needed some R&R.**

I frowned at my screen. What should I do? Tell Gil that Seton might be spinning an elaborate lie for a scam we didn't yet understand?

I hesitated and then typed, **I'll call you in the morning,** then slapped my phone's cover closed.

Django crooked his head to glance up at me. "Is there a problem?"

"Just . . . everything."

"You should get some sleep," he said. "'Sleep that knits up the raveled sleeve of care.'"

I blinked, stood up, walked my wineglass to the kitchen sink, and poured out nearly a full glass. I needed to cut down on my night drinking.

Was there a problem? Why yes, there was. I was starting to believe I'd met a man who'd been time-snatched by a witch. And now I was conversing with a Shakespeare-spouting bird.

Chapter 6

My eyes were scratchy from lack of sleep the next morning when I pressed Gil's doorbell. I was eager to listen to Seton's story again and see how closely it tracked with what I'd discovered in the newspaper. I couldn't rule out the possibility that he had read the same accounts about this missing ancestor and had, for some unfathomable reason, cooked up the whole improbable story about being time-snatched by a witch.

It wasn't that I believed him. But I didn't entirely disbelieve him, either.

Was this interest in Seton a mental diversion from the fact that I was getting married in three weeks? Not that I *needed* a mental diversion. I was glad to be getting married. I'd be even happier when the wedding ceremony itself was over with. That weddings were stressful was hardly a newsflash, but I'd assumed that diva brides were the source of the stress. I hadn't factored in all the niggling details into my wedding stress reckoning, or Wes's old flame coming back from Europe, or the strange fish-out-of-water sensation I would have around the Havermans.

I jabbed the buzzer again.

Footsteps clattered down the stairs on the other side of the door. When Gil yanked the door open, his hair, wet from the shower, stuck up in all directions, and the buttons of his shirt were done up crookedly. His bloodshot eyes looked exhausted and frantic.

"Seton's missing," he said.

I gaped in disbelief. "Are you sure?"

A ragged laugh tore out of him. "There aren't many places for a guy to hide in my apartment. Not only that, he stole a saxophone."

"He broke into your shop?"

Gil sighed. "Nah, I was an idiot. I went down last night and brought the sax up for him to try. He said it had been a while since he'd played."

Ninety years, by Seton's calculation.

"He's actually pretty good on the thing." Gil fingered through his keys and beckoned me over to the store entrance. "I could tell he really enjoyed playing. Hell, I would have loaned him one of my old beater student saxes if he'd just asked me."

"I'm so sorry. I knew he was odd, but I never dreamed he was a thief."

Never trust a guy who hijacks you. Lesson learned.

Gil unlocked the plate glass door, and we went inside the store. I'd always loved the place, with its slightly musty smell and walls covered with brass instruments facing another wall of guitars, violins, and ukuleles. The floor was crowded with music stands, racks of sheet music books, several upright pianos, and two drum kits. In the back were two small glassed-in rooms where I'd spent so many happy hours both taking guitar lessons and giving piano lessons. I never tired of coming here.

He logged on to his computer and brought up the store's inventory page, scrolling to find the serial number of the saxophone Seton stole. He scribbled the number on a scratch pad.

"I'm sorry, Bailey. If he's not back with my sax by the end of the day, I'm going to have to report him to the police."

I hadn't even realized how worried I was for Seton until I heard myself sigh with relief at the words *by the end of the day*. "I understand. Thank you so much—for everything, but especially for giving him a grace period. I'm going to look for him."

"Why?"

Was he serious? "There's a guy who thinks he's from 1930 wandering around Rochester. He believes witches are after him. He needs help."

"Why you, though?"

The question brought me up short. He was right. I could let Seton wander, get picked up by the police, and leave it to the authorities to sort him out. But the thought of that oddball trying to navigate a jail gave me chills.

"He doesn't have anyone but me." At Gil's concerned frown, I added, "Anyway, *you're* one to talk. You were going to take him to a shelter but let him stay at your place."

"And look how that turned out." He sighed. "I'd help you search, but—"

"Never mind. You've got a store to run."

Of course, I also had a job to go to. But suddenly it didn't seem as important as finding Seton.

"You might be wasting your time," Gil warned. "He could be anywhere by now."

True. Maybe he would even try to go all the way back to 1930. There was only one way he would think he could get back to his time: Esme Zimmer. I couldn't help remembering how terrified Seton had been of her. He'd begged me to rescue him from her. Would desperation lead him to seek her out again?

Or worse. What if she'd caught up with him?

I hitched my purse on my shoulder. "I'll do my best to find him. And if I can't find him, I'll pay for the sax."

"You shouldn't do that. *You* didn't steal it."

I hurried back out to my car. I had to call the office and tell them I wasn't coming in. Paige was going to love that.

I was digging my phone out of my purse when it rang.

I flipped it open without even looking. "Hello?" I asked eagerly.

"Good morning, Buttercup." Wes's warm greeting sounded as if it were coming from another life, another world. "Do you know what today is?"

"Wednesday?"

He laughed. "It's our date-iversary. We started dating exactly two years ago. I took you to the opening day ribbon cutting of our Haverman's in Utica, remember?"

"That's right. With the big organics section."

He chuckled. "Everyone said organics and Utica didn't mix, but we've showed them."

A pause crackled over the line. I was having a hard time focusing on the conversation. My head was so full of worry, it felt as if Wes's words spilled right back out of my head as soon as I heard them.

"Bailey? Are you feeling okay?" he asked.

What is the matter with me? Wes was the most important person in my life. He'd been my rock for two years. When we'd first started dating, every phone call or text from him had sent my pulse galloping. If I didn't hear from him for twenty-four hours, I started dragging around like I had the flu or something. Now here he was, being as romantic and sweet as he was on our first date, and all I could think about was some saxophone-thieving nut.

"Sorry, I've been dealing with a lot."

"If it's about the wedding dress—"

"It's not."

But that reminded me, I needed to contact the store in Buffalo about the backup dress. And I still had to call in sick to Genesee Insurance. Two years ago, two months ago, nothing would have made me believe that I would ever take a call from Wes for granted. My twenties had been a string of awful romantic experiences—single-date disasters; a brief fling with a guy who it didn't take long to figure out would rather be playing video games than actually talking to someone face-to-face; and a couple of longer-term relationships without chemistry that sputtered out.

After all that, I'd taken a dating hiatus. And then I'd met Wes. Compared to all the men I'd been out with before, he was like a white knight riding in to rescue the damsel from a life of dodging assholes and incels. He was intelligent, and actually listened, and was not only gainfully employed but successful and dedicated to his family business. Everything about him screamed marriage material.

"You're wonderful." I sighed, as much at my memories as at the sweetness of his calling me this morning. "I need to get going, though."

"Me too. I just wanted to let you know that I'm looking forward to tonight."

Alarm gripped me. "Tonight? What's tonight?"

"Dinner with the folks? Don't tell me you forgot."

"No, of course not," I lied. "I just have a lot on my plate now, so . . ."

"I'll pick you up at your office at six."

"I'm not going to be at the office today."

A pause hiccupped over the phone before he asked, "What's going on?"

I couldn't explain my worry over Seton in a way that would make sense. What could I tell him that wouldn't make him think his bride-to-be would shortly morph into the madwoman in his attic? I swallowed. "It's a family thing."

"Ah."

"I'll meet you at the restaurant," I said. The phone was halfway to my purse when I heard Wes's voice tinnily shouting, "Love you," up at me.

"Love you, too." I rang off and called the office, intending to leave a message, but unfortunately Ron was already at his desk. The receptionist patched me through before I could stop her, and I informed him that I was taking the day off.

"Taking my advice and kicking back a little!" he bellowed approvingly.

"Actually, a friend is having an emergency."

"Don't you worry about a thing." I could tell by his tone that he thought I was fibbing. "If something comes up today, I'll tell Janine to bump it over to Paige."

Oh, God. That was the last thing I wanted. "Couldn't Janine bump it over to Tim?"

"Tim's not the go-getter that Paige is."

Exactly. Tim was the kind of employee who took the expression "Ninety percent of success is showing up" at face value. He didn't have a competitive corpuscle in his body.

After ending the conversation, I headed back to Zenobia.

When I rang the decrepit farmhouse's doorbell this time, Esme Zimmer answered with a rapturous smile, as if she'd been expecting me.

"I *knew* you'd be back." She took my arm and whisked me inside.

The house seemed completely different on the inside. The living room was decorated in mid-century modern, with teal walls. My eyes needed a moment to adjust to the eye-popping retro look.

Esme blinked up at me expectantly.

"I'm not going to beat around the bush," I said. "I came here for one reason only. I know all about you."

She stepped back. Her fist tapped her breastbone as if there was something lodged in there. "Y-you do?"

"That's why I'm here. So there's no reason to be cagey. Just tell me the truth."

A typhoon of tension rushed out of her. She tottered backward toward the nearest chair and picked up a large clothes box that was sitting on it. "I thought you came for the dress. I have it here, but—" She looked up at me, lips trembling, eyes brimming with tears, and dropped the box again. "I'm so glad you know. I've wanted to tell you for the longest time."

Wariness seized hold of me. "Tell me . . . ?"

"I never forgot you. *Never.* I want you to know that. All these years, I've thought of you every day."

She thought about her insurance agent every day? "Why?"

"They all say that you should just forget and move on. And I was in very difficult circumstances, but—" To my horror, she flung her arms around me, and burst into tears. "I've dreamed of this day for so long. So so so long."

I tried without success to pry her off, but she was attached to me like a cephalopod on an undersea boulder. "What are you talking about?"

Her shoulders shook with emotion. "This is a dream come true."

I finally wriggled free and stepped back to put space between us. "Why should it be?"

Her head tilted. "You didn't come here for a reunion?"

Could finding Seton be called a reunion? I'd only met him last night.

Before I could work up a response to her odd question, she grabbed both my hands in hers.

"You said you knew." Her desperate, needy gaze fastened on me. "Izzie, I'm your mother."

Chapter 7

Her face, which had been fixed in an expression of exultant expectation, slackened. "You didn't know. But now, you must see—"

Before she could repeat the absurd assertion, I lifted my hands and interrupted her. "Please. Stop. You are not my mother."

"Your *real* mother, Is."

"Stop calling me that name!"

It was the only thing I could think of to react to at first. Her claim to be my mother was too ridiculous.

"That was the name I gave you," she said. "Isadora. Izzie. It suits you."

"No, it doesn't. You know what name suits me? Bailey. Because that's my name—the one Lloyd and Deb Tomlin gave me. My real mother lives in Rochester. She raised me. She plays bridge and gardens and thinks every minor ailment or problem can be alleviated by egg custard. She dropped me off at my first day of school and was there when I graduated from high school and college."

"So was I," Esme said.

Yikes. As if I weren't creeped out enough already. "You are *not* my birth mother." I'd only questioned Mom once about the woman who'd given me up. I could tell it had felt like a betrayal to her for me to even bring up the subject, but she told me the woman's name. Actually, Mom had called her a girl—my birth mother was seventeen when she gave me up. "My birth mother's name wasn't Esme Zimmer."

"Of course not. It was Stefanie Pickles."

My breath caught.

How could this woman have discovered that name? My birth records were sealed. Even I had only seen the birth certificate that had been issued after my adoption, listing me as Bailey Tomlin, daughter of Debra and Lloyd Tomlin.

"*I'm* Stefanie Pickles," she said. "It was a fake name."

"Why would you have called yourself Stefanie Pickles?"

She tossed up her hands. "I was stuck in a place in the country all by myself for several months waiting for you to come along, doing nothing really except eating too much and lying around in thrall to eighties TV reruns. I watched lots of *Hart to Hart*. So when I had to think of a name for a sadder-but-wiser girl giving up her baby, I guess I had Stefanie Powers on the brain. Only I couldn't actually call myself Stefanie Powers—that would have been weird. So I gave myself the surname Pickles, in honor of all the sweet, sweet gherkins I'd been devouring along with pints of Ben and Jerry's. Had a whimsical ring to it, I thought."

Whimsical? "I don't care *how* you came up with the name. Why did you have to use a pseudonym at all?"

"I was in a spot of trouble at the time." Her fingers twittered nervously. "Long story."

"A birth certificate is an official document. You can't just lie."

"Turns out, you can. I had very convincing fake IDs, of course. And it was mostly all on the up-and-up, apart from that."

Mostly? A bitter laugh burbled out of me. "Apart from completely misrepresenting yourself?"

If what she was telling me was even true. The woman was bonkers. Why, why, why had I come here? Every time I set foot on this property, it was like falling down Alice's rabbit hole.

She leaned forward. "Would you like to sit down? You're looking a little pale."

"I won't be staying." Nevertheless, my boneless legs buckled and I sagged down into the nearest seat—a stylish Heywood-Wakefield wood chair with an orange seat and back cushions.

"Care for a drink?" Esme asked me. "Tea? Coffee? Tranquilizing potion?"

"What?"

"I also make a mean whiskey sour."

Even though it was just half past ten, that last option sounded very appealing.

I shook my head. "I don't understand any of this."

She sat down opposite me, her face tensed in an expectant smile, and clasped her hands primly on her thighs. "Ask me anything you want to know. I'm here for you."

Looking at her, I couldn't forget what Sarah had said about her when I described her. *So she looked like . . . you.* She *did* look like me. The spitting image.

I wanted to cry, but not from joy.

I'd never been unhappy to be adopted, for the simple reason that I never felt anything less than adored by my parents. My dad took pictures and videos of me, and recorded every inch I grew. Every mundane milestone of childhood and adolescence had been celebrated as if it were a phenomenal achievement. When I finished kindergarten, you'd have thought I'd earned a PhD. My first piano recital, when I played "The Happy Halibut," could have been held in Carnegie Hall as far as Lloyd and Deb Tomlin were concerned. I might not have been spoiled in material possessions, but in terms of love and attention I was richer than a Kardashian.

And yet . . .

Occasionally—very occasionally—when I wasn't allowed to spend the weekend at Lake Placid when I was thirteen, or allowed to attend a concert, or when Mom made me return the leatherette miniskirt I'd bought at the mall, I'd sometimes wonder about that seventeen-year-old girl who'd given me up. Stefanie Pickles wouldn't have been an old fogy like my parents were. She would have been Cool Mom, signing off on all the school trips, okaying every sleepover, and understanding that seeing Apocalyptica at the Kodak Center was an imperative cultural event for a twelve-year-old.

And now, here she was. Stefanie Pickles. Aka Esme Zimmer. My dream Cool Mom was a kooky client who'd apparently been shadowing me for years. It was more than a little unnerving, not to mention disappointing. *This* was my flesh and blood?

My gaze traveled down to her neck, which was starting to wrinkle. My future.

That is, if she was who she said she was.

"The neck thing is genetic," she said.

My face flamed. Had I been that obvious?

"My mother's was even worse than mine," she said. "By the time she was my age, it looked more lined than a crosscut section of an old-growth sequoia. But don't despair—you've got the Zimmer coloring, but maybe in other respects you'll take after your father. Odin's a remarkable specimen."

Father? *Odin?*

"You're still with—?" I refused to say *my father.*

"Actually, that's a recent development," she said. "He and I were separated for decades—not by our own choice."

"A star-crossed lovers story?"

"Sort of. Odin was hexed out of existence for several decades."

"Hexed." Oh, God. I'd been so distracted by Esme's bombshell that I'd forgotten why I'd come here—to find Seton, who'd accused Esme of being a kidnapper, and a witch.

"There's so much to explain." She scooted forward. "It was complicated. That's why I had to let you go."

"You never considered raising me yourself?"

"They wouldn't have allowed it."

"Who is 'they'? Your parents?"

"The Grand Council of Witches." She reeled the name off as if it were a humdrum entity like a co-op board. "I was cursed."

"You said my"—I stopped myself—"Odin was cursed."

"Yes. Both of us were—different curses, you understand."

"Sure." My hands tightened around the arms of my chair.

"It's a long story, going back decades." She stopped, fidgeting anxiously. "But my real trouble started when your father was cursed. That's all worked out now. Well, mostly. He'll be able to tell you all about it." A shadow of worry fell over her face. "I hope."

"You haven't told him about me," I guessed.

Her eyes widened. "Of course I have. He's eager to meet you. It's just that I'm not sure when he'll be back."

"Where is he?"

"Right now he's still in the early twentieth century."

I should have taken her up on that whiskey sour.

"I was with him," she said, "but we got separated in 1930."

I lifted my hands. "Okay—stop. Is that how Seton Atterbury got mixed up in all this?"

She sucked in a breath. "You've met Seton? Do you know where he is?"

"That's what I came here to ask you. Seton jumped in my car

last night and spun a wild yarn about having been snatched from 1930 when he was falling out of a window."

"It's true. Odin and I were walking down the street and I saw this man falling. Odin and I both gasped, and without thinking I grabbed the falling man before he hit the pavement. It was just instinctive. I wanted to save him, and the safest place I know is my home."

My mouth opened to speak, then snapped closed. She actually believed what she was saying.

"Now I've got him here and the poor fellow wants to go back," she continued, "and I've lost track of Odin, too, so a huge responsibility rests on my shoulders alone. If I send Seton back too early, it could change history. That's a no-no. But if I return him just at the same time I found him—if that's even possible—within seconds he'll be splattered all over a Wall Street sidewalk. Talk about your ethical dilemmas."

"So you're saying you really zapped Seton into the present."

"Of course." She flicked an impatient glance at me. "How else would a person cross nine decades? Did you think he'd built a time machine?"

"Oh, no," I said dryly. "*That* would be preposterous."

She finally twigged that I didn't believe her supernatural claims. "You can't be a doubter. You must have felt the power within yourself."

"No." I shifted, forcing my gaze away from my hands. Those electric sensations I'd been having . . .

And then there was Django. Just last night I'd seen that woman Gwen talking to her cat and thought she was crazy. Then I'd gone home and had a conversation with a bird.

"I'm a rational person," I insisted. "I don't believe in the occult. I don't even subscribe to woo-woo things like karma, or love at first sight." I stood. "I don't mean to be insulting. I'm sure you mean well, and that you have many good qualities." I struggled to come up with an example. "You've been a very loyal Genesee Insurance client."

She hopped up, too. "That was all for you. To help you in the small way I could."

"We've appreciated your business," I said. "We really have. But I'm afraid I don't believe you about all this. You seem to be genuinely convinced that you're my birth mother, but you also think you're a witch, so . . ."

"I've handled this all wrong, haven't I?" Tears of frustration brimmed in her eyes. "I wish Odin were here. He's better at explaining things than I am. I spent half my life under a curse." Her expression brightened. "Of course! You *must* know I was a witch. You first saw me before. I looked completely different."

She'd looked like a crone. *That* had been her curse?

But Wes was right. Plastic surgery could easily account for the changes in her appearance.

Thinking of Wes made me want to flee back to my solid, sane life.

"I'm very busy," I said. "I really just came over because I was worried about Seton and thought he might have come back here." That seemed even more unlikely to me now. No one would come back here once they'd escaped—me included. "He took a saxophone from a friend of mine, who's going to call the police if he doesn't return it this afternoon. Please inform Seton of that if you see him again."

"You're not leaving," she said, hurrying after me as I crossed the room.

The black cat I'd seen last night was standing in the arched doorway that led from the living room to the hall. I stopped next to him.

"I thought we could have lunch," Esme said. "A mother-daughter thing. We have so much to catch up on."

She had to be joking. Hands fisted at my sides, I drew up as straight as I could and looked her firmly in the eye. "Look, I don't want to hurt your feelings. You obviously have a sincere belief"—*sincere delusion*—"in what you're saying. But I'm sorry, I'm skeptical that you're my mother, and I definitely don't believe in witchcraft."

"You *definitely* don't believe, eh?" Her face tugged into a scowl, and I glimpsed the crone she had been when I'd first seen her. "I suppose you want proof, but what will you do when you have it?"

She was a little scary when she was riled, but I'd indulged her nonsense for long enough. "I'm not worried about that. There is no such proof."

"Isn't there?" In her anger Esme seemed to swell before my eyes, her hair and skin flushing a deeper red. "You want bippity-boppity-boo, I'll give it to you." She raised her arms. "*Voilà*—the dress of your dreams."

In a flash, all the oxygen seemed to be sucked out of the room. I tried to inhale a breath, but my chest suddenly seemed made of stone. The air shimmered and fragmented like a cubist painting, and it was as though a vise were pressing me from all directions. I shrieked in pain—or did I? I couldn't hear, couldn't think.

When the atmosphere was righted again, I stumbled back in blessed relief. Then I looked down at myself and gasped in a breath. I was standing in a long white dress. I lifted my silk-clad arms. "What is this?"

Esme must have mistaken my amazement for impatience. Her lips twisted. "I forgot. You need mirrors."

"No, I—"

Before I could finish, she did the arm thing again. I flinched. Faster this time, the living room around me juddered as if the very molecules required a moment to rearrange themselves. When I blinked my eyes open, mirrors stood all around me. In those mirrors was me, in a silk shift covered with a lace overdress done in the most beautiful beadwork, giving it a vintage look. The dress was fitted to mid-thigh, then the skirt flared and draped into a train. I twisted slightly to get a view of the back, which plunged down to mid-spine. The cut was both old-fashioned and modern. Unique. Exactly what I'd hoped to find.

And it fit perfectly.

Esme crossed her arms. "So. Do you like it?"

I was too astonished to lie. "It's just what I've been looking for."

She rocked back on her heels, pleased by my reaction but completely absorbed in her handiwork. Had she made this . . . or was it really some kind of magic dress? One second I'd been in my boring clothes and the next I was wearing this gorgeous creation. It *had* been magic. I gaped at her as she frowned down at the hem.

"It'll look better when you've got the right shoes," she said. "I left yours on—I wasn't sure how much of a heel you'd want. I've got bunions myself."

"My feet are fine," I said, still stunned by it all.

"They won't be if you don't take care of them."

Were we really talking about podiatric health when I'd just witnessed sorcery?

"But you like the cut?" she asked, reaching out to tug at the waist. "It feels right? You don't want to feel constricted on your big day."

I blinked at myself in the mirrors. She'd not only conjured this dress onto me, she'd styled my hair into an updo with artistic ringlets. I hoped I'd be able to re-create those—or explain it to the stylist Joan had hired for the wedding party.

That fleeting thought of Joan Haverman was like having a bucket of cold water poured over me. *What am I thinking?*

I stepped back. "Please get this off me."

"What's the matter?" Esme asked. "You wanted a dress, and you wanted proof that I was a witch. I gave you a twofer."

"This isn't right."

"It's the back, isn't it?" She craned her head to look at my back. "Too much plunge?"

Too much witchcraft. I couldn't marry Wes Haverman in a dress conjured by supernatural trickery, by some witch claiming to be my birth mother. The Havermans wouldn't understand any of this. *I* didn't understand it. All I knew was that this woman scared the crap out of me. If what I was experiencing was real, not some crazy dream, then Esme really was a witch. And if she was right about being a witch, was she right about being my mother, too?

My mind reeled. Who was I?

"I need to go."

Her face registered disappointment. "Too much, too soon?"

I nodded, practically quivering.

She sighed. "Forgive me. I'm new at this mothering biz."

This time when she raised her hands, I welcomed the pressure and the shrieking in my ears. I wanted the vise of sorcery to squeeze all memory of this experience out of me. Maybe I would wake up in my bed, and hear Django clucking to himself on his perch in the next room.

But when the world stilled again, it was just me and Esme. I was back in the clothes I'd dressed in this morning, and she was holding a large garment bag.

"Don't decide anything just yet," she said. "Take the dress with you. Think it over. I don't expect mother-of-the-bride status, but I would like to contribute *something* to my daughter's wedding."

Mother. My mouth went bone dry.

I backed up, tripping over the black cat winding between my legs. I leapt in alarm. I needed to get out of there.

"I had the same reaction to this place at first," the cat said.

Was the cat talking to *me* now? "How did you handle it?"

"I hid under a bed for three months."

"I'm not sure three months would be enough."

He swished his tail. "The cognitive behavior therapy techniques of television's Dr. Tim were also essential to me."

I gaped at him. "You watch that charlatan?"

He bristled. "He's just my hero, but sure, go ahead and dump on him."

"I'm sorry, it's just that I—"

Oh, God. *I'm turning into them.* I was talking to animals—next thing I knew I'd be winging around the Milky Way on a broomstick. How was any of this happening?

"You can understand Griz because you've been touched by magic," Esme explained, correctly interpreting my freak-out over the cat. "It's up to the animals themselves, you know, to decide who they want to connect with and have hear them. Consider it an honor."

I continued backing away. *Touched by magic.* When had I started to be touched by magic? When this crazy woman started appearing in my life?

Esme had already moved on. "And honestly, if you don't like the dress, just bring it back," she said, pursuing me. "Or donate it somewhere." Her eyes narrowed. "But if you do decide to donate it, let me know. We need to put it through a de-ensorcellation process first."

Numbly, I allowed her to drape the bag over my outstretched arms, mostly because I didn't want to prolong this encounter another minute. The moment my skin touched the plastic, though, electricity jolted up to my shoulder. I yelped in pain.

"You get used to that," she assured me.

I squinted at her. How did she know what had happened?

On second thought, I didn't want to find out.

I pivoted and fled for the door. Unfortunately, it was covered in deadbolts, chains, and slide locks, most of which were fastened. Esme scooted past me and undid them with an apologetic shrug. "Habit," she explained. "I had to be careful for so long.

And of course, what happened when we let down our guard? A time-traveling stockbroker escapes from my basement."

"Basement?"

She nodded. "Where my laboratory is."

A witch laboratory. I didn't know what to say to that. I clasped the garment bag to my chest and fled to my car.

As I was peeling away, in my rearview mirror I could see Esme waving at me from her porch step.

Chapter 8

That was not my mother, I told myself, willing my heart to slow down. It felt as if a gerbil had taken up residence in my chest.

Witches are not real. Dresses don't try themselves onto bodies by magic. Mirrors don't appear out of thin air.

My phone pinged and I glanced down. Katrina.

Dear Lord. I couldn't think about boutonnieres now.

No, the boutonniere crisis was yesterday. Yesterday, an eon ago, when I'd thought a few wedding planning woes were stressful. Yesterday Me didn't know there was a witch lurking in the background. That she'd *always* been in the background.

If Esme was my mother, then I was either the child of a witch or the child of a crazy woman who A) thought she was a witch and B) locked strange men in her basement.

How much of this was true? How could I find out? I wished I knew where Seton was.

Questions swirled in my head all the way back to Rochester. Instead of jumping off the highway at the exits that would lead to either work or to my duplex, in a fugue state I drove farther north through town to the Charlotte neighborhood, to the street where I grew up. I needed my mother. My real one. Normal, predictable Mom. She would be able to set me straight.

If there was ever a place that screamed normal, it was my parents' narrow, two-story clapboard house, which was painted the same slate blue it had been my entire life. My parents had moved into this house two years before I came along. I couldn't help but think it was chosen to tick all the boxes an adoption agency would be looking for in prospective parents: solid middle-class neighborhood, fenced yard, three bedrooms and one and a half baths, a backyard to play in. The front was a glassed-in porch where we removed our snow boots in winter and Mom grew her seedlings in springtime.

Right now there were already tiny plastic pots of tomatoes and marigolds lined up on plastic shelves by the windows. Seeing their hopeful leaves pressing against the panes, I let out a breath and stepped out of the car. There was nothing magical here, and I meant that in the best possible way.

Mom darted her head out the porch door. I gasped. It looked like she had been body-snatched by a pixie-headed alien. Her hair had been clipped from the shoulder-length bob she'd worn for the past three decades into a short, spiky do, her natural gray spruced up with green and blue streaks.

"*Mom?*"

She brushed her shorn locks with her hand, beaming like a woman in a shampoo commercial. "What do you think?"

I pasted on a smile as I climbed the porch steps. "You look great," I said, trying to sound more enthusiastic than I felt. "So different!" Different was not what I wanted. I'd come here looking for Deb Tomlin. This woman seemed entirely new and unMomlike.

"Isn't it neato?"

Okay, maybe not *entirely* new. She still sounded like Deb Tomlin. But I'd never seen a haircut transform someone quite so starkly. She was practically glowing.

"I feel like I've been visited by a fairy godmother," she trilled. *Bippity-boppity-boo.* "Please don't mention those." I gave her a quick hug and went ahead of her into the house.

The living room with its comfy furniture and walls overloaded with pictures, knickknack shelves, shadowboxes, and other mementos greeted me like a warm hug. There was still a yarn-and-Popsicle-stick God's eye I'd made at camp hanging next to a family photo taken when I was seven and didn't have any front teeth. The sight of me there in all my awkward glory, next to my real, nonwitchy parents, comforted me so much I wanted to weep. Mom's new blue and green hair notwithstanding, here was a place devoid of weirdness. Of witchiness.

"I'm so happy you popped by," Mom said, coming up behind me. "Katrina called."

"Katrina called *you?*"

"She's worried about the dress situation."

So she called my mother? That was the worst possible thing she could have done. I was already tiptoeing through a minefield regarding Mom and the wedding dress.

"She said someone on the Haverman side was floating the idea of a dress shopping spree in New York," Mom continued. "Joan Haverman can't go because of some charity auction this weekend, so Katrina was thinking that you and I . . ."

"Don't worry." I flopped into a pea-green armchair. "There's no reason to splurge on a New York weekend so close to the wedding. I have a hundred things to do here." For instance, I still needed to track down a fugitive from 1930.

My stress levels were through the roof already. All I really wanted to do this weekend was hide in my duplex, drink wine with Sarah, and see how Django's conversational skills had progressed.

No, scratch that. I didn't want to talk to any animals. In fact, I needed to do an internet search on deprogramming a parrot.

Mom lowered herself onto the sofa, relief oozing out of her. "I'm so glad you feel that way. I'm very busy. Especially Friday night."

A muffled buzzing began in my brain, a heightened sense that something had shifted. My mom had been alternatively overly enthusiastic and hurt about my wedding plans, especially since I had told her categorically that I wasn't going to be walking down the aisle in her old wedding dress, which was from 1977 and out-dated in a way that would—hopefully, fingers crossed, please-God-please—never be stylish again. The dress was designed in the prairie style, with a Victorian neck, long sleeves that were puffy from shoulder to elbow, and eyelet fabric ruffles on the bodice and the hem of the skirt. It was basically one sun bonnet away from Ma Ingalls territory.

In the faded color photos of my parents' wedding, Mom had looked incredibly cute, especially standing next to Dad in his powder-blue tux with the ruffled front. But would I want to wear that getup in front of a pack of Havermans? Big nope.

For months, Mom's hurt mentions of the dress had made me feel guilt. So. Much. Guilt. But she hadn't mentioned it once lately.

Something was up. She was hiding something. Hiding it, but at the same time telegraphing that something was happening I wasn't aware of.

And she'd cut off all her hair. Sarah's mom had cut off her hair after she'd been diagnosed with cancer, before she'd started chemo. It was supposed to make it less traumatic when the hair started falling out.

Panic choked my throat. "Mom, what's going on?"

"Why do you think something's going on?"

"Your hair! And you haven't mentioned your wedding dress—

like you don't want to cause any friction between us right now."
Tears pricked my eyes. "Just tell me. Please."

"All right . . ." She swallowed, sat up with her hands folded
primly, and smiled. Patches of red bloomed in her cheeks. "I
have a date."

I'd been waiting for an ax to fall. And in a way it had. Just a different ax than I was expecting. "A date," I repeated.

"His name is Ed."

"Ed who?"

Her flush deepened. "I don't know."

"Where did you meet him? Church?"

Laughter trilled out of her. "Heavens to Betsy, no. Church is
mostly ladies—and most of them such squares, at that. It's certainly not a place to hook up with men."

A shudder moved through me. "Hook up?"

"Isn't that what going together is called now?"

"Not exactly."

She chuckled. "Well, it's a good thing you came over before I
meet Ed for the first time. I don't want to come out with any
boners."

"Uh . . ." I was still struggling to piece this together. "You
haven't met?" The truth finally hit me with asteroid force.
"You've been on a dating site."

She nodded. "Goldenhearts. Have you heard of it?"

"No. I have not."

"Everybody fills out a questionnaire, and when you search
somebody, the opp or app or whatever it's called gives you a
match rating between one and five hearts to show if you're compatible. Ed is a four-heart match. He's retired—well, most of
them are retired on Goldenhearts. It's specifically for mature people, which is why I chose it. I'm not looking for some cheetah-
hunting gigolo."

Cheetah? "You mean cougar."

"That's it. Anyway, gigolos aren't my scene."

I wanted to curl up on the couch with my head sandwiched between two throw pillows. "Mom, you have to be very careful. You don't know these men."

She drew back, offended. "There's no reason to take that tone with me. I didn't just fall off the turnip truck. I was dating before you were born."

"Exactly. This is different. People misrepresent themselves online."

"Bad people, yes. But not Ed SexBeast."

"*Who?*"

She laughed at my horror. "It's just a jokey handle. We all use them."

I hesitated to ask. "What's your handle?"

"DLight. *D* stands for Deb."

"None of this sounds good, Mom."

"Don't look so horrified—Ed's a very responsible person, and quite well-to-do. He works in the financial office of a Fortune Five Hundred company."

Sure he did.

"Why are you doing this?" I asked. "I thought you would have enough on your plate with the wedding coming up."

"The wedding is *your* plate." Her lip trembled. "It's because of the wedding that I'm doing this. Seeing you joining a new family, starting a new life, it's made me realize how much I'd let slide these past couple of years, since . . . well, since your father. It's time to shake things up, get out and boogie again."

I sank back down. "Boogie?"

"I don't want to be some lonely-only that people feel sorry for. That *you* feel sorry for, and that you'll make duty visits to." She sighed. "I know I haven't had a lot on the go since Lloyd died, but that's because I was in shock for so long—just figuring out the basics like getting all the bills paid was as much as I could wrap my mind around. And I thought you needed me. But now you don't." She plucked at the crease of her slacks. "You've got the Havermans planning the wedding and everything. You don't even need the wedding dress I saved all these years. . . ."

Oh, God.

She reached out and yanked a tissue out of the dispenser on the glass-topped coffee table. "Listen to me whining—Miss Self-Pity-Patty." She dabbed at her eye. "I understand about the dress. I really do. I just wish there was something I could contribute to your big day."

Her tone of disappointment echoed Esme Zimmer's. Distress gripped me. How had I ended up with not one but two mothers to disappoint?

Esme isn't your mother. I clung to that hope like a man in a thriller dangling by his fingers from a skyscraper ledge.

"You *can* help me, Mom." I pushed myself up out of the squishy cushions. "Tell me about Stefanie Pickles."

At the unexpected name, she flinched. "You mean . . . ?"

"My birth mother." Maybe Esme was wrong. It had been a closed adoption. I doubted she'd met my parents. Maybe she was the mother of some other red-haired adoptee somewhere.

Mom bit her lip. "Why do you want to know about her?"

"Because I think I might have just spoken to her."

If I'd jabbed my mother with a pitchfork, her reaction couldn't have been any more extreme. She bolted off the couch. "Now, after all these years, you suddenly felt a need to go looking for your birth mother?"

I lifted my hands to calm her. "*She* found me—at least, someone claiming to be Stefanie Pickles found me. Only that's not her real name."

"What do you mean? That was definitely her name."

"She says she gave a fake name."

"She can't do that."

"Apparently, she can, and did."

Mom looked frantic. "But how did she find you? How? Those adoption records were sealed."

"I guess not as sealed as you thought. *You* didn't give a fake name—and we've always lived at this address. She must've peeked at your paperwork, or—"

I almost said, "She might have found out by magic," but stopped myself. Instead, something else distracted me. "Wait. If the adoption was closed, how did *you* find out about Stefanie Pickles?"

Mom's face reddened, and she clasped her hands tightly together.

"Mom?"

Her hands fluttered apart again in a helpless gesture. "I was just so curious. Not that I *ever* doubted that we would fall in love with you right away, but when you're talking about, well, genetics and all that . . ."

"You wanted to find out something about my birth mother." Of course she had—she and Dad both, probably. Dad had been the most cautious man on the planet.

"Well . . . yes. The, um, lawyer told us the girl's name and a little about her. Maybe she shouldn't have."

"What exactly did the lawyer tell you?"

"She said Stefanie Pickles was a brilliant student. The brightest girl in her class—and that she was very beautiful. And she was right. We saw a picture."

"What did she look like?"

"Well, she had red hair, like yours. And brown eyes, a little like . . ."

"Mine," I said dully.

"The, um, lawyer, assured us she was very healthy and bright. And you certainly turned out to be both of those things, too."

"So you never actually met Stefanie Pickles."

"We only had contact through the . . . lawyer." Mom shut her eyes, then took a stuttering breath. "Oh, heavens. I *told* your father this was all too dipsy-doodle."

The uncertain way she kept referring to the lawyer frightened me. "Mom, is there something you're not telling me?"

"You have to understand how desperate we were. I've explained that we hadn't had much luck adopting until . . . well, until we found you. We were too old, most agencies said. And Lloyd's diabetes was a problem, even though he was very careful. Everybody wanted young, super-healthy people. Even a private adoption fell through at the last minute. And just when we were giving up hope, this, you know, lawyer contacted us."

My stomach churned. Had my parents gotten themselves involved in some black market baby racket?

"The lawyer said she'd been given our name anonymously by someone who worked at one of the adoption agencies."

Understanding crashed over me like a Pacific breaker. "Let me guess. This 'lawyer' also had red hair. Maybe she looked a little like me?"

"Now that you mention it—yes, she did. Although of course we didn't know you back then. We did think it odd that she looked so much like Stefanie Pickles."

"What was her name?"

"Matlock. Bryn Matlock."

All those months in thrall to eighties television. "And you never thought it was suspicious that the woman had the same name as a TV lawyer?"

"You mean *Matlock,* that Andy Griffith show?" My mom's face screwed up. "Bailey, Matlock was a man. This was a woman."

"A young woman?"

"Ms. Matlock said it was her first year out of law school. But the strange thing was, a few months after the adoption we tried to look her up and she'd disappeared. Like she'd never existed at all. That always worried me, but your father swore the adoption had all been finalized within the law. Ms. Matlock had all the papers drawn up and signed by all the proper authorities."

"I bet." Bippity-boppity-boo strikes again.

"I told Lloyd it all seemed too good to be true." Tears stood in her eyes. "Do you think there was something shady about Bryn Matlock, or about the adoption?"

I didn't have the energy to explain to my mom that she and my dad had made a deal with a witch. The whole scenario was just few magic beans shy of a fairy tale. "It doesn't matter now."

"But if the adoption wasn't legal . . ."

"I'm thirty-four, Mom. It's not like you have to worry about losing custody."

A kind of fatalism was taking hold of me. I was the child of a witch. *Two* witches, if Esme could be believed. And apparently, she could.

Mom crossed her arms. "What right does Stefanie Pickles have to hunt you down now, before your wedding?" She paced the length of the coffee table, then stopped. "I hope she isn't planning some kind of shakedown of the Havermans."

"I doubt that." For some reason, the defense jumped to my lips.

"Her using a fake name for herself indicates she's up to something," Mom insisted.

"The fake name was the one she gave when she was seventeen. Her real name is Esme Zimmer."

"Zimmer?" Her eyes narrowed. "I've never met anybody by that name. I don't trust it. She can't just hunt you down now like some kind of crazed stalker. What does she want?"

"She wanted to make me a wedding dress."

"Oh. I see." Too late I realized I'd blurted out the one thing guaranteed *not* to unruffle Mom's feathers. It was one mention of wedding dresses too many for her. She'd been holding it in, but now the hurt bubbled to the surface. "*My* wedding dress isn't good enough for you, but this imposter—"

"Mom, I didn't say I was going to let her make a wedding dress." The bag in my back seat weighed so heavily on my conscience, I was sure Mom could tell I was fibbing, just like she'd been able to when I'd swiped a bottle of Boone's Farm from the kitchen to smuggle into a slumber party when I was fifteen.

"I'll probably never see her again," I said. "She's very . . . odd."

"If she's running around using an alias and stalking you, I think we should go to the police."

"The alias was—" I stopped myself. What was the point? "I'm not going to the police."

I couldn't imagine what the police would make of Esme Zimmer, or of me if I walked into the station and reported that I'd found a man who'd been kidnapped ninety years ago. Of course, if Esme had more kidnapped people in her cellar, maybe I *should* alert the authorities. But narcing on the woman who'd given birth to me was something I hesitated to do.

"I see." Mom sniffed. "You're very protective of this other mother. Naturally."

It took so much effort not to groan in frustration. "That's not it at all—and she's not my mother. Not really. I don't want to be involved in any of this. *You're* my mother. You're my entire family."

"Don't say that. I talked to your aunt Janet last week. She's coming to the wedding."

Aunt Janet, Dad's older sister, was a retired schoolteacher and lived in Florida. I'd probably seen her five times in my entire life. Mom was an only child. Mom, Dad, and I had been our own little island here in this blue house. The old couple and their witch-begotten child.

Mom swallowed. "And of course, you're marrying into a well-established family. The Havermans will be your family now, too. You'll be one of them."

She spoke like a fellow castaway being left alone on a raft mid-ocean as I was sailing off into the glorious horizon on a holiday cruise ship. "Mom . . ."

She lifted her head proudly. "Don't feel sorry for me. Like I said, I'm starting a new life, too."

With Ed SexBeast? That was hardly a comfort.

"When is your date?" I asked.

"Friday night."

"You've got to promise you'll text me several times during the evening. Take a picture of his license plate."

"Oh, Bailey, you know I can't ever figure out how to do those attachment thingies."

I left her soon after, feeling more shaky than before. This visit had not provided the homey chicken soup for the soul that I'd craved. Not that I wanted Mom to remain alone for the rest of her life. I just hadn't expected her to start desperately hunting for love online. That's what people my age did.

Chapter 9

I drove without thinking of a destination, and before I knew it I was pulling into my parking space at Genesee Insurance. Why not? It was probably best that I put in an appearance and make sure Paige wasn't measuring my office for new drapes. Also, my work computer was really fast. I wanted to check online to see if there had been any incidents in Rochester involving snappily dressed vagrants with saxophones.

I thought of the blue eyes that had looked at me so pleadingly last night across the table at the Owl's Nest and it hurt my heart to think of him out on the streets, lost. The trusting way he'd spoken was fine if he was talking to me, but what if he told his strange history to the wrong person? He seemed so sweet-natured, it would be easy for someone to take advantage of him.

I supposed that was what his wife had done, the faithless woman whose lover had shoved Seton out the window. For a moment, anger rose up in me. How could she have done such a horrible thing? I would've liked to time travel back and shove her out of a skyscraper.

Not that I had any intention of time traveling. I was not Esme. And really, Seton's marital problems were nothing to me. I was overemotional about everything these days.

On the way to my office, I swung by the kitchenette to grab a coffee. Ron and Paige were standing shoulder to shoulder by the old Krups. Seeing me, Ron hopped about five feet away from Paige.

"Hello, stranger!" He got busy shaking coffee creamer into a Buffalo Bills mug. "Didn't think we'd be seeing you today."

Paige poured herself a cup from the carafe. "Back to the salt mines." She turned a dimpled smile at Ron. "Thanks for lunch."

Lunch? It was almost five o'clock.

"Great to hear your ideas about things, Paige," he called out, as if it had just been a business lunch. Talking insurance usually didn't cause someone's face to go crimson, though.

He gave her a head start and then skulked out, nearly knocking over Tim when they passed in the doorway.

"What's going on?" I whispered to Tim when Ron was out of earshot.

Tim was forty, balding, happily married, and wore a perpetually astonished expression. "With those two? Who knows—they were gone for hours."

"Do you think . . . ?" The thought was too awful to say aloud. My mother, who once was friends with Ron's ex-wife, had told me he was a Lothario, but I'd never seen evidence of it in the office. "Ron's never hit on any employees before."

"He doesn't have to hit on Paige—his challenge is to avoid colliding into her every time he turns around. She spends half of every day hanging out in the doorway to his office, like a spider." His gaze strayed to the hallway they'd disappeared down. "It's like a reverse Me Too with an extra twist of *blech.*"

Back in my office I shut my door and started combing the local network affiliate websites for news of the arrest of a strange, sax-wielding man in Rochester. Where had he gone—and why? He might have hopped on a bus and headed for New York City, for all I knew. I might never see him again.

For some reason, that thought left me with a piercing sensation in my chest. Not that there was really any connection between us. It was sort of like finding a stray cat, only to have it run away again. I was anxious for his welfare.

Nothing came up in my search for Seton, although combing through the Rochester police blotter online turned up plenty of bad characters to throw more fuel on my worries about whomever it was my mother was meeting Friday night.

Ed SexBeast. I shuddered.

Stop. I couldn't think about that right now. One crisis at a time.

Yet Seton had seemed more like a crisis before I'd discovered that my birth mother was a witch and my real mother was pursuing strange men online.

Maybe I would have time to patrol downtown on the lookout for Seton before dinner with the Havermans.

A leaden lump took up residence in my stomach at the thought of my future in-laws. What was I going to say to Wes? *About those so-called real parents of mine you mentioned last night . . .*

I couldn't tell Wes I was the love child of two witches. He would think I'd lost my last marble. I wished I could skip the dinner, but Wes had said his parents had something important they were going to give us.

I rubbed my temples, and my fingers sent a little jolt through my skull. Great. I was zapping my brain now. No telling what kind of damage an inept witch could unintentionally do to herself.

A phone call from Sarah was a welcome distraction.

"Hey," she said. "I caught an unexpected break—my last patient thought she had an abscess but it turned out just to be a piece of popcorn wedged in her gum."

"Ouch."

"Did you see the text from Martine?"

"No. Wait." I put Sarah on speaker and brought up my messages.

Martine had sent a selfie of herself in a bikini top standing in front of the bluest sea I'd ever seen. **Greece! And you should see the guy who owns this hotel where I'm staying!!!**

I sighed. That looked so nice. "I wish I were in Greece. I'd love to hole up in a villa overlooking the sea. No contact with the outside world. Just me, really great seafood, and a pile of books."

"Are you feeling okay?" Sarah asked.

I sat up straight. "Of course. Why?"

"Because you're getting married in a few weeks, and you're harboring solo holiday fantasies that people are supposed to have after they've been married with kids for twenty years."

"It's been a stressful day."

"Work been awful?"

"I didn't go to work."

"Oh—day off! Good de-stressing strategy. Where are you?"

"At work."

Confusion crackled over the line.

"I mean I just stopped by because—" Because why? Because I was suddenly like a homing pigeon whose homing instinct was about as steady as a weather vane?

"Do we need to have a wine summit?" Sarah asked.

"Wine summit" was when Sarah, Martine, and I gathered at one of our apartments to hash out whatever thorny issue was bringing one of us down. Usually Martine joined us via Zoom with a bottle of hotel minibar cabernet. These interventions had buoyed us out of the dumps, propped us up in the face of life's disappointments, and occasionally prevented us from making disastrous mistakes.

I needed an intervention now, but I wasn't sure my longtime besties would relate to any of my current troubles. In fact, I didn't know *anyone* who would.

"You know," Sarah said when my silence dragged on a fraction too long, "if I were just a few weeks away from marrying Dave, I'd be over the moon. You seem to be drowning."

"I'm not a big function kind of person," I said.

"Don't think of the function, think of what it's for. You and Wes—tying the knot! Shouldn't that be sweeping you along?"

"I guess that's it. I feel as if I'm being swept toward—"

She waited in vain for me to finish before prompting, "Toward . . . ?"

She was talking about the wedding, and I was thinking about witchcraft. "You had to take a lot of science classes in college, didn't you?" I said. "And dental school, of course."

There was a moment of confusion before she said, "Um . . . yeah."

"Do you know much about heredity?"

"You mean, genetics?" I could imagine her shaking her head. "It's three weeks before your wedding and you're wondering about Mendel's peas?"

"I'm adopted. I'm just worried that I don't know a lot of things about myself, healthwise and . . ." Witchwise.

"Is that what's been bothering you?" She laughed. "You're fine. Wes thinks you're fine. Your only problem would be if you had any doubts about Wes."

"Who could have doubts about Wes? He's a brick."

"Right," Sarah said. "So everything's okay, and this wedding isn't freaking you out in the least."

"I just don't feel comfortable in my own skin right now." That wasn't entirely a lie.

I glanced at the bottom right corner of my computer monitor. It was so late, I'd barely have time to go home and change before going out again. "I've got to run," I said. "Big dinner out with the Havermans tonight."

"Where?"

"Bella—that place in NOTA."

The Neighborhood of the Arts district was a formerly run-down area that had undergone a renaissance several decades ago. Now the old houses and former factories and office buildings comprised the liveliest area of Rochester.

"Dave took me there for Valentine's," Sarah said. "Order the cioppino—you won't regret it."

That would make one thing in the past twenty-four hours I wouldn't regret. "Thanks for calling."

"Of course! Have fun with the Havermonsters."

I laughed. "We really need to stop saying that."

"We do," she agreed. "But does it have to be today?"

Chapter 10

I was shaving it thin as I screeched into a parking spot on University and galloped up the sidewalk at seven o'clock. Wes, visibly nervous, was standing sentry at the doorway to the converted nineteenth-century factory building where the restaurant, Bella, took up part of the main floor.

"I wanted to warn you," he said. "Mad's here."

I was sure my face melted. "Why?"

"O brought her."

I took a deep breath. "It's okay." Madeleine was the least of my worries at the moment. "I can deal. Madeleine's obviously a problem that's not going away."

Wes let out a stuttering laugh. "No lie. She's like the lingering pandemic of my life." His brows drew together. "What happened between you two? Her foot's in one of those boot things. She said she sprained it when she met up with you yesterday."

"Her heel broke, but the shoe malfunction was nothing to do with me." Even as I said the words, though, I could feel the blood draining out of my face. Esme Zimmer had been there, too. And right after I told her who Madeleine was, those heels had disintegrated. *Disintegrated.* Why would shoes do that? "Is Madeleine telling people I put a whammy on her Louboutins?"

"She just said that you were there. She didn't *blame* you." He added a muttered, "Not exactly."

Right. Except for linking my being there with her ankle injury to all and sundry. "Well, thanks for the heads-up."

His expression morphed into worry. "Is something wrong?"

"No." The word came out defensive. "I mean, just the usual stuff. Mom. Dress." *Witches.* "Why?"

"I thought maybe you had a rough day, since you didn't have time to go home and change."

"I did, actually."

I'd been in such a hurry that I pulled out the first clean dress I had—a navy blue work dress—and had thrown a yellow cardigan over it.

"Oh. It looks . . . comfortable."

I laughed. "Django didn't think much of it, either."

"Your parrot?"

Oops. "Ha—a joke."

Actually, Django had told me I looked like I was someone passing around butter cookies in a church vestry hall. That bird was getting more talkative and saltier by the hour.

Luckily, before this line of conversation could go one step further, Wes took my arm. "We'd best go in. Mother and Dads have a big surprise for us. You'll be over the moon."

His words indicated that this gift of theirs wasn't a big surprise to him, just to me. Never mind. Right now wedding gifts hovered below Madeleine on the least-of-my-worries list.

The restaurant boasted the brick walls and arched doorways of the shoe factory that had once inhabited the building, but now the air was an intoxicating mix of garlic, dough, and other savory smells. Joan Haverman was already ensconced at the end of a long table, a large eyebrow window at her back. Flanking her were Olivia, against the wall, and Madeleine, her chair pulled out and slightly turned to accommodate the gray orthopedic boot that encased her limb from her toes to halfway up her calf. Madeleine treated me to a sour look before Mr. Haverman twisted, jumped to his feet, and squashed me in a hug. The fine weave of his jackets always smelled faintly of cigars and the cologne he wore.

"Here you are!" he bellowed. "I ordered wine—we're slumming it with Chianti. I hope you like it."

"I do."

I couldn't help smiling at Mr. Haverman. His friendly manner reminded me of my dad.

"Hear that?" He addressed the table. "She's practicing her 'I do's' already." Chuckling, he leaned toward me. "Hope you'll be as definite about the vows as you are about the wine."

I pulled away and sidestepped Madeleine's cast to make my way to Joan. Wes's mother wore a creamy pastel suit—skirt, not pants—and her ash-blond hair, as always, was pulled up and back in an almost Grecian do, with softly curled tendrils artfully escaping to frame her face.

I bent and engaged in the awkward, cheek-touch greeting she considered customary. She didn't stand, so this required me almost to kneel—and that wasn't by accident. When I'd straightened up again, she gestured to the empty spot between Olivia and Mr. Haverman. "We've put you there, Bailey."

Wes would be opposite me and next to Madeleine.

Olivia dragged her gaze up from her phone's screen. "What's up, Bailey? You look terrible."

Joan sucked in a breath. "That's no way to greet anyone."

Her daughter shrugged. "It's just Bailey, and it's true."

I scuttled into my chair, which had one of those slippery seats that made it hard to remain upright in.

Joan, of course, was never anything less than posture perfect. "*Especially* if it's true," she admonished Olivia.

"I think Bailey looks great, as always," Mr. Haverman said gallantly, even though his nose was buried in his menu as he spoke.

"It's just been a long day," I said. "Makes me extra glad to be here."

And extra glad that Wes was reaching forward to pour me an extra-large glass of Chianti. He smiled approvingly at me over the bottle. He always approved of conflict deflection. He was not a conflict person, which was why he and his first wife, Lydia, had divorced just six months after their whirlwind romance and elopement. Too much drama. *It's like we got married and suddenly discovered we were different species,* he'd told me once.

Also, Lydia had gotten a bit too personal with her personal trainer.

Did being a witch make one a different species?

I was going to have to tell him.

Not that I really *was* a witch. I mean, I didn't feel like one. Just because my newly discovered birth mother was odd—and okay, she could perform some witchcraft, I couldn't deny that—it didn't necessarily follow that I was of her kind. Unless there really was a sorcery gene.

"We need to get you over to the house, Bailey," Joan said. "Gifts are piling up in the pod."

I tried not to look at Wes. We'd had conflict over registering for gifts—I had resisted, the Havermans had insisted. Now there was a steady stream of loot being delivered to the Havermans' house, where Joan had set up an elaborate throughput system: each gift was stored in a rented pod set up in the garage until it was opened, catalogued for future thank-you notes, and had a calligraphed attribution card generated for it so it could be transferred to the gift display in the Havermans' dining room.

"It might be fun to gather the bridesmaids together to help get the work done faster," Joan suggested.

"'Fun' as in being sucked into a black hole of tedium?" Olivia asked. "No thanks."

"If it were me, I wouldn't be able to open those gifts quickly enough," Madeleine said. "All that generosity just goes to show how much people love the Havermans. It's awesome."

Joan bestowed a fond smile on her.

"You won't think it's awesome when you see the oil painting of the Freddie-Sue Bridge that somebody gave them," Olivia said.

I sucked in a breath. "That was from my friend Emily." The picture of the Frederick Douglass–Susan B. Anthony Memorial Bridge at twilight was one of the gifts I really loved.

Olivia shot a confidential look at Madeleine. "It looks like a couch-sized painting of an upside-down pastry cutter."

"Emily's a talented local artist," I said, feeling my anger rising.

Mr. Haverman set his menu and his reading glasses down and looked across the table at his wife. "Speaking of gifts, let's give it to them now, Joan."

"We haven't ordered yet, Douglas."

"I can fix that." He twisted and flagged down our waiter, who zipped over so quickly that it was obvious he'd waited on the Havermans before. Whatever their faults, they were generous tippers.

My stomach rumbled in anticipation of Sarah's recommended cioppino, and I looked longingly at the untouched baskets of bread. If I'd been with my friends, there wouldn't be a crumb left by now.

"There—we've ordered," Mr. Haverman said excitedly after the waiter left us. He reached under his chair and brought out a fat manila envelope. "Drumroll, please!"

"Just give it to them, Dad," Olivia said.

"Indulge me," he insisted.

"I'll do it!" There was an almost manic smile on Madeleine's face as she drummed against the tablecloth in anticipation of the big moment.

"Mads, you're such a good sport," Mr. Haverman said. "Under the circumstances."

Ouch. He might just as well have called her Wes's discard.

As pain rippled across the contours of Madeleine's face, I almost felt sorry for her. But why had she come back? And why had she inserted herself into this family dinner?

Mr. Haverman slid the packet toward me. "This is for Wes, and especially for you, Bailey. Joan and I hope your and Wes's marriage is as long and happy as ours has been. Welcome to the family."

A second before I opened the envelope, I guessed that this was why Wes had been so secretive about our honeymoon destination. Mr. Haverman had probably offered to pay, so long as he could draw up our itinerary. He loved to sail and was a big fan of Bermuda, which sounded great to me. Almost any destination would please me—I'd never been anywhere outside the US except for Canada, to visit Martine in Montreal. It was really sweet of him to do this. And generous. As I unbent the envelope's brad, I prepared myself to act surprised.

When I pulled out the package, though, it wasn't the expected travel brochure. On top of a stack of papers, a glossy photo of a house stared up at me. It was two towering stories of gray stone weathered almost to black, with leaded windows, a mossy slate roof, and a turret that looked slightly off-kilter. My prepared cry of delighted surprise died in my throat. Wes and I were going to be honeymooning in a Gothic mini castle?

A vaguely familiar Gothic mini castle. I'd seen this house somewhere before. Like, more than once.

The address underneath the picture caught my eye. *1248 Tonawanda Drive.* A Rochester address. Now I knew. I'd driven by this weird old house.

A glance around the table told me that I was the only one who hadn't known what was inside that envelope. Olivia was looking at Twitter, Joan's smile was tighter than usual, and Madeleine was beaming with the determination of someone desperate not to lose control and throw a weepy tantrum.

Mr. Haverman scooted his chair closer to me. "Here, take a look at the next page."

With a butterfly the size of a Toyota flapping in my stomach, I turned over the picture. The next page was a contract, signed by Joan and Douglas Haverman for 1248 Tonawanda Drive. "Wow!" I said. "You bought a house?"

"And we're going to transfer the title to you after the wedding," Mr. Haverman said.

They were giving us *a house*? I looked up at Wes. He was grinning ear to ear.

"Oh, my God," was all I could say, my voice cracking. My future in-laws—apparently with Wes's approval—had purchased a house for Wes and me to live in that looked like it was built for a suburban vampire.

Mr. Haverman laughed delightedly. "What did I tell you? Didn't I say she'd be thrilled to bits?"

"I can't believe . . ." I flipped through more of the paperwork. The original listing had been stapled to the back of the folder. Eight bedrooms, nine bathrooms.

Nine bathrooms?

I gaped across the table at Wes. "Are you expecting guests?"

Olivia choked on her Chianti and Mr. Haverman slapped me on the shoulder. "We don't expect you and Wes to be alone for long," he said. "We've got to make room for more little Havermans."

Okay, that was mortifying. And flabbergasting. An extra bedroom was never a bad thing, and Wes and I had talked about having a child or even children someday. But *seven* extra bedrooms? "Well, if we change our minds about the kids, we can open a B and B instead."

Wes laughed. "Thank you, Dads, Mother. You're so fantastic— we're blown away. Aren't we, Bailey?"

"We sure are."

"Look at the living room," Joan said. "To die for. The man

who built it brought a fireplace over from a castle in England. It's fifteenth century."

I flipped through some pictures and was astonished. It wasn't just that there were lots of rooms; each of the rooms looked bigger than my entire duplex. And the price—at least the listing price I could see—was more than I would earn in a decade.

Madeleine sighed. "I've always loved that house. Growing up, I thought it looked like a storybook castle."

"I always loved this house, too," Joan said. "Back when I was in high school, Tricia Marshall's family owned it. Tricia always thought she was hot stuff because her family made scads of money in the apple processing business. She was a real piece of work—always voted Most Popular, and then one year she was homecoming queen, too. Then, when we got to college, I heard it from several people in a position to know that she blackballed me from pledging Tri-Delt."

"That's awful!" Madeleine said.

"Well." Joan's lips stretched into a tight smile. "Later, a terrible apple maggot infestation decimated the Marshalls' over-stretched fortune. *That* knocked Tricia off her high horse. I wonder what she'll think when she learns her childhood home is now in my family's hands."

"Wow." Had she really bought this house as revenge for not getting into the sorority she wanted?

"Those Marshalls let the place deteriorate into a shameful state," Joan continued. "As you can see, Bailey, we have our work cut out for us. I've scheduled a consultation for us with my friend Shirley Benedetto tomorrow morning. Ten o'clock."

I swallowed. So much for my job, I guessed. I sent an SOS gaze Wes's way. Did he really want to take up residence in Schadenfreude Manor?

Apparently, he did.

Mr. Haverman grabbed my shoulder and squeezed. "We've been so excited about planning this surprise for you two. Joan's never gotten such a kick out of anything."

"Wow." The word kept burbling out of me like a hiccup. I knew I needed to say more. Much more. But the only thought in my head at the moment was *My mom knit us an afghan for her wedding present.* She was a fantastic knitter, but still. How was I going to explain to her that the Havermans were giving us a mini castle?

"What's the matter, Bailey?" Madeleine arched a brow at me. "You don't seem as thrilled as I would be if someone handed me a mansion."

She was horrible, but also right. What was wrong with me? In spite of the Chianti, my mouth still felt dry. I tried to think of an appropriate expression of gratitude. "I don't know how to even begin to say—"

A loud, frantic tapping cut off my thank-you speech.

I pivoted toward Joan Haverman, and then saw the figure in the window behind her. It was growing dark outside, so I had to blink a few times to make out the man tapping on the plate glass. He had Gil's saxophone hanging by a strap around his neck, and his face was almost pressed against the window. When our gazes locked, I rose out of my chair. Seton! So much had happened today that his disappearance had taken a back seat in my brain, but I was so glad to see him. Glad and relieved.

His eyes widened, and the hand that had been knocking on the glass gestured at me in an ecstatic wave.

"Bailey!" he cried. "I think I can make this work!"

Chapter 11

Heat rose in my cheeks as the curious gazes of the table and some surrounding tables turned to me.

"Friend of yours?" Olivia asked, brow arched.

"No, I—" What was I doing? I couldn't deny knowing the strange man in the window when Seton was still shouting my name through the plate glass window. "He's—my cousin. In town for the wedding."

"Three weeks early?" Wes asked. I could read the doubts in his eyes. He knew I didn't have much family, and I'd never mentioned a cousin attending the wedding.

Olivia met Madeleine's gaze across the table. "Isn't that the weird-cute guy we saw down the street on Atlantic on the way in? Playing on the sidewalk?"

Madeleine screwed up her face at me. "Your cousin came to town for your wedding to be a street person?"

"He's a musician," I said. "He's busking."

"What does he mean by 'making this work'?" Olivia asked.

Good question. "Not sure."

"I'm relieved that he's stopped hitting the glass," Joan said. "That knocking was right in my ear."

Seton had vanished from the window. Panic leapt in my chest. I pushed in my chair. "I need to find him."

Mr. Haverman stood courteously. "Invite your cousin in to join us."

"That's very kind, but—" I turned, and to my distress, Seton had already come into the restaurant, sax still dangling, the ancient case clutched under one arm. He strode toward me with a single-minded focus that blotted out the restaurant full of people gawping at him.

"Bailey! I'm so glad I found you."

How was I going to finesse this? "Seton—allow me to introduce you to *my fiancé's family.*"

All at once, his face fell. He glanced around at everyone. His lanky frame towered over Mr. Haverman, who was still on his feet.

He offered Seton his hand. "Doug Haverman. Glad you could arrange for a long visit before the wedding. Won't you join us?"

Seton's eyes seemed doubtful as he shook with Mr. Haverman. Then I caught him looking longingly at the bread.

"Yes, join us. You must be hungry after . . ." I swallowed. What had he been doing? ". . . your day."

His head bobbed, and for a moment his eagerness overwhelmed his shyness. "You wouldn't believe it—I made five dollars and sixty cents today. Playing saxophone!"

"Great." That would about cover about one half of one percent of the instrument he'd stolen.

I made introductions all around. Seton put on his most courtly smile when greeting Joan Haverman, which seemed to thaw her a little.

Seton couldn't get over his windfall. "Five dollars and sixty cents! Half a sawbuck. And all my life I assumed I'd never be up to scratch as a professional musician, but suddenly I'm hitting on all eight. Who needs Wall Street?"

The waiter, weighed down with a huge tray, came over and started delivering everyone's orders.

"That's terrific, Seton. Maybe you should put away the saxophone and we can talk about it later?"

His face suddenly reddened and he noticed everyone eyeing him. "Of course. I beg your pardon." He unhooked his sax strap and bent to stow the horn in its case. "Say, I didn't mean to rush in like this, I was just so surprised to bump into Bailey. But I see you all are just being served. I should spiff up a little."

Olivia gave him a cool, up-and-down appraisal. "You look spiffy to me. Nice suit."

He straightened up and shifted feet self-consciously. He sent me a meaningful look, asking for help. "Any idea where I can go iron my shoelaces?"

"What?" I needed a Seton interpreter.

"Powder room?" he asked.

"Oh." I waved a hand in the direction of the men's washroom.

When he was out of earshot, Madeleine asked, "What was *that*?"

"Seton's a bit eccentric," I explained.

Madeleine's gaze on me was razor sharp. "Where have you been hiding this cousin of yours, Bailey? Under your bed?"

She was so unsubtle, but the remark hit its target. Next to her, Wes shifted, and I could read the questions in his eyes. Questions that would become suspicions if I didn't clarify things for him right away.

"This is only the second time in my life that I've ever laid eyes on him," I explained. "He's a very distant cousin."

"But he's staying in that little duplex of yours," Madeleine said.

What she was implying was crystal clear. Nothing would have pleased her more than to have some long-lost love show up in my life to interrupt my and Wes's wedding plans at the eleventh hour. Short of that, she could plant ideas in Wes's head that would make him remember Lydia's cheating and think twice about me.

Still, she raised an interesting question: Where was I going to stash Seton now? I couldn't presume on Gil's hospitality again. And I couldn't send a man I'd just introduced as my cousin to a homeless shelter. Springing for a hotel room was an option, although I didn't relish throwing away money on accommodations for a guy I barely knew. Anyway, it might be better to have him at my place so I could keep an eye on him for a few days. Esme had indicated that she was working on a way to send him back.

"He arrived without notice." I returned Madeleine's smile. "I'm probably going to punt him over to Mom's."

"You can punt him over to my place any time," Olivia said in a husky drawl. "He's very cute for a homeless guy."

"He's not homeless. He's busking."

Madeleine twirled a single strand of spaghetti on her fork. "Something tells me Bailey won't want to relinquish him to you, O."

She was awful. My gaze cut over to Wes, who was chewing thoughtfully. It wasn't hard to imagine what those thoughts were.

Joan had already given up picking at her salad. "What did you say Seton's last name was?"

"Atterbury."

"Seton Atterbury . . ." Her mouth formed a puzzled moue. "I don't remember seeing that name on the wedding guest list."

"My oversight," I said. "If there's no room for him, he'll be fine with that. He's really nice. Very easy-going."

Mr. Haverman, who had been completely absorbed in a lamb shank, finally came up for air. "Works on Wall Street, did he say?"

"Yes. Until recently." *Just till ninety years or so ago.*

Seton came back to the table. Mr. Haverman asked the waiter to bring a menu and pulled over a chair from a neighboring table so Seton could sit between him and me. I scooted over. Seton had freshened up in the washroom, slicking his hair back with water. As he sat down next to me, the smell of soap wafted toward me.

"Please continue eating," Seton said to the table. "I didn't mean to interrupt. I was just so happy to see Bailey."

"We noticed." Madeleine tilted a meaningful look at Wes.

"The food looks wonderful. I'm ravenous." Seton picked up the menu, scanned it for a moment, then slapped it down again. His eyes bulged as he looked at me and whispered, "The ravioli is thirty dollars."

"It's okay," I said, trying to keep my voice low. "Order whatever you want." I pushed the bread basket toward him, and my bread plate.

Arched brows traveled around the table.

"This dinner is on us," Mr. Haverman said. "It's a special night. We've just presented Wes and Bailey with the house we're giving them as a wedding present. Show him the picture, Bailey."

Seton glanced down at the picture of the house and nodded with surprising nonchalance. "Reminds me of my grandfather's home in Newport."

The mention of Newport grabbed Joan's attention. "Bailey never told us her family owned a cottage." No doubt visions of Astors and Vanderbilts swam in her head.

"Different side of the family," I said quickly.

"Oh." Despite her disappointed tone, I could tell that the mere mention of that historic haven of the rich had lifted Seton in her estimation from wedding crasher to person of interest.

"It's gone out of the family now anyway," Seton said, looking regretfully at the house, almost as if it really had been his grandfather's.

"The Havermans' getting this house for Bailey and Wes is so exciting," Madeleine gushed. "I'd just *love* to live in a house like that." She pivoted to Wes, placing his hand on his arm. "Remember that place we stayed at in Maine? It sort of reminds me of that."

Wes grunted in assent.

"That was such an awesome weekend." She smiled at me, dark eyes sparkling.

Electricity shot through me again . . . but instead of being centered in my fingertips, that strange charge seemed to radiate out of me. Irritation at Madeleine, that's what it was. Part of me felt disgusted at myself for feeling anything but pity for her. She was so obvious, and jealousy was teenager stuff. I needed to stop.

She was the jealous one. Surely everyone could see that. She was so transparent.

I mean, how could they all not see it?

I looked down at the house again, trying to distract my thoughts. "It says here there's a pool."

Joan's lips pursed. "The pool house is a mess. But I'm sure Shirley will have some ideas for that, too."

"If it were me, I'd want a—" Olivia's words cut off with a gasp. "Omigod, Mad! What's wrong with you?"

Madeleine blinked. "What?"

We were all gaping at her now.

"You're *green*," Olivia announced, loudly.

At first I thought it was a trick of the light or something, but it was true. Madeleine was green. Not Jolly Green Giant green, but a yellow green, sallow and unhealthy like something curdled. It was as if her skin had turned to green cheese. Joan and Wes, flanking her on both sides, recoiled. I didn't blame them.

Madeleine looked at her arms, horrified. "What the hell is happening?"

"Maybe you're having an allergic reaction to your food," I said.

"To pasta puttanesca? There's nothing in it I'm allergic to."

"Is it your ankle?" Olivia was already searching her phone. "Maybe you've thrown a clot."

Mr. Haverman frowned. "You throw a clot in your leg, it can kill you, but it doesn't turn you pickle green."

Madeleine moaned.

Wes looked in exasperation at his father. "Not helpful, Dads."

Madeleine was shaking now, and the green grew even more pronounced. Abruptly, she scraped her chair back from the table. "I need to go to the ER. Can you drive me, Olivia?"

"Now?" Olivia looked down at her veal osso buco. "The ER, at this time of night? Mad, you'll be there for hours."

"But I have to do something."

Olivia sighed. "Are you really feeling sick, or are you just freaking out because you're green?"

"Of course I'm freaking out! I'm putrifying!"

Diners at nearby tables turned to see. Lots of gaping faces and flinching.

Given that this was Madeleine, I should have enjoyed the spectacle. I should have been mentally spinning wisecracks about photosynthesis to share at the next wine summit with Sarah and Martine. But like everyone else, I was in shock. And disturbed. What had caused this?

One particularly unnerving possibility occurred to me, but I dismissed it.

"Stay calm, Mad," Wes said. "I'll take you to the ER."

Joan put down her fork. "Oh, Wesley, do *you* have to go? We wanted this to be a special dinner for you."

Tears streamed down Madeleine's chartreuse cheeks. "It's okay. I'll Uber myself to the ER. I always have to manage things like this on my own."

Seton turned to me and asked in a low voice, "What is Ubering?"

"It means she'll take a cab," I whispered.

"No she won't," Wes said gallantly. "I'll drive you. It won't take long."

And much as I was loath to see Wes spend time alone with Madeleine—which was exactly what she'd wanted, after all—it would be better than my being alone with Wes and having to come up with explanations about Seton, and hiding my suspicions about why Madeleine had turned green.

There were a lot of things about this evening that I needed to sort out.

"That's so nice of you, Wes," I said.

"I'll pick you up at your place in the morning," he replied.

"For what?" I asked.

"The new house?" he reminded me, with an edge of impatience. "We'll drive together and meet Mother there."

"That'll be wonderful," Joan said.

Wes picked up Madeleine's purse for her and then took her arm to help her. The waiter zipped over to help, but then belatedly got a gander at Madeleine's leafy pallor and jumped back so violently that he crashed into the table behind him, resulting in a linguini disaster.

Poor guy. I'd have to slip him some extra bills when we left. None of this was his fault.

The question troubling me was, whose fault was it?

Chapter 12

"I only borrowed the saxophone. Gil gave me permission to play it."

Seton and I were back at my place, sitting at my kitchen table. I'd cut up a kiwi for Django, and Seton and I were splitting a slice of cheesecake from Bella, which we'd ordered to go.

"*Play* it—not take it," I said. "Do you realize how your disappearing act made Gil feel? Made us both feel, actually. Like we were idiots for having trusted you."

His shoulders rounded, and those blue eyes of his filled with contrition. "I'm sorry, Bailey. You're the last person I'd want to disappoint. You've been so kind to me since I escaped that witch."

That witch, my mother. At some point, a confession would have to be made. I was going to have to tell everyone, yet I dreaded saying the words aloud.

"Why did you run away from Gil's?" I asked.

A haunted shadow crossed his face. His eyes were focused

on Django, but I don't think he was really watching the bird. "Something happened to me last night. Ever since I was dropped here, all I've been able to think of was returning to what I knew. To my home, my time. Here, it was all witches and impossible, incomprehensible things—people looking so different, *talking* in ways I could barely understand, phones like radios, moving pictures in boxes, and music that sounds like someone hammering on my skull. A living terror. But there's also been you."

His eyes met mine, and my stomach did a somersault.

"You and Gil, I mean," he continued quickly. "You offered friendship, and connection."

Friendship. Yes.

"Because we wanted to help you. And then you ran away."

"As the terror over being here subsided, another worry's taken hold of me." His head dropped. "Panic about going back."

"I told you I wasn't going to take you back to Esme's."

"Not back to Esme's—back to my home." He leaned forward. "Have you ever been dreaming and had that sensation of something terrible happening—drowning, say, or falling? But then you snap awake, and you're so relieved not to be falling anymore that you're bathed in sweat. Yet at the same time you're confused, because you aren't sure which is real: the you of the dream, or the you lying there hyperventilating in the bed."

"You had a nightmare?" After what he'd been through, that wouldn't surprise me.

His eyes had a feverish look. "No, I didn't sleep at all because I started to wonder if all the life that I'd known before was the nightmare. I lost my parents, took the boring job, married the wrong woman, trusted the wrong friend—and then I tumbled out the window."

"You said you were pushed."

"Yes, but don't you see? I was living a somnambulist life. Maybe *this* is me woken up. This is reality. I mean, *you're* real, right?"

"Yeah . . ."

"And you're pretty wonderful." He swallowed. "I mean, you and Gil have been wonderful to me. So suddenly I wanted to see if I could function in this brave new world. And that's why I took the saxophone, the one thing that was familiar to me from my old life, and set off to discover whether I could survive here."

Explained that way, it almost made sense. Given the slim chances that Esme could send him back, he just might have to find a way to support himself here.

"You can't survive on five dollars per day, though," I said.

"No. Apparently, that won't buy a single ravioli anymore."

"I'm sure there are other things you could do to make a living. It sounds like you were a big success before."

He shook his head. "Let's face it—even if my old firm still exists, I doubt they've held my job open for me for nine decades."

"You could do other jobs, though. Or you could go back to school."

"Ha! A twenty-eight-year-old Joe College?"

"It's not that unusual now." I bit my lip. Before I got him on board for continuing ed, I needed to be honest with him about his other options. "Actually, if you're worried about going back just because of the falling-out-of-the-building thing, there *might* be good news for you."

He sat up. "I could use some good news."

"Don't take this the wrong way, but I went to see Esme Zimmer this morning."

Silence settled over the room. Even Django stopped smacking his kiwi and tilted his head, observing us with his small reptilian eyes.

"I trusted you," Seton said accusingly.

"I was worried about you. I thought maybe Esme had found you again, or that you'd tried to get her to send you back."

He jumped up and his chair scraped back with a shriek that was met by an answering cry of surprise from Django.

"Hey! I'm eating here!" the bird said, annoyed.

The exclamation startled both Seton and me.

"He's a witch bird." Seton grabbed the back of his chair, as if to have something solid to keep between us. "You really are one of them."

"No I'm not." Honesty forced me to retrace my verbal steps. "That is, I didn't think I was, but today I discovered that Esme Zimmer is the mother who gave me up for adoption when I was a baby. But I swear I didn't know anything about her being my mother, or about witchcraft, till this morning."

"Then why were you at her house last night?"

"She'd offered to make me a wedding dress. I didn't know who she really was."

His eyes widened as a thought occurred to him. "Holy mackerel. That woman tonight in the restaurant—did *you* do that?"

My gaze cut away from his, and I watched Django work to grab a chunk of kiwi and then steady it with his toes as his beak chipped away at it.

Ever since we'd left the restaurant, my brain had been skittering away from speculation about what had happened to Madeleine. Thinking about Seton's problem seemed less disturbing to me. Which reminded me, I still needed to call Gil and tell him that I'd found Seton and the saxophone. . . .

There. I was doing it again. Sorcery avoidance.

"I think it was Esme," I said, trying to piece events together. "Yesterday, she caused Madeleine to sprain her ankle. And today I saw her . . . do other things. I think Esme hexed Madeleine."

He swallowed the last of his cheesecake and pushed his plate away. "I should go. I don't mean to hurt your feelings. You've been very kind, but . . ."

A heaviness settled inside my chest. I'd been the one person in the present whom Seton trusted, and now he didn't.

"You can't leave," I said. "You don't have enough money for a hotel, and you probably haven't slept in who knows how long."

"I took a nap today in the park." He shook his head in amazement. "Ninety years later and there are still Hoovervilles."

Like most cities, we had clusters of homeless people with nowhere else to turn but to makeshift tents and boxes in parks. But Seton was a babe in the woods; he knew nothing of the modern world. "Sleeping in a park isn't safe."

"It's safer than a house with a witch in it. The daughter of Esme Zimmer, no less."

That knee-jerk reaction to stand up for Esme kicked in again. "Esme Zimmer saved your life—you said so yourself."

"And what if she snaps her fingers and sends me back to my sidewalk-splattering fate?" His eyes widened. "Or what if *you* do?"

"Don't worry about me. I have no powers. You might not need to worry about Esme Zimmer, either. She's a kook, but she seems to have a few scruples where you're concerned. She said she's not going to send you back until she can find a way to return you *before* you were pushed out of the window."

He sank back down in the chair. "Would that be possible?"

"Apparently, she and some other witch have time traveled before, but in rescuing you, she left him back in your time. He seems to be the one with the real expertise, and she's trying to find him and bring him back. But even if they work out the bugs in their time traveling, I don't think she'll return you to 1930 unless you're ready to go."

He thought about this. "And she really thinks she could plunk me into to my old life, pre-defenestration?"

"Well . . . I imagine there will always be substantial risk involved."

The very deadly possibilities inherent in those risks played across his face. "So now I'm presented with two options: stay here and lose everything I knew, or go back and possibly lose my life."

"That's about it."

"And what about Burt? If I just leave him back there, who knows what he'll be up to next? He said he was in love with Ruthie, but after the October crash Burt didn't have a bean to his name. That day at the office, when he pushed me, I told him that I'd divorce Ruthie only if she accepted fault, and in that case she wouldn't have a dime from me." He shook his head. "The next thing I knew I was flying out the window."

"So maybe Burt's pushing you wasn't premeditated."

"That doesn't excuse him for killing me." He shook his head. "Poor Ruthie. I wonder if she knows that she's in the clutches of a fortune-hunting murderer."

"Technically, you weren't murdered. You disappeared. No one could figure out what happened to you—not even Burt. For all Ruthie knew, you deserted her."

"How do you know all this?" he asked. "Do you have witch hindsight?"

"No, I have the internet."

His brows drew together. "I keep hearing that word. What does it mean?"

How could I explain something I barely understood myself? "Imagine if you could pick up the telephone and ask not just to call someone, but also research anything about history, or watch a movie, or find out just about anything. That's what the internet does."

His jaw dropped. "Bell Telephone managed all that?"

"It really doesn't have much to do with phones. I just used that as an example."

He thought for a moment. "Are you telling me that you were able to find out what happened to me on this interphone contraption?"

"Internet." I shouldn't have mentioned phones. Maybe I should have steered clear of the whole subject of looking up his past. I wasn't sure if he was ready to read about all the fallout from his disappearance. But I couldn't hide it forever.

I retrieved the computer from my desk nook and powered it up. "I was able to search for your name in old newspaper accounts."

His eyes bugged. "You found *me* in the newspapers? That's impossible. The only time I was ever in the paper was when I was with Boyd and His Hot Beavers, and I doubt the notices ever mentioned me particularly."

"These articles weren't about your college days. They were written after you disappeared."

Seton flinched at the screen as it brought up the first newspaper article about him, with his picture. As his eyes scanned the page, tension seeped out of his face, replaced by sorrow. "They all think I just walked away from everything?"

I couldn't bring myself to affirm this, but instead retrieved the second article. The one announcing Burt and Ruthie's marriage.

After reading it, he sank back down in the chair, dejected. "I knew Ruthie and I were unhappy, but I never would have dreamed she'd want to marry the man who murdered me." He drummed his fingers, frowning. "Although, for all I know she was in on the scheme to push me out the window. She might have planned it!"

"Don't jump to conclusions. It's possible that she wasn't even aware of what Burt was up to."

Not buying it, he let out a breath of disgust. "And now they're in my house, and she's married to Burt, while I'm lost in this crazy, noisy, horrible world."

I felt so bad for him. "A few minutes ago you were saying that the present has its good points, too."

"I was trying to look on the bright side." His jaw worked from side to side. "Then you told me that maybe I'd be able to go back. And *then* you gave me those newspapers, which made me think that there's nothing to go back for—except to divorce the woman who might have been involved in my murder." His lips trembled into a weak smile. "You certainly know how to keep a fellow unsteady."

"I'm sorry. I know there's a lot of confusion for you right now."

"And how."

We sat drinking our coffee for a few minutes.

"*Your* fiancé seemed very nice," he said, breaking the silence. "He treated the green woman very courteously."

"Wes is great."

He studied me. "Are you troubled by something, Bailey?"

I nearly laughed. Where to start? "Well, let's see. I'm getting married in a few weeks, but Wes has no clue about Esme Zimmer, or witchcraft, or even that I found my birth mother. When I do tell him I'm descended from witches, he'll think I've lost my mind. Meanwhile, my real mother—my adopted mother, I mean—has taken leave of her senses and has jumped headfirst into the world of online dating."

He had no idea what I was talking about.

"Pursuing men she meets on a dating site." When that explanation didn't take, I added, "Imagine mail-order brides, only a thousand times dodgier."

I got up and cleared our dessert plates. After that, we all migrated to the living room. Django liked to perch on the back of the couch and take an after-dinner nap or watch a little TV with me. We all settled on the couch, but the TV remained off.

"I was just thinking about what you said about Esme being responsible for Madeleine turning green," Seton said. "When I was at Esme's, I stayed in the basement, mostly. There were all sorts of creatures in terrariums down there. Frogs, toads, and lizards. I gathered that they're her test subjects. I think she's able to manipulate creatures as well as time." He paused, then added, "Green creatures."

"You think Esme was trying to turn Madeleine into a toad or something? Why would she do that?"

"You say Esme's your mother. Maybe she views Madeleine as a threat to you."

It was ridiculous. Madeleine wasn't my favorite person in the world—far from it—but I didn't want her to suffer. I just would have preferred her to stay in Europe until after my wedding.

I felt exhausted. "I think I should go to bed."

"I don't mind bedding down here on the davenport," Seton said.

He looked several inches longer than the couch. "It's not big enough for you."

"I'll curl up. It'll be jake."

That wasn't any real alternative. I certainly wasn't going to ask him to curl up with me. As soon as the thought entered my mind, a wave of heat rushed through me.

I hopped up. "Perfect."

From my bedroom closet, I unearthed some sheets and an old blanket, and I grabbed one of the pillows off my bed. Good thing I hadn't started packing up everything yet.

No, that is not *a good thing.* Every day that went by without me filling up a box or two just meant that I would have more to do eventually.

I presented Seton with the sheets and with a spare toothbrush from the pile of dental freebies Sarah had given me. Then I realized he was wearing the same clothes he'd had on last night . . . and had been wearing every day since he'd gotten up to go to work on the day his best friend shoved him out a window.

"I've got some shorts and a clean T-shirt you can sleep in, and I can scare up some real clothes for tomorrow—although the pants might be a little short. We'll have to buy you a few new things."

"Dungarees?" he asked. "They seem to be what everyone wears now. I wouldn't mind getting a pair myself. I confess I've been feeling a little out of place."

A little? "By tomorrow night we'll have you looking just like everyone else, if that's what you want."

He seemed inordinately pleased with the idea. "That'll be swell."

If he really wanted to fit in, we might have to work on the vo-cabulary next. One thing at a time, though.

"I hope you didn't mind my introducing you as my cousin tonight," I said. "I didn't want the Havermans asking more ques-tions about a strange man hanging around me a few weeks before my wedding." I frowned. "Of course, now I have to explain a cousin appearing out of the blue."

"You don't have cousins?"

"I never really had much family besides my parents."

"Same here. After my father died, I was alone." He frowned. "That's probably the reason I was in such an all-fired rush to marry Ruthie. Didn't take me long to discover that there's noth-ing lonelier than living with someone you don't love with all your heart."

"You must still care for Ruthie a little. Just a little while ago you were talking about traveling back to save her from the clutches of evil Burt."

"That was before I discovered she married the man who shoved me out a window. Whether she knew about it or not, a thing like that puts a damper on your feelings."

He looked so forlorn, something in me couldn't help reaching out to him. I took his hand, ignoring the expected shock. "I'm sorry, Seton. Things will look better in the morning."

His gaze rose to mine. "They don't seem entirely bleak right now."

That strange, electric sensation I'd felt earlier tonight swirled through me. *Sorcery*. That's what the attraction I felt toward this man was. It wasn't real.

But it felt real.

"Strange," he said, his voice slightly scratchy, "how you can cross decades, and still meet someone so . . ."

Strange how the cadence of a voice could affect me. My chest rose and fell as if I'd just huffed up a flight of stairs. Suddenly, I wanted to lean in, just to find out what would happen.

My face heated. That's what people who didn't have fiancés did, people who weren't weeks away from the altar.

I pulled my hand back and turned away, hoping he wouldn't notice the fire in my cheeks. "Someone so congenial," I finished for him, in a ridiculously bright, unsexy, schoolmarm voice. "It's so nice that we can get along so well, given our different experiences."

"Yes," he agreed, the spell broken.

I really needed to screw my head on straight. I'd heard of women getting wedding jitters and then becoming so mixed up they ran out and slept with inappropriate men and completely blew up their engagements. *I* had no intention of doing that. Especially not with a man who didn't even know which century he belonged in.

I looked over at Django, who was watching us very intently. "Come on, little guy, time for bed."

He squawked and flapped before stepping reluctantly onto my arm. "'Our doubts are traitors,'" he said as I walked him to his cage, "'and make us lose the good we oft might win, by fearing to attempt.'"

I popped him onto his branch and locked the door. "Good night, Laurence Olivier."

Chapter 13

By the time I was up and dressed the next morning, Seton was having a mini breakdown over the coffee maker.

"I don't know how your percolator works," he said, standing in the pair of boxers and Genesee Insurance Team Building Day T-Shirt I'd given him. "I poured water in the pot, put the coffee in, and punched the On button, but all it does is sit there."

As a coffee addict, I could sympathize with the frustration of leapfrogging over a century of brewing technology. I washed out the pot, set up the filter again, and explained drip coffee makers to him. The task made it easier to face him after the little hiccup of attraction between us the night before.

For some reason, this small technology setback seemed to have depressed him almost as much as the newspaper article announcing his wife's remarriage had. I tried to pep him back up by pulling out the other clothes I'd unearthed for him—ones Wes had left at my place. I sent Seton to take a hot shower and change while I made us and Django some breakfast.

Django got a ramekin of parrot pellets, which he clicked over to inspect, unimpressed. "You couldn't add a berry or two?"

"You can't live on fruit."

"Mm. And when you scarfed down two donuts last week, did I say anything?"

"No, because you *couldn't* say anything."

"I could, and did—you just weren't listening." He snuffled through his beak. "It's been bloody frustrating."

"Where did you learn to talk like that?"

"You're not my first Wiccan rodeo," he said. "My last master was an actor—a great tragedian."

I supposed if a CPA like Esme could be a witch, so could an actor. "Anyone I've heard of?"

"Fame is not the only measure of a thespian's success."

"So . . . a very talented witch waiter?"

"'He jests at scars that never felt a wound,'" Django grumbled.

I leaned against the table and let out a long sigh. "What's happening to me?"

"Magic," he said. "Is that such a bad thing?"

"It's not who I am."

"Why would you want to limit yourself to being lesser?"

"It's not *lesser* to not be a witch." I straightened, and cracked an egg to start the pancake batter. "I'm not a witch."

"Fine. You do you. I'll just mind my own business over here and eat my tasteless parrot pellets."

I scowled at him, then turned to the fridge and picked two strawberries out of a carton. I plunked them on top of his pellets.

A short while later, Seton came back to the kitchen looking cleaner, happier, and more relaxed. He was lankier than Wes, so the jeans hung loosely on his hips and ended above his bony ankles, which themselves were sticking out of his old-fashioned pointed leather dress shoes. The sleeves of Wes's Syracuse

Lacrosse Club sweatshirt hit above his wrists. Even so, he seemed thrilled with his outfit—or maybe he was just happy to be washed, shaved, and in clean clothes.

"You look good," I lied.

"So do you."

I laughed. The stained DOES NOT BAKE WELL WITH OTHERS bib apron I'd put over my work clothes had been a gift from Sarah.

"If you'll give me your dirty clothes," I said, "I'll throw them in the washer."

This led to another twenty-first-century teaching moment as I showed him the stacked washer-dryer hidden in a hallway.

"Wonders never cease," he said, astonished. "Can I try it?"

We started a load of laundry, and for a few minutes he watched the water and suds toss against the washer door, as riveted as a cat in front of a bird feeder.

I finally dragged him back to the breakfast table and presented him with a plate of pancakes.

Seton didn't hold back on the maple syrup. It looked like overkill, but after one bite, he gave me an ecstatic look. "These hotcakes are delish."

"They're one of the few things I can make."

"That's more than I can manage. Cooking is like alchemy. I don't know how women manage it."

I laughed. "You could find out—all you have to do is pick up a cookbook. Or you could even take a cooking class."

"They have those for men?"

It took me a moment to realize he was completely serious. *1930*, I had to remind myself.

"They're for both sexes. Most classes are nowadays."

After chewing a bit more, he said, "Maybe I'll take you up on that advice. I'd like to learn to do something useful."

"I'm sure you were useful to a lot of people in what you were doing before."

"Oh, yes. I bought and sold whatever my clients asked me to." He shook his head. "It pays well, but it's not the most fulfilling work."

"I know what you mean. I sell insurance, but my heart isn't always in it. I mostly went into the profession because my dad encouraged me to. I work at the business he started."

"Men cooking and ladies selling insurance." He said it with awe. "It's a world of wonders."

"Wait till you see spray cheese from a can."

His face broke into a smile, until he realized I was serious. "Really?"

He looked befuddled and . . . kind of adorable. My gaze strayed down to his lips, and then I looked away and forked another pancake onto my plate as if I were ravenous, which I wasn't. My stomach felt fluttery and uneasy.

I like him, I thought. It didn't go any further than that. That I found him good-looking in a completely antique way meant nothing. It had just been a long time since I'd been in a domestic situation with any guy besides Wes. Novelty was a drug. It was why people had affairs.

Not that I was thinking of having an affair.

He put his fork down. "Bailey?"

I looked up. "Is something wrong?"

His face was solemn, soulful. "Whatever happens to me, or wherever I end up," he said, "I want you to know that I think you're the berries."

A flush crept up my neck. "Seton, that's sweet of you but"—I was *pretty* sure being "the berries" was a good thing—"I'm engaged."

"I know. And I'm married." He bit his lip. "Sure, she tried to kill me—but you know what I mean."

"Of course," I said. "Well, maybe not exactly. Since I'm not married. But I am engaged." *Shut up, Bailey.* I kept blurting out that I was engaged, like a talking doll.

A knock sounded at the door. It wasn't nine o'clock yet. Surely Wes wasn't here already—we weren't due to meet his mother until ten.

When I pulled the door open, Mom brushed past me. "Oh, good—I'm so glad I caught you before you went to work."

"Did you think of calling me?" I asked.

"I couldn't talk on the phone. I'm too upset." She stopped. The sound of cutlery against china reached us, and she drew back. Her voice dropped. "I'm sorry—I didn't see Wes's car outside. I assumed you were alone."

This was going to be fun to explain. I waved her through to the kitchen.

"So many boxes, Bailey," she noted, squeezing between the parrot cage and some packing boxes. "When are you going to—"

At the kitchen doorway, she stopped in her tracks.

Seton rose politely to his feet. "You must be Mrs. Tomlin." He was making a gallant effort not to gawp at her blue hair. "I'm Seton Atterbury."

Mom's confused gaze caught my eye.

"It's not how it looks," I said.

Seton nodded. "Bailey just asked me to stay the night with her."

"On the couch," I said.

"Oh, yes—on her couch."

"How do you two know each other?" Mom asked.

Seton and I exchanged panicked glances. The cousin lie obviously wasn't going to work with Mom. "My guitar teacher," I blurted out. "We both know Gil."

"Yes, Gil," he said. "Good fellow, Gil."

Mom seemed to accept the story—actually, she seemed not to care all that much. I finally noticed that her eyes were red.

Seton pulled a chair out for her. "Allow me to get you a cup of coffee, Mrs. Tomlin. Bailey's been teaching me all about coffee makers and other appliances."

Mom, distracted, sank into the offered chair, but over her head

I sent him a head shake. We needed to steer the conversation away from everyday things that he found exotic. But my warning flustered him. He poured a mug of coffee, then sat opposite Mom and came out with, "Bailey tells me you're searching for whoopee on the interphone."

A tear streaked down her cheek.

I scraped a chair back and sat down. "Mom, what's wrong?"

She sniffed. "I got the most disturbing message from Ed this morning."

Ed SexBeast. "If he wants you to send money, don't do it," I said.

Her face turned pink.

I groaned. I knew there was going to be a scam. "How much did he ask for?"

"It's not for him—that is, not entirely."

I pulled out my phone. "Just tell me. We can call the police."

"There's no point. Ed's already with them. He's locked up."

"Locked up, as in *jail*? Where?"

"Otisville."

"Mom, that's a federal prison."

"Only low security," she said, as if this made everything okay. "It's not like he's a *real* criminal, but he says he needs money for a good lawyer."

"What's he charged with?"

Her forehead pillowed with lines. "Something about embezzling and government contracts? I told you he worked in a high-powered office. You'd think *they* would want to hire a lawyer for him."

"Not if they're hanging him out on the line to dry," Seton said.

"That's why I think I'm going to have to help him."

"No," I said, "that's why you're *not* going to help him. Be thankful you made a narrow escape."

She sighed. "He seemed so right in so many other ways. We were a four golden hearts match. He loves Agatha Christie and duplicate bridge."

"He probably said that because all the women he was targeting had those things in their profiles."

Seton topped up her mug with the carafe. "I just suffered a romantic setback myself."

"I'm so sorry to hear that." And just like that, Mom was pivoted away from her own troubles like a pinball hitting a flipper. Having someone who needed counseling or consoling fired up her momming instinct. "Is it over, or do you think that you'll patch things up?"

"There are some pretty big obstacles," Seton said.

Mom looked back and forth between us, and I could see a worry bloom in her mind. "And that's why you're staying here?"

"It's just temporary." My words probably would have gone over better if, at that exact moment, I hadn't remembered Seton and I saying good night last night, and the pressure of his hands on mine. "Seton doesn't have a place to stay right now, that's all."

Mom's lips turned down. "I'm sorry to hear that. That's a sticky wicket to be in."

A knock sounded at the door. "That's probably Wes." The tiny opera diva in my head tottered toward her fainting couch. Speaking of sticky wickets . . .

Mom pulled the spatula from my hand and nudged me out of the kitchen. "Go answer the door. I'll put on a few more hotcakes. Do you think Wes'll want some?"

Wes ate a bowl of shredded wheat every morning after he came back from the gym. "I doubt it."

"I wouldn't mind another helping, Mrs. Tomlin," Seton said.

"Please call me Deb."

On the doorstep, Wes stood alert and businesslike in a blue suit, crisp white shirt, and burgundy tie with matching pocket square. He was polished up like a kid about to receive the Best Attendance prize at school. His face drooped as he gave me a full north-to-south inspection. "You're not ready."

"It's just an apron. Mom dropped by—we're making pan-cakes."

Brightness returned to his eyes. "Did you tell her?"

"About what?"

"The house."

I hadn't thought about the house all morning. "No—we've had other things to deal with."

Embezzlers, time travelers . . .

"Well, let's tell her. Maybe she'll want to come along."

He barreled past me, tripped over a box of bubble wrap on the way to the kitchen—and then skidded to a halt when he took in the sight of Django on the table, Mom with her blue hair and her spatula, and Seton standing next to her by the stove.

"Good morning, Wes," Seton said.

"Good—" Wes shook his head as the lacrosse club logo regis-tered. He turned to me.

I spread my hands. "Seton had nowhere else to go, so he slept here last night."

"I thought he was staying with your mother." He spoke as if the other two weren't even in the room.

"Of course he's staying with me," Mom piped up. "Any friend of Bill's is welcome in my home."

Wes's eyes widened. "Who's Bill?"

"Gil," I corrected.

A laugh trilled out of Mom. "Gil. Any friend of Gil's, I meant."

Django, eyeing me, piped up in his parrot voice, "Go. Go now."

"Right—we should go." I looped my arm through Wes's. As perilous as it was to leave Mom and Seton alone together, it seemed better to get Wes away.

It was harder than I expected to tug Wes to the door, though. His legs were moving, but his eyes were fixed on Django. "Did that bird just say something to you?"

I frowned. The world had gotten so crazy in the past day, the fact that my parrot was giving me orders barely registered now. "Bird belch," I explained. "He just ate breakfast."

Django squawked in outrage as I shut the door behind us.

The atmosphere in the Escalade was chilly on the way to the new house. Too late, I remembered that Wes had intended to ask my mom to come along, but I'd rushed us out before there was a chance to tell her about the house. Well, maybe Seton would explain it to her. She might absorb the reality of the Havermans' extreme largesse more easily if it came from a disinterested party. Plus, she'd seemed to take a shine to Seton.

Fingers crossed that Seton had sense enough not to talk about what had happened to him in too much detail.

At a stoplight, Wes sighed and drummed his palms on the steering wheel.

"Is something the matter?" I asked.

"Yes. The way we rushed out of your place back there, for one thing."

"I'm sorry. Did you want pancakes? I'd assumed you—"

"No." He blew out a breath. "You have to admit things looked awfully cozy back there. That guy, Seton, was wearing my clothes."

"Do you mind?" I asked. "You weren't wearing them, and mine wouldn't have fit him."

"Why can't he wear his own?"

"Because the clothes he was wearing last night are in the laundry."

"And he didn't have anything else? What kind of guy travels with just the clothes on his back? Is your cousin some kind of hobo?"

"His stuff . . . got lost in transit."

More steering wheel drumming. Then, "Your mother said he's a friend of your guitar teacher, not a cousin."

"He knows Gil, and he's a very distant relation. I never dreamed he'd turn up without a place to stay."

"That's another thing. What kind of person shows up weeks early for a wedding?"

I didn't have an answer for that, which was almost reassuring to me. Lies had started tripping off my tongue a little too easily for my taste.

"Light's green," I said.

He pressed the accelerator. A half a block passed before he said, "I hope you'll show more enthusiasm about the house this morning than you did last night. My parents were a little hurt, Bailey."

"I'm sorry—I was just so surprised." Why was I apologizing? "A house is a big deal, Wes, and you obviously knew. Why didn't you warn me?"

"They asked me not to."

"But this is going to be our house—and yet you just decided to let your mother pick some old place because it once belonged to a woman who kept her out of the sorority she wanted to pledge?"

"Okay, first thing: it's not just *some old place*. You heard what they said. It's a landmark."

"And it's also a mess, if the pictures are anything to go by."

"Mother's already busy fixing it up."

"Don't you see how presumptuous that is?"

"No, because, unlike you, I'm focused on how extraordinarily generous it is. Do you think houses grow on trees?"

"Of course not. And it *is* astonishingly generous. It was just so . . . unexpected."

"You acted as if you didn't even care. Like it was a duplicate toaster or something."

"Come on. I wasn't that bad."

He side-glanced a stern look at me. "Mad was more enthusiastic than you were."

Oh, God. Madeleine. I hadn't even thought about her this morning. I turned in my seat. "What happened to her? Is she okay?"

"Yes, fine."

"How long were you two at the ER last night?"

"Not long at all. We'd barely checked in before she started to de-green."

I gulped back an inappropriate laugh. "That's good. Did she see the doctor?"

"No, once she faded a little, she insisted on leaving. I think she was embarrassed. You know how it is—you finally get to a doctor and your symptoms suddenly disappear."

I leaned back against the leather seat, relieved. I doubt the doctors would have been able to detect a witch hex, but it was just as well that the process of elimination hadn't begun.

"You were nice to take her to the ER," I said.

"It was actually good to touch base with her. She told me why she'd left Europe early."

I couldn't wait to hear this. "Paris in the spring just can't hold a candle to Rochester?" I guessed.

He smiled. "She broke up with some guy over there. Phillipe somebody-or-other. He sounded really awful. Good riddance, I think."

And best of all, she was back just in time to participate in our wedding.

"She told you all this while you were at the hospital?"

He flipped on his blinker. Did I sense a slight hesitation? "Mad wanted to see the new house, so we drove by."

"A midnight tour?"

"We just parked in the driveway."

Amazing. Madeleine had parlayed a hex into a whole evening with her ex. Esme's green spell had backfired in a big way.

I had to admire Madeleine's crust, though. "She didn't ask you to show her around?"

He shook his head. "That's why she wanted to look at the place last night. She told me she'd been dying to ask if she could come tour the house this morning with us, but she didn't want to step on your toes. Said this should be your moment."

This time my laughter would not be stopped. "Wow—so thoughtful."

He turned a wry smile toward me. "She's a pain in the neck,

but she can be surprising sometimes, too. It's why she's stayed a family friend all these years."

I made a game show buzzer sound. "Wrong. She's stayed a family friend all these years because of you."

"She's Olivia's friend."

"Because you're Olivia's brother. I wouldn't take anything she says at face value. I doubt there's even a Phillipe."

He seemed astonished that I could be so cynical. "Why would she lie?"

"For the same reason I suspect she'll be unable to stay away this morning."

"You're wrong. Mad was *very* definite about not wanting to crowd in on your moment. I mean, that was the whole point of my driving her over there last night."

Right. The moonlight had nothing to do with it. "She'll show up."

He shook his head.

I threw down the gauntlet. "I'll bet you a double cone at the Latest Scoop that she shows up."

Wes wasn't big on sweets, with the exception of ice cream. The Latest Scoop was his favorite place.

"I'll take that bet," he said.

"Good, I want pistachio and Mexican vanilla."

He glanced over at me, puzzled.

"I'm putting in my order now," I explained. "For when I win."

Chapter 14

The pictures really hadn't prepared me for the house. It looked like a mini castle in the photos, but the photos hadn't shown how it stood set apart from its neighbors on a double lot. The yard was spectacular, with overgrown shrubs flanking a circular brick driveway. The stone was much darker in person, almost a charcoal gray.

"Like Manderley after the fire," I said.

"Mother has so many ideas, and she's already got workmen here. Just wait."

It was true. Several paneled vans stood in the driveway, next to a trio of SUVs. The crowd surprised me. How many people were here?

Joan flung open the front door, welcoming us in a powder-blue suit with a flowing, floral silk scarf. "Welcome home, you two lovebirds," she called out with uncharacteristic enthusiasm.

In the next moment the catalyst for Joan's gusto became clear: the cameras were rolling. A guy with bloodshot eyes wearing army surplus camo gear followed her out the door, a handheld camera mounted on his shoulder. He swung his lens my way as I was closing the car door. My smile froze. What was this?

Katrina popped out the door behind him. "Just act natural." She hopped on her toes to direct us. "Natural and ecstatic!"

Katrina was a petite person, but not in a delicate violet way. In school she'd been a gymnast, and she still had the pistol quality of someone capable of running at a vault full tilt. A manic pixie forged in iron.

"Wes, move in closer," she directed, pressing her hands together in front of her and then squaring them up like a camera viewfinder, à la Steven Spielberg. When Wes walked toward his mother, she added, "Closer to Bailey, I mean. Jerry here is helping me put a love story video together to show at the reception. This scene will be the two of you discovering your future home!" She lowered her voice and said to Jerry, "Don't close in on Bailey's right cheek. Blemish minefield there."

"M'kay," he said.

Having a guy dressed for a war zone following us with a camera made it even more awkward to exchange the usual air-kiss greeting with Joan.

Through the front door we walked into a fantastic black-and-white-tiled foyer with a chandelier the size of a refrigerator suspended from an elaborate medallion in the ceiling. The lights weren't on, but the morning sun shining through the windows around the front door hit the chandelier's hundreds of teardrop crystals, creating prisms of light everywhere. It was dazzling. On either side of the foyer were double doors of leaded glass—one led to a large room with dark paneling, an intricately patterned parquet floor, and a stone fireplace that seemed too large even for that spacious room. That must be the mantel from the fifteenth-century castle.

Boxes were stacked everywhere, and folding tables, and cellophane-wrapped gift baskets. Were the old owners still moving out?

"That's the living room," Joan said.

Actually, she was practically yelling, because the doorway opposite the living room had been sealed off with heavy plastic and tape. Looking like a white blur through the plastic, a guy in overalls running an industrial-sized machine was creating a deafening noise.

"The workmen are polishing the floors in the ballroom."

"Ballroom?" I asked, narrowing my eyes on the plastic.

Joan put her hand on my arm. "That's where I attended my first big dance when I was a teenager. Tricia didn't even invite me until the last minute, when she realized Doug Haverman wanted to escort me." She drifted off on a cloud of memory, and for a moment I had the sensation of playing a supporting role in someone else's dream. Then she snapped to. "They swear to me the painting will be done by tonight, which means everything will be ready, set, go for Saturday."

"Great," Wes said.

I'd missed something. "Ready, set, go for what?"

"We're holding the Garden Club's silent auction here," Joan explained. "All the boxes you see stacked around are donations. We were supposed to be having it at May Keller's, but she called me late last night and said they had a sewer main leak in front of her house and the place is all torn up. So I told her just to bring it all over here and we'd work it out. We'll restrict visitors to the first floor and the yard, which shouldn't be a problem if Carlo and his men stick to the schedule Shirley and I have mapped out for them. Shirley's in the kitchen."

A wide staircase swept up to the second floor, and to its side was a corridor that Joan led us down. Jerry and Katrina brought up the rear.

I don't know what I was expecting from Shirley—I guess another Joan. Instead, a stout woman in a pantsuit and cat-eye glasses attached to a silver chain waited for us. "And here's the lucky couple!" she said when we were introduced. "You must be over the moon."

I agreed that I was over the moon. But mostly I was staring at the kitchen, which was also piled high with boxes. "Isn't all this stuff in here a bit of a fire hazard?"

Shirley dismissed my fear with a wave of her hand. "Don't fuss over details like that. You've got big decisions to make, starting with this kitchen. Or I should say, this den—because that's what it *should* be. You see, when the house was built, the kitchen was downstairs, in the basement. Some lunatic back in the twentieth century thought it would be a good idea to move it up here."

"Some lunatic in Tricia's family," Joan couldn't help interjecting.

"Of course, this room could be a bedroom, as well." Shirley jabbed an index finger toward the floor. "You'd just have to move the kitchen back downstairs—where it originally was and still should be—knock out this closet they've been using as a pantry and expand the half bath to a full bath. Simple."

Simple? That sounded like a year's remodeling job.

"Aren't there eight bedrooms already?" I asked.

"Never hurts to have another bedroom on the first floor," Shirley said. "You'll thank yourself when you're eighty and your knees are shot."

"We should go outside and see how the tables can be set up for the auction," Joan said.

"And get some nature shots of the happy couple," Katrina added.

The backyard was breathtaking. A lawn sloped gently down from the house. The property's perimeter was lined with old maples, rhododendrons heavy with buds, and azaleas, some of which were already in bloom. An outbuilding in the same stone as the house stood to one side. "What's that?" I asked, pointing. It looked like a mausoleum.

"That's the old pool house," Joan explained. "It was a mess even back when Tricia had parties there. It might make a good guesthouse someday, though."

Donated statuary, lawn furniture, and decorative garden items had already been delivered and were scattered around the lawn, awaiting Saturday.

"We can set up chairs and tables over here," Joan said, pacing off the area. "Even if it's still a little chilly—I've hired some of those heat lamps." She frowned at an ancient swing set in one corner of the yard. "We'll need to get rid of that eyesore."

"A swing!" Katrina clapped her hands together, back in Katrina B. DeMille mode. "That's perfect for the movie. Bailey, get in the swing. Wes, you push her."

Wes headed toward it but I dug in my heels. For one thing, the swing set was made for little kids. It was also completely rusty. "I'm not touching that thing without a tetanus shot."

Katrina made a frowny face. Even Wes seemed to be impatient with me. Was I being a pill? Madeleine would have leapt into that swing, tetanus or no tetanus.

I needed to be a better sport. I started to cross toward them.

"Look at this, Bailey." Joan waylaid me and gestured to three birdbaths that had been donated for the auction. "The one in the center. Isn't it magnificent?"

It was magnificently ugly, I'd give it that. What was supposed to be a bald eagle carved into concrete formed the base. The bird had a coronet or a halo or something over its head, and that's what the bowl of the birdbath rested on. Was this some kind of bad taste test?

I smiled, hoping that my suppressed *You-have-got-to-be-kidding* thoughts didn't show in my eyes. "It's . . . unique. But is it appropriate for a birdbath?"

"Why not?" she asked. "It's a statue of a bird."

"But don't eagles kill other birds? Little birds might freak out at having their bath be on top of their scariest predator."

Joan met that observation with a flat stare.

"But maybe I'm overthinking it," I said.

"I just love it." She actually put her hand on her heart, which then slowly dropped mournfully to her side. "Of course, *I* can't bid on items. Some pesky conflict-of-interest rule about the people running an auction not being allowed to bid prevents me."

All of a sudden, something dropped out of a maple nearby and landed on the wide bowl of the birdbath, causing Joan and me to jump. A squirrel, reddish in color, chittered at us.

Joan glared at it. "Aggressive little beast. I hate squirrels. They're just rats with floofy tails."

The squirrel rose on his hind legs and chittered even more angrily.

"Shoo!" she said.

The squirrel turned, flicked its tail as a parting insult, and sprinted across the yard. It scrambled up a holly bush near the house and leapt onto the roof.

I left Joan to join Wes and Katrina, although I couldn't help glancing back at the squirrel. High on its perch on a second-story gutter, the irate rodent continued to vocalize, although I was the only one paying attention now. Those vocal clicks sounded like a warning to me.

Rochester didn't have red squirrels, did it? Gray, yes, and black. Occasionally I'd spotted an albino. This one definitely had a red hue to his fur.

Something Seton had said scratched at the back of my mind. *I think she's able to manipulate creatures as well as time. . . .*

Wes squeezed my arm. "Pistachio and Mexican vanilla?"

I frowned at him. "What?"

He nodded toward the back gate Madeleine had just hobbled through. "Oh, here everybody is!" She was wearing a pale-blue suit—skirt, not pants—that almost matched Joan's. She was still in her boot, and today she'd added a cane. The stick sank into the dirt as she crossed the yard, causing her to have to yank it out with each clunky step.

"I didn't mean to interrupt a family moment," she said, "but I got up this morning and realized I must've lost an earring last night when Wes and I were here."

Joan pivoted toward Wes and me, her brow arched.

Wes shifted.

I cleared my throat. "Madeleine and Wes came by last night after they left the ER."

Above me, the squirrel released a new barrage of clicks. There was definitely something suspicious about that animal. Could Esme have shape-shifted into a squirrel?

But how would she have known I'd be here?

"Wes wouldn't let me take a step inside the house before you'd seen it, Bailey," Madeleine said. "Even though I was dying for a little tour. Still am."

Joan was delighted. "Bailey hasn't seen much of the house yet, either."

Madeleine made a shocked face. "If I were you, I would have been through every square inch by now."

I was not going to let her get to me. "Shouldn't you stay out here and look for your earring?"

"Oh, no—I found it." She held up a gold hoop. "Out in the driveway, right by where Wes and I sat on that cute ornamental bench and talked last night."

All eyes were on Wes now, including mine. Earlier he'd made it sound as if he and Madeleine had just sat in the driveway in the Escalade. Bucket seats, not a bench.

"The bench!" Katrina practically did a handspring. "That's a *great* idea. Let's shoot some footage of Wes and Bailey on the bench."

"Why?" Wes asked.

"Because it's perfect—right next to the gingko tree, a little secluded, with the house in the background. A perfect romantic setting!"

Had it seemed like a perfect romantic setting the previous night? I wasn't the only one wondering.

Wes's face reddened.

"I've got a better idea—let's all go upstairs," Joan suggested quickly. "There's the most wonderful view from up in the turret. It's like a little bird's nest up there."

Back inside, we all trooped up the wide staircase. Upstairs, there were bedrooms as big as my entire apartment. What would we do with all these rooms?

A smaller staircase led up to the attic and the turret, and everyone trailed after Joan like ducklings. Everyone but me. I got sidetracked by the master bedroom. At least, I assumed it was the master bedroom. It was located at the end of the hallway and stretched the width of the house. A wide window seat looked over the backyard we'd all just been standing in.

It was my dream bedroom, if you didn't count the stained wallpaper and hideous carpet, which was gold with a swirly sculpted pattern in the pile. I knelt on the window seat and looked out. As I was staring out the leaded glass panes, a face suddenly popped into my view—the furry, mischievous face of a squirrel. Reddish gray.

I hopped back, yelping in surprise. In doing so, I slammed into someone. I turned as Madeleine stumbled backward, her non-booted heel catching on the carpet. Where had she come from? In the next moment, a strange rumbling sounded. I looked up just as the ceiling directly above us cracked, and then a large piece of it came down.

I dove, landing right next to Madeleine as Sheetrock hit the carpet mere inches from us, accompanied by an explosion of dust and ancient insulation. I flung my arm in front of my face to shield my mouth and nose from the foul, toxic cloud, but I don't think Madeleine's reflexes were fast enough. As soon as her shriek of surprise ended, coughing and cursing took over.

"What the hell just happened?" she said. "What did you do?"

As if *I* had caused the ceiling to collapse.

I hadn't, had I?

Of course I hadn't. I hadn't done anything. I hadn't even known Madeleine was there. I'd just been looking at—

The squirrel.

"Did you see that squirrel?" I asked.

Madeleine gaped at me. Dust covered her face everywhere except her eyes, creating a raccoon-like effect. "A squirrel? Did you not see the roof collapse on us?"

"The ceiling."

"Whatever." Coughing, she struggled to her feet. "We need to get out of this room before it kills us."

She wasn't wrong. If one section of the ceiling could collapse, who was to say that the whole thing wouldn't come down on our heads? And no telling what we were breathing.

At that moment, Jerry the videographer glided into the room, camera trained on me. Ancient insulation dust still floated in the air around us. I was probably coated in it almost as much as Madeleine was. Before Jerry could turn his lens toward her, she poked her cane toward the camera. "Don't you dare," she warned. "Turn that thing off."

Wes sprinted into the room. "We heard a noise. What happened? Are you okay?"

He hurried over and pulled me to my feet, hugging me.

"That's perfect!" Katrina said, stopping on a dime just behind Jerry. "But try not to close in too much on Bailey."

Madeleine slapped the dust off her now-filthy dress. "I'm fine, everyone," she muttered. "Thanks for asking. *Really* enjoyed my house tour."

"I thought I saw that squirrel," I said, still trying to piece it together.

"What squirrel?" Wes asked.

Madeleine whacked her hands against her now-filthy suit in a vain effort to beat the dust out. "Her house fell on me and *she's* obsessed with a rodent."

Still holding an arm around me, Wes stared up at the ceiling. "I don't think squirrels could have had anything to do with this. Maybe there's water damage on the ceiling. We need to check the roof tiles for leaks."

Joan came in and put her hands on her hips, her gaze traveling between Madeleine and me. "What did you two get up to in here?"

"Nothing," I said quickly, with the defensiveness of a kid who's just been caught making a mess.

Madeleine smirked. "Bailey thinks a squirrel tried to kill her."

It was worse than that. I suspected my birth mother had almost killed me—by targeting my nemesis. First the shoes. Then Madeleine turning green. Now the ceiling collapsing. The attacks on Madeleine were escalating. I needed to intervene before someone really was killed.

Chapter 15

I took a deep breath before ringing the doorbell at the old farm-house in Zenobia. This time I knew what I was up against. Or I assumed I did.

Instead of Esme answering the door as I expected, Gwen appeared. The cat was draped around her shoulders like a fur stole. Both seemed surprised to see me.

"I didn't expect you to come back here again," Gwen said.

"I need to speak to Esme."

"She's unavailable at the moment."

"Please. It's urgent."

She took in what must have been desperation in my eyes. "You'd better come in, then."

Inside, the living room had been totally transformed since yesterday. Mid-century modern had given way to a more traditional look, with an accent on Arts and Crafts decorations—burnished tones, deep mahogany wood grains, and Tiffany glass.

"Some people stress bake," Gwen explained. "Aunt Esme stress decorates."

"What was she stressed about?"

She looked as if she were about to say one thing, then had a change of heart. "I'm sorry—I can't pretend I don't know who you are. Aunt Esme was so distraught after you left yesterday that the whole story about you came spilling out. You and I are cousins. My mom is Esme's little sister."

"Just what you need," the cat deadpanned to her. "Another cousin."

"There are more of you?" I asked, intrigued in spite of myself. Even after Esme had told me who I really was, it hadn't occurred to me that I had more witch relations out in the world. Cousins. Real ones.

"I never had cousins," I said. "Or much family at all."

Her face brightened. "You should hang out with us sometime. In addition to being a teacher, my cousin Trudy runs a home business called Enchanted Cupcakes, so we usually meet up at her place every week or so and make a dent in her day-olds. We call it our cupcake coven—Trudy, me, and our cousin Milo. Sometimes we play games, or just talk. Sometimes our partners join us."

Something inside my chest swelled. Cousins. Cupcake coven! It was a glimpse of an alternate life I'd missed.

"You're all"—I couldn't bring myself to say the word *witches*— "like Esme?"

"None of us have her expertise. I consider myself Aunt Esme's apprentice. We weren't even able to practice till recently, when we were granted a provisional go-ahead while Odin finds proof that our family did no wrong in the past." She stopped and shook her head. "It's a long story, and Aunt Esme said you didn't think you were one of us anyway, so maybe I should just shut up. Unfortunately, right now she isn't . . . reachable."

"I know about the basement," I said. "Seton told me." I was curious to see that place for myself.

"I can't really—"

Whatever she was going to say was lost in a house-shaking explosion. The floor buckled beneath my feet, sending pictures dropping from the walls and tchotchkes toppling off shelves. I dove under the nearest table and assumed the duck-and-cover position as the world slowly stabilized. Then, from somewhere beneath us, a guttural curse rose up, followed by a clatter of steps that grew louder until Esme burst into the room dressed in what looked like burlap sack. The garment was filthy, and visibly ripped in places. Her frazzled red hair stood on end, coated in dust. She shook herself like a wet dog sending out a spray of dust and dirt, and let out something between a howl and a whoop.

"Hoooooly crap!" she rasped. "Screw up a few coordinates and time travel can go very, very wrong." She leaned over and rested her hands against her thighs, panting like a sprinter.

"Where were you?" Gwen asked.

"Not Manhattan in 1930, that's for darn tootin'." Her hair dropped a few leaves as she shook her head again. "Or maybe it *was* Manhattan and I just got my BCs and ADs mixed up. I might have been a few zeroes off, too. I'm pretty sure I saw a woolly mammoth."

"Cool," Gwen said.

"Not so cool when there are also saber-toothed tigers running around." She shuddered, then let out a sigh. "Well, live and learn. But I didn't find Odin—that's the worst part."

"I'm so sorry." Gwen cleared her throat. "Actually, you returned in good time. You've got a visitor."

She nodded toward me as I crab-crawled out from under the table. Esme had been so discombobulated by her time traveling misadventure that she hadn't even noticed me. Now she stepped back in alarm, obviously distressed to be caught looking less than her best. Her mouth pulled into an unnatural smile, and she smoothed down her wild tangle of hair in an attempt to assume an air of normalcy. "Izzie! I'm so happy to see you again."

"Not my name," I said.

"I mean Bailey." She gave herself a pretend thump on the forehead, which dislodged a plume of dust. "You know Gwen?"

"We met a few nights ago."

Gwen and the cat looked from Esme to me. "I was just making tea," Gwen said. "I'll bring us some."

After she left, silence stretched between Esme and me. What I'd overheard about her time traveling not only astounded me, it made me doubt my assumptions of what had been happening in my own life.

"How long were you gone?" I asked.

"It's hard to say." She fidgeted with her hands and seemed to be struggling to find some way to improve the impression she was making. She finally hit upon manners. "Would you like to sit down? You can have the glider chair."

I lowered myself into it a mission-style chair mounted on a gliding rocker mechanism. Actually very comfortable for an antique.

"Why is it hard to say how long you were gone?" I asked. Our last meeting had just been yesterday.

She sat on something that looked like a Victorian fainting couch. "The minutes stretch like decades when you're scrambling around a wilderness populated with wildlife that looks way more Jurassic Park than Central Park."

Nothing about this was boosting my confidence in her time traveling skills. It certainly wouldn't boost Seton's. But he wasn't my primary concern at the moment.

I gestured around the living room. "You probably spent a lot of time doing all this"—I gestured around the room—"yesterday afternoon?"

"No, it doesn't take me long, especially when I'm in an emotional state. I was . . . well, upset after you left. Our first real meeting hadn't gone as I'd always dreamed it would."

I hoped she wasn't under the impression that I'd come here to

have a big reconciliation. "I'm trying to piece something together. Things happened last night."

"To you?" Her eyes flashed with mother bear anger. "Is someone threatening you?"

Gwen came in with a tea service rattling on a tray. She set
the tea things down on the coffee table and began to pour cups
for us.

"No one's threatening me. All the incidents seem directed at
someone I know—that woman you saw with me the other day in
front of the bridal boutique." My gaze narrowed on her. "Whose
heel you broke."

"You pieced that together, did you?" Mischief glinted in
Esme's eyes. "I couldn't help it. She's one of those women who
walks around with a stick up her butt. Then, when you told me
she was your fiancé's ex, the temptation to mess with her was irresistible."

"As irresistible as the temptation was when you turned her
green at the restaurant last night, or this morning when you almost killed her?"

Esme sputtered at the accusations. "I did no such thing."

Of course she would deny it. "When did you leave on your
trip?"

"Yesterday evening. Around six, I guess."

That brought me up short. She couldn't have been in present-
day Rochester and prehistoric Manhattan at the same time.
"Then you didn't have anything to do with turning Madeleine
green?"

"No." She laughed. "Sounds wonderful, though."

I was baffled. "If you didn't, who did?"

Esme's and Gwen's eyes met as the latter handed cups around.

"Sugar?" Gwen asked me.

There was something these two weren't saying.

Gwen settled on the other side of the settee from Esme and
took a sip of tea. The cat hopped up on an armchair and watched

us expectantly, as if intensely curious to know what would be said next.

"If it wasn't you, who could it have been?" I asked.

Gwen stirred her tea but didn't meet my gaze. "Can't you guess?"

There was no mistaking the implication in her tone.

"*Me?*" I crashed my cup down in its saucer. "Madeleine's awful, but it never would have occurred to me to turn her Margaret Hamilton green."

Esme cackled at the Wicked Witch of the West reference. "Oh, that's too good. Honestly, I couldn't be prouder. And you call yourself a nonbeliever!"

"I *couldn't* have done it."

Gwen eyed me sympathetically. "Pigment spells are pretty rudimentary. It's possible you tossed one off without thinking."

"Subconsciously, you mean?"

"Like a natural. I'm so, so, proud." Esme took a long slurp of tea and sighed happily. "I can't tell you how much I needed that," she told Gwen. "All the water smelled of sulfur back there. I was afraid to drink it."

"Wait," I said. "Just because you're my birth mother, that doesn't make me a witch, does it? Gwen was just telling me something about apprenticing . . ."

"But you're no ordinary witch," Esme told me. "You have a pedigree to be quite proud of—including a father who's one of the most brilliant witches of his generation."

Uh-huh. In her tattered burlap dress and with her crazy hair, she wasn't giving off Super Witch vibes. Also my so-called wizard of a birth father seemed to be stuck in the early years of the Depression. The parental units were not exactly covering themselves in supernatural glory.

"If I was born a witch, why did it take me nearly thirty-five years to turn someone green? Why wasn't I doing it in elementary school?"

"You didn't know you had powers," Esme explained. "And I

took care to hide you with the most even-keeled, levelheaded couple I could find. I was trying my best to protect you. I didn't want you coming to grief like your father."

"Grief?"

A cloud fell over Esme's expression. "Our family's had a few problems."

"The Grand Council of Witches issued an edict against anyone in our family practicing many decades ago," Gwen explained, "so we all were forced to let our powers go dormant, or undeveloped. When they started to awaken, it was often in unexpected ways. Our cousin Trudy had the most trouble. She turned her husband into a rabbit." She bit her lip. "But Trudy was under a lot of stress. Marital difficulties."

If she'd been having marital trouble, turning her husband into a bunny couldn't have helped matters.

"Aunt Esme defied the edict and kept practicing," Gwen continued, "but even she had to keep her witchcraft under wraps."

"Hence, the basement laboratory," I guessed.

Esme scooted forward. "How did you know about that?"

"Seton told me."

"You found him, then? Good. How is he?"

"He isn't sure if he wants to stay or go back."

She heaved a sigh. "It's a quandary."

I was struggling to absorb what they'd been telling me about my own situation. It just didn't make sense to me. "Even if I was somehow able to unconsciously turn someone green, I *know* I wasn't responsible for this morning's attack. A ceiling collapsed and could have seriously injured not just Madeleine, but also me. I was standing right next to her."

Esme's dusty red brows drew together.

"I think I was lured up to the second floor by a squirrel," I said.

I'd expected them to look at me as if I'd cracked up. Instead, the interest in their expressions ramped up a notch.

"I thought the animal was trying to tell me something," I continued. "To be honest, I suspected it was you."

Esme drew back in distaste. "Turn myself into a squirrel? Yeesh, I would never do that." She stopped to consider. "An otter, maybe. I like otters."

"The point is, that squirrel's chattering seemed to be a kind of incantation," I said. "Like a malign spirit speaking through him."

As the words left my mouth and echoed around the silent room, I cringed. Squirrels and malign spirits? What was happening to my brain?

But the atmosphere in the room shifted. Esme and Gwen both put their cups down. The cat arched its back, hissing as if it had just detected a mortal threat.

Alarm zipped through me. "What's going on?"

Their gazes remained locked.

"Tannith." Gwen's voice had an edge as she spoke the name.

The cat hissed again, and the air around us crackled with tension.

"Who is Tannith?"

Esme and Gwen held themselves stiffly, neither willing to speak.

"Is this some big witchy secret that's not for the uninitiated?" I asked.

My question spurred them to speak, but not to me. "Maybe it's not her," Gwen told Esme, her voice shaky.

"It's her."

"But how could she know . . . ?"

"She just knows."

Griz interjected, "I'm not going back to her."

"Oh, God." Gwen picked him up, enveloping his furry body in a strangling hug. "No, you're not, Grizzle. That's not happening."

My heart pounded a bass drum of fear. "Who's Tannith?"

"A witch." Esme bit her lip. "And not a good one."

"I grew up with her," Gwen explained. "The Grand Council of Witches forced my parents to take her in. It didn't turn out well."

"What does that have to do with me?" I asked.

"I should have stayed away from you," Esme lamented. "But I couldn't. With you getting married, it seemed a perfect time to connect."

I had to do some reading between the lines. "You're saying that this evil witch latched onto me through you?"

"I'm *so* sorry." Esme's eyes filled with tears, and she reached out and took my hands in hers. "I'll help you. We will get through this as a family."

I snatched my hands back. "But I don't know Tannith. Whatever problems you have with her, it's nothing to do with me."

"It is if she knows you're my daughter," Esme said.

Gwen nodded. "Or my cousin."

"She hates us."

I still didn't get it. "Okay, but if there's this Grand Council or whatever you call it, can't I write to them and get them to issue a cease and desist letter, or whatever the witch equivalent is?"

"It's not that simple." Gwen stroked Griz's back. The poor animal looked terrified. "The Council doesn't know Tannith's missing."

"Where is she?"

"We don't know," Gwen explained. "I put a disappearing hex on her."

I felt like a slow student. "Which means . . . ?"

Gwen took a breath. "Last year we were having a big argument, and I made her vanish."

"Like a magic trick?" I said.

Esme sighed. "A magic trick with permanent consequences. No one's seen her since last Halloween. And we aren't likely to, either. Whatever hex Gwen pulled out of her butt that day is a mystery to me."

I was having a hard time processing this. "So where is she?"

"Nowhere and everywhere," Esme said. "And in a squirrel, evidently."

I looked over at Gwen. Next to Esme she seemed just like a nice, regular person, but to hear them tell it, she'd basically committed witch murder.

"Don't blame Gwen," Esme said, reading my thoughts. "She was a novice, and concocted some indecipherable hex under pressure." She raised her hands in a what-can-you-do gesture. "That's what happens when you suppress your talents. Mistakes are made."

Mistakes? "You made this woman disappear from the face of the earth."

"The woman is pure evil," Gwen said. "At the moment it happened, she was threatening us all. It was hex or be hexed."

"She's out in the ether, but apparently she's discovered you're one of us," Esme said. "Maybe she knows I found you and has decided to get her revenge on me by messing with you."

"Lovely," I said. "Guilt by association." With people I never asked to be associated with. "So if you can't unhex this person, can you at least let her know that I'm innocent?"

Gwen snorted. "Like Tannith cares about that. You don't know her."

"Protect yourself," Esme urged. "Embrace your inner witch."

These two really were barking mad. "What good would that do? You've embraced your inner witches, and as far as I can tell, all you've managed to do is make muddles like you've gotten poor Seton into."

"He's not dead," Esme pointed out, "which he would have been if I hadn't intervened."

"No, he's not dead, he's just a lost soul. How is he supposed to live in the modern world? He's a permanently displaced person." Not as displaced as Tannith, evidently, but still . . .

"Maybe not permanently," Esme said.

"What, do you have plans to send *him* back to be a saber-toothed tiger snack?"

"That's not a mistake I'll make again," Esme said, her tone defensive.

I crossed my arms. "Why exactly was your family not supposed to practice witchcraft?"

"We had an ancestor who—allegedly—made a mistake," Gwen said.

"What was the mistake?"

She sighed. "They *said* he caused the Dust Bowl."

I sputtered.

"But it was a mix-up," Esme said. "That's why your father is back in time, trying to collar the culprit so that the edict will be officially struck from the records. And I'm sure it will be." She bit her lip. "If he ever makes it back."

Heaven help me. Of all the witch families in all the world, I had to be born into one that was hopelessly, supernaturally incompetent. No wonder the Grand Pooh-Bahs of Witchcraft or whatever they called themselves hadn't wanted this messed-up family practicing sorcery. They were a menace.

"So Tannith is trapped in the ether and her only recourse is to body-snatch squirrels and bring ceilings down on people's heads? I can't say I blame her for being a bit pissed off." I got to my feet. "As far as I can tell, the best way to protect myself is to get as far away as possible from you people and your crackpot supernatural powers."

Gwen flinched. "That's a terrible thing to say."

Esme shook her head at her niece. "No—let her speak freely. Honesty is best. You can't force feeling. Or trust. Or . . . love." She couldn't hide the hurt look on her face when she turned back to me, though. "I'm just trying to help you."

Help? "Even by your own account, all my troubles started

when you went out of your way to find me. Which is nothing I ever sought. I *have* a family—well, I have a mother, at least—and I'm going to marry into a very traditional, proud family who would not understand these bizarre, not to mention dangerous, shenanigans."

"It's not shenanigans," Esme said. "It's serious business. Think about the ceiling coming down. You said yourself that it could have hurt you, maybe even killed you."

"Yes! That's why I'm begging you to leave me out of your witchy politics and vendettas. I'm going back to Rochester, and I'd really appreciate it if you would give a psychic shout-out, or whatever you people do, to let Tannith know that none of her current woes are my fault and that she should just leave me alone from here on out." I huffed out a breath. "Is that too much to ask?"

The words had spilled out of me, and it wasn't until I stopped talking that I saw the effect my speech had on Esme. She seemed to have shrunk before my eyes. Her features looked older, forlorn, and her body took on the hunched, cronelike posture I remembered from years ago. I'd wounded her.

I swallowed past a lump in my throat. She was, after all, my mother. A freak, maybe, but my flesh and blood nevertheless. And I'd just told her I wanted nothing to do with her.

But it was the truth. What else could I do? None of this was my fault.

Guilt coursed through me.

I put my hand on her slumped shoulder, ignoring the jolt I felt in my fingertips. "I'm sorry to be so blunt. You did the right thing all those years ago. Mom was telling me about it—I know you used subterfuge to find a good home for me, with kind people who really wanted me. And they did. I'll thank you for the rest of my life for the sacrifice you made. But I can't suddenly accept you into my life as my mother, any more than I can accept that I have supernatural powers. That's not who I am. I like security—risk really isn't my thing. I sell insurance, for Pete's sake."

A tear made a muddy path down Esme's cheek, which was still dusty from her time-traveling misadventure. She tried to say something, but it came out as a hiccup. Gwen, pale, remained seated and fixed me with a cool stare.

Even the cat eyed me disapprovingly. "You don't know Tannith," he said, flicking his tail.

"No, I don't. And I'll be happy if I never know her."

Gwen shook her head. "Griz means that Tannith won't give up. She holds grudges."

"Again, your fight with her has nothing to do with me. Please tell her that—however you can. In the meantime, I have a wedding to plan."

"Did you decide to keep the dress?" Esme asked in a pathetically small voice.

I sighed. "Yes. Thank you. That can be your contribution to the wedding, but that's *all* I need from you."

The cat swished his tail. "Harsh."

There didn't seem to be any more to say, so I headed for the door. Belatedly, I realized it might not be a good idea to burn *all* my bridges here.

I made myself turn back. "I hope you won't hold any resentment against Seton for what I said here today. He's a victim in all this. You owe it to him to try to make things right and return him to his life. If you can think of a way to get him out of the fix he's in, then you know where to find us."

Esme rushed forward, eyes still moist. "No resentment," she rasped. "Never resentment toward you. And I *will* make things right for Seton. On my honor as a Zimmer, I'll dedicate my last drop of energy to that task until we find a way to return him to his rightful time." She paused, then added, "Unsplattered."

I let out a breath. "Thank you."

I hurried out the door and back to my car. Behind me, Esme called out, "Love you, Bailey!"

Oh, God. She was even using my right name.

Why did I feel such guilt for jumping into my car without being able to say the same thing back to her? I *didn't* love her. How could I? She'd descended on my life like an affliction.

I just needed to get back to my real life. My normal life.

I drove away without another word or a backward glance.

Chapter 16

Dreams of a normal life died the moment I dragged myself through the front door.

"Well met, mistress!" Django called from his cage in the dining room.

My eyes narrowed as I headed toward the voice. Django was in his cage, perched on his favorite branch, eyeing me in that disarming way he had.

"Door, please?" he prompted.

I opened it and offered my arm, which he hopped on immediately, climbing up to my shoulder.

"Did Seton come back today?" I asked.

"No, it's just been me. 'Alone and palely loitering.'"

"What?"

"Keats," he explained in disgust.

Articulate *and* literary. I set him on the counter while I prepared myself a vodka and orange juice. As much as I loved Django, it was unnerving to be talking to a bird whose language skills had rocketed from incoherent babble to Nobel laureate overnight.

I wasn't normally a pre-dinner drinker, but today I was making an exception.

He cocked his head my way. "Isn't it customary to offer others refreshment?"

I tore off a grape from a bunch sitting in a bowl and handed it over.

"Thank you."

I expected him to tear right into it, but he waited for me to finish mixing the screwdriver.

I tapped my glass against his grape. "Cheers." I couldn't help smiling. If not for Wes, I probably could have stayed a crazy single parrot lady for the rest of my life.

Wes. A chill ran through me. How was I going to explain the new, improved Django to Wes? Or to anyone? "We're going to have to work out some things here. There are people around me who won't understand why you're suddenly so chatty."

"Don't worry, I won't talk to Wes," he said. "Seton, yes. I like him."

I was about to ask him why when my phone pinged. It was a text from Sarah.

Okay if I come over? Having a crisis.

Of course! I wasn't sure I was in a fit mental state to counsel anyone, but it would be a relief to hear someone else's problems. And I was worried about my friend. **Any time.**

Someone knocked on the front door, and I slapped the phone closed. I wondered if this was my landlady, Dottie, who lived in the adjoining unit. She'd complained once about Django squawking.

I headed to the door but stopped and turned back to Django. "Act normal," I said. "Parrot normal. No smart-alecky showing off."

He tilted his head and said in a Stupid-Pet-Tricks parrot voice, "Polly want a cracker?"

I rolled my eyes and went to answer the door. Sarah stood on the porch.

"I texted you from the driveway," she explained.

In the kitchen she took in the screwdriver fixings out on the counter and sagged onto a barstool. "I'll have what you're having."

I wasted no time preparing a drink while she greeted Django in a loud, slow voice that probably set his beak on edge.

"Hel-lo, Django!"

She didn't seem to notice the dead-eyed stare Django leveled at her.

"Pretty birdie!" she continued. "Are you enjoying your grape?"

He tilted a glance at me. I half expected him to start reciting Hamlet's soliloquy, but he just let out a sound that might have been *sheesh* or an avian attempt at something worse.

Sarah straightened, exasperated. "You said he'd started to talk."

"It's like asking a dog to do tricks for company. They always choke when people are watching."

She regarded Django clumsily spearing the grape with his beak. "That bird's not as bright as you seem to think he is."

He released a guttural growl.

I handed her the drink glass. "What's the crisis?"

She took a sip and leaned back. "It's Mark."

Sarah and her boyfriend, Mark, had been together since she'd opened her own dental practice around the same time he'd hung out his orthodontist shingle. Her only gripe about him was that he was marriage-phobic. They'd been dating seven years.

"When my last appointment canceled and I realized I'd have free time this evening, I called Mark to see if he wanted to go have an early dinner and then a movie—weeknight date sort of thing. That's when he dropped the bombshell on me."

Oh, no. Sarah had spent the better part of a decade nudging

this relationship along. She loved Mark, and when I saw them together it always seemed like he really cared for her, too.

"He didn't break up over the phone, did he?" I asked.

"Break up?" She tensed in panic. "What makes you think we broke up? Has he said anything to you about breaking up?"

"You just said he'd dropped a bombshell on you."

"Right. Get this—he told me he can't make it to the wedding."

"My wedding?"

"Yes, Bailey. *Your* wedding. What other wedding am I attending this month?"

"That's not such a big deal, is it?"

She looked at me as though I'd lost my wits. "I've got the nicest dress I'll own until I get married myself, *if* I ever get married, and yes, I care if he's not there to see me all decked out. Weddings are supposed to beget more weddings, but that can only happen if attendees are there to be begat."

"I'm beginning to think it would be better if Wes and I eloped," I said.

Her brow furrowed. "Are you okay?"

I nodded out of habit. And really, what could I say? *An evil witch is out to sabotage my life—and oh, by the way, I'm a witch, too.* Sarah was my best friend, but how could I expect her to understand? She was a rational person, just as I had been mere days ago.

"There's a lot going on at the moment," I said, then switched back to her problem. "Did Mark give you any reason for wanting to skip the wedding?"

She puffed out a breath. "There's an orthodontics convention in New Mexico that he suddenly swears he can't miss. He's leaving me in the lurch to spend a weekend learning about new techniques in palatal expansion."

"Maybe he really thinks it's important?"

She shook her head at my credulity. "He's *fleeing.* I tell you, he's been getting more and more nervous as this wedding approaches." Her neat fingernails beat a tattoo on the tabletop. "Like he suspects it's all a big trap and he'll wind up hog-tied and dragged off to the altar himself."

"Well, we'll have fun anyway. Martine'll be here." It was always a blast when our old roommate winged in from her exotic life into ours.

Sarah released a wistful sigh. "You know, when Martine first told me that she was going to be a flight attendant, I told her she was crazy and would be sick of traveling around after a year or two. Like those people who love ice cream until they get the job at the ice cream store."

"I don't think she ever will be tired of traveling."

"No." Sarah took a sip of her drink and frowned. "Come to think of it, I probably wouldn't get sick of ice cream, either."

I smiled.

"What?"

"I was thinking of a bet I made with Wes. He owes me a cone."

She glanced around as if she expected Wes to pop out of the woodwork. "I'm surprised you two aren't out tonight."

"I don't think he's that wild to see me more today." I outlined some of what had happened since I saw her yesterday afternoon, omitting any mention of witchcraft. When I got to the part about the Havermans' gift, she yipped in surprise.

"Say that again?" She gaped at me. "Wes's folks are giving you *a house*? And you didn't mention this to me?"

"I'm still having a hard time processing it. I suspect Joan only wanted to buy it because it once belonged to her high school nemesis. And the place is all gray stones and turrets, and a little dilapidated, to tell the truth. Like an old house where mod English people get possessed by demons in old Christopher Lee movies."

The amazement in her face intensified. "The Marshall house?"

"You know it?"

"It's a landmark, Bailey. It's been for sale for months. You're going to live *there?*"

Was I? It didn't seem real.

"I can't believe you didn't mention this to me first thing."

"I was worried about what was going on with you. Plus, I've had bigger things to deal with."

"Bigger than a really big house?"

I told her about Mom trying online dating, and Madeleine popping up everywhere, and then, weirdest of all, my birth mother showing up out of the blue.

"That's . . . a lot," she agreed. "Your birth mother! What's she like?"

"Not really someone I want to hang out with." *Totally crazy-sauce.*

"I used to fantasize that I was the love child of someone famous and they would come claim me," Sarah said wistfully.

"You're not adopted," I said.

"No, but I have the kind of family that makes a person dream of being adopted."

"Liar." She had two brothers and two sisters, and she was right in the middle in age. As far as I was concerned, she was resting right in the middle of a perfect family sandwich. "I've always envied you your siblings. More than dreaming of my birth parents, I used to think about having brothers and sisters."

"And I used to dream of having my parents' undivided attention."

I'd had that, all right. My dad had been a helicopter parent before helicopter parenting was a thing—telling me which activities I should be involved in, monitoring my progress, dictating where I should go to college and what I should study. I'd always wanted to pursue something musical, but he thought that was madness. A business degree, he'd insisted, would be more prudent. He did his best to take care of me by making sure I could always take care of myself. He'd worried that I wouldn't be able to support myself if something happened to him.

And then something had happened to him.

During college, I'd chafed at Dad's philosophy of incessant carefulness. I didn't love business classes, so I took as many fun electives as time would allow. I gave up studying piano but spent my free time attending college recitals and other performances. Then, during my senior year, Dad suffered his first heart attack and it felt as though our little family unit that I'd taken for granted for so long was under attack by a hostile force. Like Dad, I suddenly embraced caution. As soon as I finished college, I accepted an entry-level job in his insurance firm.

Mom, surprisingly, was the one who worried about my returning home. Over my dad's objections, she'd helped me find the duplex so I'd have some independence. Later, when I told her I missed music, she encouraged me to pick up a new instrument.

"I never seriously wanted any other parents," I said. "At the same time, I wonder if I didn't suspect that there was a war going on inside me all the time."

"A war?" Sarah's forehead wrinkled. "What are you talking about?"

Oops. I shrugged. "Oh, you know—between my practical side and my creative side."

"Are you sure you're okay, Bailey?"

"Of course," I said. "And I don't think you should worry about Mark. You might have lost your plus-one, but we'll have fun anyway. It'll give you a chance to kick up your heels. You'll have more time to hang out with Martine."

The prospect cheered her. "Have you heard from Martine?"

"Not recently."

"She texted me last night from Amsterdam—no cute innkeeper there, she said."

"It'll be so much fun to see her again. I envy you guys getting a few days to hang out together after the wedding."

Sarah tilted her head. "Yeah, but you'll be on your honeymoon. Has Wes told you where you're going?"

"Not yet."

"I bet it's something really exotic."

A few days ago I would have thought so, too. Now my definition of exotic had shifted somewhat. Bermuda—or New York, 1930? Paris, or prehistoric Earth?

Putting witchy things behind me was going to be easier said than done.

Chapter 17

"Visitors for you, Bailey."

I was planted in front of my work computer the next morning, preparing renewal documents for a client with a chain of shoe stores, when Janine, the receptionist, buzzed me.

My daily planner app didn't list any more appointments until the afternoon. But of course, Janine said these were visitors, not clients.

At my hesitation, Janine said, "You'll want to see these people. They've brought treats."

At the mention of treats, my stomach rumbled. It was almost lunchtime and I was ready to devour anything that came across the desk. I stood.

Moments later, Gwen came in dressed in jeans and a cotton sweater, much as she'd been when I'd first met her at Esme's house. A woman with her looked about five years older than me, and I liked her open, friendly expression at once. She clutched a white pastry box. Next to her was a slim, dark-haired, handsome

younger man wearing a dark suit with a pale coral shirt and pais-
ley tie.

Was this the cousin coven Gwen had spoken of? I stepped out
from behind the desk, veered around them, and shut my office
door. My coworkers didn't need to listen in on the conversation
between me and my witch family.

"This is Trudy," Gwen said, gesturing toward her cousin like a
game show hostess, "and that's Milo. Guys, this is Bailey."

I muttered a perfunctory "Pleased to meet you" at them on
my way back to my desk chair. Why were they here? My last
leave-taking from Gwen hadn't been particularly friendly. I
beckoned them to sit down in the visitor chairs.

"We brought a peace offering," Trudy said, pushing the box
across the desk. It bore a logo of an anthropomorphized cupcake
with one of those veiled cone hats that fairy-tale princesses wore
sticking out of its icing-topped head. *Enchanted Cupcakes* was
printed beneath it in fancy script. Unable to resist, I broke the
seal on the box and opened the lid, revealing a dozen cupcakes
nestled together. The aroma wafting toward me made my mouth
water.

"Today's specials," Trudy said. "Tender Loving Caramel and
Mellow Chocolate Mint."

It was hard to resist tearing right into the cupcakes, but that
would be rude to do without asking them to join me. I wasn't
sure I wanted these people in my office for that long. I'd made
my feelings clear to Gwen and Esme yesterday. Did they think a
few cupcakes would lure me over to the dark side?

"They smell wonderful," I said. "Thank you."

"You're welcome—and congratulations on your upcoming
marriage!" Trudy beamed. "We're having a big year for weddings."

I took in their smiling faces, feeling clueless. These people
were my family, and I knew next to nothing about them. "Is
someone else getting married?"

Milo flashed a gold band on his left hand. "My husband Brett and I tied the knot in February. Your usual cliché Valentine's wedding."

"There was nothing cliché about it," Trudy said. "It was a gorgeous ceremony."

"Brett's mayor of Zenobia," Gwen told me.

Milo was already scrolling through his phone. He scooted around to my side of the desk and swiped his way through dozens of pictures of the big day.

His husband was astonishingly good-looking. "Brett looks like a movie star," I said.

Milo sighed. "I know. *Barefoot in the Park*–era Redford, right? I'm still feeling a little swoony, to tell you the truth."

Gwen leaned forward. "The reason we're here, Bailey, is that I felt bad about how you left the house yesterday afternoon. That's why I called up Milo and Trudy. They suggested we come meet you."

"Why did *you* feel bad?" I was the one who'd announced that I didn't want to have anything to do with my witch family.

"I thought maybe you felt overwhelmed. Aunt Esme can be a little off-putting."

"She's better now than she used to be," Milo said.

"Oh, yes, she used to be awful." At the negative sound of her words, Trudy shook her head. "But of course, she was cursed. And until just recently none of us knew that she was carrying so much heartache over Odin"—my supposed father—"and you."

Milo cleared his throat. "Long story short, we wanted to meet you and answer any questions you might have, so you can make a more informed decision about whether you really want to turn your back on your powers."

I shifted in my chair. "It's very nice of you all to come this way, but I don't really have questions."

Three owl gazes blinked back at me incredulously.

"None?" Gwen asked.

"I'm not a witch," I said, shoving down in my consciousness—way down—my electric fingers and the Shakespeare-spouting parrot familiar waiting for me at home. "I've never had any witch tendencies, and I don't want to start now. I'm getting married in a few weeks, to a very nonwitch family. That's all I really have time to concentrate on at the moment."

"Girl, you turned a woman green," Milo reminded me.

Apparently, Gwen had told them everything she'd overheard between Esme and me. "*If* it really was me who turned her green," I said, "it was completely unconscious on my part. I've been under a lot of stress."

"See, Bailey, that's what got *me* into trouble." Trudy looked pained, as if she were trying to explain algebra to a toddler. "I started casting spells without even being aware I was doing it. I'm sure Gwen mentioned the trouble *that* caused."

The rabbit husband, I remembered. "I'll make sure to be careful," I said. "I've never had anything odd happen to me at all . . . until just recently. And honestly, I was happier before the weirdness began. I like being a normal, nonwitch person."

The air crackled with disbelief.

"Well." Trudy took a breath. "If that's how you feel—"

"Wait a second," Milo interrupted. "Don't forget Tannith. She's out there, and she's found you. Without flexing your powers, you'll be like a lamb tied to a stake as the wolf circles."

I lifted my hands. "I've got no bone to pick with Tannith. If she's as all-knowing as you say, she'll realize that—which she must have done, since she hasn't been successful in attacking me, despite being the hypervillainess witch you've warned me about."

"A witch has some resistance to being hexed—especially a witch with your blood."

Oh, brother. "Esme and Odin are a power witch couple, are they?"

"They could have been, if they hadn't been suppressed for so many years," Gwen said. "Even so, a single witch won't be able to hex another witch on her own very easily. It would take the tacit agreement of a community of witches to allow harm to come to one of their own."

"What about what you did to Tannith?" I asked.

She flushed. "That was terrible. My back was to the wall—and I honestly don't know exactly what I did. That's the problem."

I thought about it. "Okay, so what you're telling me is that I've got some kind of witch Teflon coating protecting me?"

"You have some immunity," Trudy said. "But the people around you don't."

I would take my chances. "I appreciate that you're trying to help, I really do. But I've come to the conclusion that the best way to stay out of trouble is to stay away from witches."

Though I couldn't show it, it hurt my heart to send people away who should have been my friends from childhood. Part of me wanted to ask if I could belong to their cupcake coven without being a witch. It wasn't witchiness I yearned for, it was belonging.

But of course, being a half witch wasn't an option. And from what I kept hearing about this Tannith person out in the ether, getting involved with this particular witch family came with significant drawbacks.

I stood.

"Thanks for the cupcakes." I herded them toward the door.

They left, although a few minutes later Milo was back. He riffled through cards in his wallet, picked one and then thought better of it, and pulled another out. "I'll give you my witch card. If you ever need a landscape designer, I give generous family discounts. Even to nonwitch family."

Landscape Magic by Milo, the card read.

"And if you're ever witch curious, my deets might be of interest, too."

Studying the card more closely, I saw it listed a Zenobia address, a phone number, and then:

Follow me on Cackle: @MiloMagic

Like my BrewTube channel: Milo'sMagicalLandscapeDesigns

"BrewTube?" I asked. "Seriously?"

"Sorry—forgot you're a total newbie." He snatched the card back, took a pen off my desk, and scrawled on the back. "I'll write down my personal Cackle handle for you, too. And this is the code to get on our social media . . . just in case you want to do some exploring. Be *very* careful not to give it out to anyone else, though." He handed the card back to me. "Doing so would have the Grand Council of Witches dropping us *both* in a cauldron of boiling oil."

"You're kidding, right?"

He laughed. "Of course!" His smile faded and he lowered his voice. "But seriously, keep that code to yourself."

I would probably stick it in a drawer and never look at it again, but I didn't want to tell him that. He was being nice, even after I had been not-so-nice.

"Thank you." I walked him out to reception, where Gwen and Trudy were waiting. We all said a second round of goodbyes.

After the glass doors shut behind them, Janine's gaze clocked Milo across the parking lot. "Nice."

"Married," I said, remembering those joyous photos he'd showed me.

"Isn't that always the way?" She sighed. "Oh well, at least he brought you cupcakes."

A whole box. Left to my own devices, I could probably devour them down to the last crumb. "I think I'll put them in the break room for everybody."

Her eyes lit up. "Really? Give me a heads-up so I'll have a fighting chance at one."

"Will do."

I returned to my office. Had I been wrong to send my cousins away? What if they were correct about the whole suppressed-powers thing? I didn't want to go around turning people into Technicolor specimens every time I got stressed out.

Work beckoned. I looked at the template I'd pulled up on my

computer, a form I'd completed a squillion times, and wished the blanks would fill themselves in. *If I were really a witch . . .*

I stared intently at the screen, willing the information to type itself. But the cursor sat stubbornly in its place, heedless of the strong vibes I was sending its way. Maybe my witch powers just weren't PC compatible.

My stomach rumbled. I peeked at the cupcake box on my desk. Unable to resist, I broke off a little piece of one and took a bite. The moment it touched my mouth, I realized this was the best cupcake I'd ever had. What did Trudy put in those things? The cake was fairy light, the flavor chocolatey-minty without being after-dinner-mint cloying. A feeling of well-being oozed through me, like the best sugar high ever.

My phone rang, and when I saw the caller I closed the cupcake box, leaned back in my chair, and did something unusual: I took Katrina's call.

"I'm texting you an address," she said in answer to my greeting. She was wound up about something. "I need you to get in your car and meet me there right away. It's an emergency."

I stretched, then crossed my legs at the ankles. "What's up?"

"A champagne flute disaster," Katrina said. "The caterer misunderestimated the number of champagne flutes in the pattern you picked out. You'll need to pick out a new pattern."

"Wow, you want me to drive across town for champagne flutes." I was more amazed than annoyed.

"Stemware is important."

"Couldn't we just mix in another pattern?"

A puff of irritation reached my ear. "Sure—or, hey, we could just put out Dixie cup dispensers and let the guests help themselves."

I laughed. "Mismatched crystal to Dixie cups seems like a big leap."

There was a pause. "Bailey, are you really committed to this wedding?"

"Well . . . yeah."

"Really?" Her agitation grew hotter. "Because I'm busting my hump like some wedding planner Oompa-Loompa, and you're doing *nothing*."

"That's not true."

"Oh, please—you can't even manage the simplest thing, like picking a dress."

"I have a dress."

"You told me that you would send me a picture of your dress as soon as you found it."

I smiled. For once, I had this. The dress was still in my car. "I'll do better than send a picture. I'll bring the dress when I come meet you and you can get a picture of it yourself."

"Really?"

"Sure, not a problem." I had an appointment early in the afternoon, but suddenly nothing seemed as rushed and urgent as before. "I'll mosey over there right now."

"Mosey quickly, I have a million things to do."

I ended the call, grabbed my purse, and headed for the door. Belatedly remembering the cupcakes, I doubled back to get the box and take it to the break room. Thinking of Janine, I wrapped one of the Mellow Chocolate Mint cupcakes in a paper towel and presented it to her on my way out.

Her eyes flashed with happiness. "Yum! Thank you. Where are you off to—must be somewhere fun, by the smile on your face."

I was smiling to run off to meet Katrina. Amazing.

I should have known right then that something was profoundly wrong.

An hour later, with the champagne flute crisis handled, the dress choice finally set in stone—how hard was that, really?—I strolled back through the doors to Genesee Insurance. Unexpected silence made me pause at reception. The place seemed deserted . . . until I detected a faint noise. A snore? I peeked over the top of the desk. Janine was there after all, her face planted on her mouse pad, mouth hanging open.

I glanced around. The client whose appointment I'd gotten back in time for was nowhere in sight.

Where was everybody?

"Uh, Janine?" When I reached over the desk, it was like giving a sleeping puppy a nudge. She was so relaxed, she was practically boneless.

I repeated her name, and she lifted her head with effort. Her mascara was streaked and her skin had creased on the side that was against the desk. She squinted at me. "Oh, hey," she said. "You're back."

I kept my voice low. I liked Janine and wouldn't want to see her get into trouble for sleeping on the job. "Where is everyone?" I asked. "I don't want Ron to see you zonked out."

She yawned and stretched her arms. "No worries. They're gone."

"Who?"

"Ron and Paige."

"You mean they went to lunch together?"

"Purportedly." One brow arched. "Although to be honest, I don't think food was foremost in their minds."

I did not want to think about that. "Any message from Dale Wagner of Wagner's Shoes?" I asked.

"He's here."

I scanned the empty seats in reception. "Where?"

"I'm . . . not sure. I set him up with some coffee and a cupcake. He seemed like a happy camper."

"Maybe he's in the washroom or something," I said. "I'll check around."

As I walked back, I flipped my phone open. I hadn't received any texts or voice messages from Wagner. I checked the break room and the hallways, but there was no sign of him. He'd probably had to leave.

I returned to my office, fighting the urge to put my head down on my desk like a kindergartner at nap time . . . or like Janine. My brain felt like a saturated sponge.

Someone tapped at my door. When I called out, "Come in," my coworker Tim reeled in and flopped into a chair.

"What's going on?" I asked.

"I'm not sure. One minute I was explaining travel insurance policies to some lady in Syracuse, and the next minute I was waking up on my office carpet."

"I'm not feeling too good myself," I said. "Do you think there's some problem with the ventilation?"

"It's those cupcakes. The one I ate hit me like a mint tranquilizer dart. Where did you buy them?"

"I didn't. Some friends brought them over."

"Are your friends potheads? I haven't felt anything like this since Spring Break 2002."

"I don't think they're potheads. They're just . . ."

My words died as a vision of that logo swam before my eyes. *Enchanted Cupcakes*. They'd mentioned Mellow Chocolate Mint . . . and Something Something Caramel.

Tender Loving Caramel.

A horrible suspicion crept into my brain.

"Were Ron and Paige eating cupcakes?" I asked.

Tim tipped his head back and squirted drops into his eyes. "We all had one."

My phone buzzed. "Hey, Bailey," Janine said. "More visitors for you."

"Is it Mr. Wagner?"

"Nope, it's another guy." She lowered her voice. "Another hottie."

"Really?"

"Before you get too excited, he's with your mother."

Seton and Mom. I smiled. "Thanks—send them back."

"Would you like me to bring you all some cupcakes?"

"No!" I wasn't sure whether mint-chocolate buttercream icing could be considered a Class A substance, but in this case it probably should be.

"I'll leave you to it," Tim said, heading for the door.

Mom breezed in first, followed by Seton. I was still trying to adjust to her hair, but today she was also wearing a dress I'd never seen—canary yellow with a cute pink-and-blue embroidered bolero jacket. She looked ten years younger.

But by far the biggest surprise was Seton. He was wearing a long-sleeved shirt, no tie, and a pair of jeans that actually fit him. *And how*, as he would have said. Mom had taken him to a barber, who'd managed to put a side part in his hair and cut it so that it was short, yet still a little floppy on top. I could see what Janine meant.

Seton shifted self-consciously. "Do I look odd to you?"

"The receptionist just told me you looked hot."

His face screwed up. "How can I be hot? I feel half dressed. The man at the store said I didn't even need an undershirt."

Mom sent me a look. "Isn't that a hoot? I haven't seen a man wear an undershirt since my father's day."

"It doesn't feel right." Seton squirmed as if he was about to jump out of his skin. "Is there a mirror here?"

I pointed him down the hall.

As soon as he was gone, Mom hurried toward me, propping her hip on the corner of my desk. "Seton is such a doll. Where did you find him?"

"He just sort of popped up."

"He's a fantastic dancer. You should see him Charleston!"

"You were dancing?"

"Well, I had to do something to cheer him up. He watched a documentary on the internet and got so depressed. Apparently, he'd never learned about World War Two." She lowered her voice. "And he says he has a college degree. I don't know what they're teaching in school these days."

"He might have skipped a few years," I said.

"I'm planning to give him some of your father's old Ken Burns documentaries to watch while I'm out tonight."

"Where are you going tonight?"

"I have a date."

The horror of this warred with the general well-being I'd felt for the past hour. "You said Ed's in jail."

She lifted her chin. "Just like you have a backup dress, I have a backup man. RC, aka Mr. NiceGuy."

"RC? You don't even know his name?"

"Maybe his name *is* RC, like the cola. Lots of men use initials."

I groaned.

"Don't look so horrified," she said. "I had Seton look at RC's profile, and he declared him very suitable. Goldenhearts calls us a five golden heart match, which was even higher than Ed's four hearts."

"So why were you wasting your time with Ed?"

"RC didn't include a picture, while Ed did. Ed's a hunk."

An incarcerated hunk. "So you have no idea what RC aka Mr. NiceGuy looks like?"

"No, but guess where he suggested we meet?"

I shook my head.

"McAllen's Steakhouse—your father's favorite restaurant. Now, doesn't that seem like a good omen?"

It seemed horrible to me, actually. Horrible and borderline sacrilegious. She'd be on a date with some strange man, possibly at the same table where my father had eaten his last porterhouse?

"Seton said he thinks the setup seems copacetic to him."

My voice looped up. "Seton didn't even know what online dating was until yesterday."

"That doesn't mean he can't tell a good egg from a bad one." Mom clucked at me. "Now, don't make a fuss. I only told you because I wanted to know if Seton could come over to your place tonight."

"Why?"

"RC might think it's odd that I've got a strange man living with me."

My blood temperature dropped thirty degrees. "Please tell me you're not planning on bringing RC back to your place. That would be a bad idea. Colossally bad. Anyway, Wes is taking me out to a nice dinner tonight. We've hardly had a real date in weeks, it feels like."

"Maybe because you keep running off to Zenobia." She sighed. "Seton said you'd gone back to see that woman."

"Just once." I wasn't going to let her change the subject. "You've got to promise me to not bring Mr. NiceGuy anywhere near your house. And don't go back to his place, either. We need to get his license plate, a picture, and do a criminal background check."

"Bailey, you're being paranoid."

"You can't be too paranoid."

Someone walked by my office and then doubled back. Ron ducked his head in, a big smile on his face. I tried to push aside the idea that the smile was somehow a product of his long lunch with Paige. Ron smiled all the time.

At the sight of Mom, though, his usual bonhomie faded. The change in her appearance obviously startled him, too. "What happened to you?"

"What do you mean?" Mom asked.

"Your hair! Have you decided to become a rock star?"

She laughed mirthlessly. "You're one to criticize anyone for acting young."

It never ceased to amaze me that the two most aggressively friendly people in my life couldn't stand each other. Ron resented the fact that she wouldn't sell him my dad's share in the business, and I supposed she'd never forgiven him for dumping his first wife, Kathy. "Mom just dropped by to say hello," I said.

Seton scooted by Ron. On his arm was Paige, of all people,

giving him the kind of heart eyes she usually reserved for flirting inappropriately with our boss.

Seton flushed crimson as he met my gaze. "Your coworker says I'm the cat's pajamas in my new rags."

Paige chuckled. "I *love* how you talk."

What had happened? I'd thought it would be safe sending Seton to the washroom on his own. But of course, the washrooms were next to the break room, and the break room . . .

Cupcakes. Tender Loving Caramel cupcakes.

Ron looked whiplashed by Paige's quick defection.

Mom, catching the vibe, plucked her purse off my desk and scooted over between Paige and Seton. "Seton and I are going ice-skating this afternoon," she announced.

"Since when do you ice-skate?" Ron asked, taking the words right out of my mouth.

"Since I was nine, Mr. Smarty Pants." She looped her arm through Seton's. "A little brisk activity will be just the thing to get Seton's mind off Hitler for a few hours."

They breezed out. Ron watched them from the doorway, looking a little forlorn, especially when Paige trailed after them to say goodbye to Seton.

He turned back to me with a bewildered frown. "Are that guy and your mother . . . ?"

"No."

"Because blue hair or no blue hair, she seems a little old for him."

And boss or no boss, I couldn't stop an eye roll. Age differences mattered to him now? "Seton's just here for the wedding."

The phone buzzed. It was Janine. "Hey, Bailey, we found your client. Mr. Wagner's asleep by the Xerox."

I sighed. Another cupcake casualty.

Ron and I headed for the copying room, where other employees had gathered. Mr. Wagner was in a heap on the floor, a buttercream-stained napkin held against his mouth like a baby's binky.

"Tim," Ron said, "help me carry him to my office. He can finish his nap on my couch."

"Are you sure?" Tim asked. "Maybe we should call someone from Wagner's Shoes to come get him."

Ron shook his head. "I don't want to embarrass him. He's carrying a lot of policies on those stores."

As they hauled my client away, Janine sidled up to me. "That guy with your mom sure was cute."

I hated to burst her bubble again, but it had to be done. "Married."

"Oh." She sighed. "When you find a good one, he's always out of reach."

I nodded.

So out of reach he isn't even from your century.

Chapter 18

The first thing I did once everyone left was dispose of those cupcakes. Then, remembering the card Milo had given me, I got online. Yes, I was doing family business on work time, but since my client was zonked on pastries, I cut myself some slack.

As Milo had predicted, logging on to Cackle was a no-go without the secret code he'd given me. As I entered the ten-character mix of letters and numbers—it looked like gobbledygook to me—I couldn't help sneaking guilty glances at the door, as if I were visiting some nefarious dark site of the internet. It did seem to be dark—literally. Cackle's home page was black, its logo a crow silhouette in gray and purple.

A quick search for the address Milo had given me brought up his business site. It was very professionally done, and not at all witchy—except for a reference to magical herb gardens. The personal account he'd handwritten—@WarlockHolmes—was livelier and more focused on witchy matters. Warlock Holmes, aka Milo, was currently involved in a long thread of witches arguing over the many inaccuracies of witch representation in television shows and movies. I scrolled for a few minutes, shaking my head. Strident opinions abounded, insults were volleyed back and forth, and no one ever seemed to budge an inch from their original opinions.

Same as regular social media, then.

The only difference was that these people were getting *very* riled up about witchcraft, which would have seemed ridiculous to me a few days ago. Now I'd witnessed the harm witchcraft could do. I didn't want to be puritanical, but there needed to be some restraints. Hexes, time traveling, enchanted food—all of these things could be harmful, especially to the unsuspecting.

I brought up the Cackle page for Enchanted Cupcakes, but when I tried to leave a comment, a prompt appeared, telling me I needed to sign up for an account to take part.

I blew out an exasperated breath. More accounts and more passwords. Still, I'd come this far.

I created an account for myself and was finally allowed to leave my comment. I didn't want to hurt Trudy's business, but witches needed to realize that their spells had real-world consequences.

I frowned.

I was on a secret witch website. Could I speak as a representative of the real world anymore?

I logged out and shut down the page. *I'm not really one of them.*

I moved on to the other mess on my horizon: Mom and her blind date. She had no idea what she was stepping into—and she'd be all alone.

An idea occurred to me. I called Wes and told him that I wanted to shake up our evening plans a little—omitting my ulterior motive.

He wasn't wild about the idea. "McAllen's Steakhouse? Isn't that kind of casual? Katrina's supposed to be joining us tonight, with that cameraman."

"During our dinner?"

"She said the wedding video lacks date footage."

Come to think of it, having a cameraman present might serve me well.

"It would mean a lot to me to go to McAllen's tonight, Wes."

"All right." He'd heard me mention that I used to go there with Dad. "I'll call Lord Essex and cancel."

Guilt pricked my conscience. He was being amenable because he assumed this was about my dad, and I was going along with it. "Thank you so much. I'll call McAllen's and make a reservation for us—and I'll let Katrina know about the change."

The employee on the phone at McAllen's seemed bemused by my request for two adjacent two-person tables, but she put us down for seven o'clock.

Next, I phoned Katrina, who was not at all enthused about downgrading Wes's dinner reservation selection. "Wow. Okay. Why not Red Lobster?"

"It's personal," I said. "It was my dad's favorite."

I waited for a lightning bolt to strike me. *Shamelessness, thy name is Bailey Tomlin.*

Shamelessness, though, was right up Katrina's alley. "Sentimentality—I like it! That'll be great for our wedding video."

"Can you give me Jerry's number? I'll let him know."

She was more than happy to offload that task on me.

"Oh, hey." Jerry seemed surprised to hear from me. And uncomfortable. "What's up?"

I told him about our change in plans. "Cool," he said. "I like that place. Good seafood bisque."

"Really?" During all my years going there with my dad, I'd always wondered who ordered the seafood bisque at a steakhouse. "The thing I'm calling about is this: there's someone I need you to photograph. My mom will be at the restaurant with someone. Do you have a camera with a good zoom lens?"

"Isn't there an easier way to get a photo of your mom?"

"It's not her I want the picture of. She'll be sitting at a separate table from us. With a man. I need you to take a clear picture of the man."

"Oh, um . . ."

"It's okay," I said. "Katrina won't mind."

"But I'm more of a what you might call an artist, not a private detective?"

"Fifty dollars extra. For one good picture."

Money was the magic word. "M'kay."

"I'll email you a picture of my mom. Her hair's blue now, though. With green streaks." I frowned. "Or green with blue streaks."

"Got it."

After my barrage of phone calls, I was ready to go home. But first I needed to make sure my client had recuperated from his cupcake.

I arrived home with just enough time to get myself freshened up to go out again. Django would not be happy with me. He was only going to have a half hour or so outside his cage before Wes arrived.

I let myself in, calling out my usual "I'm home" as I shut the door behind me.

"Hi!" Seton was standing in my living room with Django perched on his shoulder.

I sagged against the door I'd just shut, clutching my purse to my chest. "You scared me! What are you doing here?"

"Your mother dropped me off."

"I asked her not to do that."

He looked disappointed by my reaction. "I won't be any trouble. Deb gave me some of those little records to play on your motion picture box. They're all about history. It's pretty swell watching newsreels in your own home."

"You're welcome to stay, but I'll be gone most of the evening."

"That's all right. I'll have Django."

At his words, Django gave him a tender nip on the earlobe.

It was ridiculous, but the sight of them together made attraction shiver through me. Wes and Django didn't get along at all.

Not that the comparison meant anything.

I excused myself so I could take a shower and change into a dress. My favorite little black dress would be inconspicuous, I decided. I also pinned my hair back to make the red less flashy.

When I emerged from my room, Django gave an appreciative whistle.

"You're looking snappy," Seton agreed, staring in a way that made heat pool in the pit of my stomach.

"Thanks." I headed to the fridge and poured a glass of white wine. I offered him one, too, which he accepted.

He smiled as we clinked glasses. "Here's how."

My stomach felt fluttery. I put it down to nerves over this evening's plans.

"Esme's niece came to see me today," I told him. "She said Esme's working twenty-four-seven to find a way to get you back home."

"That's good, I suppose."

He supposed? "That's what you want, isn't it? I mean, if it can be done safely."

"Of course." His gaze sought mine. "Do you think I should go back?"

"It's your home." I thought about how attached I was to all the things I'd grown up with—my parents, my parents' house, this place. If I had been airlifted out of my life, I'd definitely want to go back.

"I'd like to go home, of course," he said, sounding less than certain. "There are people I miss. I didn't have much family to speak of, though, aside from Ruthie. I'm not sure there's much hope of patching things up with her."

For some reason, thinking about him trying to go back and repair his marriage with that woman—who actually might have been part of a plan to kill him, for all we knew—wrenched my heart. Seton deserved better.

Someone knocked. The appreciative smile on Wes's face when I opened the door seemed like a good omen for the evening. Then he looked over my shoulder and his smile faded.

"Seton's staying with Django this evening," I explained.

He wiped his feet and came inside. "I didn't know parrots needed babysitters."

"I haven't been spending as much time at home with my bird as I used to."

"I'll say," Django said through a squawk.

"Attention hog," I scolded him.

Wes glanced in confusion between me and the bird. "Were you talking to your bird?"

Heat crept into my cheeks. "Doesn't everybody?" Changing the subject quickly, I said, "I just need to show Seton how to operate the DVD player, and then we can go."

I demonstrated the DVD player and the television and had Seton try it a few times until he got the knack of it. Wes paced behind us, his impatience a palpable thing in the room.

When I finally had Seton set in front of his war documentary, I grabbed my purse.

On the way to the car, Wes was shaking his head. "Couldn't even figure out a DVD player," he said. "Why doesn't he just stream that show?"

"Mom had the DVDs, that's why."

It was another of those drives.

A few blocks of silence was all I could stand.

"What is it?" I asked him. "Something's obviously bothering you."

"You tell me," he said. "You've been acting so strangely. It's like I don't recognize you."

Damn it. I should have known that I couldn't be a member of a notoriously inept clan of witches and not have it show. I struggled to find some way to explain what I was going through without actually mentioning what I was going through.

Before I could speak, though, Wes started in. "The changing of the reservation didn't make sense to me at all, but I went along with it because, hey, why make waves over one dinner? You have to admit I'm fairly easygoing."

"Yes." Though not at the moment.

"But what really gets my goat is that Seton character hanging around at your house all the time. You said he's staying with your mother, but he always seems to be at your place."

"He *is* staying at my mom's. She just didn't want him there during her date."

"Your mother's dating someone?"

"Sort of." I explained about Goldenhearts.

"Is she stark raving mad?" Wes asked. "Doesn't she understand that people who call themselves 'nice' are probably the most likely to be Charles Manson types?"

For the first time since learning about Mom's Goldenhearts situation, I felt more understanding toward her. "She's hardly the only woman in the world to use a dating site. I think she feels lonely."

He took my hand. "No wonder you seem like such a basket case. I would be, too."

That might have been the perfect moment to admit the evening had been planned to spy on my mom's date, but I was too focused on my hand, which was as inert as a dead fish under his. The electricity thing seemed to come and go.

When Wes pulled into the restaurant parking lot, Katrina's car was already parked there, but not my mom's. Perfect.

McAllen's had stood in the same building for over fifty years. The very bricks gave off an odor of charred meat. Inside, the half-timbered interior was comfortably old-school, with red leatherette chairs and booths. Katrina and Jerry were already installed at one of the adjacent reserved banquette tables, and I arranged myself with my back against the wall, which gave me a great view of the restaurant's entrance. Jerry and his equipment sat next to me.

"You two just act normal," Katrina said to Wes and me. "We don't need a ton of footage from here. This is all going to be filler."

Jerry caught my eye, then nodded at the camera he'd brought, which was sitting on the table.

M'kay, I thought. All set.

It occurred to me that RC, aka Mr. NiceGuy, might be in the restaurant already. I peered around at all the other tables, but none of them were occupied by a single man. I finally spotted a booth several tables over that had a *Reserved* marker on it. Perfect.

"Where's the dude?" whispered Jerry.

Katrina overheard. "What dude?" she asked, full volume. "Who are you talking about?"

"Bailey's mom's date."

I groaned. I'd failed to ask him to keep this under his hat. Stupid.

"*Jerry* knows about your mom's date?" Wes looked puzzled, and hurt. "*I* just found out."

Luckily, the waitress came over to take orders. My eye was on the door, so I'd already lost track of what was happening around me when silence fell and Wes gave me a nudge.

I blurted out the first thing that came to mind. "Seafood bisque."

The woman frowned. "For an appetizer?"

I swallowed, realizing belatedly that she'd only intended to take our drink orders. "Sure. And a glass of whatever the house white wine is?"

After the waitress left, Katrina jumpstarted the conversation. "You wouldn't believe how fabulous the downstairs of your new house looked today when I popped by. And Joan had gardeners up in the trees stringing fairy lights outside. So pretty!"

While Wes told her how much the auction made each year, I

was distracted by movement at the restaurant's entrance. Mom walked in, her gaze darting about uneasily. I scooted down and ducked behind my menu, holding my breath as she scanned the tables. Mom knew Wes, so if she saw him, the jig would be up. Luckily, he was sitting facing me, with his back to her. And she was looking for a lone man.

The hostess escorted Mom to the reserved table. The diners between us hampered my view, and I found myself hiking up in my chair to try to see around Wes's left shoulder. As subtly as I could, I gave Jerry a pointed look and gestured my head toward Mom sitting at that table. She'd dressed well for the evening, I'd give her that. She had on a classic navy-blue dress with a portrait neckline and half sleeves. Around her neck was a hummingbird pendant Dad had given her for their thirtieth anniversary.

As I recognized it, it felt as if my heart were being strangled. She was wearing my dad's pendant to a date?

Then she pulled a book out of her purse. The little hardcover had a red rose sticking out of it for a bookmark. My breath caught.

"Bailey, what's wrong?"

"Nothing, I—" My hand, which was shaking, lost hold of the water glass. It slipped, sending a mini flood spilling across the table. Wes jumped back before it splashed him. He hopped up, the scraping of his chair loud against the wood floor. Everyone looked over—Mom included.

Her glance took in Wes, then me. At first, her eyes widened in disbelief, as though she felt she was staring at a mirage. But in the next moment she scooted out of her booth and marched over to us.

Wes, who with Katrina had been using his napkin to dam up the water spill, looked up in shock at her. "Mrs. Tomlin—what are you doing here?"

"That's the question I want to ask my daughter." Her arms were akimbo, in classic disapproving mom position. "Did you come here to spy on me?"

I so obviously had, I didn't deign to answer. Besides, I was still shaken by that book—and the rose.

"How dare you," I said.

Mom recoiled as if I'd slapped her. "What have *I* done?"

"You're using the old flower trick from *The Shop around the Corner*." The old Jimmy Stewart movie had been my dad's very favorite film. We'd watched it every Christmas. In it, Jimmy Stewart and Margaret Sullavan's characters had met on a blind date using a flower to identify themselves. Margaret Sullavan had even carried a book with her. "Dad's favorite movie. Who else would think of that?"

"If you must know, RC suggested it."

"Oh, sure, this guy you don't know *just happened* to suggest Dad's favorite restaurant *and* a plot point from Dad's favorite movie?"

"Who's RC?" Wes asked, baffled.

"Mr. NiceGuy," I explained.

Mom flashed a disappointed look at me. "No matter what manner RC and I choose to communicate in, you have no right to judge us, much less spy on us."

"What else could I have done? You were doing all this Goldenhearts stuff on the sly."

"I was not," she said. "I told you about it."

"Only once it became clear you couldn't hide it anymore, just before one of your anonymous paramours got hauled away to the hoosegow."

Wes choked. "You never said anything to me about prison."

"It's a low-security facility." Mom's face flushed crimson again as she glared at me. "You're a fine one to talk about keeping secrets. You certainly weren't going to tell me you'd been to see Esme Zimmer again. I had to learn that from Seton."

"Who's Esme Zimmer?" Wes asked.

Mom's eyes widened. "You mean she hasn't told you about finding her birth mother?"

"She didn't tell *me*, either," Katrina interjected. "And that would have been fabulous for our video! A real Oprah moment."

Wes was speechless.

It was then that I noticed that Jerry had lifted his video camera and was picking up everything, including the curious stares of onlookers who'd abandoned their sirloins and baked potatoes to watch the floor show we were providing.

Our waitress, balancing a loaded tray, stopped at our table. "Are we all doing okay over here?"

I almost laughed.

She forced a smile. "Okay, well, I'm going to put your drinks and your bisque here, and I'll run and get a mop for the spill, and some more napkins for you."

All of us muttered a tense "Thank you" at her as she scurried away.

Mom turned to Wes. "Your fiancée has been sneaking off to Zenobia every day to meet with this other family of hers."

I reddened. *Your fiancée?* She couldn't even bring herself to say my name now?

"You never told me about your birth family." Wes's disappointed gaze bored into me. "Who are these people?"

I wasn't going to explain about my witch origins now in the middle of a steakhouse. Instead, I tried to wrestle the conversation back to the important matter at hand. "I was worried about you, Mom. I probably shouldn't have come here tonight, but I know how dodgy online dating can be. I don't want to see you get hurt."

Katrina let out a soft "Aw," but Mom remained unmoved. "I'm sixty-six, not sixteen."

Someone interrupted us. I assumed it was going to be the restaurant's manager asking us to either sit down or leave, but this voice was very familiar, and out of place. An office voice.

Ron stood in a blue suit, a bemused expression on his face.

"Announcing your age to the whole restaurant, Deb?" he joked, clearly not reading the room. "Expecting a senior discount?"

Mom looked horrified to see him here. At first I guessed it was because she didn't want her late husband's best friend there as a witness to her first date since she'd become a widow.

Then I saw the red rose in Ron's buttonhole, and it dawned on me.

Ron was RC, aka Mr. NiceGuy. This *was* her date.

They gaped at each other, each growing redder by the second.

"You sneak!" Mom finally said.

He drew back. "*I'm* a sneak? You put a fake picture up to lure men in."

She glared at him. "That photo was a professional glamour shot. I assure you it was very real."

"Really air-brushed, you mean. And now you've got blue hair—you never mentioned *that*."

I was incensed on Mom's behalf. "Her hair is gorgeous."

Jerry, who still had his camera rolling, shifted to get a better angle of us all. Ron pointed at him.

"What is this? *Candid Camera*? Why's this guy filming us? Stop that."

"Keep going, Jerry," Katrina said from behind him, eyes gleaming.

Mom marched up to Ron and poked him in the chest with her index finger. "You're a fine one to insult my hair when you didn't even bother putting up a picture. And then you have the crust to call yourself Mr. NiceGuy. Mr. Big Cheater, is more like it."

His head moved slowly from side to side. "Oh, come on, Deb. After all these years? You're still jealous because I dumped you for Kathy?"

I froze. What was he talking about? Kathy was Ron's ex-wife. "What?"

Ron smiled at me. "Your mom never told you? She and I were a couple till I met Kathy. Deb married Lloyd on the rebound."

I turned back to my mother. "Dad was your rebound from *Ron*?"

Tears in her eyes, she picked up the seafood bisque from my table and tossed the contents of the bowl straight at Ron's face.

Out of the corner of my eye, I saw the restaurant manager making his way over to break up what was turning into a brawl. A bowl of bisque in someone's face wasn't going to help matters.

Reaching out my hand, I stopped the bowl—but not by touching it. A wave of energy shot from my fingertips, and the bisque stayed in the bowl. The bowl stuck to Mom's hand.

Mom stared in confusion at the bowl and the congealed liquid it contained.

Her mouth opened and closed like a goldfish. "What just . . ."

She wasn't alone in her surprise. Wes was staring at me. I'd been so caught up in what had been going on, I'd almost forgotten he was there. Eyes wide with shock, he looked from my face to my hands.

Before he could say anything—and before the manager could boot us all out—I lifted those hands and tried to think of something to explain away what had just happened.

In the next moment, the lights went out.

Chapter 19

If I were going to write down the story of Wes's and my courtship for our children and grandchildren to read, I decided I would title it Uncomfortable Moments in the Escalade. The drive back to my place was just as silent as the drive to the steakhouse had been, but now there was an extra frisson of tension in the air.

I was so discombobulated that I was almost beyond caring what Wes thought. Mom and Ron had been a longtime item, and she'd never mentioned this to me? All my life, I'd thought my parents were the perfect couple—a love so deep that the only thing that had been lacking between them had been me, until they'd miraculously found me. Now I knew that the source of that miracle had been both supernatural and suspect, and that their marriage had only been a desperation measure to begin with.

Well, maybe that wasn't the whole story. They really had loved each other. I was sure of that. Or I knew that Dad had been devoted to Mom. She, on the other hand, had simply been dumped and sought out the nearest port in a storm: her boyfriend's best friend.

Over halfway home, I said, "That did *not* go as I intended."

Wes flicked a glance my way. His jaw was clenched tight.

Just as we'd never discussed possibly going somewhere else for dinner to make up for the aborted steakhouse meal, the subject of us going to his place as we usually would have after a date never came up. It was just assumed he'd drop me off at mine. Drop me off like a package containing plastic explosives, to judge by the wary glances he kept flicking my way.

"I haven't seen any power outages anywhere else in the city," he observed.

I sank down in the leather seat. "No. It must have just been in that one spot—maybe a wiring problem in the restaurant or something?"

I was such a liar. I didn't know how to explain that I'd hexed a restaurant's electricity . . . and hadn't been able to fix it. Turns out, hexing was apparently much easier than unhexing.

"You should have told me that you were going to ambush your mother on her first date with Ron."

"Apparently, that *wasn't* her first date with Ron," I grumbled. "All my life I heard how Ron cheated on his poor wife. Now I find out that he and his ex-wife probably cheated on my mom when she and Ron were dating."

"Whatever happened between Ron and your mom happened a long time ago. I'm more worried about . . ."

Half a block went by before I realized he wasn't going to finish his sentence.

"Worried about what?" I asked.

His jaw, already tight, worked from side to side. "Never mind. I was probably imagining it."

No, you weren't.

We turned onto my street. A light shone from the inside of the duplex. Poor Seton. I'd told Mom that he could stay the night with me. She hadn't looked in the mood to have a stranger in the house.

I was sure Wes had overheard that conversation, but he hadn't said a word. He didn't say anything now, either, even though he probably noted the television lights flickering behind my window shades.

He pulled up to the curb without turning the engine off. Panic surged through me. Was this the end? I twisted the engagement ring on my hand. One disastrous attempt at a dinner out couldn't sink an entire engagement, could it?

Maybe that would be for the best. I wouldn't have to worry about the wedding, and I wouldn't have to explain about my newfound other family.

"About tomorrow," Wes said.

I closed my eyes. Suddenly, it felt like I was on one of those rides where you spin around in a drum while the floor drops out from under you.

I swallowed, unable to believe the thoughts that had been flitting through my mind. Wes was my rock. The man who'd stood by me during the worst moments of my life. What would I do without him?

For a fleeting moment, a vision of Seton came to me as he'd been this morning, freshly showered, smiling at me. Where had that come from? Seton was nothing to me—he meant no more to me than a strange puppy would have. He was only in my life by accident, and he wouldn't be there for long.

"We should arrive early," Wes continued. "I know Mother's hostessing the auction, but it's our house."

Our house. He wasn't ending it.

Relief filled me, followed by a chaser of puzzlement. I didn't want to call off the wedding. That would be horrible. But what were all these doubts popping up? Was it just the confusion of finding out I wasn't who I thought I was—that I had an entire witch family a half hour away? A family who'd somehow brought a strange man into my life, too.

Still, I felt like a convict who's just been granted a reprieve. He wasn't dumping me, whatever he suspected about what happened tonight with the lights and the *bisque*. "What time, then?"

"The reception begins at five, the auction starts at six."

"I'll email your mom and ask when she wants us there," I said with a new determination to make this all work. "I can help set up, bartend, anything she needs."

His mouth screwed up at the corners. "There will be caterers and workmen there to do stuff like that, Bailey."

"Oh, right." Silly me. Havermans didn't *set up*. They hired that done.

He smiled tightly. "I'll see you tomorrow then."

"Right." I had my hand on the door handle, but I still hesitated.

He leaned over and kissed me on the lips. When we pulled away, I looked into his eyes, which were gazing to the side, as if he were in a hurry to get going. I had a feeling he was still thinking about that bowl of unspillable seafood bisque.

In the duplex, Seton was sitting in front of a television while Tom Hanks's voice narrated over vintage photographs. Before I could speak, he lifted his hands to his lips. "Django's asleep."

That was surprising. I glanced back at the partially covered cage. "He usually likes to hang out on the back of the couch while I watch television."

"He said he'd already seen this movie before."

That was the thing about adopting adult pets. You never really knew about their histories.

Seton paused the television. He was a quick study with the remote. "You're back sooner than I expected."

"Dinner didn't really go well." As I went to the kitchen for a glass of wine, I gave him an abbreviated version of the steakhouse disaster, ending with the fact that Mom wouldn't be picking him up.

"You don't mind sleeping on the couch again, do you?" I asked as I rejoined him in the living room.

"Not a bit. I'm relieved, actually. Your mother's swell, but it's a little hard staying with her and having to hide who I really am."

I sank down on the couch next to him. "I know exactly what you mean."

"Do you?" He frowned. "I guess I should be happy that someone shares the feeling with me, but I'm not. You seem so troubled."

At his expression of sympathy, a tear rolled down my cheek. It was ridiculous, but the evening had been so tense, and most of what went wrong had all been my own doing.

"In the past three days, all the underpinnings of my life have come apart," I confessed. "An alternate family has come out of the woodwork, suddenly I've got supernatural powers I don't even want, and tonight I discovered that assumptions I'd made about the family I did know—my mom and dad—weren't right, either. I thought my parents were the perfect couple, but it turns out that it was really a rebound marriage."

"A what?"

"She married him because her heart was broken by his best friend."

"That doesn't mean that they might not really have loved each other, though. They stayed together, right?"

I thought about it, then sighed. "I always thought they were devoted to each other. And he obviously was to her."

"Maybe her devotion just started a little later than you thought."

I remembered my mom's grief when Dad died so suddenly. Seton was right. At some point, she must have fallen in love with my dad. And now I was acting like a judgmental fool because she hadn't traveled the path to get there that I assumed she had.

Another person to make amends to.

Suddenly, I felt foolish for going on about my problems. Seton had been wrenched away from his world in ways I couldn't imagine. "I'm sorry. My problems seem miniscule next to yours."

He shrugged. "Well, I don't have to worry about being a witch, but I can sympathize with having all the assumptions of your life suddenly called into question. I'm not even sure I exist."

"Of course you exist. You're here."

"But what if I go back? Will I have ever existed here?" He looked at me. "Would you remember me?"

"Of course I would," I answered without hesitation. And the selfish part of me wanted to say, *Don't go back.* Because I enjoyed having him here.

As a friend.

He looked back at the television. The brand logo was ponging around on the screensaver background. "So much happened back in that time—my time—that I didn't get to live yet. Did you know the economic depression continued on for a whole decade?"

"It's called the Great Depression. We study it in school."

He blew out a breath. "Greatly depressed is how I feel thinking about what happened to my money once Burt took over my life." He sighed. "You're lucky that all you have to do is decide what you want. Everything is within your reach. You have so much to hold on to here, and you don't have to depend on witches to get you where you want to go."

I just had to worry about witches undoing all my plans. . . .

We sat watching the screensaver a moment longer, probably both of us superimposing our own desired scenario across it. *Everything is still within reach.*

He was right. Things were a little topsy-turvy at the moment, but nothing had fundamentally changed. Mom was still my goofy mom. Wes and I were still engaged. Yes, a little witchcraft had been injected into my life—I hadn't expected that—but so far this evil, unseen witch they'd warned me about was nothing I couldn't handle.

"Thank you." Impulsively, I leaned over and kissed him.

Drawing close, I got a whiff of soap, and when I pressed a hand against his chest I realized how solid he was. Solid and strong. When my lips touched his stubbly cheek, the contact sent sparks through me.

We both hopped apart.

"Sorry!" I said. Also, lip shock. Ouch.

He rubbed his cheek. "Why does that keep happening?"

"I'm not sure. Maybe it's just as well, though, since I—"

I gulped back the idiotic thing I was about to say. Thank God.

His eyes, so brilliant and blue, registered every bit of awkwardness in my statement. He knew that for an instant, I'd really wanted to kiss him. Of course he knew. A few kind words from him, a simple touch, and I'd been ready to throw myself at him and blow up every plan I'd made for my life. As if things weren't chaotic enough already.

What was the matter with me? Kissing him—really kissing him—would have been a terrible thing to do on so many levels. I'd be betraying Wes and jeopardizing our future life together, to say nothing of our wedding. It wouldn't be fair to Seton, either, who had enough past problems to sort out without being dragged into my present-day ones.

And wasn't that the heart of the matter? We were two people whose lives had just been stirred up by witchcraft. It was natural that we would be confused, and turn to each other. But nothing had changed since this morning: I was still engaged, and he was married . . . or something. Maybe his wife was unfaithful and possibly homicidal, but that was something he needed to work through. Having a fling with someone from the twenty-first century would just muddle everything more for him.

Because that's all it could be, right? We'd only known each other a few days. He was attractive and I'd rescued him, and now we were drawn together. But that wasn't the basis for anything lasting. We didn't even know if Seton would be here tomorrow, or be zapped back to the past.

The thought sobered me. And saddened me.

I rose to my feet. "I should go to sleep. I put your bed linens in the storage cupboard in the hallway, next to the laundry."

He looked away. Was he as relieved that the awkward moment I'd introduced with that cheek kiss was over?

"Thanks," he said. "I'll tend to everything myself. Would you mind if I watched a little more of this before bed?"

He nodded at the DVD sleeve.

Maybe he hadn't wanted to kiss me at all; he'd just wanted to watch television.

"Not at all." I forced a smile. "Welcome to the twenty-first century's favorite pastime—binge-watching."

I hurried to my room, got ready for bed, and climbed under the covers, shaky with relief to have finished the day without having completely, irrevocably screwed up everything. I felt like a tightrope walker who managed to make it slipping and wobbling to the end of the act. But would I be any less shaky the next time I was tested?

Chapter 20

I woke up full of resolve to shake off the confusion of the past few weeks and get my head on straight again. Today would be a better day. I drew up a to-do list while I sipped coffee and shared a bit of toast with Django. He clicked over to inspect what I'd written.

I put my pen down. This was nonsense. "You can't read."

"Not your hen scratch, I can't." For a bird, Django had a pretty snobby attitude toward poultry. "What are you planning?"

"There are some people I need to make amends to." Starting with McAllen's Steakhouse. I didn't have a lot of money saved up, but I was going to drop off an anonymous donation to make up for shutting off their electricity the night before.

"Good morning." Looking uncharacteristically rumpled, Seton stumbled into the kitchen. He headed to the coffeepot, poured himself a cup, and then sat down opposite me. My insides did a somersault. Hunger, I told myself. Nothing to do with how his heavy-lidded eyes were looking at me, or the way that light stubble on his jaw made me long to reach out and touch it.

"I'm sorry if I woke you," I said.

"I couldn't sleep," he said. "After watching that movie about the war, I was up half the night, wondering what became of everybody I know." He took a sip of coffee. "*Knew*, rather. I suppose everyone's gone now."

Maybe Mom shouldn't have given him those documentaries. They seemed to have brought out a maudlin streak in him.

He sank down in his chair. "It would be nice to know, at least, that Burt got his comeuppance. Preferably in the electric chair at Sing Sing."

An idea occurred to me. "Sarah can probably help you find out some things."

She volunteered on weekends with the local genealogical society. When I got hold of her on the phone, she was already at their research library.

"My cousin Seton is in town and wants to do some research on family and old family friends," I told her.

"I didn't know you had a cousin!"

"Very distant."

Her voice was bright. "Bring him over today. We'll set him up on a terminal."

"He's not what I would call tech-savvy."

She laughed. "I can't wait to meet him."

The excitement in her voice rattled me. I was becoming too adept at lying to people I loved.

"Joan's charity auction is tonight, don't forget. It's at the Marshall house."

"You mean *your* house," she corrected me. "Fun! Dave and I will swing by."

When I hung up, I remembered that I hadn't acquainted her with the events of last night. A week ago, I would have been on the horn first thing to tell her all about the ill-fated steakhouse episode. Now it felt as if there were so many things I couldn't share with my best friend.

* * *

When I arrived at the Marshall house that evening, it looked a hundred times better than it had the last time I'd been there. A decorator had come through and festooned the yard with pots of annuals and urns with flowering shrubs. Azaleas lined the now-lighted pathway to the front door, which had been repainted red. The interior of the house had received paint and touch-ups, too. Every piece of crystal on the chandelier had been cleaned, and now the magnificent fixture was radiating light like the space-ship in *Close Encounters of the Third Kind*.

Madeleine and Olivia were manning a table in the front hall where visitors could sign in, pick up bidding slips, or make a donation to the Garden Club, which raised money to beautify Rochester's parks and other public spaces. They were both staring down at their phones, but the second I walked up, Madeleine slapped hers closed and sent a thousand-watt smile my way.

"Hey, Bailey, you're looking nice tonight! I almost didn't recognize you."

I pretended that was a compliment. I was wearing a fitted dark-green dress with long ruched sleeves. I'd intended to put on something flowery and springy, but Django had insisted that I needed to look striking.

I couldn't really see what Madeleine was wearing, although her orthopedic boot was sticking out prominently. Now that I knew her injury had been caused by something Esme had done on purpose, I felt indirectly responsible. She seemed to be a witchcraft magnet. In fact, I was a little surprised to see her there. The last time she'd been at the house, a ceiling had fallen on us. *Tannith*, Esme and Gwen had called the evil witch who was supposedly out to get me. Nothing had happened since then, though, so I assumed we were all safe.

"I was hoping you'd bring that weird but also weirdly yummy cousin of yours," Olivia said.

"I left him with Sarah, doing some genealogy research."

"Saturday at the genealogical library," Olivia deadpanned. "Fun."

Wes appeared, lugging a red duffel with a white cross on it. He dropped it when he saw me. "You look nice." His smile was bright, but I sensed a wariness in it, too. It reminded me of his expression in the car last night.

My gaze was focused on the duffel. "What's that for?"

"It's a first aid kit. I thought we should keep it up front here." He scratched his jaw. "After what's been happening around us lately . . ."

Around *me*, he meant. Guests started to swarm in behind us. A member of the Rochester city council pulled Wes aside to confer with him about a city zoning question concerning one of the Haverman stores. I ducked outside to make sure there weren't any witch-possessed squirrels lurking around.

I didn't find any supernatural rodents in the backyard—just guests in semiformal attire drinking wine and circulating among the lawn statuary and other garden items that were on display as part of the auction. It was a gorgeous late afternoon, with perfect seventy-five-degree weather. The only thing marring the day was intermittent chain-sawing going on next door.

Joan was standing near that eagle birdbath she coveted, with her hands on her hips, staring up at the workmen visible in a tree next door. "I asked them to stop," she said, "but they said they're on a schedule and can't stop for a party—even if it's a Saturday."

"Well, dead trees can be dangerous," I said.

Wes came over, practically at a gallop. "Here you are, Bailey. Is everything okay?"

I tilted a glance at his worried face. "Why wouldn't it be?"

"I lost you. I was concerned."

"I'll leave you two alone," Joan said. "I think there's a reporter here who wants to talk to me about the Garden Club fund."

"Is everything okay?" I asked Wes when she was out of earshot. "You look a little frantic."

He swallowed, and lowered his voice so that the guests circulating nearby couldn't hear. "To be honest, last night freaked me out a little."

No wonder. "I know. That scene with Mom and Ron was totally bonkers."

He stared at me, and I sensed he felt that I'd missed something in what he'd said. "I just want things to go smoothly today with no . . . mishaps. Do you know what I mean?"

"You want things to go smoothly," I repeated. Did he think I didn't?

"Last time you were here, Mad was almost hurt."

"So was I."

"She already can't walk very well, Bailey."

"That wasn't my fault," I said.

"For Mother's sake, I want this evening to be a success," he continued. "She's worked so hard. I don't want any, you know, disturbing occurrences."

"I want this to be a good event for your mom, too." I had an idea then. "You know what? She pointed out a piece in the auction that she likes. It might make a nice thank-you gift for all the effort she's putting into the house and the wedding."

He seemed heartened by the idea. "That would be so nice. It would mean a lot to her."

Before I could show him the eagle birdbath, a couple who worked with Haverman's Foods came up to talk to Wes. Wes was a veteran schmoozer, and with this crowd of his mother's invitees and local bigwigs, he was going to have a busy evening.

Out of the corner of my eye I spotted Sarah with Seton over by a catering table. What was *he* doing here? And where was Dave?

"Dave couldn't make it," Sarah explained when I scooted over to greet them. "Oral emergency, he said, but I think anything involving you and Wes just gives him wedding nerves."

"But it's not his wedding," I said. "And he's not even coming."

"I know. It's something he just needs to work through."

"Meanwhile, Sarah's stuck with me as a sidecar today," Seton said.

Sarah seemed eager to change the subject. "This is such a great place!" she exclaimed, then frowned as the sawing started up next door. "But that's awful."

"The noise isn't so bad inside," I said. "I'll give you a tour of the house—right after I put in a bid for the world's ugliest birdbath." I took her over and started filling out a bid sheet. I didn't have to worry about bidding too much—the jar next to it was conspicuously empty.

Sarah was disturbed by my choice. "Why?" she asked as she frowned at the eagle.

"It's a gift for Joan."

She nearly choked on a tiny profiterole. "Aren't you supposed to make your in-laws like you?"

I folded my bid and put it in the bid jar on the birdbath's bowl. "I told Joan that birds might not feel comfortable letting their hair down next to their most dangerous apex predator, but she loves it anyway."

Sarah looked around. "Speaking of apex predators, here comes Olivia."

She was slinking across the yard, making a beeline for us. In her black jacket, black silk capris, and black heels, she resembled an exclamation point in motion.

"Hey, Sarah!" Her voice rose in an enthusiasm never before heard from Olivia. Then her eyes locked on Seton with transparently fake surprise. "Oh! Seton—great to see you again."

He glanced at her warily. "Hello."

"Where's Madeleine?" I asked.

Olivia shrugged. "I left her in the front hall. She's fine—it's good practice for her to be on guest book at your wedding."

An uneasy feeling snaked through me.

Madeleine, alone.

She's a witchcraft magnet.

"Excuse me, I need to check on something." I hurried inside, gripped by a premonition of doom.

I took a shortcut through the kitchen, which was packed with caterer boxes and cartons of wine, then passed through the newly painted ballroom, around which folding tables had been set up and laden with all sorts of items and gift baskets that had been donated. In one corner, Wes and Joan were speaking to a woman I recognized from the local news. A cameraman stood nearby. A news station would have to be desperate for content for a Garden Club auction to rate a mention. On the other hand, this was Rochester, so slow news days were never out of the realm of possibility.

I sent Wes a furtive wave and hurried on. Just as the double doorway between the ballroom and the foyer came into view, I saw Madeleine standing near it, craning to see the reporter interviewing Wes. She was standing directly under the foyer chandelier.

And that's when it happened. The earth shook, and the chandelier above Madeleine trembled. Madeleine's face bloomed in surprise at the jolt.

My heart jumped into my throat. The evil witch, Tannith, wasn't going to be satisfied having a little chunk of ceiling drop. This time she was going to bring down an entire chandelier.

Madeleine was a sitting duck.

"Watch out!" I cried.

I tackled her, wrenching her out of the way of danger. She let out a shout of surprise, as did a caterer standing nearby, who managed to bolt out of the way, though not without sending a tray of tiny quiches spilling to the floor. Madeleine wheeled her arms and then lost balance. We went down together, sliding on the newly polished floors toward the staircase.

When we stopped, I clutched my hands over my head, waiting for the crash of the chandelier hitting the floor nearby. Instead, when I peeked an eye open and looked up, the fixture was still hanging from the ceiling, its luminous teardrops winking down at me. Also looking down at me were dozens of pairs of eyes, and the lens of the Eyewitness News cameraman.

"You lunatic!" Madeleine said, glaring at me. "I can't move my arm."

I took in the strange angle of her arm in her shoulder.

That did not look good.

This time, Madeleine waited at the ER until a doctor was able to see her.

"What the hell, Bailey?" Wes said to me. We were standing in a hallway outside the treatment room where a doctor was sedating Madeleine to put her dislocated arm back in its socket. "You *tackled* Madeleine at an important social function. Do you realize the mayor was there?"

I blew out a long breath, trying to stay calm. Wes was angry, but I could see his side. We were both under stress from the upcoming wedding, but he didn't know that there were malign forces at work. The whole situation had to seem bewildering to him.

"I thought we were having an earthquake and that the chandelier was going to fall on Madeleine's head."

"It was a tree."

"Sure, I know that *now*."

The workmen next door had dropped an entire center section of a tree trunk, causing me to believe a witch earthquake was bringing down the house.

He blew out a long breath. "Strange things keep happening to poor Mad. I can't tell you the crazy suspicions I was starting to have. I even wondered if you weren't engaging in some, I don't know, hocus-pocus. But this, today, was just a farce."

"I thought she was in danger," I said. "I was trying to help."

"Help!" He shook his head. "You've been so erratic lately. In fact, you've been acting oddly ever since that guy showed up."

Seton, he meant.

Wes's first marriage had been a classic movie-of-the-week drama, so I understood where his suspicions were coming from. And I wasn't being honest with him. I wanted to tell him that there was no affair, just a witch. But if I said the *W* word now, everything would probably be over. Witchcraft was a concept a person needed to be eased into accepting.

"There won't be drama from now on," I promised. And, since the house rattle had been caused by a tree, not Tannith, I felt confident that it would be smoother sailing from now to the wedding. My witch paranoia was causing more harm that the wicked witch herself.

Wes stayed at the hospital to drive Madeleine home, so I Ubered back to the house to pick up my car and Seton. The auction had ended and the place was emptying out.

Sarah, who'd bid on and won a wine-and-cheese gift basket, was loading it into her car when I drove up. "Where's Wes?" she asked.

"Taking Madeleine home." I sighed. "She can't drive."

I'd been texting Sarah from the hospital, so she knew the whole story. She had been doing her best to soothe Joan for me by taking over Madeleine's place at the front table.

"Good news," she said. "You won the eagle birdbath."

That actually was good news. Now more than ever, I needed a peace offering for my future mother-in-law. "Is Mrs. Haverman here? I'd like to get it into the car without her seeing." I wanted to wait till things had cooled off a little to present it to her.

Sarah and I walked around the side gate to the backyard. We found Seton in the stone pool house building.

"What are you doing out here by yourself?" I asked.

"Hiding from Olivia."

It was a good choice of hiding place. From the outside, the pool house was off-putting. Inside, though, there was a small, empty swimming pool in spectacular blue painted tiles, like an oversized delft pottery bowl.

"This is incredible," Sarah said.

I agreed. Around the empty pool the architect had constructed a little cathedral to natation—stone walls featuring high leaded glass windows and whimsical carvings of fish and mermaids. A Gothic-style ceiling arched over the pool. Ancient, rusty furniture lay around the deck of the pool, along with a few piles of leaves that had blown in over the years somehow. It must have been a spectacular pool in its day, but for the past twenty or thirty years probably only a few mouse families had enjoyed it.

"We need to pick up the birdbath and go," I told Seton.

The eagle birdbath was the only auction piece left in the backyard.

Now I had to figure out what to do with it. Would the thing even fit in my LEAF? "It looks heavy."

Sarah inspected it more closely. "The bowl comes off."

Sarah and I removed the cement bath bowl and carried it across the grass toward the back gate. Seton followed with the base. We stuffed the bowl into my little hatchback's trunk, which left the back seat as the best place for the eagle statue base. We tilted it almost upright and secured it with the shoulder belts.

Finally done, I hugged Sarah and thanked her for everything, and Seton and I got into the front seat of the LEAF.

"Well," I said, not without sarcasm, "that all came off pretty well."

"At least there was no wicked witch attack," he said.

"No—just me attacking Madeleine. Very old school."

Maybe my relatives in Zenobia were worrying about nothing. Could it be possible that they were mistaken about Gwen having made Tannith disappear? Perhaps Tannith was just in Hawaii or something. And now anytime something bad happened, they blamed their misfortune on the malevolent Tannith. Unseen foes made great scapegoats.

I had just turned onto a wide city road when I felt something strange in the air. I shot a glance at Seton. He was tapping out the rhythm of "Happy Feet," the song playing on my streaming jazz channel, totally absorbed in the music.

I drove on, but a few moments later I caught a movement in my rearview. My heart skipped a beat.

You're imagining it. Ever since that night when I'd seen Seton in the rearview mirror, I'd been jumpy in the car. But Seton was right next to me blissing out on old trad jazz, and all I saw when I looked in the rearview mirror now was—

Eyes. Raptor eyes.

I screamed.

The eagle in the back seat had shed its cold gray concrete and transformed into a terrifying creature of wing, beak, and talons. His newly freed wings flapped, though there was nowhere near enough room for them to reach their full span. Talons lashed out between the bucket seats, and the eagle let out a blood-curdling shriek.

Seton and I were both yelling, and his yells became more frantic when the great bird pecked at his head and tore at his left arm with his razor talons.

The car was swerving all over the road, despite my white-knuckle grip on the wheel. I'd lost control of the steering. The brakes were not responsive no matter how hard I mashed down with my foot. Nothing I did seemed to slow the car down or get it over to the shoulder. It was a lucky thing the road wasn't crowded, because we were barreling and swerving along at death-defying speed.

"Stop it!" Seton cried.

"I can't!" I called back, although I wasn't sure if he'd been yelling at me or the bird.

The car was a lethal missile of steel and feathers, and as we plowed ahead, my stomach roiled. *We're going to die.* Joan's bald eagle birdbath had come to life in my back seat and was going to crash the car.

A long dark stretch of road lay ahead. Off to the right, beyond the shoulder, stood a large old maple. The car accelerated.

Seton and I unleashed terrified screams as the LEAF ran off the road, hurtling straight for the tree.

Chapter 21

The car stopped so abruptly, all the airbags in the front seat inflated. I slammed forward and then back again, the breath knocked out of me. I was suspended in shock, chest aching, eyes squeezed shut, body braced for that tree to come through the windshield.

Yet there was only stillness.

Cautiously, I opened my eyes. The windshield was not shattered. The car wasn't wrapped around the tree—the trunk of which appeared to be half an inch from my front bumper.

Next to me, Seton groaned. He was flattened against the seat as I was, although he was in much worse shape. His shirt was shredded from his fight with the bird, and blood streaked from his temple where he'd been pecked.

The eagle. Crooking my right arm over my eyes as protection, I pivoted toward the back seat. The terrifying raptor had become the ugly cement eagle again, but even that panicked me.

I nudged Seton gently. "Are you okay? Can you move?"

He murmured and opened his eyes.

"We need to get out of this car, Seton. Now." More important, we needed to get the cement bird out of the car before it decided to attack us again.

We opened our respective doors and stumbled into the darkness. The place we'd ended up was far beyond the shoulder of the road, out of the arc of light thrown by both car headlights and the intermittent streetlight poles. It was doubtful that anyone had seen what had happened to us.

I went around to the passenger side, leaned in to the glove compartment, and grabbed a little packet of tissues and a mini bottle of hand sanitizer. Pulling out a few tissues, I tried to stanch the bleeding on Seton's head cut.

We were both still rattled. That eagle had been trying to shred him to pieces, but it was impossible to look at how close the car had come to hitting that tree without concluding that the bird's real intent had been both our deaths.

My mind replayed those terrifying moments. "I lost control of the steering. The brakes weren't working." I studied the minuscule space between the car and the tree again. "So why aren't we dead?"

"You must have done something right," Seton said.

I let out a ragged laugh. "I haven't done one thing right all week." Ever since my first encounter with Esme, I'd had my head buried in the sand, trying to pretend that if I could just make it to my wedding day, I could ignore this witchcraft nuisance.

How could I have been so stupid? My witch family had even warned me of this eventuality. But I'd assumed I knew better than they did.

I was humbled now. Humbled and desperate. Desperation made it clear what my next steps should be.

I opened the car's back door. "Give me a hand with this," I said.

Seton, daubing a Kleenex at a painful-looking cut on his hand, frowned. "What are you doing?"

"I'm not driving anywhere with this hellbeast perched behind us."

We heaved the eagle out of the car and dumped it on the ground. Esme might have a de-ensorcellation process, but I just wanted the thing gone. For good measure, I also took the top half of the birdbath out of my trunk and plopped it down in the muddy grass. Cars on the road zoomed past, but either no one could see us or they assumed we were up to no good.

I reached into the front seat and fished my wallet out of my purse, which was on the floor. I still had Milo's card, and now I whipped out my phone.

"Who are you internetting?" Seton asked.

"The only people I know who can really help us now."

My witch family.

Milo gave me directions to Trudy's house, where apparently a meeting of the cousins' cupcake coven was underway. Over the phone, there had been laughter in the background until he'd shushed them all in order to hear me better. I doubted anyone would feel like laughing when they saw Seton. Despite our efforts with Kleenex and hand sanitizer, he was still a mess, and he also still seemed a little disoriented.

Did eagles have poison in their talons?

Of course, if the eagle was a witch, I imagined it could deliver any toxin it wanted to.

What had I gotten myself and everyone I knew into? Even though I'd discarded the birdbath, as I drove down the road it was hard not to keep looking in the rearview mirror, dreading what I'd see there. My whole body vibrated with fear.

Trudy lived in a picturesque neighborhood near Zenobia College, where I'd gone to school, so I had no trouble finding the place. Hers was one of the many Arts and Crafts houses on the tree-lined block. It was surrounded by beds of rhododendrons filled with spring flowers barely visible in the dark. On any other night I would have loved to stop and appreciate the beauty, but right now my first thought was Seton. He looked weak.

I helped him get out of the car and gave him my shoulder to lean on as we headed to the door. My legs were still shaking. As we stepped onto the porch, a policeman came out of the house.

"Whoa," he said, studying Seton's face. "That *is* bad."

Who was this? I wasn't sure how much I could say.

The cop crooked his head toward the door. "Don't worry, they'll fix you up. Go right in—they're waiting for you."

"Thanks."

"I'm Marcus, by the way."

"I'm Bailey, and this is Seton."

"We'll be seeing each other again, I expect. I'm Trudy's partner."

He trotted down the stairs to a police cruiser, which I hadn't noticed parked down the street.

Before I could knock, Trudy swung the door open. "I thought I heard Marcus talking to someone out here." She pulled us inside. I was so glad to see people, I practically fell over the threshold. Soon, we were surrounded. The cousins helped a weak Seton over to a cheerful green couch.

While they hovered around him, I looked around. The living room was open concept, with both a comfortable living area and a separate space for a long dining table. Right now the table was covered in some kind of world-building game which they'd probably abandoned after receiving my phone call. The kitchen was obviously the focal part of Trudy's life. It was set off with a long granite-topped island on which sat a KitchenAid stand mixer and a platter of cupcakes.

A rabbit hopped past my feet, followed by the strangest bird I'd ever seen. It resembled a mutant goose, only it didn't have webbed feet.

"Seton's lethargy seems out of proportion to the amount of blood he's lost," Gwen said.

I felt rattled. Gwen owned a handyman business. She wasn't a doctor. "Do you think I should take him to the ER?"

She waved a hand. "They wouldn't know what to do. Just sit down and take some deep breaths. You're safe now."

"But if he's been poisoned, he needs help."

"We'll help him," Milo assured me.

"I've made you some tea," Trudy said from the kitchen, as if this would fix everything. "Would you like a cupcake?"

I glanced distrustfully at the platter on the counter. No telling what these were laced with. I needed to keep a clear head.

"Just the tea would be fine."

Gwen retrieved towels and bottle of what I assumed was alcohol from the bathroom and went to work cleaning the wounds.

"You say this statue just came to life right in the car?" Milo asked.

I nodded. "It also seemed to take control of my steering and brakes. We ran off the road."

"That's not good." Milo steepled his fingers. "Tannith, wherever she may be at the moment, is apparently able to possess two entities at once—the bird *and* your car. She may have been lost in the ether for six months, but she's been gaining spell strength."

"Spell strength?"

"The amount of force a witch possesses for spellcasting," Trudy explained. "We all have talents, but it's only through learning and practice that our abilities are honed and strengthened."

It was on the tip of my tongue to make a joke about Hogwarts, but then I remembered how hostile witches on Cackle had been toward anything in the Potterverse. With Seton in such terrible shape, I didn't feel much like joking anyway.

I glanced over at him, then did a double take.

His wounds weren't just cleaned, they were almost gone. "How did you do that?"

Trudy brought a cup a tea around to me, took my arm, and led me over to an armchair. "Gwen'll be done in a moment."

It was then I realized that the other two had been distracting me while Gwen performed some kind of cleaning-healing ritual.

I lowered myself into the chair. Magic was happening right before my eyes and I didn't see it. It made me wonder what else I was missing.

I did a double take at the rabbit, remembering that Trudy had once accidentally turned her husband into a rabbit. "Are you two still married?" I asked, amazed.

My cousins laughed.

"That's Peaches," Trudy said. "Laird doesn't live here anymore. He's not a rabbit anymore, either."

The bird waddled across the room again and dipped his beak around our feet, as if he was used to scavenging for crumbs. He was about two and a half feet high, gray brown with a long bill that turned down sharply at the tip, and the strangest blue eyes I'd ever seen on an animal. His feet were four-toed, like chicken feet, but his walk was even more ungraceful than a duck's.

"What is that?" I asked.

Furtive glances ricocheted around the room.

"His name's Dwayne," Gwen said, finishing wrapping a bandage on Seton's hand, where there had been a particularly nasty defensive wound. "I brought him over from Esme's for the evening. He's very sociable."

"He looks like . . ." *A dodo.* I felt silly for even thinking it. I'd only seen drawings of a dodo when I was a kid, in a picture book called *The World That Was,* full of watercolor pictures of extinct creatures.

Extinct was the key word, of course. As I sipped my tea, it was hard to take my eye off the strange creature.

"I gave Seton something to help him rest." Gwen crossed to an armchair nearer me, while Trudy and Milo dragged chairs over from the dining room table. "It will also allow us to talk over a plan for you in private."

"A plan?"

Trudy lifted a teacup to her lips and sipped. "You need to get yourself trained up to deal with Tannith."

They made it sound like preparing for a witch decathlon. "I was hoping there would be some protection spell you could cast over me."

Gwen shook her head. "That would only take you so far. To save yourself from a force like Tannith you have to be ready to go on the offense. You'll need to hone your inner witch."

I swallowed. "I'm not really sure I have one. So far all I've managed to do is stop something from spilling, shut off some restaurant lights, and turn someone green."

"You saved yourself and Seton tonight."

I gestured toward the couch. "That's what you call saving us?"

"Tannith isn't merciful," Trudy said. "Why do you think your car didn't actually hit that tree?"

"It wasn't anything I did."

"It wasn't anything you purposefully did, maybe, but you still managed it."

Could that be possible? In my mind I relived those scary moments when the car was hurtling toward the tree. When I realized nothing was working, I'd almost given up. I just remembered screaming. If I'd yelled the right words or sounds or curses to save us in that split second, it was *very* subconscious.

"Honing one's inner witch sounds like a lot of work," I said. "I'm just trying to save my loved ones for the lead-up to the wedding—and that's in two weeks. I don't have much time to hone."

"That's why you should start now," Trudy said. "While you were driving here, we drew up a preliminary plan."

Milo laughed. "School's out for summer, but Trudy still loves to draw up lesson plans."

Trudy handed me the sheet of paper. At the top of the page, they'd divided up their teaching duties in a kind of three-prong approach.

Spellcraft + practical hexes (Gwen)
Herbs and enchantments (Trudy)
Social + self-defense and deflection (Milo)

"We'll need to see you for an hour or so every day to get you started. But you'll have to study and practice on your own."

Time was the one thing I didn't have much of right now. On the other hand, if I didn't do as they directed, my time might be cut permanently short. Innocent, nonwitch people could be harmed. What if Tannith's malevolent spirit came after Seton again, or Sarah, or Mom?

I released a pent-up breath. "Please, tell me what to do."

Milo leaned forward. "Okay, first thing—we'll set you up with social media accounts. It might seem trivial, but when you're on your own, these can be good sources of information."

Trudy nodded. "You can learn how to hex anything on Brew-Tube."

"You can also learn how not to," Gwen warned. "There are some real idiots on there."

"I'm already on Cackle," I confessed. "I signed up the other day."

"Great, what's your handle?" Milo asked.

I blushed, remembering. "NotWitchyPoo," I said.

Milo glanced up from his phone, his dark brow arched in a perfect inverted V.

"It was just something off the top of my head." To distract from my dumb Cackle handle, I nodded at Dwayne. "Did you know that bird looks like a dodo?"

The three of them exchanged uncomfortable looks again.

"It *is* a dodo," I guessed. "But how could that be? Did you bring it to life from a feather or something?"

Trudy almost spat up her tea. "You must think we're real wizards."

"Dwayne was Esme's doing," Gwen told me. "She's been frantically trying to decipher Odin's notes on time travel so she can figure out how to get Seton back, but she's made a few errors. A few days ago she ended up in the sixteenth century and rescued Dwayne from a Spanish galleon. She doesn't have the heart to send him back."

"She's going to land us all in hot water if she keeps this up." Trudy shook her head. "Time travel's not for the softhearted."

The poor creature was stuck being a misfit in the present or going back to doom. *Like Seton,* I thought sadly, looking over at him lying shirtless on the couch, asleep.

Milo sucked in a breath.

"What?" we all asked in unison.

He darted an accusing look at me. "You left a nasty message on Enchanted Cupcakes's page?"

Trudy gaped at me. "That was *you?*"

Heat flooded my face as I remembered my sharply worded review. "It was after your Mellow Chocolate Mint cupcakes knocked out half my office. And those Tender Loving Caramels could have precipitated a sexual harassment lawsuit."

Milo scrolled and groaned. "You called Enchanted Cupcakes 'purveyors of hocus-pocus criminality.'"

"I'm sorry—I was dealing with a bad situation."

He shook his head. "Well, you gained one follower—Voldemort666—but then you were reported for being a troll and Cackle locked your account." He sighed. "We'll have to start over."

Talk about your shaky starts. I hadn't brewed my first potion yet, and the witch community had already canceled me.

While Milo tackled my social media, the other two launched my apprenticeship.

"We'll begin with the easiest level," Gwen said. "Calm."

My skepticism was hard to shut off. "So, you're going to teach me to breathe deeply?"

Her mouth screwed up in disapproval. "Being defiant is only going to slow you down."

She was right. *Open mind*, I told myself.

Trudy was more patient. "Let's start in the kitchen. I'll show you how to brew a basic calming tea."

"Like, chamomile?" I didn't mean it to sound as snarky as it came out.

Gwen folded her arms. "No, like the stuff you drank that turned you from the blithering wreck who walked in the door to a woman who knows she needs to take steps to protect herself."

I looked down at my cup, then remembered the state I'd been in before I'd drunk it.

She pulled a small cast-iron cauldron from a bottom cabinet. "It's a spare," she told me. "You can take it with you. It's been pretempered."

For the next hour, she talked me through basic herbs, roots, and powders, explaining their properties, giving me samples from her pantry, and taking me step-by-step through her basic calming brew. Gwen aided her, putting herbs in ziplock baggies, writing instructions on index cards, and quizzing me at each step over what Trudy had just said. It was late, and all of this seemed baffling, so a lot of the information whistled right past me.

When I confused the properties of valerian with those of elderberry, Gwen turned in frustration to Trudy. "She's not getting it."

"Maybe you've forgotten *your* learning curve, the one Esme would say we're all still on?"

Gwen's lip twisted. "Right. Sorry."

She went over the herbs with me again, but by this time I was panicked. "What if I'm one of those backward witches who just never gets it?"

Trudy handed me a cup of our brew. "Nonsense. Drink this."

I sipped the stuff, which was pungent and rooty, but slightly sweet from the honey she'd stirred in for me. Within moments, a wave of well-being washed over me.

"See?" she asked. "*You* did that."

It was like a mom giving a kid credit for baking a cake when all the kid had done was lick the spatula. But I saw her point. I'd seen it done. I'd taken part. With practice, I could do it.

"I'm sorry I'm such a mess."

Trudy laughed. "I teach eighth graders. You're fine."

She poured the tea into a thermos, cooled off my cauldron in the sink, and then boxed up everything in a plastic tub.

"Here's your witch kit," Gwen said, handing it over. "I've written a few assignments and taped them to the lid. Come over to Esme's tomorrow. We'll start spell work in the basement."

Tomorrow was supposed to be a wine summit with Sarah and Martine. I'd have to postpone it. This was more important.

Milo put a sheet of paper on top of the box. "These are the passwords for your social media accounts, with some suggestions for the most helpful basic BrewTubers to follow."

"Thank you." I turned toward the couch, where Seton was just beginning to stir. "Will he be all right?"

"The cuts should be healed up by tomorrow," Gwen said. "Minor scarring at worst. The toxins have been drawn out of him, but if he starts to act oddly, let me know right away."

That *oddly* sounded ominous, but I was so relieved to see him recovering, I didn't press further. What would I have done if he hadn't survived the eagle attack? Just the possibility opened up a hole of grief inside me. *But he did survive*, I told myself.

They helped me load Seton into the car, and then Trudy handed me a thermos. "Here's the calm tea. Drink some before bed. You need to get some rest."

"Right," Milo said. "Take care of yourself like you're in training."

And they were my coaches, I thought as I drove off down Trudy's leafy street. My crew. My coven.

During the drive back, my gaze kept darting to the rearview, fearing to see the face of the screaming eagle—or perhaps some new, unexpected terror. But there was only dark highway. I turned on the jazz station and let Tommy Dorsey and His Clambake Seven serenade us home.

When we arrived, we both were ready to collapse physically, though neither of us felt ready for sleep. My brain was buzzing from all that had happened. We went through the motions, brushing our teeth, changing out of our auction party clothes, making sure the house was locked up. If only I could be sure that the locks would keep Tannith out.

Sometime in the past week, Seton had acquired a pair of cotton broadcloth pajamas in thin blue-and-white stripes. They had darker piping around the collar, cuffs, and the left breast pocket. In a normal world, those pajamas should have spelled the death of desire, but my normal world had set sail the day Esme had breezed into my life. Now I was staring at a hundred-plus-year-old-man wearing grandpa pajamas and felt as if I needed to take a cold shower.

They must have been what he was used to wearing, because he looked more at ease in them than he did in the T-shirts and boxers he'd been sleeping in until now. The classic look did suit him, and there was something casually sensual about the way he leaned against the counter, arms crossed, long legs stretched out, waiting for the calming tea to reheat in the microwave.

I stood next to him—wearing T-shirt and boxers—feeling anything but at ease. His cuts were already healing. I studied his face, memorizing its features: his eyes, the plains of his cheeks, the slight cleft in his chin, his lips . . .

Stop it.

"I hope nuking the tea doesn't kill its calming properties," I said.

He glanced uncertainly at the microwave. "I have no idea how that dingus works."

"I'm not sure, either." It might as well have been powered by sorcery, for all I knew. "Trudy advised us to drink another cup of this relaxing tea before bedtime." It sounded ridiculous now. "My cousins talk as if I can just do a few exercises and brew some hot drinks to protect myself from supernatural interference. In Zenobia, I believed it. Here, I feel more vulnerable."

A muscle in his cheek popped. Maybe he wasn't as at ease as I thought. "This is where I should promise to protect you, but I wasn't much use against that eagle."

"Nobody would have been."

He swung to face me, eye to eye, and electricity sizzled through me. "Back in the car, when it looked like we were going to crash, my life passed in front of my eyes."

A joke about how little faith he must have in my driving was on the tip of my tongue, but the emotion in his voice squelched my glib reply. "You saw Ruthie and Bert?"

"No—I saw you."

My mouth went dry. "We've only known each other a short time."

"I know, but when it felt as if I might die, I kept thinking, 'What if I don't get any more time with Bailey?' It didn't seem fair."

"Our minds think crazy things when we're stressed."

He nodded, still looking into my eyes intently. "I was thinking about kissing you. Does that seem crazy?"

"No . . ." *I'm thinking the same thing right now.*

Gently, he took my hand and drew me closer, so that I was leaning against him now, not the counter. His body was warm, and I suddenly needed that warmth. Needed him.

Just kiss him, I thought. Nothing serious—just to satisfy my curiosity. It didn't have to mean anything. It would be better to go ahead and kiss rather than wondering about it.

I slid my hands up his chest, around his nape above the soft collar of his pajamas. He looped his hands at the small of my back, pulling me even closer against him. He dipped his head and our lips touched, and the shock of it nearly took my breath. His lips, the taste of him, shocked me. I hadn't expected it to feel so right. To feel as if we just . . . fit.

It's not real, I told myself. This was just a reaction to all that had happened. It was the adrenaline. We'd been through so much—we both could have been killed.

And why was that? Because of me.

The microwave sounded off. *Saved by the beep.*

I pulled back. "Seton . . ."

He kept hold of my arm and looked as if he might reel me back in. And how would I respond if he did?

I stepped back and held out my hands, palms-out. "Please, don't say anything. It's been a crazy night, and we've both got survivor energy. But nothing about our situations has changed— except that I've put you in danger."

"I don't care about that. You're the one I'm worried about." He reconsidered that and added, "Well, and me too, a little bit."

It was wise to be nervous. *I'd* brought this down on us—or my family had. And now the only way to deal with Tannith was through studying with my family and trying to get strong. Spell strength, Gwen had called it. Until I had that, I'd never be safe, and neither would the people around me. I had to practice, to become the best witch I could be.

I grabbed the two cups from the microwave and handed one to Seton. "There, drink this down."

He frowned down at the liquid.

"After a good night's sleep, hopefully we'll be able to wake up tomorrow and put this long, confusing night behind us." I raised my cup and he reluctantly clinked his to mine.

We both gingerly sipped the hot, slightly bitter brew.

I hoped the calming spell would have quick action. I tried to think of Wes, who would be here long after Seton was back in his own time. "Nothing's changed," I repeated. "For either of us." It was starting to sound like my new mantra, where Seton was concerned.

He shook his head, looking as if he might contradict me, but he repeated, "No, nothing's changed."

Except that I was lusting after a guy who was living on my couch. That needed to stop.

Chapter 22

During the week that followed, I went through the motions of my real life during the day: going to work, answering Katrina's increasingly urgent texts about final guest counts, confirming centerpieces, finalizing catering delivery times, making a dent in the Haverman garage pod of gifts. In the evenings, I worked on becoming a witch, visiting my cousins in Zenobia and not returning until after midnight sometimes.

At home, Seton and I settled into a housemates relationship. Yes, there was attraction between us—that brief kiss stayed stubbornly in my mind—but we were being adults.

Still, I'd resisted any suggestion that he go back to Mom's. After the eagle attack, I needed to keep an eye on him. Or so I told myself.

Toward the end of the week I met Wes for dinner at the country club with Judge Taylor, a friend of Mr. Haverman who was going to officiate at the wedding. He and Wes talked golf while I surreptitiously attempted to levitate the salt shaker a millimeter or two. According to Gwen, levitation spells were elementary, but it was still a gratifying skill to practice.

"Bailey?"

Wes's voice broke my concentration, and the salt shaker came right back down. I covered the movement by knocking it over. "Sorry!"

The gray-haired judge flinched at my clumsiness, but Wes's eyes narrowed. Had he seen what I was doing?

"What were you saying?" I asked.

"I suggested going outside to take a look at the ceremony site," Judge Taylor said. "Unless you'd like dessert?"

"No, a stroll sounds wonderful."

Outside, we walked over the grounds where the ceremony would take place. I half listened to Wes and the judge discussing what we wanted from the ceremony—simple, short, nothing too flowery—while the other part of my brain was going over the self-defense lesson I'd had with Milo. He was teaching me about hex deflection and protective shields. Like levitation, these were concentration exercises, which I found challenging.

As part of self-defense, we practiced casting spells on the fly. He'd introduced me to a game called hex tag, which was like freeze tag only with the added challenge that whoever was "it" was being chased by witches tossing actual freezing spells at him. Once I got the rudiments down, the coven gathered to play a round of hex tag in Trudy's backyard. It felt like high-stakes PE. At the end of three rounds, I'd been numb from being the target of freeze bolts.

After Judge Taylor left, Wes and I stayed behind and looked out at the boats on Lake Ontario. I was still a little stiff from the hex tag game. It was probably good to be taking an evening off.

Wes darted an anxious look at my face. "I'm sorry for the harsh way I spoke."

I'd been so lost in witchcraft thoughts that I must have missed something. "To the judge? What did you say to him?"

He frowned. "No. On Saturday, at the hospital."

"Oh." We hadn't been alone much since that night of the auction, which seemed a lifetime ago. I'd been so absorbed by my witchcraft, I hadn't given any thought to the scene at the hospital. "It's okay."

"Are you sure?" he asked. "It feels like you've been avoiding me."

"I've been busy." Even now, surveying this beautiful, serene scene, all I could think about was what Tannith would do to disrupt our day. If she was as strong a sorceress as everyone said, could she send a wave from the lake up the bluff to drown us out? Whip up a hurricane-force wind? What exactly did I need to protect myself against?

He hesitated, then said, "Mad suggested you might be getting cold feet."

He'd been talking to Madeleine? Of course he had. Wes was the reason she'd come home.

I laughed. "I'll bet she's said more than that."

Blotches of red sprang to his cheeks. "Can you blame her? You're basically living with another man now. I realize he's your cousin, but O says he's sexy."

I think so, too. I shook my head. "A lot of people are attractive. But I'm marrying you." It was so frustrating. Everything I was doing was to ensure that the wedding went off with no major mishaps.

"I told you what I went through with Lydia." He raked his fingers over his hair. "The doubts, the deceptions. I couldn't stand that a second time."

"I'm not Lydia." *Or am I?*

"I know you're not, but—" He buried his hands in his pockets.

I lifted my chin. "Do you want to call it off?"

"Of course not," he said quickly.

And what would I have said if he'd answered yes? A few

nights ago that prospect had set off a hurricane of confusion in me. Now . . .

There was no difference now. Seton was still married and looking to return to his world. I had to hold on to what I had.

"Good," I said. "I'm focused now on making sure the wedding's a success."

And for the next few days, I really was laser focused. There was so much to do between now and the wedding. I felt as I had back in college, cramming for final exams. At work, whenever I could steal a moment, I shut my door and practiced what Gwen, Trudy, and Milo had taught me. After a few days, I could levitate a stapler. I transformed a pile of forms on white paper into a cheery periwinkle color. I worked on a calming shield that got me through the world's most tedious Zoom meeting with a client.

There was so much yet to learn. At night I drove to Gwen and Esme's to work on spells or to Trudy's house to mix potions. There wasn't time enough in the day for everything and everyone. Something had to give, and I was afraid I was neglecting Sarah. I did see her once or twice, but only because she was helping Seton with his genealogy research, which occupied most of his time. And when he wasn't with her, he would visit my mom's to watch television.

"Deb seems sad," he told me one evening as I was putting the last touches on what was supposed to be an energy potion. God knows I needed it. After several days of witch study and work, my energy was flagging.

"I think you should talk to her," he said.

I blew out a breath. "I'm so busy. What I'm doing—the witch-craft training—is really important."

"You're telling me," he said, reaching for the faint scar on his cheek where the eagle had slashed him. It gave him a more rugged look. Unluckily for me, he seemed more handsome than ever.

I looked away, trying to shrug off the discomfort I felt. *I'm not Lydia.* "Maybe if I work hard enough at my witchcraft, I'll be able to send you back to 1930 myself."

His face paled at that idea, and the scar stood out more. "Get rid of me yourself, you mean."

"No," I said quickly.

My words hadn't come out right at all. I'd been so careful around him this week—that was another good thing about witchcraft training. It kept me away from Seton. By the time I got home I was usually so tired that all I could do was say a quick good night and stumble off to bed. But I couldn't lie to myself. The prospect of his leaving upset me.

"You're . . ." I swallowed. "My friend. I don't want you to leave."

My words didn't seem to move him much. "Speaking of friends," he said. "Gil called. You missed your guitar lesson again."

Oh, no. And Gil had been so understanding about the stolen saxophone, allowing me to rent it for Seton for as long as he stayed. "I'll pay him for the missed lesson," I said.

"It's not the money that bugs him most, Bailey. It's being forgotten. People are starting to wonder what you're doing."

"I'm trying to protect them."

"*I* know that." He pulled a beer out of the fridge. "But Gil, your mom, and Sarah don't."

Sarah. A wave of guilt hit me.

"Any joy with your genealogy research?" I asked him.

"We're still trying to find out what happened to Ruthie. Sarah can't locate a death record, but I doubt Ruthie's lived to be a hundred and twenty-five."

"What about Burt?"

"Burt died in that war I watched the show about, on a battleship." A puzzled shadow crossed his expression. "Why did he join the navy? He couldn't even swim. Neither of us could—we laughed about it once when we were on the Staten Island Ferry.

Strange to think that in the end he was buried at sea, or maybe drowned."

"How do you know?"

"He's listed as one of the casualties of the *Houston*, which was sunk early in the war. A lot of men drowned." His gaze went distant. "Why did Burt enlist at all? He was younger than me, but by then he would have been old for enlisting."

"Patriotism," I said. "A lot of older men joined."

"That's what confounds me. Burt pushed me out a window, and then twelve years later he sacrificed himself for his country. A hero." He shook his head. "It's like reading the end of a novel when you've skipped twenty chapters."

"I guess it just goes to show that people can change for the better. It just doesn't happen often enough."

His brows knit. "I wonder what kind of person I would have been."

That was easy for me to answer. "The best kind."

Our gazes met, and that sharp, totally inappropriate attraction poleaxed me again. I looked away. *Idiot*, I scolded myself. Seton didn't want me. He was just a lost soul, looking for a place for himself.

And what are you? a voice inside my head asked.

Seton emptied the rest of his beer in the sink. "I should go to bed early tonight."

"Me too."

He paused in the doorway. "Things have been calm, at least. No more eagles."

"Thank goodness," I said. "Hopefully, all of this witch work I'm doing is an exercise in futility."

I didn't like to work late in the kitchen when Seton was trying to sleep in the living room. I gave Django a few pellets, put the cover over his cage, and went into my room. I changed into shorts and a T-shirt to sleep in, then noticed my guitar leaning in the corner. Another friend I'd been neglecting. I picked it up and strummed a G chord lightly. Then, from memory, I played a song I loved, "I'll See You in My Dreams." It was probably my favorite recording of Django Reinhardt's—although of course I was light years from being able to play like he did. He was in a class all his own.

Rusty from not practicing, I picked out the melody of the song slowly. On the second chorus I managed better, and then a strange thing happened. From the next room, a saxophone echoed my song, and then played a gentle harmonic riff along with me. The bluesy saxophone sound added extra plaintiveness to the music. The words ran through my head.

I'll see you in my dreams,
Hold you in my dreams . . .

I wondered, since Seton knew the song, if those words made him think of anyone. Ruthie, maybe? Or someone else?

We finished our duet, and I leaned the guitar against the night table. "Good night, Seton," I called through the wall.

"Good night."

I crawled under the covers and mentally extinguished my overhead light. For some reason, a tear trickled down to my pillow as I dropped off to sleep. *Just tired,* I told myself.

Hours later, from a deep sleep, I snapped awake to an assault on my eardrums: the soaring, piercing sound of a demented Irish tenor voice singing "Danny Boy" at the top of his lungs.

I leapt out of bed in a single bound, tripping over the guitar and my shoes in my race to the door, which I flung open. The lights were on and Seton was standing in the living room in his boxers and T-shirt, bleary and wild-eyed.

"What's happening?" I screamed over the racket.

"It's Django."

In the dining room, I whipped the cover off the parrot cage. Sure enough, he was puffed up on his favorite branch and belting out the second verse now.

"Shhhhh!" When that didn't shut him up, I yelled, "Stop it! Now!"

"I won't be silenced!" he taunted me. And then he started the song all over again.

I rounded on Seton. "Did you do this? Have you been playing music to him?"

"*That* kind of music? No."

Django's piercing voice reminded me of Joe Feeney, the Irish tenor on *The Lawrence Welk Show*, which my dad would watch on reruns on PBS when I was a kid. Having that voice live, right in my ear, filtered through parrot vocal cords, was like nails on chalkboard.

And not just to me.

Someone pounded on my front door.

When I opened it, my elderly landlady and neighbor, Dottie, stood in her bathrobe, her eyes bloodshot with exhaustion and anger, her mouth screwed up in outrage.

"It's three o'clock in the morning!" she yelled at me.

Abruptly, Django switched his tune to "Three O'Clock in the Morning," which failed to amuse Dottie.

"How can one little bird make so much noise?"

"In the wild parrots have to communicate with each other across dense forest canopies," I explained.

"This duplex is not in a dense forest," she snapped.

"I'll quiet him down," I promised.

"If you don't, I'll call the police." She turned on her heel and stomped back to her side.

Inside, I crossed to the parrot cage and got a handhold underneath it. "Grab the other end," I told Seton.

Eager to do something, anything, he joined me. "Where are we taking it?"

"My bedroom has a big closet," I said. "I'm going to shut him up in it for the night."

Quickly we lugged the unwieldy parrot cage through to my

bedroom. I yanked armfuls of hanging clothes off the rod in the closet and heaped them on the bed. Then we stuffed the parrot cage in and closed the door.

Seton and I fled back to the living room. Even having two shut doors between us, we could hear Django's grating rendition of "Come Back to Sorrento." Hopefully, Dottie couldn't hear it.

We fell onto the couch, exhausted. Then we looked at each other and laughed.

"What am I going to do?" I despaired. "Now I don't even have anywhere to sleep."

"Come here." He pulled me toward him.

"This won't work." The couch was too small for even one of us.

But I scooched against him anyway. Our legs intertwined, and my hands pressed against his chest. Our mouths were so close. Just inches away. And that quickly, I knew. He hadn't forgotten about that brief kiss the other night, either. His blue eyes telegraphed his desire in no uncertain terms.

We melted into each other—lips together, my hands snaking around his neck, his looping around my waist. We pulled closer, kissing each other as we'd wanted to for days. He still had the faint taste of beer, that forbidden drink from his past. Now this felt forbidden, too. Forbidden and irresistible.

As I wriggled to get impossibly closer and to not fall off the too-small couch, he looped his hands against my lower back, anchoring me against him, and then his hands slid lower. This was wrong on so many levels, wrong to so many people—people we loved—and yet here we were. Kissing like these were our last moments on earth. Savoring each stolen second, yet feeling more and more dissatisfied as the moments passed. He slipped a hand underneath my shirt, and the feel of his hand against my bare skin caused me to arch against him.

So wrong, and yet his hands and lips anticipated what I wanted before I knew I wanted it. He wasn't rough, but he wasn't reticent. His lips brushed the sensitive skin of my neck, and I let out something between a gasp and a sigh.

"I've dreamed about this," he murmured.

"Me too." This was real, though, wasn't it? Maybe not smart, irresponsible, but every nerve ending in my body felt alive. How could that be wrong?

Lost in sensation, Seton shifted, and I moved with him, forgetting for a moment where we were. I rolled off the couch and bumped onto the floor.

Bumped back to reality. That was the trouble with dreams. They inevitably ended with the realization that the wonderful thing you'd experienced wasn't real.

I rubbed my hip, which had taken the brunt of the spill. "Ouch."

Seton reached down to pull me back up, but I pushed up at the same time, landing on the couch myself. Next to him, this time, not on top of him.

He reached for my hand. "Bailey . . ."

His voice was a caress, but seemed to presage an apology, which was the last thing I wanted. What *did* I want? For Seton to sweep me off my feet and tell me that I couldn't marry Wes because he, Seton, was madly, hopelessly in love with me? It would never work. There were too many uncertainties and obstacles. I wasn't a risk-taker.

I swallowed, but didn't pull my hand back. Not all at once. "It's okay. We lost our heads."

Again.

He dragged in a ragged breath. "Yes, we did."

"It's okay. Irish tenor parrots have a maddening effect on people."

"I'm married," he said. "Or not married, depending on the century. But if I go back—"

I cut him off, a little more sharply this time. "You don't have to explain that again."

Star-crossed didn't begin to describe our dilemma. We sat listening to the end of the muffled "Come Back to Sorrento."

"*Now* what are we going to do?" I said. "I can't sleep in that room."

Seton hopped up. "I'm going over the top!"

He tore down the hall, flung open my bedroom door, and charged inside. I followed and found him tugging the mattress off the bed frame. I transferred the heap of clothes to the floor, and together we wrestled the mattress, bedding and all, out of the room and slid it down the hall. There was barely enough real estate to flop it down between the coffee table and the television, but it did fit.

When we were done, I flopped down onto the mattress while Seton made another trip into the bedroom to retrieve my pillows.

"Thank you," I said when he tossed them down to me.

He flicked off the light. "Good night, Bailey."

I grunted sleepily in return, and heard him pad back over to the couch. We were on different levels, not touching, yet I felt attuned to his every movement and breath.

What if I *weren't* risk-averse? I could throw caution to the wind and climb back up on the couch—or better yet, pull Seton down to the mattress and finish what we'd started. So what if he was a married, unemployed stockbroker from another century, and I was in the final stages of wedding preparations? Engagements were broken, weddings canceled. His being displaced in time was a thornier problem, but couldn't love overcome all obstacles?

Not that he'd ever mentioned love. I frowned. *Love,* that thing I'd felt for Wes until . . .

Until when? When Seton showed up, or until I'd met Esme and she'd introduced witchcraft into my life? The two things seemed inseparable.

I started to doze off, until Django began singing "The Rose of Tralee."

I flopped over onto my stomach, muffling a groan. I preferred him spouting Shakespeare to this. Where had my parrot picked up this repertoire? And how long could he keep it up? It was torture.

My eyes blinked open. *Torture.* Of course.

Tannith had returned.

Chapter 23

"That needs to stop," Esme declared, wincing as Django launched into his third chorus of "When Irish Eyes Are Smiling." She snapped her fingers and the sound ceased.

Django nearly fell off the chair back he'd been perched on. "Thank you!" the bird said. "That was exhausting."

"You're telling me," I said. The drive to Zenobia with that singing in the back seat had seemed to take hours.

He floofed his feathers indignantly. "It wasn't my fault. Believe me, if I were a singer, I'd choose grand opera. Pavarotti." He sang a few shaky bars of "La donna è mobile" before Esme shut that down, too, leaving him flapping his feathers in mute outrage.

"You can't do that," I said. "It's cruel."

She wasn't backing down. "No—bird opera is cruel. To us."

We were down in Esme's basement laboratory, which had been painstakingly carved out of the rock the house stood on. The space had no windows, but I hadn't noticed at first because the long room boasted high ceilings and white-painted floors, lending it a feeling of spaciousness. The walls were done in a creamy pink. Against one stood a massive, antique apothecary's cabinet, and another was taken up by floor-to-ceiling bookcases filled with hardbound volumes. In the center of the room were several chrome-topped worktables covered with terrariums of frogs and newts, hot plates, and cauldrons.

Esme had just returned from another of her trips. "I'm very close to solving Seton's problem," she assured me. "If I could just find Odin again, we'd have him back in a snap. But even without Odin, I might be able to swing it on my own."

When she mentioned Seton's name, I kept my face pointed toward Django, who was bobbing in outrage at being silenced. This morning Seton and I hadn't said a word about what had happened on the couch the night before. We'd kept the focus on the other thing that had disturbed our sleep: Django. Seton was the one who'd suggested taking the parrot to Zenobia to fix the problem.

I hadn't expected to find Esme here. And she, having just materialized herself before I rang the farmhouse bell, was surprised to see me rush in, completely familiar now with her secret laboratory. Gwen got her up to speed on what had happened after the silent auction.

"That's good," Esme said. "Now you need to learn to manage Django's voice yourself."

"Me?" I asked. "I'm still at the levitating staplers stage. I don't want to experiment on my bird."

Esme looked accusingly at Gwen.

"It's only been five days," Gwen said in our defense.

"And it's been mere hours since Tannith found a way *into Bailey's home* and put a nuisance hex on her bird, and Bailey wasn't able to do anything about it. We need to move things along, people."

She marched over to a cage, pulled out a small gray mouse,

and plopped him on a chrome-topped worktable. "Okay, if you're afraid of hurting your bird, we'll try something else." She fixed me with a stern look. "Change this mouse into a toad."

I froze. "Why would you want him to be a toad? He's a sweet little mouse."

Esme spoke to the ceiling. "Can this really be my own flesh and blood, and the blood of Odin Tiberius Klemperer?"

"I just feel bad for the mouse," I said. "He might not want to be a toad."

She rolled her eyes. "You can change him back." A moment passed before she added, "Probably."

Oh, God. The mouse, which I swore had the most expressive eyes I'd ever seen on a rodent, looked up at me pleadingly.

"I'm not sure I know how," I said.

Esme planted her hands on her hips and looked impatiently from me to Gwen. "You two haven't covered this yet?"

"We went over the chapter in *Moribundus Veritudus*," Gwen explained, "but Bailey's been taking in a lot. We haven't been able to practice everything."

Esme turned toward me with a commanding glare and snapped her fingers. "Tough love. No excuses. Mouse into frog. Go!"

She looked so fierce, I feared a refusal might make her turn *me* into a toad.

Panicked, I reached back in my memory for the strange words I'd seen written in the book. I closed my eyes.

Before I could utter a syllable, Esme rushed over, took my hands in hers, and lifted them. "Hands up, fingers pointed at subject," she instructed. "Now keep your eyes open and concentrate."

She was right. Having my hands up helped. The position put a fire in my fingers that seemed to connect me and the poor mouse with his nervously twitching whiskers. *Here goes nothing.*

"*Rana . . . hinein . . .* um . . . *oris?*"

My words were hesitant, but I finished the spell with a flour-

ish of my hands, as Gwen had taught me, and was rewarded with
a satisfying puff of smoke where the mouse had been. When the
smoke cleared, though, the mouse was still there, very much a
mammal. Disappointment filled me . . . along with relief. I lowered my hands.

Then the mouse opened his rodent little maw and croaked.

The room fell completely silent. Gwen and I braced ourselves
for a withering rebuke from Esme.

When I braved a glance over, though, tears stood in my birth
mother's eyes. She clasped her hands, joy radiating from her like
beams of light. "Look at you—my little girl, casting spells! I
could bust with pride!"

Really?

"But he's not a toad. He just sounds like one."

She waved a hand dismissively. "Baby steps. He's not meow-
ing or oinking, at least."

She put me through more of my paces, testing my color spells,
object movement, and the protective shield spell Milo had been
helping me with. Then she took me through the steps of revers-
ing the stop spell she'd cast on Django, which I managed to perform perfectly on the second try.

"I am not a guinea pig!" the parrot pronounced irately when
his voice returned.

"You're not immortal, either, so watch your mouth." Esme
looked at me apologetically. "Sorry, I didn't mean to step between you and your bird, but you have to be firm or these critters
will take over your life."

As she spoke, Dwayne the dodo waddled over to her. She bent
down and almost touched her nose to his beak. "Isn't that right?
Who's a good little extinct flightless birdie-birdie-birdie? You,
that's who!"

Rolling her eyes at the display, Gwen brought over a little of
the energy potion I'd brewed for Esme to sample. After a sip of
it, Esme practically bounced to the ceiling. "Bottle that stuff, and

you'd be a millionaire." She patted Gwen on the shoulder. "You all are doing good work." Me, she enveloped me in a smothering hug. "When I come back, I'll have something really special for you. A wedding present you'll never forget."

"Where are you going?" I asked.

"Nineteen twenty-something, I hope. I told you I was getting closer. Tell Seton we'll have him back in no time."

Her optimism caused a stab of alarm. So soon? I'd been assuming Seton would be around for a while.

With a final swig of energy drink for the cosmic road, Esme began to spin, making the air in the laboratory shimmer. I closed my eyes as matter around me bent and snapped. Just from my few attempts at transforming spells, I realized that what she was doing had an extremely high level of difficulty, and couldn't be easy on the body. How could a person put herself through that multiple times in a week?

And she was doing it for me.

I needed to thank her. But when I opened my eyes, she was gone. *Here one minute, and the next—where?* Her disappearing act unnerved me.

Gwen went on with her activities as if a person dematerializing before her eyes were no big deal. "Trudy texted," she told me. "She wants you to drop by." She glanced at the parrot. "I think we're done here."

"Good," Django said. "I've never been so mistreated and insulted in all my life. You should be ashamed—"

My cousin snapped her fingers, shutting him up. "Yup, done."

When I stopped by Trudy's, she greeted me in her Enchanted Cupcakes apron. As soon as I was inside, she shut the door and spoke in a furtive voice, as if the walls had ears. "I've got some samples and a recipe for you, but you need to be careful who you share them with."

"Why?"

She bit her lip. "Well, the other day you were telling me that there was tension between you and your fiancé. Love potions aren't looked on favorably in our world—there are too many ways they can be abused, and so much harm can result." She lifted her shoulders. "But if you know the recipient is someone who's meant for you . . . I mean, if you're trying to *repair* a relationship, not manufacture one that maybe shouldn't exist, what's the harm in that?"

"In the wrong hands, it might lead to romantic trickery."

"But my Lavender Love cupcakes can mend any relationship. Isn't that a good thing?"

I was wary. "If it's illegal, I probably shouldn't do it. I'm new at this."

"You're doing so well, though," she said encouragingly. "Tell you what. I'll give you the recipe, just in case." She considered the box she'd wrapped up for me on the counter. "And take a few cupcakes, too. Aside from having good magic, they're lavender vanilla, and delicious. They're not love-inducing so much as *infused* with love." She smiled such a motherly smile, no one would suspect that this woman could cast a whammy with those cupcakes of hers, if she had a mind to. "You don't want unnecessary conflict before your wedding, do you?"

No, I didn't. I took the box and the recipe, and thanked her.

Genesee Insurance had become the calmest part of my life, which was amazing, since I was avoiding Ron and he seemed to be avoiding me, as well.

The work was so routine to me, I could sit in my chair filling out paperwork and going over my witch lessons in my head. Today, though, I was distracted by thoughts of how gratifying it had been to have Esme help me with my magic. It felt as if there might actually be a path for us to have a relationship. Maybe not a lovey mother-daughter bond, but something.

Which reminded me . . . I hadn't heard from Mom recently,

except for a terse reply to one of my texts checking on her, when she'd assured me that she was fine.

The tension between us made me uneasy. Throughout my life, she had been every bit as much my champion as Dad had been, cheering in the audience, bucking me up when I stumbled, encouraging me. And, unlike Dad, she had wanted me to guard my independence, to be my own person. It was she who'd insisted that I find a place of my own when I returned to Zenobia after college, rather than live at home. I never gave her enough credit for that. And when the time came for me to be equally supportive toward her, I'd fallen short.

While I was lost in thought, Paige appeared. She barely tapped before sweeping into my office, closing the door behind her. Then she marched to my desk and stood with her arms stiffly at her sides, like a gunslinger ready for a showdown.

"Anything I can do for you?" I asked warily.

"Yes. Stop trying to undermine my path forward with Ron."

"What have I done?"

"You've been throwing obstacles at me since I arrived here," she said. "You've never wanted me to get ahead."

"Ahead of what?" It was hard not to laugh. "We sell insurance. It's a small office."

She lifted her chin. "An office is as small as the vision of the people in it."

"Wow—what TED Talk did you pull that little nugget from?" She really was amazing. "And if you have such a winning vision for Genesee Insurance, why do you think it's necessary to vamp the boss to secure your position here?"

Her eyes were like lasers. "Maybe because my daddy didn't secure a nice cozy berth for me in his business?"

Heat flooded into my face. "I've worked here for over ten years."

"Sure, if you call being a warm body in a chair working." She shook her head. "Why are you always coming between me and Ron?"

"Oh, please. Name one single thing I've done to interfere with you two."

"Bringing your mother in here, all dressed up with that young guy?"

She was thinking about cupcake day—which had also been right before Ron and Mom's disastrous blind date. I hooted. "I don't think you have to worry about my mom standing between you and Genesee Insurance rep glory, Paige."

"That's all you know. Ron's funny about her."

My smile melted. "Ron talks about my mom to you?"

"Not often, but *way* more than necessary when he's out to lunch with someone younger and—sorry, but it's true—hotter."

Paige seeing my mom as a romantic rival was just head shaking. "You know he dumped my mom years ago. There's nothing there."

She rolled her eyes. "Like people never have regrets, never change, never grow." Her mouth twisted. "Maybe *you* should listen to a TED Talk sometime. You might find something to get you out of the rut you've been digging for yourself for the past decade. But in the meantime, stay out of my way."

With a final glare, she turned on her heel and marched out of the office.

Rut?

Screw her. I belonged here. It was the only real job I'd ever had. The job my own father had wanted for me, which he'd encouraged me to take so I'd have a secure life, instead of running off pursuing la-di-da musical pipe dreams that, sure, might have made me happier in brief bursts while things were going well, but what would they have led to? Here I had an office, a job I could do with my eyes closed, a lifetime ahead of me stretching like a—

Rut.

Schooled by Paige Wilkins. I sank farther in my chair, feeling like one of those building ruins from Seton's war documentary.

Paige had scored a direct hit on me and now I was just a smoldering shell.

I didn't warn Mom I was coming, so I couldn't complain when she answered the door dressed to go out and announced that she didn't really have time for a visit.

"Please, just a few moments," I said. "I brought a peace offering."

Trudy intended those cupcakes to be used for me and Wes, but I didn't care. This was the relationship I most wanted to repair at the moment.

Mom took in the Enchanted Cupcakes logo, then the desperation on my face, and stepped aside to let me in.

In the kitchen, she brought down two mugs and set the electric kettle to make tea.

I took a deep breath. "I want to apologize," I said. "I shouldn't have sabotaged your date, or gotten in a snit that it was at Dad's favorite restaurant, or been horrified that you dated Ron before Dad. It was none of my business."

She pulled out one of the painted wicker breakfast table chairs for me and we sat down. "You know I was devoted to your father."

"Because he was what was left after you were betrayed by your boyfriend and your best friend?"

"Why not? I fell in love with the person who was there to pick me up when my heart felt broken."

Heartbroken. Over Ron.

I had to let it go.

But I also had to ask. "Do you think Dad ever wondered if he was first runner-up?"

She laughed. "He knew he was. He also knew his friend better than I did. Ron was fun to be with, but look what happened. He and Kathy ended up miserable together. *I* was the one who got lucky."

"Yes."

"Even Ron says so."

Says? "Have you been talking?"

"He emailed me after last Friday and told me that in his surprise at seeing me there, he'd said things he regretted." She watched my face to catch my reaction. "He also asked me out again. He said he never found anyone he cared for as much as he cared for me."

I frowned. "You believe that?"

"I'm not sure." She let out a breath. "I've occasionally wondered why Ron never married again or even dated anyone seriously. He says that was because of me."

I knew I should stop interfering, but this was too important not to mention. "He and this woman in the office have been having a weird kind of flirtation. I'm not the only one who's noticed."

"Paige?" She laughed at my surprise at her knowing the name. "He told me he was flattered that someone so young would show any interest in him, but he thinks she's just buttering him up for a promotion."

Huh. Maybe he wasn't as gullible as I assumed.

Mom looked me square in the eye. "It's Ron who I'm meeting this afternoon."

"Isn't it early for a date?"

"I'm selling my shares of the business to him." When she saw my shock, she added, "I should have done it after your father died. I was just holding on . . . well, I don't know why. You know, part of me suspects it was to hold on to both Lloyd and Ron. They were my youth." She sighed. "But now I'll get a nice chunk of change out of the deal to begin the next phase of my life."

"What phase?"

"I'm thinking about selling the house and moving to Florida."

"Leaving here?" I felt as if I'd been sucker punched.

"Your aunt Janet asked me to visit. She loves it down there."

"But you can't let Ron chase you away."

"He's not chasing me away. He's being very kind." She smiled wistfully. "You know, when we were talking online through Goldenhearts, I really thought RC was great. We had so much in common, it was spooky. We were a five golden heart match."

The regret in her voice confused me. "So you're moving to get away from a man you're too compatible with?"

"Maybe. What would I do if it didn't work out?" She shook her head. "There won't be a Lloyd on the sidelines next time to pick up the pieces."

"Did you ever consider that it might work out?"

As soon as the words were out of my mouth, I couldn't believe I'd said them.

"Something might work out in Florida, too." She smiled. "Either way—I'm seeing lots of options."

I nodded, feeling as numb as I did after a round of hex tag.

"Nothing's decided yet," she told me.

I breathed in a ragged breath. I'd just been kicking myself for not seeing that I was in a rut. I couldn't very well criticize Mom for wanting to blast out of hers. "I'm happy for you," I said. "Whatever you decide you want for yourself."

"I'm glad you came over," she said, reaching for my hand. "I probably came across as angry about that woman—your birth mother. But of course I understand your being curious about where you came from." She bit her lip. "And if you want to invite her to the wedding . . ."

"No," I said. "I don't want that."

"Oh." She frowned. "I hope you're not bitter toward her, Bailey. She was only seventeen."

"I'm not bitter," I said. "She's just . . . odd. I'm not sure Wes or anyone in his family would understand her."

Mom's brow wrinkled in concern, and she looked at me in a way that made me squirm. Like *I* was a Havermonster.

I added quickly, "I mean, I still barely know her. I don't know how she would feel being plunged into a big wedding."

Mom nodded. "It's up to you. Whatever you decide, I love you, Bailey Bee. You know that."

My throat threatened to close up. "I love you too, Mom."

She checked her watch. "I really do have to go, though. We'll have to postpone our tea party."

She walked me to the door. "You'd better take my umbrella," she said, handing me a large one leaning by the door.

I was going to argue that she would need it, but I knew Mom always kept an extra umbrella under the seat of her car. And she was right. As we stood on the threshold of the glassed-in porch, the darkening sky threatened rain.

Lots of it.

Chapter 24

When I got home, the rain had started coming down harder and Sarah's Jeep was parked at the curb in front of my duplex. I hurried inside, expecting to find her and Seton way ahead of me on cocktail hour.

"Hello?" I called out.

"In the kitchen." Sarah's voice lacked its usual buoyancy.

I dropped my purse, shaking my head at what a train wreck the house seemed. Between rushing to Zenobia in the morning and then rushing to work and finally to Mom's, I hadn't had any time to tidy up from last night. All I'd done was drag the parrot cage out so Django wouldn't spend the entire afternoon in my closet.

I went into the kitchen and dropped my purse on the counter. "Hey," I said.

Django was perched on the back of his kitchen chair and flapped his wings in greeting. I gave him a quick kiss on the beak. Sarah remained seated, a cup of coffee in front of her. Ever since he'd learned how the coffee maker worked, Seton never missed a brewing opportunity.

I looked around, listening for some sound in the rest of the house. "Where's Seton?"

"He went for a walk."

"In this rain?"

"He wanted to be alone."

I didn't like the sound of that. "What happened?"

She crossed her arms. "I'm not sure. We were researching some person he was interested in, and I finally traced her and some of her family from county marriage records—he'd been looking for the wrong name. Anyway, I was able to find her death announcement after that. When I came over after work to show it to Seton, it was like I'd punched him in the gut."

I dropped into a chair. "It was Ruthie?"

She nodded. "Ruth Smith. She died in 1978—of natural causes, it said in the newspaper."

"Smith—not Lane?" I frowned. "She must have married three times."

"Who was this woman?"

"Just some woman Seton knew."

Sarah let out a confused laugh. "When, in a former life?"

Too late, I caught my mistake. "Knew *of*, I mean."

She growled in frustration, got up, and dumped her coffee down the sink as if in preparation to leave.

"What's the matter?" I asked.

"You tell me." She rounded on me; her voice was taut with anger. "I thought we were friends. I'm going to be maid of honor at your wedding, which is just over a week away, but I've barely seen you—just this weird cousin of yours who it appears you're camping out with in the middle of your living room now."

"We just moved the mattress out because of Django's singing." I tilted my head. "You think he's weird?"

Her gaze burned into me. "He didn't know what a cursor

was—he asked me if it meant someone who swore a lot. He's never heard of Madonna, the Rolling Stones, or *Star Wars*. He went pale with shock one day when a life-flight helicopter was flying overhead. He had to ask me what he was seeing. The man's either a space alien or he bolted from the Amish."

I winced. I probably should have coached him.

She lifted her arms at her sides and then dropped them again. "I'm not judging you for whatever you guys are doing, but you used to tell me things, Bailey. Seton says you spend half your time now in Zenobia with your birth family, none of whom I've met or even heard of."

"I told you about Esme Zimmer."

"Right—you said you didn't want anything to do with her, but the next thing I know, you're hanging out down there. Every. Single. Day. We were supposed to have a wine summit, remember?"

"Oh, right."

She let out a ragged breath. "Oh, right. You've been too busy, although doing *what* isn't clear. You're obviously not packing to move, and your kitchen is crammed with weird jars full of herbs and strange-looking teas, and when I asked about it, Seton clammed up and Django started reciting the witches' speech from *Macbeth*, and how is it that your parrot is suddenly reciting Shakespeare?"

"You're hearing him now, too?"

Sarah put her hands to her head and looked as if she might start yanking out fistfuls of blond hair. "What the hell is going on? Just please tell me. Right now I've got an AWOL boyfriend—if I'm losing my best friend, too, I'd like to know so that I can go home and drown myself in cabernet and Cadbury bars."

"I'm a witch." I didn't mean to blurt it out, but I couldn't think of any gentle lead-in. And it was a relief just to say it.

Sarah ceased moving, ceased breathing. Then, when I said no

more, she gulped in air. "Okay . . ." Her voice was shaky. "I think I might need that cabernet and chocolate anyways."

I retrieved two glasses and unscrewed a bottle I'd bought at Aldi—I wasn't quite a full Haverman yet.

We sat down again and I poured. She took a long drink. "Witch, you said?"

"It sounds ridiculous, I know. I didn't believe it at first. It started when I saw Esme Zimmer that day I was trying on dresses at Blanche Bridal Boutique."

Step by step, I talked her through everything that had happened—Esme, Seton, Madeleine turning green, Tannith, the collapsing ceiling, the eagle, the cupcake coven, the song-possessed parrot . . . all of it. "I didn't tell you at first because I could hardly believe it myself, and then when the truth finally did sink in, it seemed too bizarre and complex to explain."

"But you just did."

"Right. And do you believe it?"

"I'm not sure." She looked at Django. "I definitely heard him recite Shakespeare. But all the rest . . ."

"All right." I searched for a way to prove it to her. My eye fell on the Eiffel Tower coasters Martine had given me for my birthday. "Keep an eye on that coaster." Concentrating as hard as I could, I raised the coaster six inches—a record for me.

Color drained from Sarah's face. "Holy cow, Bailey. You're a witch!"

Her words broke the spell and the coaster plopped back down on the tabletop. "Pretty basic stuff," I said. "My cousin Gwen was levitating her Barbie when she was six."

Sarah was still impressed. "I can't believe it. I mean, I can. I know you're not a liar, even if you haven't been telling me the truth for the past two weeks."

"I'm sorry. I didn't know what to do. Plus, there's been all the stuff with my mom going on."

Her brow wrinkled. "So that woman, Ruthie Smith . . ."

"Was Seton's wife. Her second husband died in World War Two, and after that she must have gotten married again."

"She must have been something."

Unexpectedly, jealousy stabbed at me, which was ridiculous. Ruthie wasn't even alive . . . except in Seton's heart, evidently. Even though the woman had cheated on him, and might have conspired to kill him, he still wasn't over her.

But he'd kissed me . . .

Sarah took a sip of wine. "So I'm guessing you haven't told Wes you're a witch, either."

I sighed. "I don't know what to do."

"You see, you needed that wine summit."

"Yes, because now I'll have to explain all this again to Martine." I frowned. "Where is Martine?"

"Athens again. I Skyped with her last weekend. She's back at that inn." She opened her phone and brought up a selfie Martine had taken of herself with a very tanned, extremely attractive man with thick, curly black hair. They were both wearing sunglasses and grinning like mad.

"I hope she can drag herself back," I said. "I can't wait to see her."

"So you *are* going to tell Wes?"

"Of course." I took a long drink of wine. "Eventually."

"After the wedding?"

"It won't be a huge deal. It's not like I plan on making witchcraft my life's vocation."

Sarah raised a brow at the contents of my witch kit spread across my kitchen counters. "What's all this, then?"

"Protection, I hope."

The front door opened and a few moments later Seton appeared, drenched. He looked strikingly like Mr. Darcy in that *Pride and Prejudice* movie, the one with Keira Knightley. My racing pulse made me feel in need of a calming potion.

The man is grieving. That thought only made me want to reach out and comfort him, though.

"Are you okay?" I asked.

"Just wet," he lied. "I should change clothes." He disappeared down the hall into the bathroom.

"I need to get going," Sarah said. "I'll call you tomorrow. We've only got a week to go. Aren't you excited?"

"Nervous." But not for the reasons I'd always assumed I'd be nervous before my wedding.

A few minutes after Sarah dashed out in the rain to her car, Seton came out of the bathroom in a fresh shirt and his jeans, toweling his hair dry.

Even sexier, I thought, inappropriately. I started chopping food for Django's dinner. "Sarah told me about Ruthie," I said.

He sat down, and Django sidled over to him, nipping gently at his jaw. The tender little gesture made me turn away.

"It wasn't a surprise," he said. "I shouldn't even care. If we'd divorced and I'd read about her passing in the paper thirty years later, I doubt I would have been affected by the news."

"Yes, you would have. But it's fresher now."

He absently scratched Django under his beak, the sweet spot. "Ruthie died over forty years ago. But her obituary mentioned she had a daughter, Alice Lane, who was—or maybe still is—a pediatric surgeon." He looked at me. "Think of the number of lives she must have saved."

Oh. I began to see why he'd wanted to be alone.

"How can I risk going back now?" he asked. "What if something I do back then disturbs all that?"

I swallowed. The selfish part of me wanted to seize on this to tell him to stay. But what right did I have to influence him?

"You could go back and not stand in the way of Burt and Ruthie's relationship," I said.

"Give my wife my blessing to run off with Burt, you mean? *If* he'll take her with no money of her own. That's a big if. Of course, the alternative is spending the rest of my life here, as out of place in the modern world as Dwayne the dodo."

"You're not out of place."

He leveled an incredulous look at me. "In a week I won't even have a home."

"You can stay here," I said.

"After you're married?" he said. "I'm not sure I could live here without you."

What did he mean by that? "I'm sure Dottie would rent it to you."

My phone started vibrating on the tabletop. It was Sarah.

"Turn on the news," she said.

"What's going on?" I'd been so preoccupied with personal matters, I hadn't paid attention to the news for weeks.

"A volcano erupted. In Iceland, they're shutting down air traffic."

At first I didn't get the connection.

"Martine texted me that transatlantic flights have been grounded."

"Oh, no."

"And not only that, the local news is predicting torrential rain over the Genesee Valley for the next week, at least until June second."

My wedding day was June first. Coincidence?

"You know that evil witch you were telling me about earlier?"

"Tannith," I said.

"I think she just upped her game."

At that weekend's meeting of the cupcake coven, which I took Sarah and Seton to, the talk was all about the weather situation, Tannith, and what Tannith could be planning.

"I think we have to expect that she has something worse up her sleeve," Trudy said as she placed a platter of mixed mini cupcakes on the coffee table.

"Worse than a torrential flood?" I asked.

As forecasters had predicted, there had been no letup in the rain since it started. The Genesee Valley area between Rochester and Zenobia was the eye of a precipitation dump that had mete-orologists scratching their heads.

"Things can always get worse where Tannith is concerned." Milo popped a lemon cupcake into his mouth.

I still had the same difficulty with the Tannith threat that I'd had from the moment Esme and Gwen first told me about this unseen menace. "Why is she bothering with *me*?"

"Because she can't get at Esme any other way," Milo said. "Esme's cagey—but you're her weak spot."

"You said I'm protected. I've got witch Teflon, you said."

"Witches aren't invincible," Trudy told me. "Tannith could probably squish us all like bugs under the right circumstances."

"Then why hasn't she?" Sarah asked.

"Because she's ether," Gwen explained. "Esme thinks Tan-nith would need to be in a body to cast a powerful spell against one of us. She needs a host."

"Like the eagle," Seton said.

"Right," Milo said.

"Tannith's searching for a specific host, I think," Gwen said.

Sarah frowned. "Host makes it sound like some kind of body pod in a horror movie."

Except this was real.

The thought of it made me shudder. In the following minute as we chewed our cupcakes, the only sound was the rain on Trudy's roof.

"Why the rain, though?" Seton asked.

It was a good question.

"It has to be something to do with the wedding," Milo said.

"Crashing a wedding in spectacular fashion would be right up Tannith's alley," Gwen agreed. "When I turned eight, she cast a profanity hex on the clown at my birthday party. Mom spent a week apologizing to outraged parents."

"So if we believe she has some nefarious plan for Bailey's wedding ceremony," Seton said, "shouldn't we be trying to predict how she'll mess it up?"

"Something tells me it will be more serious than a profanity hex on Judge Taylor," I said.

Milo scooted forward. "What motivated these latest tricks of hers?"

"Rain will drive the wedding inside," Sarah said.

"And crowds are easier to control indoors," Milo said. "It's harder for people to escape."

Gwen's lips twisted. "Yeah, but a volcano?"

"Maybe she isn't responsible for the volcano," I said. "They've happened before."

"It seems an awfully big coincidence," Sarah observed.

"But it doesn't really affect the wedding, except that Martine, one of my bridesmaids, might not be able to make it."

"Where is she?" Trudy asked.

"In Greece," Sarah said. "With a hot Greek innkeeper."

Milo shook his head. "Poor baby."

Gwen picked up a cupcake. "It'll be interesting to see if Martine manages to make a miraculous appearance at the ceremony after all."

The suggestion horrified me. "You mean Tannith might possess Martine?"

"It's one possible scenario," Trudy said. "The volcano could hold 'Martine' up until she can only fly in at the last moment— and by then you'll be so busy and preoccupied that you probably won't even notice that there's a witch at your wedding, in your bridal party."

"That would be a lot of effort to go through to body-snatch someone," I said. "She'll have inconvenienced thousands of people and crashed airline stocks just to get at one of my bridesmaids?"

Milo nodded. "Sounds like Tannith, all right."

* * *

By Monday, the Havermans were in even more of a swivet about the weird weather events than the cupcake coven had been. Joan invited everyone for tea at her house, and we gathered around the long polished table in her formal dining room of the Haverman mothership. Joan's housekeeper, Mona, served us finger sandwiches while we stared out the double doors at the endless rain pattering down on the back patio. Surrounding us, the wedding gifts were arranged on the two buffets and other tables brought in especially for display purposes. Calligraphy cards denoting the giver leaned against each piece, lending the room the air of a high-end hock shop.

I found myself staring at the large painting of the Freddie-Sue bridge. I couldn't unsee the upside-down pastry cutter now.

Wes's older sister, Wendy, had arrived from California with her two children, Parker and Aida, who were practicing their wedding repertoire in the adjoining den. Pachelbel's Canon on an out-of-tune cello and oboe made a fitting serenade for this gloomy day. Wendy shared Olivia's blond hair and porcelain skin, but in personality she reminded me more of Wes—there was nothing lackadaisical about her. No matter that she'd just arrived the day before, she was ready to be Joan's right hand.

Also present were Katrina, Olivia, and Madeleine, who was still in both her boot *and* her sling . . . although I suspected the sling was pure theater at this point. Wes was also supposed to be there but was running late. I'd called Mom to tell her about the tea, but she'd never answered.

Katrina, who was at the end of the table opposite Joan, tapped on her iPad as if bringing a meeting to order. "The rain shows no sign of letting up before this weekend, and the country club is being *very* stubborn about not renting us their indoor banquet hall," she announced.

Joan sighed. "The club's inflexibility is outrageous. Havermans have been members there for decades."

"Can't Dads just talk to someone?" Olivia said. "That usually works."

"They've already rented the banquet hall for that entire afternoon, to a local club," Katrina said. "The Antique Car Association of Western New York."

The Havermans looked baffled, not to mention disgusted, to be refused in favor of car geeks.

"Can't we just keep the ceremony outside but use canopies?" Wendy asked.

Olivia laughed at her sister. "Canopies? Wenster, this is, like, *torrential* flooding. Even if the canopies managed not to collapse under the weight of the deluge, the sound of the raindrops on the fabric would drown everything else out."

On the upside, it would also drown out Parker and Aida slaughtering Pachelbel.

"I have the most perfect, elegant solution," Joan announced. "Wes can get married at the new house."

Delighted gasps went up around the table.

"Judge Taylor will lead the ceremony in the living room," the matriarch continued, "and we can hold the reception in the ballroom."

"That is such an awesome idea!" Madeleine said.

The talk turned to apprising the guests, the caterers, and the rental companies of the change of venue. Katrina was on it, of course. "Mark my words, Joan, this will still be a beautiful day. All the floral arrangements, the catering, and the decorations will remain the same."

"The house is better than the boring club anyway," Olivia declared.

"Excellent!" Katrina said, happy to have the venue matter resolved, "that leaves only one question about Saturday. The third bridesmaid." Everyone swiveled toward me, which almost startling. So far, they'd been doing fine without my input.

"What is the word on our absentee bridesmaid?" Katrina asked.

"She's stuck in Greece at the moment."

Wendy frowned. "So that leaves three groomsmen and only two bridesmaids?"

"Martine hasn't said she definitely won't make it," I said. "It depends on the airlines."

"The news said it will be a week before they open up air traffic from Europe," Joan said.

"A friend of mine was stuck in Provence for two weeks the last time that volcano erupted," Olivia chimed in.

Expectation hung in the air, as if I was supposed to make some executive decision.

I didn't see the crisis. "We could just have three groomsmen and two bridesmaids. Does it matter?"

Katrina choked on her tea. "The whole ceremony will be lopsided."

"I can't tell Martine she's canceled as a bridesmaid just because planes are grounded," I said.

"Why not?" Katrina surveyed the other faces around the table. "If she can't make it, she's sort of canceling herself, isn't she?"

Nods all around.

"If symmetry matters so much," I said, "and Martine really can't make it, then we'll have to get rid of one of the groomsmen."

"Wes would never do that," Joan declared. "It would be monstrous to ask him to."

Monstrous.

"You've got Martine's dress here," Olivia said, as if the answer were obvious. "Just stick someone else in it."

I felt a knee-jerk resistance to the idea. "Even if I were okay with kicking Martine to the curb, which I'm not, I don't have anyone else I feel close enough to, to replace her with."

Olivia shrugged. "*We're* not close."

I struggled and failed to find a diplomatic response to that.

"Anyway, we can't stick just anyone in any dress. Martine's tall and slim."

Madeleine used her free arm for balance as she maneuvered herself to her feet. "Excuse me." She hobbled toward the door, trying to assume her usual loose-gaited strut, despite her clunky boot. She had a model's build and carriage.

Like Martine.

After she left the room, the others stared at me pointedly.

"No," I said.

"It makes sense," Wendy said. "Mad's so close to the family."

And for that reason I was supposed to tell Martine she'd been supplanted as bridesmaid by Wes's ex-girlfriend? No, no, no.

"The swap would also work, shoe-wise," Wendy said. "A substitute bridesmaid wouldn't work if the shoes you dyed for Martine didn't fit—and what would be the chances that they would? But Mad can wear unmatching shoes and everybody'll just chalk it up to the boot."

"I'll tell Jerry to keep her feet out of the pictures," Katrina said. "Easy-peasy."

I shook my head. "Madeleine is not usurping Martine as bridesmaid."

Joan sighed. "Well, of course she's not going to *usurp* anyone, Bailey. If, by some miracle, your friend Martina—"

"Martine."

"Exactly what I was saying—if Martina braves the sooty skies and makes it here in time, of course she'll be your bridesmaid. Madeleine's just going to be an alternate."

"Like that extra figure skater they always send to the Olympics," Katrina explained brightly.

Olivia stood and stretched. "Are we done? I'll let Mad know she's in."

"Wait just a second," I said. "I did not agree to this."

"There's nothing to agree to," Wendy said. "It's just a matter of practicality."

"And symmetry," Katrina said.

"Right." Joan stood now, too. "There's oodles to do in a very short amount of time—we all need to get busy, busy, busy. I've got a facial in fifteen minutes."

I was bleating into the void. It felt like one of those nightmares when you're trying to talk to people and nobody hears you and you realize you're invisible.

As the others were on their way out, Wes appeared, all apologies. "Sorry—my meeting with one of our distributors went on forever, and then one of the neighborhood roads was washed out and I had to take a longer route." He kissed his mom's cheeks. "Everything sorted?"

"The wedding's going to be at the new house and Madeleine's taking Martine's place as bridesmaid," Katrina summarized.

"No she's not," I said.

"She's the alternate," Katrina corrected quickly. "Like in skating."

"That's terrific," Wes said. "That way the numbers of bridesmaids and groomsmen will stay even."

Et tu, Wes?

Just then, Madeleine came thumping back in, dark eyes sparkling, her generous mouth pulled into an ear-to-ear grin. She went straight for Wes like a magnet sucked toward an iron pole. "Did you hear? I'm going to be up at the altar with you."

Wes gave her a hug. "That's so great."

Looking at them, a frisson of apprehension crept up the back of my neck.

You won't even know that there's a witch in your bridal party, Gwen had warned me. That had been when we thought Tannith would be using Martine as her host. But we were wrong. Madeleine was the one we had to watch.

"I'm *so* psyched." Madeleine kept her arm around Wes as she looked down at me, now seated alone at that long table. "I get to go to the bachelorette party now too, right? When is it?"

The bachelorette party? My mouth felt dry. "The night before the wedding, was the plan. That's all been left up to Sarah and Martine."

"Fun!" Madeleine hopped with glee on her one good leg. "Hen party! Can't wait!"

So now I had to inform Sarah that Madeleine was embedded in my wedding party—and that Tannith was possibly embedded in Madeleine.

Chapter 25

"Your turn, Olivia."

The bachelorette party was not going well.

Olivia, dressed in a tight black Hervé Leger dress that had looked fabulous at the quick wedding rehearsal Katrina had run us through at the house, uncrossed her bowling shoe–clad feet and heaved herself out of her molded plastic chair with a glare at Sarah. "When you said bowling, I thought there would be some twist to it—like male stripper bowling or something. I didn't think it would just be, you know, *bowling*."

"Me neither," Madeleine said.

I couldn't help looking at her and wondering if Tannith were inside her somewhere, observing me through Madeleine's eyes. The thought gave me a shiver.

Madeleine had more reason to pout about bowling than Olivia did. It was clear that she'd had high hopes for this evening—either to meet up accidentally with the bachelor party taking place concurrently, or to discover some compromising nugget to whisper into Wes's ear at the last minute. Also, she was still in an arm sling and a boot, so an evening at King Pin Lanes probably wouldn't have been the best choice of entertainment from her perspective even if she hadn't harbored ulterior hen night motives.

Sarah's choice surprised me, frankly. In all our years as friends, we'd never once been bowling. Now we were out in party clothes, wedged in a lane between bowling teams called the Rochester Rollers and the Lucky Strikes.

"We were going to take Bailey zip-lining," Sarah explained over Van Halen playing at deafening volume and the crash of pins in the next lane, "but with the rain, obviously that was out."

"Speaking of out, I'm leaving," Olivia declared. Then she looked at the pins lined up for her. "Right after this frame."

There really was something addictive about bowling, once you were there.

Sarah's mouth twisted into a disappointed frown. "Leaving already? I have the lane reserved for another hour."

We all watched as Olivia heaved a bowling ball off the carousel and proceeded to fling it and herself down the lane. Even so, she managed to hit the seven pin, which gave her the high score of the evening. Sarah and I whooped and cheered. Madeleine rolled her eyes, impatient now that Olivia would be bowling for the spare.

Sarah turned to her. "I'm so sorry, Madeleine. You don't seem to be having much fun. Would you like some more Tater Tots? Another Pabst Blue Ribbon?"

"No." She started gathering her things and had just managed to get to her feet when Olivia returned after her gutter-ball spare. "Come on, O. We're dressed up, we might as well hit one club tonight."

Sarah bumped my knee—a silent directive to remain seated. "Too bad," she said. "Maybe next time we can plan something you all will like better."

As if there would ever be a next time.

The two of them skulked off to return their shoes.

Sarah kept her eye on them as they dealt with the man at the rental counter.

"I've never seen Olivia that pissed off," I said, watching them stalk out. Actually, it was more emotion than I'd ever seen Wes's sister display about anything. "Well done."

"They stuck it out for an hour! I thought I was going to lose my mind."

"How long were you expecting?"

"Twenty minutes, tops?" She read something on her phone and then snapped it closed. "Okay, it's all set."

"Are we going somewhere?" I asked.

She laughed. "You didn't think we were going bowling for your bachelorette party, did you? I just wanted to shake those two without letting them know they were being shook."

"So where are we going?"

"It's a surprise."

During the drive in Sarah's Jeep, I drummed my fingers on the passenger door armrest, worrying. Since being named alternate bridesmaid, Madeleine had been throwing herself into her role—running interference with Katrina's last-minute checks, arranging for bridal party mani-pedis, and helping sort through the piles of gifts arriving at the Havermans'. She'd been on bridesmaid hyperdrive, a woman possessed. Literally, I assumed. I tried never to be around her without doubling down on my protection spell.

But she couldn't stick through an evening of bowling?

"Something's not right," I said as Sarah drove us through a residential neighborhood.

"I told you it would be a surprise."

"I'm not talking about our destination, I'm talking about Madeleine. We've been assuming she was Tannith's body pod. So why would she just walk away tonight?"

"Maybe Tannith doesn't like bowling, either."

The tingling in my hands grew stronger. Magic afoot. I checked the rearview mirrors to see if anyone was following us. But the neighborhood streets were quiet.

I thought I was ready for any surprise Sarah could throw at me, but I was speechless when she pulled up to the mini castle on Tonawanda Drive.

"Here we are." Sarah opened her door and was readying herself to make a dash through the rain, while I just sat in the front seat looking through the rain on the windshield at that big house. We'd already had the quick walk-through rehearsal tonight. The thought of going back in there made me queasy.

Which was probably not a good sign.

Sarah twisted back to me. "What's the matter?"

"This is Schadenfreude Manor. Now that we've ditched Olivia, I was hoping for my last Haverman-free evening."

"Okay, confession time. I did a little consulting with your Zenobia coven." She was giddy with excitement. "Tonight we're trespassers here. Come on."

The cupcake coven was here? That quickly, my spirits lifted.

I liked the idea of being a formal trespasser on Haverman property.

Sarah dashed ahead of me, not toward the front door, but to the side gate. As we entered the backyard, a sound other than that of rain pelting the nylon of my flimsy umbrella hit my ears—music, very faint. Jazz.

Our destination was the outbuilding where the old pool was. At the thick wood door, Sarah knocked in a peculiar pattern—three, one, two—before it was opened by a handsome, dark-haired man in a tuxedo. "Welcome to the Pool House," he said.

The mausoleum had been transformed. Gone were the leaves and the rusty furniture. The pool was scrubbed clean and filled with clear water, on top of which colorful paper lanterns floated. Urns of greenery and bougainvillea stood everywhere. At the far side of the pool, on a platform partially obscured by a line of pot-

ted palms, a group of musicians were playing a classic arrangement of "Limehouse Blues." Snowy-clothed tables and chairs
dotted the deck around the pool, most filled with people dressed
in vintage twenties clothes. Most wonderful of all, a perch had
been set up by an empty table, and Django, in a mini bow tie and
tuxedo dickie, bobbed on top of it to the infectious, jazzy tune. I
had to run over to say hello to him.

"This is living," he said.

I laughed. "How did you manage this?" I asked Sarah.

"Esme, mostly."

Esme was back again? She hadn't been kidding about liking to
decorate.

Milo, clad in a tux like all the other men, zipped over to me.
"It's about time the guest of honor arrived."

"Who are all these people?"

"You're always saying you won't have much family at your
wedding," Sarah said. "Well, meet your family."

"Family, or friends of family." Milo took my arm. "For starters,
our doorman for the night is Jeremy, Gwen's boyfriend."

Jeremy and I exchanged greetings. I liked the looks of him.
Gwen had told me he was a history professor at Zenobia College.
She hadn't mentioned he was adorable.

"And of course, that extraordinarily handsome man waving at
us is Brett Blair, Mayor of Zenobia."

Brett beamed his million-watt smile my way.

Damn. He really did look like a movie star.

Milo proceeded to lead me around to all the tables, introducing me to Jane and Tom Engel, Gwen's parents. Trudy and Marcus were at another table, along with Trudy's twin daughters,
Molly and Drew, just home from college for the summer and
looking adorable in flapper outfits. Other tables had more distant
cousins, which I assumed was the case of a woman alone at a
table not far from the empty table intended for me.

The older woman, whose head was in a turban, looked vaguely bewildered.

I laughed. Someone I actually knew, and I hadn't recognized her at first.

"Aunt Janet!" I sank into a chair opposite her. We hadn't seen each other in person since Dad's funeral. "How are you?"

"I'm fine. Your friends invited me to this party. I must say, it's quite . . . strange."

Dad's big sister at a witch party. Now I'd seen it all.

"Where's Mom?" I asked.

She blinked at me. "I haven't seen Deb today. She forwarded the invitation to this party to me, so I came here from the hotel."

"I sent an email invitation to your mom, Bailey," Sarah explained, "but I never heard back."

Strange. I hadn't heard from her in . . . how many days?

"I'll sit and talk to your aunt while you circulate," Sarah told me. "I think there's someone who'd like to say hello."

I turned, and there was Esme, resplendent in a dark blue velvet drop-waisted gown with faux black monkey fur lining the draping arms. A string of pearls a mile long hung from her neck. On her head perched a feathered headpiece with a starburst pendant in front. She enveloped me in a hug. "What do you think of your speakeasy party?"

"It's amazing. How did you do it?"

"It was a snap." Her eyes were bright. "I told you this would be a wedding present you'd never forget. And I've got amazing news for you, too." She pulled back and inspected me from head to toe. "But first things first—you are *not* dressed quite right."

Knowing what was coming, I braced myself for the crushing feeling, the shimmering of molecules. Judging from the shriek coming from the next table, Aunt Janet was *not* prepared. When she saw me decked out in a drop-waisted satiny silk dress with a long pleated skirt, her skin paled.

"Oh, my," she breathed. "I think these cocktails are stronger than I'm used to."

My gaze sought Esme's, but she waved away my worry. "Forgetting spells are easy. She'll be fine."

The band started into a rousing rendition of "Fascinating Rhythm."

"This music is incredible," I said. "Where did you find this group?"

"Nineteen twenty-four," she said.

I could feel my brow crinkle. "You aren't supposed to do that, are you?"

"I just borrowed them. I'll take them right back tonight—they'll be back before dawn their time." She bobbed on her satin-bowed shoes. "That's my big news, Bailey. I've finally cracked the code. Seton can go home."

Her words were like a bucket of ice water over my head. Now Seton really could choose to leave. And soon.

Too soon.

Esme squinted at me. "Is something wrong?"

"No—no, that's great." I plastered on a smile. "Where is Seton?"

Esme pointed a red-nailed finger toward a table partially hidden by bougainvillea blossoms. In his formal attire, Seton was heart-stoppingly handsome, but he didn't appear to be in the mood for a party, even one that seemed tailor-made for him. "You might want to have a word with him. He's feeling rather blue, for some reason." She fixed her eyes on me. "Sometimes getting what you think you want doesn't make you as happy as you expect it to."

The lively song had gotten the guests to their feet, and I threaded through the dancers to reach Seton's table. "Ask me to dance?" I said.

He looked up, eyes widening, then stood. "Gosh, you're lovely." The way he said it, though, made it sound like the worst news in the world.

In unspoken agreement, we both sat down. It was no use pretending we weren't preoccupied with Esme's news. "So you can go home." I couldn't force a smile. He would have seen through it anyway.

He nodded.

"You don't want to go?"

He cupped the glass in front of him and fixed his eyes on the amber liquid in it. "No."

"Oh."

"I don't have any right to say any more," he said. "I busted in on your life, I know."

"You certainly did." Heat spread through me. I couldn't tell which was the stronger emotion in me at that moment, happiness or fear.

"And tomorrow you're going to be married."

Something shifted in me then. All my years of caution, of risk avoidance, came crashing around my ears.

"I'm *supposed* to be married tomorrow."

The dullness cleared from his expression. "What are you saying?"

What *was* I saying? "Just that tomorrow is still a night away."

Hope sparked in his eyes. The same hope that was blooming in me, and made me feel lighter than I had in weeks.

"Let me start over." He reached across the table. "Dance with me?"

Whether it was fate, or magic, the band started playing "I'll See You in My Dreams."

We stood, and Seton put his arms around me. Mom was right—he was a wonderful dancer. I wasn't, but neither of us cared. I hung on and followed his lead. It was the eve of my wedding to another man, the moment when Seton should be celebrating going back to his proper time, but none of that mattered. Somehow, despite everything, this felt right.

"What does this song remind you of?" I whispered.

He looked into my eyes. "Dropping off on a couch, wishing I had the nerve to knock on your door."

He put his cheek to mine, and held me closer. After a moment, he said, "Actually, I used to play this song."

"Did you?"

"It was a hit. In fact, we played this very arrangement—right down to that trumpet riff Arnie used to play."

"It's nice. The sax reminds me of how you play saxophone, too."

His footsteps slowed, then stopped. He pulled back, a stricken, confused expression on his face.

That look frightened me. "Seton?"

He shook his head, craning to see around the palms. Then his skin went chalky. "That's Boyd and His Hot Beavers."

I laughed. "Your college band?"

"No, really."

"They can't be." I glanced over at the band of seven young men. One of them caught my eye—the saxophone player—and I felt the blood from my face drain to my heels. It was Seton. Nineteen twenty-four Seton. Like the Seton standing next to me, he was wearing a tux. Only his hair seemed slightly different—the same center-parted, pomaded mess that Seton's had been when I'd first encountered him.

Sweat popped out on my Seton's forehead. He looked as frantic as he'd been when I first encountered him in my rearview mirror. "How can this be happening?"

"Esme said she heard them when she was traveling and brought them back for my party."

"But that me *can't* be here," Seton said, growing agitated. "*I'm* here."

I tried to imagine running into myself. I would probably freak out, too.

"Find Esme," he said. "She has to send him back."

He strode toward the dais. I grabbed at his suit jacket to stop him, but he was laser focused.

"Boyd!" he called out. "Boyd, it's me!"

The music fizzled to a stop. The conductor took in Seton,

then stared at his identical saxophone player, confused. His baton hand dropped. "What . . . ?"

The saxophone player stood up then and hopped down from the stage. The two Setons circled each other. "You can't be here," my Seton said.

"Who *are* you?" asked the other.

Esme bustled toward me in a flurry of velvet and fur. "Is there a—" She spotted the problem. "Oh, dear."

"You have to send him back," Seton said. "Or . . ."

"I was hired to play this gig," the 1924 Seton said. "I'm not going anywhere."

"But you must, don't you see?" Seton was beyond agitated now. "You're ruining everything!"

I tugged on his sleeve again. "It's okay, Seton."

"No, it's not—we can't *both* exist, can we? If something goes wrong with him, what will happen to me? To us?"

Esme's hands rose in front of her in a faux fur flutter. "We'll work it out. The band will just have to go back."

Now Boyd was angry. "Wait a minute—we haven't been paid yet."

Before anyone could act, the younger Seton took a swing at his older self. Seton grabbed the other Seton's jacket, and together, the two of them launched into a knock-down, drag-out fight. They swung at each other, but, well matched, neither seemed to get the upper hand. Finally, they stopped swinging and began wrestling at the edge of the pool. In a tangle of arms and legs, they fell into the water.

Esme shook her head. "This is not good."

"You've got to do something," I urged her. "Zap that old Seton back to 1924."

"Which one?" she asked as they flailed in the water, still fighting.

And then I remembered. *We laughed about it once when we were on the Staten Island Ferry.* Seton couldn't swim. They weren't fighting anymore—they were drowning.

I pushed forward to the edge of the pool and, without another thought, dove into the water. Inserting myself between two drowning men was not a smart thing to do. I got dunked, too, and inhaled a lungful of water before I felt someone else come up behind me. Milo and Brett were also in the pool now. From the deck, Marcus helped fish the two Setons out.

The men lay coughing, half drowned.

"I'll get him back to 1924 as soon as possible," Esme said. "But which one?"

They were two identical, drenched men in tuxes, so at first it was hard to sort out. I knelt between them, and finally one of them took my hand. He looked into my eyes. "Bailey," he said, and he squeezed my hand, sending an electric pulse straight to my heart. "I'll see you in . . ."

He closed his eyes.

"No!" I cried.

Marcus tugged me away and started first aid.

Chapter 26

We took Seton back to the duplex while Esme tended to returning 1924 Seton, Boyd, and the rest of the Beavers to the past. Gwen and Sarah helped me with my Seton, but as we laid him on the bed in my room, I could tell from the grim set of Gwen's jaw that the situation was as fraught with potential disaster as I feared it was. "What if Esme gets it wrong?" I asked.

Gwen shook her head. "She said she was sure she had cracked the secret of pinpointing time."

I couldn't banish the memory of Esme after she'd returned from her prehistoric error. "She could accidentally send him back to be eaten by a tyrannosaurus, or accidentally materialize him during a plague year. And if something happens to Esme's Seton, what will become of my Seton?"

"Don't worry about that now."

"Just tell me, Gwen. If Seton's 1924 self dies, what will happen?"

She swallowed. "I imagine he'll . . . expire."

Seton had never really recovered from nearly drowning. Now he lay on the bed, inert.

"To have him taken from me just as . . ."

He *couldn't* die. Not when we'd decided to try to make a start of . . . something.

Sarah wrung her hands. "Oh, Bailey. I'm so sorry."

"No one's taken him from you yet," Gwen said. "Trust Esme."

I took a deep breath that threatened to become a ragged laugh. "And to think I was worried about Tannith." This was a thousand times worse than any wedding threat.

"We still have to worry about her," Gwen insisted.

I didn't even care about the wedding anymore.

Gwen and Sarah wanted to stay, but I insisted that they go home. To have everyone sitting around my living room now, faces pinched with worry, felt too much like a death watch. Or a wake.

Around one a.m. I went through the motions of putting Django to bed and clearing the kitchen, although every five minutes I had to run and check to see that Seton was still stable. He breathed regularly, but he was suspended in a deep sleep.

The doorbell rang and I ran to get it, hoping it would be Esme with good news.

It was Wes. "Hey, Buttercup," he said, but the endearment sounded forced and wooden.

"What are you doing here?" I said, unable to keep the impatience out of my voice.

"Aren't you going to ask me in?"

Reluctantly, I stepped aside. "You'll have to be quiet. Seton's not feeling well."

"Seton." He ran a hand through his hair. "So he *is* still living here."

"Yes."

"That's what Mad said." He shook his head. "Bailey, what's going on?"

I crossed my arms. "What do you mean?"

"Mad and O met up with us tonight. Mad was so upset. They said you made them go bowling. How could you? You know Mad has a sprained ankle and a bad shoulder."

I couldn't help it—I laughed. Olivia, Madeleine, and bowling were so far from anything I cared about right now.

"Why are you acting so strangely?" he asked. "You're in some wild getup and you look like you got soaked. Is that what you wore to go bowling? Did you walk home or something?"

I looked down at the flapper dress I hadn't bothered to change out of. The wet satin had dried—almost—to a crinkly mess. "I fell in some water."

"What is going on?" His face was anguished. "Please tell me, Bailey. We haven't been close for weeks, and to me it feels as if just as we're getting married, we're coming apart."

At the anguish in his voice, shame suffused me. I'd already let him go, but I hadn't told him. I hadn't even admitted it to myself until tonight. But deep down a part of me had always known I could never be a Haverman. For weeks I'd been operating under the delusion that I could keep my witchiness under control the way my father had managed his diabetes. But this wasn't a condition, or a disease. It was me.

"I'm a witch," I said.

The impatience in his face melted into shock. "A what?"

"A witch," I said. "My parents adopted me from a witch. My mother is Esme Zimmer of Zenobia, and my father is Odin Klemperer of . . ." I frowned. ". . . Somewhere. He's one of the most formidable witches of his generation."

Wes's neck crooked. "Is there a Who's Who of witchcraft?"

I set a calming shield around myself. It had taken almost crashing into a tree for me to believe I was really a witch. I couldn't expect Wes to swallow the whole story all at once. As logically and rationally as I could, though, I laid out my proof, much as I had for Sarah, pointing out all the things that had happened, large and small, over the past weeks.

And Wes listened. He really did. At times I could tell he was biting his tongue in an effort not to interrupt. His face flashed between pale and uncomfortably red, and his eyebrows kept shooting up into his forehead. But he heard me out.

"So you're saying that this"—he gulped at the ridiculousness of it, as if it pained him even to form the words—"this *wicked witch* caused the volcano that has shut down traffic on two continents, and is flooding our city, just to stop our wedding?"

"Not to stop it. We—my family—think she has something planned. She's trying to corner Esme into a moment of vulnerability, through me."

He sucked in a breath and closed his eyes. He seemed to be holding something back, trying not to speak, but he couldn't help himself. "Mother warned me that you weren't like us."

Heat crept up my neck. "Your mother knew I was a witch?"

"God, no." He shook his head. "She thought you were in over your head. That's why she arranged for Katrina to help you, and for Olivia to be a bridesmaid. She wanted our people around you helping you."

There was so much to unpack in what he'd just said. But the first thing that came out of my mouth was, "She thought Olivia would be *helpful?*" I laughed. "Olivia won't even drive her best friend to the ER."

"My point is, I underestimated just how much the stress would affect you."

"This isn't about wedding stress. This is me—and from what you're saying, you and your family had plenty of doubts about me already." I mean honestly. *Over my head?*

"Just mother. And Olivia." He crooked his head, considering. "And Wendy."

If I gave him more time to think about it, he'd be telling me that Parker and Aida didn't like me, either.

"What did you really come here to say, Wes? Just tell me. Because I'll be frank. I don't want to marry someone who doesn't accept me, witchy warts and all." Now that the truth was spilling out of me, I decided I might as well go for the full Niagara Falls. "And you were right about Seton. He's living here. He isn't my cousin, he's a time traveler from 1930. I haven't cheated on you with him, except for a couple of kisses. But he's made me realize that there would be nothing worse, nothing lonelier, than living with someone I don't love with all my heart."

Wes looked down. He didn't really need to speak now. I'd always known the one thing he couldn't stand was cheating. It was over. For a moment it felt as if the earth rumbled. Maybe earthshattering moments were a literal thing.

I didn't feel shattered, though. Regretful, yes. We'd both been dancing away from the truth for too long now. And then there was the practical side of things to consider: undoing a wedding was bound to be as tricky as planning it, and I doubted I'd have Katrina helping me out through the undoing part.

But then Wes looked up again. And he was smiling. "It's okay, Bailey."

I nodded, already tugging off my engagement ring. "I know. We can always be friends."

He laughed, reaching forward and clasping my hands. A jolt of electricity shot up my arm. "No—I mean it's *all* okay. I admire you for your honesty, and I love you just as you are—witch and all."

Confusion muddled my brain. "Really."

"Yes."

"What about Seton?" I asked.

"A crush?" He lifted his shoulders. "*Everyone* looks. We're all human, aren't we?"

"Wes, I'm telling you that I would happily have slept with Seton tonight if . . ." Well, that required a lot more explanation than I had the energy for.

"But you didn't, did you? That's fidelity, Bailey."

No, that was falling for someone who met with a tragic timetraveling mishap.

"The only thing I wouldn't be able to accept is if we weren't married tomorrow." Wes swallowed. "Today."

This was fishy as hell. Wes, understanding my lusting after another guy?

And what was with the hands? He'd never set off my electric hands, had he? That jolt had come from *him*.

I proceeded carefully. "And what about my family?" I asked, keeping my voice steady. "My witch family, I mean."

"They'll be welcome in our lives, too."

That decided it for me. The Wes I knew would never be excited to have Esme—or anyone claiming to be a witch—as an in-law.

"Your parents might not be so enthusiastic about that."

"I'll talk to them. Anyway, I'm sure your family will be able to win them over." He grinned. "Aren't witches good at enchanting people?"

I forced a smile. Esme Zimmer charm Joan Haverman? The sky would be thick with flying pigs before that happened. Wes would know that.

"So we're good?" he asked.

It was difficult, but I pushed the ring back onto my finger. "Of course. I'm so glad you understand."

He grinned, and enfolded me in a hug. "I can hardly wait for tomorrow, darling."

He'd never called me darling before.

"Today," I corrected.

He kissed me.

Correction: Possessed Wes kissed me. This was not him. It took my entire calming shield not to jump out of my own skin at the grossness of it.

As soon as I pushed him away, protesting that I needed my beauty sleep and that after tonight we'd never have to spend another night apart, Possessed Wes turned and left, practically skipping down the walkway to his Escalade.

First I wiped my mouth with my crinkly satin sleeve. Then I pulled my phone out of my pocket and speed-dialed Gwen.

"How's Seton?" she asked at once.

I hurried to my bedroom doorway and looked in. "The same."

"Okay . . ." She was understandably confused about why I was calling.

"You know how you told me that we still needed to worry about Tannith?"

"Yes."

"I just heard from her," I said. "She'll be at the wedding today. As the groom."

Chapter 27

Schadenfreude Manor was decorated to the nines by the time I arrived the next day. The rental people had shown up bright and early to set up chairs and tables. The floral bower looked slightly out of place but still beautiful in the living room; as Katrina had said, it was paid for and it would be a shame to let it go to waste. Flowers and ribbons festooned every surface. The house buzzed with caterers getting ready in the kitchen and setting up for the reception in the ballroom. The wedding gift display had been transferred from Joan's dining room to this house's dining room.

Katrina had been so occupied directing the various tradesmen all morning that she seemed to automatically assume I was one of them when she spotted me in the foyer loaded down with my garment bag and a tote bag full of toiletries, shoes, and several liter bottles of potions. Then she did a double take.

"Oh, it's you!" She gestured with both hands to the stairs, like airport crew marshaling a jumbo jet to the airstrip. "I have the bridal party up in the blue bedroom. I've set out hanging racks, two full-length mirrors, and a double-wide portable vanity table supplied with curling iron, emergency sewing kit, veggie tray, mineral water, and a bottle of Veuve Clicquot for you and the bridal party. Please don't overdo the champagne. Drunk bride is never a good look."

"Is everything okay?" I asked. She looked a little frantic.

"I'm fine, although I have to say there are more people here than I expected." She pointed to a man in coveralls passing through who winked at me as soon as Katrina looked away from him. "I think that's a gardener, but I don't know who he belongs to."

The he in question—Jeremy—belonged to Gwen. The Zenobia clan were all going to be there today, blending in as gardeners, florists, catering staff, and guests. Tannith might sniff them out anyway, but as Milo said, why make it easy for her?

"More hands make lighter work," I told Katrina.

She gave me a thumbs-up. "I like that briditude!"

I hurried upstairs, found the blue bedroom, and laid down my stuff on the vanity table so I could check my phone. Marcus had agreed to stay with Seton during the wedding.

No change, he wrote in response to my last inquiry about Seton's condition.

That was disappointing, but not unexpected. Seton's fate depended on Esme's success in the past, but not one had heard from Esme since she'd dematerialized with the band last night.

I scrolled down and found a message from Mom. She'd called me this morning to tell me she'd gone to Aunt Janet's hotel to pick her up for the wedding and discovered her in a daze, complaining of memory loss from the night before. She was taking her to the ER, but hoped to be in time for the wedding. Now she was sending me updates.

Janet in with doctor.

And then, later: **Janet in Xray. LOL.**

I felt bad for not being able to tell her the truth. How many healthcare dollars were spent each year trying to diagnose witch-craft-related issues?

At this point, I would have preferred that Mom *not* make it to the wedding. She'd be safer staying away. But the coven thought it was best to proceed as normally as possible. Tannith was supposedly targeting my birth mother, not my real mother, but she might have realized she'd been twigged if I advised my own mom to stay away.

With nothing else to do now, I went ahead and got into the wedding gown Esme had made for me. I twirled in front of the mirror. The dress looked just as good as it had when Esme had first put it on me. I loved the way the beadwork looked, and the graceful drape of it. Esme really was a sorceress with a Singer.

Sarah burst into the room like a tangerine-colored sunbeam. "He's here!" she shouted, then stopped in her tracks. "Holy moly—you look fantastic! You really did find the perfect wedding dress."

"Unfortunately, I didn't find the right groom." I went over to my tote bag and pulled out a tumbler and some of the strength potion I'd found a recipe for on BrewTube late last night. I'd made some to give to Seton if he ever woke up—but then I realized Sarah might need some for the ceremony. She'd been apprised of the fact that this was not going to be a real wedding, and that the groom was possessed. None of us knew exactly what would happen. I wanted to give her any hex protection I could.

I handed her a glass of the brew. I'd poured some for myself, too, and we clinked glasses. "Bottoms up."

And that's when I saw it: a diamond, winking on her finger.

I let out a cry of shock. "Are you kidding me? What happened?"

She held out her hand, admiring the ring. "Dave didn't go to Albuquerque after all. He said he couldn't stand to be away from me, and that the next time he went to a conference on palatal expansion, it would be with me at his side."

I gave her a hug. I was so happy for her.

"I told you weddings were lucky," she said. "We're thinking of merging our practices."

"That's so great." I reached for the champagne bottle. Now we really had something to celebrate. "Were you not going to tell me?"

Her smile faded. "I'm just so worried about you, Bailey. Are you sure you don't want to just cancel all this?"

I struggled with the cork. "I thought about calling it off last night when I was talking to Wes, but then I realized Tannith had gotten to him. I can't just leave him like that."

"Maybe Tannith would vacate him if you canceled the wedding, though."

"Right—and then who would she attack next? Seton again—or you? This is my best chance to have a showdown with her. And I'll have my coven with me."

I popped the champagne cork just as the door banged open and Olivia came slinking in, followed by Madeleine, thumping along in her boot. Madeleine's face was pale, her eyes bloodshot. Both of them were loaded down with tote bags, although they were already made up and dressed in their seafoam-green and pink bridesmaid dresses, respectively.

Seeing my bridal party all together for the first time, I realized Olivia wasn't wrong. They really were Necco Wafer colors.

Olivia was stunned by my dress. "Where did you find *that?*"

"It was custom-made."

"Damn—I wish you'd had it made before we wasted all that time sitting around bridal shops."

"Guess what?" I held up Sarah's hand. "Sarah's engaged."

"Really?" As if she needed convincing, Olivia moved closer to inspect the engagement ring. "That's a good-sized chip. Congratulations."

Madeleine's lips pursed. "Is that what we're drinking to? Because I could use some of that champagne."

I poured out four glasses.

Madeleine couldn't even bring herself to congratulate Sarah, or even raise her glass. She gulped hers down and asked, "Has anyone seen Wes today?"

"It's bad luck for a groom to see the bride." Sarah shot me a look as if to say, *And we've had enough bad luck already.*

"Why are you asking?" I wondered if Madeleine had seen him—and sensed the change.

Two patches of red appeared in Madeleine's cheeks. "I just thought he might have done some thinking since last night. When I was telling him about the bowling, he seemed really upset that you'd be so insensitive to someone with my disability."

"A sprained ankle isn't a disability," Sarah said.

"That depends on how much fashionable footwear means to you." She sniffed. "These past two weeks have been *very* difficult for me. Wes understands that."

Olivia sighed. "Come on, Mad. Buck up." She sent us a look that was pure exasperation. "She was like this the whole time we were at Anton's getting our hair done. It's pathetic."

"I did not consent to be a bridesmaid just to be insulted," Madeleine said. "It's bad enough that I'm wearing the yellow dress when Sarah gets to wear tangerine, which is *my* color."

Olivia plopped down, uncapped a can of hairspray, and sprayed enough to guarantee that no hair would dare step out of line. "Is Seton coming today?"

I hid my distress behind a cough. "He's not feeling well."

She released a languid sigh. "Too bad—seeing him was the only thing about today that seemed worth looking forward to."

Madeleine sank into the chair next to her and downed half a flute of champagne. "This is the worst day of my life."

If I'd been looking forward to getting married to Wes, the time might have dragged. As it was, I was so nervous about what might happen today that it felt as if the minutes were slipping away too fast. I texted Marcus again and was stunned by his reply.

He opened his eyes.

Without thinking, I let out a bleat of happiness.

The others turned to me.

"Seton's feeling better," I explained, unable to control the out-of-control hope blooming in me. I just needed to get through this day.

Madeleine clunked her glass down. "You are shameless."

"Because I'm happy that my cousin's feeling better?"

She snorted. "Your 'cousin.' Please." She drank the rest of her champagne and poured another glass.

Sarah looked nervously between Madeleine and me.

A knock sounded at the door, and in the next moment Mom breezed into the room. She took one look at me and burst into tears.

"Oh—you're so beautiful. You were absolutely right about the dress."

I gave her a hug, then handed her some strength potion in a champagne flute.

"I'm so glad we made it—I was beginning to worry." She drank some and nearly gagged. "That champagne's flat."

"Where's Aunt Janet?" I asked.

She put the glass down. "Downstairs—I went ahead and got her seated, poor thing. The doctors couldn't find anything wrong with her." She lowered her voice, darting anxious looks at Madeleine, who was swilling champagne. "One said she might have been a little too free with the hotel minibar."

"Seton said you were out of town," I said.

She blushed. "Ron and I went to New York to catch a show and stayed over an extra day at the Marriott."

I swallowed. "Wow. When was this?"

"We decided to go that day I saw you last—you know, when I went to see him about the business shares?"

I frowned. The day I'd gone over with the peace offering of cupcakes.

Love-infused cupcakes. "Oh."

She squeezed my arm. "You were so understanding. It made all the difference to me. Ron said I seemed to have a new confidence."

"What happened to your Florida plan?"

She laughed. "I said I was going to keep my options open."

But my stupid cupcakes had steered her toward Option Ron. How could I have forgotten the cupcakes? I should have taken them with me. And poor Mom didn't even know that she'd been duped by a love spell. A love spell that seemed to make her very happy, but still . . .

"Mom—"

Katrina poked her head in the door. "It's showtime, folks!"

Madeleine stood. "Already?" There were tears in her eyes. "Is Wes here?"

"Wes, the groom?" Katrina frowned. "Um, yeah. Did you think he'd be getting married via Zoom?"

No, she hoped he wouldn't be getting married at all.

We lined up at the staircase and waited for Parker, installed with Aida in an alcove down below, to start sawing those first notes of the Pachelbel Canon in D on his cello. Butterflies flapped against my stomach. I almost wished I'd agreed to walk on Mr. Haverman's arm after all; I felt alone and exposed right now.

Strangely, the sight of a cater waiter standing behind Jerry the videographer in the foyer bolstered my confidence. The older man, who was handsome despite being egg bald, looked up at me with startling blue eyes. I didn't know him from Adam, but he sent me an avuncular smile and even an encouraging nod of his head.

The music began and my Necco Wafer attendants and I started down the steps. My legs felt shaky as I reached the bottom of the staircase. But not as shaky as Madeleine's shoulders. She'd forgone her sling for today, so I wondered if that had something to do with her visible trembling. It wasn't until I heard a loud sniff that I realized she was sobbing.

"For God's sake," Olivia hissed at her. "Grow. Up."

Poor Madeleine. I would have liked to reassure her that this wasn't the worst day of her life, but to be honest, I didn't know what was going to happen. When we entered the flower-bedecked living room and I found myself walking toward Judge Taylor and the tuxedoed men waiting by the bower, I could tell at a glance that the glassy-eyed Wes standing there was Tannith within Wes. *Game on, Wannith.*

The only question now was when Tannith was going to make her power play.

I looked away from that disarming gaze and glanced across the gathered guests. Most of the blur of faces were Haverman invitees, whom I didn't know. I picked out my mom and Ron up toward the front, twisted in their seats to grin at me encouragingly. Aunt Janet, dazed, sat next to Mom. And Dave, so over his marriage phobia that he'd rented a formal morning suit with tails for the occasion, only had eyes for Sarah. The Havermans were across the aisle, and next to Joan and Mr. Haverman was an ancient woman. Was Wes's grandmother still alive? He'd never mentioned her. Looking at the elderly woman, and knowing she'd probably had a difficult time getting here for this sham of a ceremony, I felt guilty. The Havermans hadn't asked for any of this. They were Havermonsters, but I didn't bear them any ill will.

The bridesmaids turned to the left at the bower as we'd done at rehearsal—all except Madeleine, who stopped in front of the judge as if prepared to stand her ground. Olivia grabbed her friend's arm and tugged her to the side, like a stage manager giving a bad comic the hook. Sarah smiled at me nervously and gave a subtle eye roll.

I hoped her strength potion held up.

What was Tannith waiting for?

When I was finally standing next to my possessed groom, Judge Taylor took a deep breath and looked out over the rows of guests to begin. "Friends—"

"I object."

All eyes turned to Madeleine, who hobbled back toward Wes and me.

Judge Taylor looked baffled. "It's not time to object. That comes later."

Madeleine wasn't backing down. "I object right now." She pushed me aside and clomped right up to Wes. "I love you. I've always loved you. Yes, I slept with that lacrosse player, but I was twenty and it was spring break. Do you honestly think I would have jeopardized our entire future together if it hadn't been for those Long Island Iced Teas?" A tear ran down her cheek. "Those are strong drinks. And no one over the age of twenty-one drinks Long Island Iced Tea anyway, so it's not like I was ever going to do that again."

"You really do need to stand aside," Judge Taylor insisted.

She stomped her booted foot, then winced. "I have a right to object." She lifted her chin. "You're a judge—you should know that."

I was curious what real Wes would have done in this circumstance. Wannith seemed torn. Tannith had intended to ruin the wedding, I was certain of that. But here was Madeleine, seizing control of its ruination from her. Finally, her interruption became too much for Possessed Wes.

"Sit down," he said, in a voice that practically breathed fire.

"She doesn't even love you, Wes," Madeleine insisted. "She's in love with that so-called cousin of hers. Everybody can see it."

"No, Madeleine, everyone can see you making a big fool of yourself." He turned back to Judge Taylor. "Go on with the service."

Another voice shouted, "I also object!"

A murmur went through the guests. The old lady sitting next to the Havermans, who looked frozen in horror, leapt to her feet with unexpected agility.

"Who are you?" the judge asked with growing irritation.

The old lady pulled off her gray wig, revealing a thick head of brassy orange hair. Aunt Esme! I hadn't spotted her. Spinning, she raised her hands and cast a spell, freezing the well-dressed guests as she waved her arms across the rows. "I am Esme Zimmer of Zenobia," she announced, pinning the groom with her sharp gaze. "Tannith, show yourself!"

Wannith shook his head as if to deny the crazy accusation, but then, lightning fast, he raised his hand and Esme was shot into the air. The speed of it, the violence, made me gasp. I wasn't the only one caught off guard. Esme's eyes blinked in shock but her voice had been silenced as easily as she had once silenced Django.

Frantically, I looked around me. The room was a tableau of statue-still bodies. All the Haverman invitees, Mom and Ron, Jeremy, Sarah and Olivia, weeping Madeleine, Katrina and Jerry, and even Parker and Aida in the back with their instruments—none of them could move. This left only the members of my coven, who I assumed were all still present and unfrozen.

My family hadn't been overstating Tannith's powers. In Wes's voice, she addressed the furious, kicking Esme dangling near the ceiling.

"Esme Zimmer, because of you and your relations casting an illegal disappearance spell, I've been forced to possess this body. But it's not this body I want."

Quick as a viper, Wannith whipped out a hand and grabbed me. My whole being felt the shock—so much that I feared it might stop my heart. "If my own corpus is to be lost, I demand the possession of this witch, Bailey Tomlin, descendant of Esme Zimmer. Corpus for corpus."

What was she saying? That *I* was going to be her body pod, now and for the rest of my life? I looked pleadingly up at Esme, but her voice had been cut, and her feet kicked in fury.

Wannith smiled. "Just nod if you agree, Esme."

Gwen, who with Trudy had been hiding among the guests, stood. "I'm the one who disappeared you, Tannith. Take me."

Wannith sneered. "Your pathetic shell holds no appeal to me. I will embody the daughter of Esme Zimmer. If this is allowed me, I will not approach the Grand Council of Witches to report the unlawful, dangerous spellcraft employed by the Zimmer-Engel clan and reinstate the ban on your practice of witchcraft."

"What illegal spellcraft?" Trudy asked. "You have no proof."

"*Hello?*" Wannith said. "I've been a poltergeist for the past six months. You think *that's* okay?"

"That was just supernatural error," Gwen said.

Wannith smirked. "Okay, how about this little guy?" She snapped her fingers and a hologram of Dwayne the Dodo appeared next to Esme. "How many laws of spellcraft are broken to bring an extinct creature forward from the past?" She sighed. "Once the Council finds out, they'll be making your little friend extinct again."

There were so many reasons to hate her, but somehow her glee at the idea of Dwayne's being put down made me as angry as anything.

Gwen looked up at Esme, then back at Wannith. "We would never allow you to take one of our own."

"Even if it meant the death of one of your own?"

Was she talking about me? My death? Of course, being Tannith's body pod was a kind of death, too. From my point of view, this was starting to feel like a big lose-lose situation. I struggled to free myself from Wannith's grasp, but fighting just sent more pain shooting through me. My protection shield was woefully inadequate.

In a cater waiter uniform, Milo appeared at the back of the room. "Possessed Wes is it!" he yelled.

Suddenly, as if it were a life-and-death game of hex tag, Milo, Gwen, and Trudy were shooting freezing spells toward the bower. Some of them hit me, but Tannith managed to deflect them all. And not only deflect, but to throw even stronger freeze hexes in return. I could only watch in despair as my cousins dropped, one by one. Above us, Esme's face went crimson in fury.

And then the bald man I'd seen by the staircase stepped forward. A spell shot out of his arm and rocketed toward us like a lightning bolt. In less than a blink, it slammed into Wannith's chest. The grip on me released and I stumbled to the floor. So did Wannith. Before she could grab me again, I scrambled to my feet. Anger shot out of me like sparks—literally. I pelted Wannith with my own baby bolts, which probably were nothing more than pinpricks in the grand scheme of things.

The bald man put his hand on my shoulder, not so much to calm me as to center me. I was wasting energy.

"Witches," he said, summoning the rest of the cousins to pick themselves up. "Gather."

Trudy, Gwen, and Milo rose and approached us, and we all formed a semicircle around the bald guy and Possessed Wes, who still lay on the ground, inert.

With an incantation of words I'd never read in any of the books in Esme's laboratory, the bald man cast another spell at Wannith, whose body began to convulse. And then a form rose up out of Wes's body—partially materialized, part spirit. I could make out kaleidoscopic fragments of green eyes, shimmering dark hair, long fingers with blood-red nails like talons. Muffled curses emanated from the flashing, fragmented vision, which swirled before us like a funnel cloud.

We cousins focused all our energy on the Tannith cloud. Our focus hummed through my body; the more intensely we concentrated, the faster the cloud spun and condensed until it gained speed and began to fold in on itself. The sound that shrieked out from the cloud made me want to cover my ears, but my hands were forward, all power within me directed at making that last smidgeon of Tannith implode. I squinted my eyes closed so that I barely saw when the spirit winked out completely.

We lowered our arms, but it took a moment for my coven to recover. Especially me. I felt wrung out, boneless. Had we just defeated Tannith? I couldn't quite believe it.

The one witch who required no recovery was the bald man, who turned immediately toward Esme, still dangling—although now her arms were crossed, the expression on her face impatient. With great care, he brought her back to the ground.

When the two of them hugged, I knew. This man was Odin Klemperer, my witch father.

Esme disentangled herself from his embrace and rushed toward me. I found myself smothered in a hug. "Thank the Great Tree you're all right! Didn't I tell you that your father was a force to be reckoned with?"

Odin winced modestly. "Esme told me I'm your father, Bailey, but she also told me about your real father. Those are shoes I could never fill."

I swallowed. It felt strange to be having this family reunion in front of an entire roomful of unconscious people, including my own frozen mother.

"You saved my life," I said. "That's a good start."

Esme put her hands on her hips as she mock glared at Odin. "I don't know why you had to leave me dangling up there for so long, though."

He shrugged. "We have to give the kids a chance to do hands-on work, Es."

Esme harrumphed as she took in Gwen and Milo, standing up and stretching out the hex effect. I was feeling it myself. "We're going to have to redouble our training. That was the sorriest show I've seen in all my witch years."

"But what happened to Tannith?" I asked.

Odin frowned. "Tannith has gone back in time. Way back. She can tangle with velociraptors now."

Esme scanned the room and started flexing her fingers in anticipation of more witch work ahead. "Now we just need to figure out how to unhex all these guests and make our escape before they wake up. I haven't cast a delay spell in a while."

I looked at my friends over in the bride's corner. "I hate to leave them. What will they all think?"

Milo smiled at me. "That you came down with the world's biggest case of bridal jitters."

"That's actually true." I was still shaky.

Trudy took in the scene of the old, paneled room covered in flowers, the bower, and the frozen guests in their wedding finery. She sighed. "It's too bad. It really was going to be a beautiful ceremony."

I nodded. And yet I was *so* glad that things were different. I was already itching to check my phone for any update on Seton.

Esme noticed Madeleine, her face still frozen in a plaintive pout. "This one has a lot of nerve, though. I wouldn't mind treating her to a parting hex."

She was probably joking, but I put my hand on her arm. "Leave her alone. I think she and Wes might really belong together after all."

Esme's lips twisted from side to side as she considered this, and then she laughed. "Well, she was right about one thing. You really do have to be careful with those Long Island Iced Teas."

Chapter 28

Martine sent me a picture of herself and her innkeeper, Christos, toasting my happiness on a sun-bleached patio by the Mediterranean.

I replied with a big thumbs-up.

Right now Mom was sitting on the armchair in my living room. She'd come by to check on me, and to drop by the things I'd left at Schadenfreude Manor in my hurry to flee before all the wedding guests woke up.

"It was a little uncomfortable with the Havermans." She regarded me first, then Seton. We sat on the couch together, along with Django. "Everyone felt sorry for Wes. That poor man really looked like he'd been through the wringer."

"I'm sorry I left you to deal with the aftermath," I said. "I was in a hurry to get back to check on Seton. He wasn't feeling well."

Mom smiled. "He looks better now—and I can guess why."

Not in a million years. Esme swore she'd returned Boyd and His Beavers exactly where she'd found them, and it seemed to have worked, because Seton was his normal self again. But Mom obviously thought he'd popped back to perfect health because I wasn't marrying Wes.

Come to think of it, that news had perked him up, too.

"Doug Haverman was telling me that they were probably going to use the honeymoon tickets to send Wes somewhere to recuperate." Her eyes widened. "Oh—you were going to Cancun on your honeymoon."

"Dollars to donuts Madeleine will just happen to come across a bargain flight to Mexico," I said.

Mom nodded. "When it was discovered that you were gone, she was suddenly able to walk without her boot again. It was a wedding miracle."

I laughed. "Today seems to have been a lucky day for all sorts of couples."

"Weddings are supposed to bring people together, aren't they?" Seton asked.

Mom cleared her throat. "What are you planning on doing now, Seton?"

He glanced at me, then looked away quickly. "I'm not sure. Gil mentioned my helping him in his store. I think I'd enjoy that."

"And I'm going to start teaching piano again in the evenings," I said.

"'If music be the food of love, play on,'" Django said joyfully.

Mom's brow scrunched. "That bird *is* clever. If you worked with him a little and maybe taught him a song, you might get him on one of those late-night shows."

"And have him become more insufferable than he already is?" I asked. "No thanks."

Django flapped at me.

"Well, you know best." Mom sighed and got to her feet. "I'd better go. I left Ron back at the house with your aunt Janet. We're taking her to the airport tomorrow morning. Maybe you could come have breakfast with us."

"I will," I said.

"Oh, and I slipped a little treat into your tote bag—those cupcakes you brought over the other week. I had a few left over that I put in the freezer. They're awfully good. Ron liked them, too."

I debated telling her the part those cupcakes might have played in her romantic life, but decided against it. I was starting to believe in second chances—no matter how they came about.

When she was gone, I went back in and collapsed onto the couch. Seton drew me to him. "Are you sure you're okay?"

I sank against his chest and he slipped his arm around me as if we'd been cuddling all our lives. The past day had been an emotional cyclone. In the past twenty-four hours, I'd nearly lost Seton, almost been body-snatched by an evil witch, and managed to defeat that same evil witch with the help of a family coven that had been totally unknown to me just three weeks ago.

But right now, calm oozed through me. It hadn't even required swallowing a potion. All it took was the right chest to lean against. "Never better. This is perfect."

He didn't say anything.

Belatedly, I realized I might be taking a little too much for granted. I looked up at him, "I mean, I realize you're still working things out. But you're welcome to stay here as long as you want."

"Would forever be too long?"

I didn't trust myself to speak.

"Of course, we've got a few obstacles to overcome," he said.

"A ninety-year age gap, for one thing," I said.

"Actually, I'm only twenty-eight." A brow arched. "Technically, I'm a *younger* man."

I laughed. "Then, according to my mom, I'm a cheetah."

He pulled me to him for another kiss. Liquid fire moved through me. "I've wanted you since that first night," he murmured. "Even in that bewildering place you took me to."

I looked up into his blue eyes. "It's called a bar."

"It wasn't like any bar I'd ever seen. And you weren't like any woman I'd ever met."

That made me smile—as if Seton had cut a swath through the eligible flappers of New York. "A regular Valentino, were you?"

He waggled his brows in mock matinee idol. "I don't know about Valentino, but I knew my way around a rumble seat."

"In the Owl's Nest, you looked like Gary Cooper, only terri-fied."

"All I was thinking about was going home. I didn't know I'd found a new home."

I nodded. "You told me then that there was nothing lonelier than living with someone you don't love with your whole heart."

"I don't think either of us needs to worry about being lonely again," he said.

I tilted my head up and he kissed me again. The kiss deep-ened. It was hard for me to believe that we had all the leisure time in the world now that these moments between us no longer had to be furtive and guilt-laden. I felt suddenly that we needed to celebrate.

I pulled back. "I know—let's go to the city."

"Manhattan?"

His uncertain expression made me want to kick myself. "Un-less you think it would be too painful. The city's changed a lot. And you've got a lot of memories there, I'm sure."

"Everyone has memories, and even ghosts." His lips quirked. "Mine are just a little further back."

"So you'd like to go?"

His answer was cut off by the doorbell. Expecting Mom had forgotten something, I crossed the living room to open the front door.

"Olivia!"

She had the painting of the pastry cutter bridge propped in front of her. "The family asked me to bring you the gifts." She heaved the painting toward me.

I took it, and then noticed that out in my driveway the large storage pod from the Havermans' garage was now blocking my car in the driveway.

"Mother's emailing you the names of the senders and their addresses." Her lips turned up in an amused sneer. "Have fun processing one hundred and eighty-two gift returns."

She turned and slouched toward her car.

I picked up the painting and was lugging it inside when Seton joined me. He looked anxiously out the door at that pod before taking an end of the painting, kicking the door shut, and helping me walk the picture into the living room. "Did she say 'one hundred and eighty-two gifts'?"

I nodded, feeling despair well in me.

"We'll get it done, don't worry," he said.

I'd never been happier to hear the word *we*. I set down my end of the painting and leaned into him.

"Didn't your mom mention something about cupcakes?" he asked. "Maybe we should fortify ourselves before tackling the pod."

Trudy's love-laced lavender cupcakes. The baked goods that might have accelerated my mom's relationship with Ron. And now there were some in my house.

The pod could wait. I wound my hands around Seton's neck. "Cupcakes are always a good idea."

Acknowledgments

Most authors write alone, but it takes a village to make a book. I'm very fortunate to have some creative, capable people in my village. Many thanks to John Scognamiglio, Carly Sommerstein, and all the other wonderful, imaginative people at Kensington for their work on the Cupcake Coven books.

I'm also grateful to Annlise Robey and all the support I receive from the folks at the Jane Rotrosen Agency.

Visit our website at
KensingtonBooks.com
to sign up for our newsletters, read
more from your favorite authors, see
books by series, view reading group
guides, and more!

Become a Part of Our
Between the Chapters Book Club
Community and Join the Conversation

Submit your book review for a chance to win exclusive
Between the Chapters swag you can't get anywhere else!
https://www.kensingtonbooks.com/pages/review/